A SHADOW IN THE NIGHT

The room was dark, but not so dark that Amanda couldn't see the huge, dark silhouette as the door opened wider. A hot, damp scent of herbal soap tickled her nose as she sat there in bed, paralyzed, not really certain that she hadn't once again retreated into her dreams.

There was light in the bathroom, and it leaked briefly into her bedroom before Daken closed the door silently behind him. He was naked except for a towel draped around his waist. His silver hair looked dark, plastered against his head.

"I wanted to see you." His voice was low and husky and she could actually feel his discomfort.

But now she could feel something else as well: that same alien, primitive feeling she'd had when he'd come to the cottage in Wat Andara. It washed over her in waves, inundating her.

"I didn't mean to frighten you," he said, apologizing but not leaving.

The charged silence that followed was broken by the cries of wolves. They were distant, far off in the mountains. She turned toward the window and shuddered.

"They were very close earlier," she said without turning back to him. "It sounded as though they were singing."

He said nothing. She felt him waiting and felt his hunger reach out to touch her, envelop her, push her back to the dream. In a slow motion that seemed to take forever, she turned back to him.

"Yes," she said, then "yes" again, the words running together in the electric silence. And she suddenly felt the power of that single word—and its irrevocability.

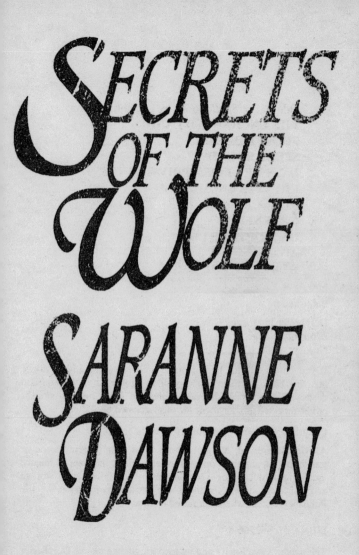

SECRETS OF THE WOLF

SARANNE DAWSON

LOVE SPELL BOOKS NEW YORK CITY

LOVE SPELL®

May 1998

Published by

Dorchester Publishing Co., Inc.
276 Fifth Avenue
New York, NY 10001

ISBN 0-505-52260-8

The name "Love Spell" and its logo are trademarks of Dorchester Publishing Co., Inc.

Printed in the United States of America.

SECRETS OF THE WOLF

Prologue

Amanda saw the stranger for only a few seconds—just before the lights were dimmed in the large auditorium and her Uncle Steffen's lecture began. Other latecomers were hurrying through the doors as well, but it was his image alone that remained with her. There was nothing surprising about that, however, because he was a man who would have commanded attention in any crowd.

He towered over the others, and his great height was matched by the breadth of his shoulders. His dark clothing contrasted sharply with his thick silver hair, which was worn rather long and curled at the ends. She never really got a good look at his face, but an impression lingered of boldly masculine features.

She turned around and tried to settle comfortably into her seat as her uncle began to speak, but her curiosity had been aroused and she had to fight to keep from turning around again. Steffen's lecture was entitled "Mankind's Enduring Legends and Myths," and although she had heard it before, she still listened with interest as he led the audience through a series of tales of vampires, zombies, lost continents and vanished peoples.

"And finally, to complete our survey of myths and legends, we come to what may be the most intriguing myth of all: the legend of the Kassid. Many folk historians believe that the legend of the Kassid gave rise to later myths about werewolves that have come down to us in horror fiction and films.

"As I've already demonstrated, all enduring myths have at least some basis in fact, even if those facts tend to become distorted in the telling and retelling over the centuries. Generally speaking, a careful search of historical records will reveal something of the source of that legend.

"However, because of the special circumstances pertaining here, that avenue of exploration is not open to us where the Kassid are concerned. What little information we do have is, at best, secondhand, and for that reason, many historians have tended to discount the legend of the Kassid completely.

"What we do know is that the legend arose more than two thousand years ago in the region shown on this map—the last unexplored part of the world.

"About seven hundred years ago, the region was struck by the worst natural disaster in human history. It began with a very powerful earthquake, which then triggered a series of violent volcanic eruptions. The result was that the land believed to have been the home of the Kassid, as well as of several other tribes, was completely destroyed.

"A land that had undoubtedly once been home to thousands of people slowly became over the centuries a thick and impenetrable jungle, where tremors and volcanic eruptions persisted until less than fifty years ago. Ancient maps unearthed in neighboring lands showed a coastline totally different from that which exists today. As you can see from these photos, the present coastline is a sheer rock wall, varying in height from a half mile to more than a mile.

"Still, the region certainly would have been explored if it hadn't been for persistent political unrest. The three nations that border the ancient home of the Kassid and their neighbors have all laid claim to this land, and all three countries remain in the thrall of long-standing tribal and religious enmities.

"About thirty years ago, an international team of explorers did gain permission to search the offshore waters in hopes of finding the remnants of the vanished civilizations. But their efforts were unsuccessful, and when warfare broke out again in the region, the explorations ceased altogether—until this past summer, when a group of us once again undertook this guest.

"The results, as you all know by now, have given rise to a renewed determination to search for the lost civilization of the Kassid. The following series of slides show some of what we found: the underwater ruins of what may have been one of the largest cities in the world at that time—and a city far more advanced than any of us would have thought possible.

"As you can see, none of the buildings have survived intact, but what remains, plus the objects we found, suggest a civilization that was advanced well beyond any of its time. A civilization that must have enjoyed a long period of peace. We surmise this because of the high state of their arts, which extended even to objects of daily life. As a rule, throughout history, great art and craftsmanship have flourished during times of peace, when mankind is able to turn its attention to the gentler side of life.

"Gold was apparently quite plentiful among the Kassid, and as you may know, gold survives even many centuries under the sea. The following slides were made to show in greater detail the scenes depicted on some of the embossed items we found.

"And it is in these items that we see the legend of the Kassid come to life. Over and over, people are depicted side by side in peaceful coexistence with wolves, suggesting that they had tamed the creatures and perhaps kept them as pets. This, we believe, gave rise to the prevalence in the region of tales of men who could transform themselves into wolves. Tales that have evolved into the modern werewolf.

"What is most striking about all the depictions we've found thus far is that although wolves are shown intermingling freely with all people, they are most often shown with one distinctive race: a race of giants—if we are to believe the artists' renderings.

"The other thing these drawings show is that this race of giants is associated with high mountains— undoubtedly the Shegalas, which are among the world's tallest peaks. They rise now out of a jungle just at the edge of the region.

"The word 'Shegala' comes from the ancient Turvean word for 'Dark Mountains' and is an accurate description of those forbidding peaks. You've all seen pictures of them, of course, but it's impossible to capture on film the true color of the mountains because they are almost always enshrouded in mist. They appear to be composed of very dark rock and covered with dark firs as well. The tallest of them is surrounded by lower volcanic peaks that still erupt from time to time, though with far less devastating consequences than was the case in the past.

"Thus far, we've been able to photograph them only from the sea and from the air, but if our negotiations with the nations that claim this territory are successful, we will be mounting an expedition into the jungle and perhaps even into the Dark Mountains themselves next summer."

Amanda felt a thrill of anticipation as she listened to Steffen's words. It wasn't yet certain that she herself could become part of the group even if they did succeed in obtaining permission for the expedition—but she was determined. Surely Steffen would be able to persuade the others of the advantage of having an accomplished photographer in their group—especially since she was prepared to pay her own way.

She shifted in her seat and at least a dozen muscles protested simultaneously, reminding her that she still had a long way to go with her exercise routine. Climbing the sheer rock walls north of the city was the closest she could come to mimicking what would be expected of her in the Dark Mountains, but she doubted that any of them would be better prepared.

As Steffen's lecture wound down, Amanda's thoughts returned to the man she'd seen earlier. When the lights came up again, she turned in her seat and scanned the rear of the hall, but he was nowhere to be seen.

His image lingered in her mind. She wondered if her uncle might know who he was.

Chapter One

A life just didn't end this way—cut off so abruptly, with so many things left undone. That thought kept swirling through Amanda's mind as she stood beside her mother, listening to the minister deliver the final few words at the grave site.

Don't be so naive, she told herself. *People are murdered on the street every day in this city—many of them for no reason other than that they were in the wrong place at the wrong time. You know that. You read the newspapers and watch the television news.*

But none of them had been Steffen Lescoulans, her mother's brother and the closest thing she'd ever had to a true father.

Slightly apart from the small group of mourners who'd followed them here from the large memorial service stood the two detectives who'd grilled them both endlessly about any enemies Steffen might have had. Amanda was surprised that they'd come to the service and then all the way out here. Could they really believe that Steffen's killer could be one of his many friends—or one of his few relatives?

Once the initial shock of Steffen's death had begun to wear off, Amanda had decided that he was only the latest victim of random violence in a city gone mad. It seemed that the detectives thought otherwise—or perhaps they were only going through the motions.

Still, there were some troubling aspects to his murder. He lived in a quiet neighborhood that had until now seen little violence. And the murderer had failed to take either his money or his expensive watch. He'd been stabbed to death on his doorstep as he returned home shortly past midnight. The police knew where it had happened because of the blood found on the doorstep, although his body had been discovered in the foyer the next morning by his housekeeper.

Dazed with shock, Amanda and her mother had been forced to spend that day inventorying Steffen's town house to see if anything was missing. As far as they could tell, nothing was—and the police found that very strange indeed. Steffen had owned many things that should have attracted a thief: expensive stereo equipment, numerous cameras, a state-of-the-art VCR and many priceless works of art.

But Amanda's mind rebelled at the possibility that anyone could have deliberately killed her uncle. The man had no enemies. Everyone who knew him had loved him. He had had the good fortune to possess a brilliant mind in combination with a wry and often self-deprecating wit. He was unfailingly generous with his time for his students and colleagues and equally generous with his money to various charitable causes.

Through a haze of unshed tears, Amanda watched as the casket was lowered into the grave. Suddenly she hated this ritual. It seemed so pointless. Everything that was truly Steffen was already gone. The body inside the ornate casket her mother had chosen was not Steffen; it had only once belonged to him.

The minister beckoned them forward to throw in the first shovelful of dirt. Her mother complied while Amanda herself hung back. Barbarism. That was all it was. Her mother had said that it was a necessary ritual, a part of dealing with the reality of his death. Amanda didn't need a ceremony and this graveside ritual to know that Steffen was gone from her life forever.

"So you've completed the inventory of your uncle's papers?" the detective asked.

Amanda nodded. They were in Steffen's large study, the day after the funeral. "He was very well organized. I've checked everything against his list and it's all here. One of his colleagues helped me, both here and at his office. Nothing is missing."

"And you found nothing that could point to a reason for his death?"

Amanda shook her head. "The reason for my uncle's death is that we live in a time of total madness," she stated coldly, "as you surely must know, since you deal with it every day."

The detective nodded wearily. He was a rumpled middle-aged man with bags under his eyes and deep lines carved into his once-handsome face. She regretted her frosty tone as she wondered how he could survive in such a job. "I'm sorry. It's just that I'm still having trouble believing that this could have happened to him."

"And I'm still having trouble believing that this was just a random killing," the detective responded, heaving his blocky body out of the leather chair in front of Steffen's desk.

But Amanda had by now reached the point where she wanted to believe that. She knew it was irrational, but she preferred to think that, rather than being forced to consider that someone could have hated Steffen enough to have killed him.

"Maybe the killer was interrupted before he could take anything," she suggested.

The detective shrugged. "That's possible, I suppose, but once he'd dragged the body into the house, it wasn't likely that he would have been interrupted. And we've talked to all the neighbors. No one saw or heard anything."

Amanda didn't find that so strange. People were too frightened these days to let themselves become involved—as though by merely helping the police, they were risking some sort of contamination that could lead to their own deaths.

"Have you been up to his cabin yet?" the detective asked.

"No." She just wasn't ready to face that yet. "But he didn't keep anything there. That was where he went to get away from his work."

"Well, be sure to let me know if you do find anything. I'm afraid I've taken this about as far as I can right now."

She nodded, simultaneously relieved and angry

that the police were apparently writing it off. But what choice did they have, really, when each new day brought more bodies, new cases?

She saw the detective to the door, then returned to Steffen's study. It was her favorite room in his house because it had been his favorite as well.

She sank into his big leather desk chair again and stared at the large framed photograph on the wall. It was one of the aerial shots the expedition had taken of the jungle and the Dark Mountains. It was easy to see why Steffen had enlarged and framed it. The contrast was startling: black, snowcapped peaks rising out of myriad shades of green. They'd even been fortunate enough to have captured the scene on a day when the ever-present mists had thinned.

She thought that she'd cried herself out by now, but as she stared at the photograph, her eyes misted over again. In less than two months, they would have been leaving for that place. Finally, after nearly a year of negotiation with the various governments, the group had gotten permission to go into the jungle and to the Dark Mountains.

She brushed away her tears, knowing that she was now crying for herself as well as for Steffen. Now that he was gone, it wasn't likely that they'd permit her to accompany them. They hadn't said so yet, but she knew that her own chances of seeing the ancient land of the Kassid had died with her uncle.

Amanda didn't fully understand what it was about the legend of the Kassid that had always made it her favorite. After all, there was so little known about them. But from the very first time Steffen had told her the tale, she'd been enchanted.

She reflected that it was probably because Steffen

himself had liked it best. He'd told her once that it was because his family—her family, too, of course—had quite possibly come from that region.

Steffen had used all his research skills to try to trace the origins of their family, but had come up basically empty-handed. It seemed that the Lescoulan family had been world wanderers before coming here nearly two hundred years ago. Steffen hadn't been able to trace the origins of the family, but his research had suggested the possibility of Menoan ancestry.

In any event, the journey she'd been looking forward to with mounting excitement now seemed only a dream of the past.

Spring had finally come to the mountains. As Amanda drove slowly up the steep, rutted road, she could see the delicate white lace of the dogwoods that dotted the thick forest, where the pale green of new leaves mingled pleasantly with the darker hues of pine and hemlock. Up here, winter loosened its hold on the land only begrudgingly. There were certain shady spots where traces of snow could still be found into early June.

The road leveled off and she saw the cabin, squatting stolidly among the tall hemlocks. She'd been steeling herself for this moment during the long drive, but she still felt her throat tighten at the sight of the place.

Steffen had built the cabin himself from a "kit" of precut logs and an instruction book. It had been ten years ago that he had built it, after a severe winter storm had felled a giant oak, sending it through the roof of his old cabin and ravaging the interior.

Amanda had helped him construct the new dwelling. Weekend after weekend, and then for a full week, they had come up here that summer, staying at a motel in town while they worked on it. Amanda had just finished college and was torn between pursuing her art or her then newly acquired interest in photography. It had been a wonderful interlude, a time out of time, and they'd restored their former closeness that had suffered somewhat from separation over the past four years.

The cabin had been Steffen's hideaway, the place where he had come to think and to escape the many demands on his time. Even she had never been invited back after the cabin was finished—but then, she hadn't expected an invitation. She and Steffen understood each other completely in that regard. Both genuinely liked people and led active, sociable lives, but each of them had a fierce need for privacy as well. Steffen had given her a tiny cottage at the beach as a graduation present, and he had this place.

And now the cabin was hers, together with his town house in the city and an enormous amount of money.

But I don't have Steffen, she thought sadly as she pulled up in front of the cabin. She'd never been able to describe adequately what her uncle had meant to her. In a way, he'd been a father figure, stepping in to replace her real father, who'd died when she was only seven.

But somehow, their relationship had remained free of any parent-child tension. Instead, Steffen had become her best friend: not only the person to whom she confided her mundane problems, but the one who listened to her dreams, who saw the best in her and made her see it as well.

Steffen had never married, although she knew that he had led an active social life and had no problem attracting women. When she'd passed her thirtieth birthday last year, Amanda had begun to realize consciously what she'd probably known all along: that she too preferred to live alone. She had friends, she dated and she'd even had a few lovers—but never once could she have imagined wanting to spend a lifetime with any of them.

Her mother had despaired, claiming that Amanda must have inherited the family's solitary nature, a trait that she herself had fortunately escaped.

Amanda got out of her car and walked around the outside of the cabin. The past winter had been especially brutal, and she didn't think that Steffen had been up here since then. When she satisfied herself that there hadn't been any damage, she dug the key out of her purse and unlocked the front door.

A faint trace of pipe tobacco greeted her, mingling pleasantly with the stronger odor of woodsmoke. Steffen had given up tobacco several years ago, but either he'd secretly indulged himself up here or the odor had somehow permeated the very walls.

The day was still warm, so before the evening chill could set in, she hurried to the windows, opening them and then unlocking the heavy wooden shutters as well. Sunlight and a soft breeze poured in, bringing to life the simple but comfortable furnishings.

After putting away the groceries she'd bought in town, Amanda decided to try to lower the big wooden porch swing that had been hoisted up under the eaves for the winter. She was balanced on the porch railing, trying to free the chain that held the swing against the underside of the porch roof, when she had the sudden, unmistakable sense that she was being watched.

She paused in her work, bracing a hand against the corner post as she slowly scanned her surroundings. The cabin was very isolated, situated in the center of a twenty-acre plot that Steffen had bought many years ago. The land was located on the edge of a large state forest. The woods grew close to the cabin in all directions, and now, in the ruddy light of the setting sun, the shadows were already long and deep.

She stared into the woods, holding her breath as she listened for any sound. She knew there were both deer and bears in the area, since she'd seen them while she and Steffen were building the cabin. Now she listened for the sound of snapping twigs as she strained her eyes to see into the dusky woods.

Suddenly she saw movement deep in the shadows. She peered intently, but it didn't become any clearer. Whatever had been there was moving away.

She turned her attention back to the swing, wondering if the movement could possibly have been a stray dog. Steffen had never mentioned any in the area, but the shape had almost looked like that of a large dog. That thought made her slightly uneasy. She hoped it wasn't a vicious dog. She wished that she'd gotten a better look at it.

Once she finally got the swing lowered, she went back inside and fixed herself something to eat, then carried it out to the porch. Dusk was turning into darkness and the temperature was already dropping, but she'd put on a heavy sweater and was comfortable enough as she sat curled up in the big swing, letting it rock gently as she ate a sandwich.

She supposed that she really should sell the cabin. It wasn't likely that she'd use it much. But parting with it would be hard. Maybe if she could find someone who truly appreciated it, someone who wanted a hideaway as Steffen had . . .

The feeling came over her more slowly this time as her thoughts drifted back to the summer they'd built this place: suddenly she was certain that she was being watched. She set down the sandwich and began to turn slowly, scanning the darkness at the edge of the light from the porch.

Nothing moved, and the only sound was the mournful hooting of an owl deep in the woods. She was caught between her curiosity about what could be out there and her knowledge of her own vulnerability. She thought about going inside to get Steffen's gun. He kept a handgun up here, and she knew how to use it. He'd shown her.

But her pleasure in sitting out here had gone. She kept imagining some creature suddenly leaping up onto the porch behind the swing and attacking her. Furthermore, she was unnerved by the thought that she could actually sense its presence out there.

She picked up her plate and mug and carried them inside, and then came back out, this time with the big flashlight that Steffen kept at the cabin. Standing on the edge of the porch, she swept the area with the bright beam. Nothing—and yet her sense that something was there, just beyond the reach of the light, persisted. There was a strange, primitive quality to what she was feeling, as though some long-dormant sense had been awakened.

Laughing at her fanciful notion, she went back into the cabin, deciding that she'd try in the morning to find some tracks that might identify the creature.

After lighting a fire in the big stone fireplace that had been Steffen's proudest achievement when they had built the cabin, Amanda settled down on the comfortable sofa with the latest mystery by one of her favorite authors.

It was past midnight when she closed the book, yawning. The fire was burning low and there was no more wood in the cabin. She picked up the wood carrier and went out back to the small shed where Steffen kept the firewood he had cut the previous fall. There were electric heaters in the bedroom and bathroom, but the rest of the cabin depended on the fireplace for warmth, and the nights up here were still below freezing.

Her breath steamed in the frosty air as she gathered up some logs. The moon had come out and she paused to stare at it. It was nearly full, and its light silvered the tops of the tall trees, leaving the forest floor in darkness. Here and there, the dogwoods gleamed with a ghostly light. The silence was nearly palpable—especially to one accustomed to the endless sounds of the city.

Her thoughts returned to the animal she'd glimpsed and then sensed earlier. Then suddenly the feeling came again—even stronger this time. And then she saw it. She froze, her arms clutching the firewood to her chest. Standing atop a small hill off to one side of the woodshed was a wolf.

There was no doubt in her mind that a wolf was what it was, even though she'd never actually seen one before. It stood there motionless, watching her, clearly outlined in the moonlight. Even though a part of her was screaming a warning, Amanda felt no fear. What she felt instead was a sense of awe.

Later, in the safety of the cabin, she would wonder what it was about a wolf that had inspired such a very different feeling than if it had been another wild creature—but at this moment, all she knew was that it felt different.

The creature remained utterly still, its tufted ears pricked as it stared at her. It was huge—or at least much larger than she had thought a wolf would be. Its thick fur was a dark gray tipped with silver, and although she couldn't be sure at this distance and in the pale moonlight, it seemed to have light eyes.

Woman and wolf stared at each other for a time that seemed to stretch out toward eternity. Fear continued to nibble at the edges of her consciousness, but a long time passed before she gave in to it and began to edge cautiously back toward the open cabin door. Still the creature didn't move.

Inside, with the door closed and bolted, Amanda began to tremble. But even now the sense of wonder remained. She went over and peered out the kitchen window. It was gone—and now she began to wonder if it had been there in the first place.

She threw some logs onto the fire and then went into the bedroom, moving automatically through her nightly routine as the image of the wolf lingered in her brain. Only when she was in bed, safe and warm beneath the covers, did she draw the connection she should have made before. How very strange that she should see her first wolf now, when the expedition to the land of the Kassid was so much on her mind.

She slipped slowly into sleep, wondering if it could

be an omen. Her last conscious thought was that maybe she could still find a way to persuade Steffen's colleagues to let her join their expedition.

He waited patiently in the darkness, watching the cabin. One light went out and another came on. Then it too went out, and the only remaining light was a reddish glow from the fireplace.

He thought about her—about her red-gold hair and her delicate, fine-boned features that still somehow projected a strength belied by her diminutive size. There was a quality to her that drew him as no other woman had for a long time. What was it? Was it her faint resemblance to the portrait at home that never failed to capture his attention? How many times had he caught himself staring at it without quite understanding why?

When the cabin had remained in darkness for a sufficiently long time, he crept toward it, moving soundlessly as he approached a window. He was hoping that it would be unlocked and he could make his search without disturbing her sleep.

Surely what he sought would be here—if it existed at all. There'd been nothing at Steffen's home or at his university office, so he was inclined to think that no record existed. But when he'd come across a picture of the cabin, he'd begun to watch her, hoping she would lead him to it.

A copy of Steffen Lescoulans's will had been in his files, so he knew that everything had been left to his niece, Amanda Traynor. He'd found pictures of her, too—including ones of her and her uncle building the cabin. So he'd guessed that she would come up here, and he'd waited impatiently for her to leave the city.

He pushed at the window carefully, and smiled as it slid up almost soundlessly. A few seconds later, he was inside the cabin.

Amanda opened her eyes and turned to the glowing clock on the nightstand. She hadn't slept long. Had something awakened her? She lay there in the darkness, thinking about the wolf and listening for any sounds.

Finally she turned over in bed, seeking sleep once again. She was safe in here, regardless of what might be prowling around outside.

She was just drifting off to sleep again when she heard something. Fully awake now, she sat up in bed. What was it? Could it simply have been a log falling in the fireplace?

She got out of bed quietly and slid open the drawer on the nightstand. She'd discovered Steffen's gun in there earlier. He'd taught her to use it the summer they built the cabin. She hadn't touched a gun since, but she found its cool metal reassuring as she crept toward the doorway and then out into the short hall.

Most of the cabin was one big open space that included the living room, a small dining area and an equally tiny kitchen. Steffen had set up a study of sorts in one corner of the open area: an old desk and some built-in bookshelves.

The only light was the flickering glow of the fire, and as she reached the end of the hallway, a log snapped in the fireplace, momentarily freezing her in place. Surely it was a similar sound that had awakened her. It seemed very loud in the night's silence.

Feeling less uneasy now, she stepped out into the big room—and immediately felt a cold draft. She was sure that she hadn't left any windows open, and turned to seek the source of the cold air.

The window behind the desk was open—and standing near it, with his back to her as he went through the books on the shelves, was a man. Amanda was stunned. She even blinked several times, certain that she must be imagining him. She wasn't aware of having made any sound, but perhaps she had, because he turned abruptly to face her.

He was holding a tiny penlight, and as he turned, it briefly lit his face before he switched it off. Amanda recognized him immediately. It was the man who'd drawn her attention at Steffen's lecture last fall. Although she hadn't seen his face clearly then, she had no doubt that it was him.

He was huge—easily six and a half feet tall, with broad shoulders and features that couldn't really be called handsome, but were certainly unforgettable. Apart from his size, what made her so certain that it was indeed the same man was his thick silver hair, worn rather long and curling slightly at the ends.

Amanda simply stared back at him. She'd never seen a man who was so uncompromisingly . . . male. At some level, she knew she should be terrified at finding this huge stranger in the cabin, but what she felt instead was an overwhelming sense of his maleness—and her own femaleness. Fear just didn't play a role in it. She'd completely forgotten about the gun in her hand.

Strange, erotic thoughts teased the edges of her mind, sending tiny curls of heat through her until her legs began to tremble. An invisible thread connected them across the room, powerful but fragile. His face was now in the shadows, but his hair gleamed in the firelight as he stood there, as motionless as she was.

Then he raised his hand and made an odd, graceful movement, as though he were writing something in the charged air between them. Amanda watched, and then turned and walked back to the bedroom, where she placed the gun on the nightstand and got into bed again. She was asleep within seconds.

"Must have been a coyote. There haven't been any wolves around these parts for years."

Amanda opened her mouth to protest that it had been a wolf, but changed her mind and closed it again. "Perhaps you're right."

"They're damned nuisances," the man went on as he filled her gas tank. "Always chasing deer. Sometimes they attack livestock, too. But they won't go after humans—at least not when there's other food around."

Amanda thanked the man for his information and paid for the gas. She hesitated as she started to pull out of the gas station lot. Across the street was the municipal services building—including the police. Should she talk to them? Finally, she turned onto the highway and started back to the cabin.

It was a dream, she told herself. It had to have been a dream. If the man had actually been there, she certainly wouldn't have simply gone back to bed.

His shadowy features swam back into her mind's eye once again. It was strange, though, that the man she'd dreamed about was a man she'd seen only once before. She recalled that she'd had a powerful reaction to him then, but over the intervening months, she'd all but forgotten about him. Or so she'd thought. Obviously her subconscious hadn't forgotten him.

She abruptly recalled Steffen's reaction when she'd asked about the stranger. Her uncle had immediately asked for details she hadn't been able to provide because she hadn't seen the man all that clearly. Steffen had then said that he had no idea who it might be, but Amanda had been left with the impression that he'd thought—or perhaps hoped— that it could be someone he knew.

She returned to the cabin, uneasy. She still couldn't quite convince herself that it had been only a dream, and she was very troubled by her inability to separate a dream from reality in a concrete manner.

She spent several hours roaming through the woods near the cabin, looking for prints but finding nothing on the pine needle–strewn floor of the forest. On the hill behind the shed, where she'd seen the wolf, she did find faint indentations in the hard ground, but that was all. And not once did she have a recurrence of that sensation that she was being watched.

Finally, she turned to the task of packing up Steffen's books. Most of his vast library was at his city home, but there was a rather large collection of fiction here at the cabin, and when she'd stopped earlier at the small local library, they'd said they would be happy to accept a donation.

Amanda was amused to discover that Steffen, whose collection in the city was limited to scholarly works and the classics, had had a secret cache of crime fiction up here. Still, it fit with the purpose of this place, where he'd come to forget about his work for a time.

As she put the books into boxes, Amanda's thoughts returned to that strange dream. The man had been going through Steffen's books. On the surface of it, that fact seemed to argue even more strongly that it had been a dream. Why would someone break into the cabin to check on Steffen's reading material?

On the other hand, though, what if he'd been looking for something specific: something he thought Steffen could have hidden among the books?

Stop it! she ordered herself. It *was* a dream. And yet, she began to sort through the books, studying titles, shaking them to see if anything might fall out. And when she had finished with the books, she went through his desk. The drawers were nearly empty, containing only some notepaper, several pens and pencils and two keys.

She picked up the keys. One of them turned out to be for the drawer in which she'd found them, but the other one puzzled her. It wasn't a spare key for the cabin; she could tell that without checking.

Then she remembered the hiding place. When Steffen had built the cabin, he'd installed a metal strongbox beneath the floor in the bedroom closet. She'd teased him about it at the time, suggesting that maybe he was turning into the proverbial eccentric bachelor uncle who planned to hide his money there. But he'd said that since he came up here so infrequently and there was always the chance that the place could be burglarized, it was good to have a hiding place.

29

Several pairs of old shoes and boots sat on the closet floor, concealing the opening to the strongbox. She moved them out of the way, and tugged on the small metal ring that opened the flap. The key fit the lock in the strongbox, and she opened it, not really expecting to find anything. But inside the box lay a manila envelope with her name on it. Puzzled, she took it out. Why would Steffen have left something for her here?

She sat down on the edge of the bed and opened the envelope, then withdrew several pages of lined yellow paper with Steffen's writing on them. She read them slowly in the waning light of the day, and as she read, a feeling of disbelief crept through her.

Steffen was a man of impeccable reputation among his peers, and after reading and rereading the few pages, Amanda immediately understood why he had hidden this and left it for her eyes only.

Contained in the six densely written pages was a story that could have ruined his reputation and turned him into an object of scorn among his colleagues and a subject for supermarket tabloids.

He had written about his first and, as it turned out, only expedition to the land of the Kassid: the underwater expedition that had uncovered the ruins of that lost city.

Unlike several other members of the expedition, Steffen had been an experienced diver. It was a hobby he'd taken up years ago for purely recreational purposes, one that had come in handy on this journey.

They were diving in pairs for safety reasons, and several days into their search—just after they'd discovered the first ruins—his partner, a novice diver, had panicked, and Steffen had helped him get back to the boat. The others were all off somewhere, so Steffen had gone down again—alone this time. It was, he wrote, a risky thing to do, but his excitement at their discovery overrode his normal caution.

Swimming through the ruins of what had apparently been a very large building, he discovered a section that was in far better condition than anything they'd yet seen. It contained a veritable maze of rooms and staircases that led ever deeper. He had refilled his air tank, and now paused only to mark his way as he swam deeper into the ancient ruins.

Finally, after following yet another staircase into what he surmised must have been deep cellars, he came to a closed door of dark, intricately carved wood, surprisingly well preserved after centuries in the sea. He'd seen no other doors like it; the other rooms he'd passed had had no doors at all. But this one was so well preserved that it still sealed whatever lay beyond.

Excited by his discovery and hoping that behind the door might be some treasures from the past, he set about getting it open with the tools he'd brought with him.

The room had indeed been well sealed. Water rushed past him into the room as he hovered in the doorway, trying to see inside with his powerful underwater light.

What he saw astounded him. The bright beam of the light seemed to be swallowed by the darkness in the room, but all around him he saw the glitter of gold.

He swam into the room and actually bumped up against a wall before he saw it was there. The gold he had seen turned out to be writing on the black stone of the walls. A close examination showed that the stone had been carved and then the ridges filled with gold so carefully that his hand could not detect the difference.

Steffen was an expert in ancient languages, but he could not begin to decipher the strange writings on the walls. But prominent among the writings were the carefully drawn figures of wolves. Amanda's heart beat faster as she read her uncle's account, but she continued reading.

"I was certain right then and there that this was the most important thing we'd yet found, and I was eager to find my colleagues and bring them here.

"But something happened—and as a result, I told no one else about my discovery. A part of me wanted very much for them to experience what I had, but I decided that the whole matter required some careful thought.

"It's impossible even now to describe the feeling that came over me in that dark place that glittered with gold writing. The only thing I can say is that I felt something then: a presence, if you will. Not evil and not good—just very ancient and very powerful. I had the thought then—and have it still—that I had intruded into a world that had existed long before mankind appeared on this earth.

"All of this came to me as thoughts, appearing full-blown in my mind as though planted there. I was not aware of having given birth to those thoughts myself.

"I had stopped my examination of the room and was hovering in the very center, when I felt, rather than heard, a deep vibration. My first thought was that the entire structure was about to collapse around me, but before I could move, a great sense of well-being came over me: a sort of tingling warmth.

"I may have blacked out for a short time, but it couldn't have been for long, because afterward, when I checked my tank, the remaining air indicated that it couldn't have been more than a minute or so.

"One minute, I was treading water in that strange and wonderful room—and in the next instant, I was in a dry room, but one that appeared to be identical in all other respects. I removed my breather and found the air to be cool and slightly musty, but otherwise fine.

"Too curious now to be feeling much fear, I took off my flippers and began to explore. Like the underwater room, this one appeared to be deep underground. I walked through empty hallways, passing empty rooms, and climbed several sets of stairs. And then I began to hear voices in the distance, speaking in a language I could not identify.

"Finally, I emerged into what must have been storerooms, filled with wooden crates that were marked in strange writing that seemed to bear some similarity to the gold writings I'd seen before. And there were men there.

"There is no doubt in my mind that these were the people pictured in the drawings we'd already seen. The shortest of them was at least six-foot-two, several inches taller than me. And they were dressed in the manner we'd seen in the drawings: heavy, fitted tunics of what seemed to be a very fine, shiny wool, and loose trousers with high boots. They were dark haired and dark eyed, except for one man who had very pale blue eyes.

"There was something about them—apart from their size and dress—that kept me rooted in place when I should have fled. I felt as though I were seeing men who were not mere humans. I cannot describe it any other way.

"It was clear that they were as startled to see me as I was to find them there. And of course, since I was wearing my diving gear, I must have looked strange indeed to them.

"One of them drew a knife from his belt. The blue-eyed one put out a hand to stop him, and then spoke to me in heavily accented English. He asked who I was and how I'd come to be there.

"At that point, I panicked. The other man still held his knife and one of the others drew his as well. The blue-eyed one seemed to be the leader, and he was more curious than angry, but I couldn't be sure of the situation.

"So I turned and ran back the way I'd come. I could hear the blue-eyed one calling to me as they came after me. He was telling me to wait, that he wanted to talk to me. But I ran back to the black room—and once again, I must have blacked out, because then I was back in the original water-filled room.

"For a time, I was too frightened to move. I

checked the gauge and saw that I still had plenty of air, so I just waited until the paralyzing fear passed, expecting that at any moment, I could find myself in the other room, facing knife-wielding enemies.

"But nothing happened, and I finally made my way back through the maze of rooms and staircases. My flippers were gone, so it took me longer to get to the surface, which was probably just as well, since it also gave me time to think."

Steffen's continued his narrative, agonizing over what he'd experienced. Was it real—or only a strange hallucination? The only evidence he had that it was real was his missing flippers. He'd taken them off before he went exploring in that other place.

He had thought about returning to the strange black room, but he had never had the opportunity to dive alone again. And in any event, the beginning of the typhoon season soon brought an end to their expedition.

"As I write this, nearly a month after the fact, I still don't know whether it was real or only some strange hallucination. My rational, scientific mind tells me it couldn't have happened, but it seems that some darker, more primitive part of me believes that it did.

"If it did happen, the implications are mind-boggling. It would mean that either those two rooms are some sort of wormhole through time itself—or that the underwater room is somehow magically connected to another place in the present world where the Kassid still survive—perhaps in the Dark Mountains.

"Of course, I can't be certain that the men I saw are in fact Kassid, but I believe they were. And if indeed they still survive, they have obviously not remained totally isolated, since at least one of them spoke English.

"As you must realize by now, it would be far better to believe that I simply hallucinated—but I do not believe that to have been the case.

"In any event, it is in your hands now, to do with as you wish. If you are reading this, rather than hearing it directly from me, it will be because I am gone. You know that I am not a man given to gloomy thoughts or dire predictions, and I'm certainly not psychic, but I felt very strongly when we left off our explorations that I would never be able to return.

"Knowing you as I do, I feel certain that you will want to do something. I know too that you've always shared my interest in the Kassid, and if there is to be another expedition, you will want to participate. But I would caution you that none of my colleagues—despite the respect they have for me—will believe my story. And I would also warn you that any investigation on your part could be dangerous if, in fact, my experience was real."

The journal ended there, but there was one final page. Amanda saw that it was a map showing a detailed part of the ruined underwater city. A big red X marked the spot where he'd discovered the room.

Amanda finally set aside the journal and the map and wrapped her arms around herself to ward off the chill she'd begun to feel. Such a tale coming from the pen of anyone else she would have dismissed out of hand. But this was Steffen, an eminently sane and logical man not given to flights of fancy.

She went out to the big room and lit a fire in the fireplace. The last of the day's light had faded and the evening was already growing cool. When she had finished laying the fire, she turned, and her gaze fell on the corner of the room Steffen had used as a study. Seeing the boxes of books she'd packed reminded her of her own strange dream. Suddenly she felt as though she were being stabbed by shards of ice, and she sank onto the sofa with a cry of shock.

Thoughts tumbled through her mind crazily. The man she'd seen in her dream. He didn't fit the description of the men Steffen had described because his hair had been silver, not dark. And he hadn't been dressed like them, either. He'd worn ordinary dark clothing. But he was huge, like the men Steffen had seen—and Steffen's description of his reaction to them had a certain familiarity, even though her own reaction had been all mixed up with a strange eroticism. And then there was the wolf. . . .

"No!" she said aloud. It was madness. And yet . . .

Steffen had been transported to a strange place and had seen strange men—or else he'd had a hallucination. She had seen someone here—or else she'd dreamed it. Wasn't that too much of a coincidence?

Throughout the long evening, Amanda thought about these things—and added to them the fact that Steffen had been killed, an event that he seemed to have almost predicted. And she thought again about his keen interest in the man she'd glimpsed at the lecture last fall: almost certainly the same man who'd been here at the cabin, or in her "dream."

She picked at that "dream," trying to find something she'd missed or forgotten that would establish its existence as a figment of her imagination. And once again, she decided that it must have been a dream, since it had, in effect, no ending.

But then, finally, she recalled something: that strange gesture he'd made at the end, almost as though he'd been writing in air. Had he also spoken? It now seemed to her that he had, but she couldn't recall what he'd said.

So she concentrated on that gesture, closing her eyes and willing the image into her mind's eye. And when it did, an even deeper chill came over her. She'd always been fascinated by tales of sorcery and black magic, and she now realized that what she'd seen had been described in some of those stories. She'd read that sorcerers often summoned magic by tracing ancient symbols called runes in the air to invoke their powers.

Black magic had no place in the modern world—if indeed it had ever had a place. Amanda knew that, and clung desperately to that knowledge. Steffen had hallucinated. She had dreamed. Coincidences did happen.

Before she went to bed, she reread Steffen's journal one more time and stared at the map as well. She very nearly threw it all into the fireplace, as though by destroying it, she could forget it. But at the last minute, she changed her mind and instead tucked it into her bag.

Then she poured herself a healthy dose of Steffen's fine old brandy and hoped that she could find a dreamless sleep.

Chapter Two

Amanda woke up slowly, feeling so groggy that at first she could not remember where she was. Something had awakened her, but what was it? She was struggling to reconstruct the past twenty-four hours when two things happened nearly simultaneously.

She smelled smoke—and a second later heard a loud, unnerving howl from somewhere close outside. The wolf was back—and apparently very near the cabin. But the smoke? Was it only the odor from the fireplace?

She dragged herself from bed, still too groggy to be truly alarmed. But she woke up in a hurry when she saw the glow in the hallway. And now she could hear it: the sound of flames greedily devouring something. Outside, the wolf howled again—even louder this time. Something struck the shutters. She'd closed all of them and locked them before going to bed.

A second loud thump against the shutters sent her to the doorway—but she immediately shrank back again. The entire front part of the cabin seemed to be ablaze.

She closed the bedroom door quickly, threw on a jacket to cover her near nakedness, then started to gather up her things. But just as she was reaching for the gun in the nightstand, the flames began to erupt around the edges of the door frame, and thick smoke poured into the bedroom.

She flung the window up, unlocked the shutters and dove out, landing in a heap on a dirt pile beside the cabin. For a few seconds, she lay there coughing. Then she remembered the wolf—and the gun she'd left behind. She picked herself up and raised her eyes to find herself staring into the beast's pale eyes.

The wolf was only about six feet away, standing motionless in the flickering light from the fire. It stared at her for a long moment, then abruptly turned and vanished into the darkness. Shaking with fear, Amanda stared after it until a sudden noise drew her attention back to the cabin.

The entire front part of the cabin had started to collapse, and the flames were now reaching out toward her through the open bedroom window. Luckily, Steffen had built the cabin in a clearing, and there was little combustible material to conduct the fire to the nearby forest. Strangely enough, what came to her mind at that moment was that she'd lost Steffen's journal and his map—never mind the fact that her clothes and her purse and her car keys were in there as well, and she was miles from the nearest help.

She staggered around to the front of the cabin and got into her car. Fortunately, it was far enough from the cabin that it was not in danger of being consumed in the blaze. She sat there, huddled in the front seat, and watched the cabin burn. From time to time she peered into the light created by the blaze to see if the wolf might still be there.

A long time passed before she heard the sounds of sirens in the distance. And then the fire trucks were there and the firefighters were pouring water onto the ruined cabin. The chief led her to his car, telling her that she was lucky to have gotten out alive and then asking her if she knew how the fire might have gotten started.

She told him that she'd added logs to the fire before going to bed, but that she'd put the screen in place and doubted that it had started that way. When he gave up questioning her and went to join his crew, she began to ask herself some very different questions.

How *had* she gotten out? Had she smelled the smoke even in her sleep—or had the wolf awakened her? She shuddered, recalling that moment when she'd stared into the creature's eyes. And she thought too about the thumps against the shutters. Was that the wolf as well?

But she made no mention of the wolf—not that night and not the next morning, when the fire chief and the state fire marshal came to the motel to tell her that the fire had clearly been deliberately set.

"They weren't even very professional about it," the marshal told her. "There are ways to set a fire that can be real hard to detect afterward, but this one was started by pouring gasoline or some other flammable liquid on the outside walls. He probably ran out of fuel before he got to the rear—and that's what saved you."

What saved me was the wolf, Amanda thought, but didn't say. The more she'd thought about it, the more she became convinced that the wolf's howls had awakened her, and that the sounds she'd heard were made by the creature flinging itself against the shutters.

"Do you know of any reason why someone would want to burn the cabin—or harm you?" the marshal asked.

Amanda hesitated, then told him about the man who might have been real—or might have been a dream. She described him, but admitted that she wasn't at all sure that she hadn't dreamed the whole episode.

"This was the night before last?" he asked.

Amanda nodded. "I didn't report it to the police because I just wasn't sure it had really happened—and I'm still not certain." But she was thinking now about the coincidence of someone having broken into the cabin, apparently seeking something—and then the fire the following night. Too many coincidences.

"Well, from your description, it shouldn't be too hard to find him—if he exists, that is."

"The man I saw definitely exists. I've seen him before. He attended a lecture my uncle gave last fall." But even as she spoke, she was rejecting the notion that this man could have tried to kill her. Why she would think that, she didn't know—but the feeling was very strong.

"Are you going back to the city now?" the fire marshal asked.

She nodded. With all its violence, the city still seemed a lot safer than this place right now.

The woman who owned the motel had been kind enough to get her some clothing and lend her some money, and as soon as the two men left, Amanda went to thank the woman again. She then drove off, eager to put this place behind her.

She hadn't really intended to return to the cabin, but found herself turning in that direction. Somehow, in the bright sunlight and under the deep blue sky, the ruined cabin looked even more frightening than it had the night before. She walked around the edges of the charred mess, hoping that she might find something intact. But it was all gone.

Then she turned and scanned the woods, searching for the wolf. "I wish you'd come back, so I could thank you," she said aloud, then laughed at her foolishness. Her life had become surreal enough without her beginning to talk to wolves—or believe that the animal had deliberately saved her life.

All the way back to the city, she thought about the silver-haired man, the wolf and Steffen's journal. And by the time she reached her home, she knew that Steffen had been right. This quest could indeed be dangerous, but she couldn't let it go.

"I'm willing to help finance this expedition, Professor Whitely. Steffen left his entire estate to me, and I know that he would be pleased to have some of his money used for this purpose."

The professor nodded. He was a lean, wiry man in his mid-forties with a surprising shock of carrot-colored hair. Following Steffen's death, he had been named to head the expedition. Amanda knew that although her uncle had respected his scholarship, he had also fretted about Whitely's reputation as a publicity seeker.

"Steffen had already volunteered to finance the expedition if it became necessary," Whitely said. "You see, we hadn't any idea how much we would have to pay to the governments that lay claim to that territory, in order to obtain their permission. Unfortunately, it's proved to be quite a lot. We need all of their permission, and as soon as one government found out what another had demanded the stakes were raised."

Amanda did her best to conceal her pleasure at that bit of news. Reprehensible as they were, the demands of those corrupt regimes might well be responsible for her joining the expedition.

"As I said, the only demand I make is that I be allowed to join the expedition. And since Steffen had already obtained the group's permission for me to come along . . ." She smiled and shrugged eloquently.

"I have to be honest and tell you that we all agreed reluctantly," the professor replied. "We will be confronting the unknown on a daily basis, and sometimes living in a very primitive manner."

Sensing some sexism in his words, Amanda reminded him that she wouldn't be the only woman in the group.

"That's true," he acknowledged. "But Miriam Daniels has been on many digs, and she was also with us for the undersea expedition."

"I'm well prepared for this, Professor Whitely. I've gone scuba diving with my uncle for years, and I've been rock climbing in preparation for the other part of the expedition.

"Perhaps you're unaware of the fact that I worked as a photojournalist for several years, during which time I covered wars in Eastern Europe and in Africa." She paused for a beat, then, keeping in mind Steffen's remark about Whitely's love of publicity, threw out what she hoped would be her pièce de résistance.

"I've already spoken to the editors at several major newsmagazines who used my pictures in the past, and they're very interested. I know that you already have a photographer among your group, but there's a big difference between taking pictures for scientific purposes and doing newsworthy photography."

"I see," was his only comment, but the sudden light in his bright blue eyes told her that she'd succeeded. Furthermore, she couldn't really blame the man for thinking she might not be up to the rigors of the expedition. Most people saw her delicate features and her large gray-green eyes and assumed that she was a fragile creature totally unsuited to rigorous work. She'd had to fight against that image all her life.

"Well, of course I must consult with the others, but I believe that they will be willing to keep our commitment to Steffen."

Amanda managed to restrain herself until she had left his office. Then she let out a whoop of joy that turned a few heads as she hurried across the campus. She knew that the others would agree, if for no other reason than that they needed Steffen's money. And she had no doubt that she could prove her worth.

She hurried across the ivy-draped campus to the huge library. They would be leaving in less than a month, and she had a lot of catching up to do. She'd read some of the articles written by Steffen and the others after their previous expedition, but now she was determined to become an expert on the lost civilization of the Kassid.

It was early evening and her stomach was growling in protest over a missed meal, when she finally set aside the pile of articles. Unfortunately they'd all been written for other academics, so now she had a growing list of other, previously published articles to find and read. Tomorrow she would go back to the library and continue her research.

What interested her most at this point was a reference to the Sherbas. Amanda had heard of them, but knew very little about them. They were a mysterious religious order that had existed for many centuries and were said to have amassed great wealth. One of Steffen's colleagues had suggested that they could be the black-robed figures portrayed in ancient art unearthed in a country that bordered the Land of the Kassid, a nation that had in ancient times been called Turvea and was supposed to have had strong ties to the Kassid.

After discovering that her refrigerator held nothing of interest, Amanda pulled on a heavy sweater and set out to find dinner. It was dusk and the streets were still filled with people, but she nevertheless felt a wariness that she'd been feeling ever since Steffen's death—a nervousness that had only increased after the fire at the cabin.

She filled her stomach with good Italian food at a small restaurant several blocks from her home, before starting home through the cool darkness. There were still people about, but far fewer than before. She moved along purposefully, her mind on the phone call she'd had earlier from the fire marshal.

No one had seen the silver-haired stranger, either before or since the fire. It was difficult for her to believe that such a man could have passed unnoticed anywhere, let alone in a rural area, which led her to decide that she must have dreamed him, after all.

Still, there was the matter of the fire itself. Someone had set it, and as far as she was concerned, the silver-haired giant was the most obvious suspect. The man did exist, after all. She certainly hadn't been dreaming the first time she saw him—at Steffen's lecture. That established his interest in Steffen's work, and if he really had broken into the cabin, it must have been to find the hidden journal. Perhaps, since he hadn't found it, he'd started the fire in the hope that it would be destroyed.

But it was all pure speculation, based on very shaky evidence. She knew that, and yet she could not let go of the thought that everything that had happened had occurred because Steffen had found that strange room. Perhaps even Steffen's death had resulted from that discovery. The silver-haired stranger could be at the root of it all.

Walking home through the darkened city streets, she scanned each and every passerby, half expecting the man to reappear at any moment. The more she thought about him, the more she became convinced that he was there somewhere, lurking in the shadows. It reminded her of the times when she'd sensed the presence of the wolf.

She turned onto her street, noting that, as usual, most of the street lamps were out. Big bags of trash were piled at the curb, and several of them were spilling their contents into the gutter. A car went past, adding the stench of exhaust to the odor of rotting garbage. Across the street, a homeless man or woman—she couldn't tell which—had appropriated a recessed store entrance for the night. A battered shopping cart piled high with his or her possessions was parked across the entrance to the shop.

Amanda wondered again if she should give up her precious loft and instead move into Steffen's town house. It was certainly a better neighborhood, but that fact hadn't saved Steffen.

More and more, Amanda was coming to hate this city that she'd always loved. From time to time she thought about leaving it and moving to some quiet artists' enclave. But crime happened in those places, too, even if they weren't so dirty and polluted.

The world is going mad, she thought. *The very fabric of civilization is being torn to shreds*. Perhaps that was why she found the lost civilization of the Kassid so appealing. But then, their world had also gone mad—and in a much more cataclysmic fashion.

She reached the street-level entrance to her loft and was just taking her keys from her purse when she heard a sound behind her. She whirled around quickly, and pain exploded against the side of her head. Just before she was plunged into darkness, she saw two figures. One of them, rushing at her out of the night, was the silver-haired giant.

*   *   *

Amanda awoke on her sofa. When she tried to move, excruciating pain shot from the side of her head down along her neck to her right shoulder. She fell back against the cushion, struggling to make sense of the situation.

It began to come back to her slowly. She'd been attacked just as she was about to enter her loft. There were two men. She'd gotten a somewhat better look at the one closest to her. He was of average height and rather slim, with dark hair and a thin, pale face. She also had a vague recollection that he'd been wearing a chain around his neck, with something dark hanging from it.

The second man, the one who had seemed to be running toward her when she blacked out, was the silver-haired stranger.

She sat up carefully, grimacing at the pain and wondering if she should seek medical attention and if she should report the attack to the police. It was perhaps an indication of her confused state of mind at the moment that she had actually staggered to her feet before it occurred to her that something was missing from her memory.

How had she gotten up here? The last thing she remembered was the attack downstairs—and yet here she was, on her sofa. And her purse and keys were right there on the table.

She sank back down onto the sofa and reached for her bag, certain that she would discover her money gone. But the contents of the purse were intact. She looked around the large, open space. There was her stereo, her TV—all her possessions. And nothing appeared to have been disturbed.

Moving very slowly, she searched the entire loft and found nothing missing or out of place. Then she forced herself to go back downstairs in the big iron elevator cage. The street door was locked, except for the chain that could only be used from the inside. Cautiously, she opened the door and peered out into the empty street.

Then she closed the door and fastened the chain and returned to the loft. Already she was wondering if she'd actually seen the second man—or had the silver-haired giant somehow become her personal bogeyman? Who was this man who seemed to be walking along the edges of the place where her dreams and reality met? And why, despite the fact that she was certain he was trying to kill her, could she not forget that strange attraction she'd felt toward him?

The pain had subsided to a dull ache by the next day, when Amanda went back to the university library to research the Sherbas, that mysterious religious order that might or might not be connected to the Kassid.

Anyone watching her would have thought she was paranoid, as she stopped frequently and scanned her surroundings, seeking either the thin, dark-haired man or the silver-haired giant. But she saw no sign of either man, and soon lost herself in her research.

The Sherbas were fascinating. There was a fair amount of information available in the library archives, although she soon discovered that most of it was speculative in nature. No one knew their origins, although the first mention of them in historical accounts could be traced back to ancient Menoan and Turvean writings.

They were a small sect, but apparently a very wealthy one. It was known that they maintained secret residences all over the world—elaborate compounds with very tight security. Many attempts had been made to learn about their beliefs, their means of support and their recruitment methods, but none had been successful. Those who had, from time to time, spied upon the compounds and the comings and goings of the members believed that whole families were involved.

One of the articles she found discussed their influence in the countries bordering the land of the Kassid. It was believed that this influence was very great, although it appeared to be exercised in secret.

It wasn't until she came to the final article that Amanda saw a photograph that had been taken of several Sherbas entering one of their compounds. She drew in her breath sharply as she stared at the picture. The two men were dressed completely in black. One had turned toward the camera, and she saw that he wore a black jacket similar to that worn by Catholic clergymen, but without the white collar.

But what really caught her attention was the long chain he wore around his neck with what appeared to be a black stone suspended from it.

A chill swept through her as she stared at the somewhat grainy photo. Her one attacker had worn a chain she was fairly sure looked identical.

She left the library deep in thought and unable to rid herself of that bone-deep chill. And yet, as she walked along the city streets, it was nearly impossible for her to believe that she might have stumbled into an ancient mystery, filled with wolves and giants and a mysterious religious order—and sorcery. All around her, the great city was poised to leap into the twenty-first century, while she felt herself falling into the ancient past.

Amanda had her first glimpse of the land of the Kassid from the deck of their chartered boat. They were about five miles offshore in calm waters, moving slowly toward the site of the submerged city. The others were talking about their planned dives, but Amanda's gaze was locked on the distant mountains that rose beyond the dense green jungle. The Dark Mountains drew her even more powerfully than she'd expected.

The day was clear and very dry, with the sharpness that came with low humidity. She had borrowed a pair of high-powered binoculars from one of the group, and she brought them into focus. *Dark* didn't really describe the great mountains. They were black, not the smudgy charcoal she'd seen in the photographs. One craggy peak after another rose to touch the blue sky, and the tops of several were tipped with glistening white. Even in summer, the snows lingered there. No accurate measurements had ever been done of the Shegalas, but they were believed to be among the highest mountains on earth.

Strangely, Amanda didn't find them forbidding. She felt a sense of awe, but not fear. She imagined great waterfalls and deep ravines and the coolness beneath the dark firs: a timeless place, but not a threatening one.

In front of them lay the thick jungle, fed by rich

volcanic soil. Wisps of what could be smoke were visible above the tops of the few of the lower peaks. The volcanoes had been quiescent for some time now, although no one could say how long that would last.

She put down the glasses and let the Dark Mountains recede into the distance. But even when she turned her attention to the discussion about their upcoming dive, the mountains remained in her mind's eye, silent sentinels guarding ancient secrets.

They would be spending the next four days here, diving to the submerged city. Then they would return to the harbor from which they'd sailed, and from there would begin the long overland journey into the jungle.

Someone in the group mentioned Steffen's name, and Amanda felt a sharp pang of regret that he wasn't here with her now. If he were, they could dive together to that strange room that had so disturbed him. As it was, she could only hope to have the opportunity to dive alone and try to find it, her memory of his map her only guide.

She wanted and needed to find that room. If she did, perhaps she could unravel the mystery that surrounded her life now. She'd told the others nothing of Steffen's journal and of the strange occurrences that had followed her discovery of it.

Amanda was a woman of the twentieth century, and she very badly needed to make some sense out of what seemed to defy logic.

"They have arrived at Ertria."

Daken nodded. "According to our information, they will be there for four days, and will then return to Menoa. They've acquired some native guides who will lead them into the jungle, and the guides have been well paid to see to it that they find nothing of importance."

"But what if they find the room again?"

"That's unlikely," Daken stated. "Steffen Lescoulans never told anyone about his discovery; they would have been swarming around here if he had. Now he's dead. But I will post a guard down there, just in case someone stumbles upon it as Lescoulans did."

The others were obviously relieved, but Daken, despite his words, was not. He knew that the red-haired woman, Amanda, was with them. She was Lescoulans's niece, and the information he'd gotten indicated that the two had been very close. If Lescoulans had told anyone of his discovery, it would be her—and that would explain her presence now. What other reason could there be for an artist to join the expedition?

"They'll never give up, Daken," one of his advisers said, breaking into his thoughts about Amanda. "Unless we see to it that there are no more expeditions."

"You already know my feelings about letting the Sherbas stir up any more trouble in Turvea and Menoa. We cannot justify fomenting wars just to protect ourselves."

No one said anything, but they didn't have to. This issue had been a chief topic of debate ever since he'd become leader of his people. He was sworn to protect them—but could he justify keeping the neighboring lands in a constant state of turmoil to do that? His predecessors had, but Daken found it reprehensible.

Nothing is easy anymore, he reflected as he stood

staring out at the jagged black peaks of his home-
land. The Sherbas had become a serious problem.
His people were fearful and restive. Sooner or later,
no matter what he did, the world beyond the Dark
Mountains would encroach upon them.

There were times when the burden of leadership
sat too heavily upon him. Elected for life by his people, Daken felt the responsibility keenly. He was not
a cruel man, and yet circumstances sometimes
forced him to take actions he knew were just that.
The matter of Steffen Lescoulans had been one such
occasion—and now there was Amanda.

His gaze went to the huge painting on the wall of
the council room. The great leader for whom he was
named stared implacably back at him. More than
eight hundred years ago, the first Daken had led his
people out of their self-imposed isolation into a
golden age. And now, here he was, the first leader
since then to bear that revered name.

He stared at the woman in the portrait: Jocelyn,
who'd won the heart of his ancestor and persuaded
him to leave the Dark Mountains. And now another
red-haired woman had come to the land of the Kassid.

Amanda swam slowly through the underwater
maze, her diving partner at her side. This was their
final day here—and her last chance to find that
room.

For four days, she'd been agonizing over whether
she should tell the others of Steffen's discovery. Her
conscience was troubling her greatly because she
knew they'd be very excited about the room, even if
it was no more than that. But there was no way to

tell them about it without being forced to explain Steffen's failure to do so—and she refused to allow her uncle's name to be subjected to scandal.

She moved on through the ruins of ancient buildings encrusted with algae that gave off a strange greenish glow. The others had all spoken excitedly about the ruins, but Amanda felt only a deep sadness for the loss of so many lives. At times, it almost seemed to her that she could feel the horror of those final moments, when the people who had lived here faced their doom.

The building where Steffen had found the room lay just ahead. The others were certain that it must have been a palace or home to whatever form of government they'd had. Yesterday they'd even reached what Amanda was certain must be the beginning of the maze that Steffen had followed into the cellars. But a decision was made not to explore further because of the questionable stability of the structure. She hadn't known whether to be relieved or frustrated, and was a bit of both.

She glanced at her diving partner. He was an experienced diver, so she had no qualms about deserting him, but she knew that he'd resist any suggestion that they split up.

The search thus far had yielded very little—and nothing really new. Since this was their final dive, everyone was desperate to discover something.

As she thought about her predicament, her eyes were constantly scanning the bottom of the sea, searching for peculiar shapes that could be hidden treasures. Then, just as she saw something interesting, her partner tapped her on the arm and pointed in that direction.

She nodded and they both swam over to the silt-covered heaps. As near as she could tell, they were inside a building, though only a small portion of broken walls remained. They began to brush the debris of centuries from the objects, which appeared to be the size and shape of large trunks. There were a lot of them. The room, if that was what it was, must have been filled with them.

For a few moments, the water became opaque as they swept off the silt, and then they were staring at what was indeed a trunk. Her partner began to examine its edges carefully, probably to determine whether it could possibly be airtight after all this time. Then he nodded excitedly to her and swept an arm around at the other trunks.

Amanda shared his excitement—but she also saw her opportunity. As soon as they reported their discovery, everyone would be down here, trying to get the trunks dislodged and lifted to the boat. And that just might give her the chance to slip away for a while.

He took out a flotation marker and tied it to the trunk before setting it free. They both watched as it bobbed upward toward the surface, and then began to make their own slow ascent to tell the others.

Within a half hour, they were all diving to the spot, eager to haul the trunks aboard the boat. Their excitement convinced her that her plan would work. It would take quite a while to dislodge the half-buried trunks, and as long as she rejoined them before they'd completed the task, she wouldn't be missed. Their full attention would be focused on the prospect of treasure, and no one would be counting the number of divers present.

Soon after they had all congregated at the spot, the water was once more murky from their attempts to free the trunks. Amanda slowly worked her way to the edge of the group—and then took off.

She found the large building again without difficulty, and a short time later reached the half-collapsed archway that marked the entrance to the cellars. Pausing only a moment to consider the danger of descending into that maze, Amanda swam past the archway and down a broken staircase. She hoped that she would be able to find the marks Steffen had made for himself, but if not, she would have to trust her memory of his map.

She confronted her first problem at the foot of the broken stairs. A hallway led off in both directions, and she saw no markers. Desperately, she tried to recall Steffen's map. Her instincts told her to turn left, so she did—and when she reached the next intersecting hallway, she saw the first of the markers.

From that point on, it was easy. She went deeper and deeper into the ruins, knowing the risk she was taking, but knowing too that she had to find that room.

And then she was there, facing a massive, age-darkened door at the bottom of the stairs. This had to be it. Steffen's mark had clearly directed her down this staircase, and nothing lay ahead of her now but the door. According to Steffen's journal, it had been closed. Now it was slightly ajar. Perhaps once the water had rushed in, he'd been unable to close it.

Now that she had found the object of her search, Amanda was brought face-to-face with her own ambivalence. She wanted to believe that Steffen's experience had been real, but if it had been . . .

She swam toward the door, ignoring her fears as she wriggled through the opening, thrusting her powerful lantern ahead of her.

It was exactly as Steffen had described it, but still, she was unprepared for the sight before her. The beam of light traveled only a short distance before being swallowed by the blackness: a blackness that glittered faintly, as though fine threads of gold hung suspended there.

She turned slowly in the water, sending the beam out in all directions, and discovered that even the ceiling was covered with the indecipherable writing—and sketches of wolves. The moving beam of light created the unnerving effect of motion, as though the writing and the wolves were moving to and fro, now toward her and then away.

She began to wonder if Steffen's experience might have resulted from this optical illusion, but before the thought had finished forming, she felt something. The water around her seemed to be vibrating, pressing ever more relentlessly against her. Her body felt heavy, rather than buoyant as it should have. She panicked and started to turn toward the door, but before she'd even completed the turn, she found herself sprawled on a cold stone floor in a small puddle of water.

For a few seconds, she just lay there—unable, despite Steffen's warning, to believe what had happened. Her brain sought frantically for a rational explanation, but could find none. The room was dry except for the puddle around her, and the beam of her lantern showed the strange writings even more clearly now without the filter of seawater.

In that moment, something changed forever for

Amanda. She understood that she was no longer living in a rational world that obeyed the laws of science. There were holes in that orderly world—and she'd fallen through one of them.

She pulled herself up into a sitting position and carefully removed her mouthpiece. The air was as Steffen had described it: cold and slightly musty. She took off her flippers and stood up, her gaze still drawn to the strange gold writing—and to the wolves. They were everywhere, drawn in great detail and in a variety of poses. They leaped and stood and lay down. They stared at her or presented their profiles. The quality of the drawings was astonishing. Her artist's eye appreciated the work of a master who had created incredible beauty in what must have been a very difficult medium.

She peeled off her gloves and reached out to touch the wall nearest her. It was very smooth. The gold had been poured into the etchings so carefully that her fingers could not detect the difference.

The black stone intrigued her as well. Its matte finish was a perfect foil for the glittering gold. She wondered if it might have been painted, but when she scratched it, nothing came away.

She set down the lantern and began to take pictures with her special underwater camera, making adjustments she hoped would result in good shots. The film came to an end before she had finished the first wall.

During this time, she'd also been listening for any sounds beyond the heavy carved wooden door, but had heard nothing. Now she walked over to it and listened more carefully. The only sound was that of her own breathing and her thudding heart.

Without the buoyancy of the water, her air tank had become heavy and cumbersome. If she was going to follow Steffen's explorations, she'd be better off without it. The speed she would gain without its weight should more than make up for the time required to get it back on again if she had to leave in a hurry.

After unstrapping the tank, she paused, remembering that she was utterly at the mercy of the forces that had brought her here. And if they chose not to let her return . . .

Once again, she chose action over thought and opened the door cautiously, half expecting to find a knife-wielding giant waiting for her. But the long corridor beyond the door appeared to be empty.

Clad now only in her wet suit, Amanda started down the unlit hallway, knowing that the beam of her lantern would give her presence away to anyone in the vicinity, but preferring the light to the darkness of this unknown place.

She passed room after room, most of them empty, but a few filled with big trunks that looked very much like the ones they'd just discovered beneath the sea. Then, as she went farther still along the hallway, she reached an intersecting corridor that was lit by oil lamps affixed to the stone walls. She quickly extinguished her own light. Steffen hadn't mentioned any oil lamps, so perhaps he hadn't gotten this far. His encounter with the men must have occurred in one of the storerooms she'd passed.

Directly across from her as she stood uncertainly in the place where the two hallways intersected was a large room half-filled with wooden crates. She moved toward them, and saw that there was writing on the sides. The writings on the black walls had been more like hieroglyphics, while what she saw on the crates bore a strong resemblance to the writing she had seen on some of the artifacts recovered from the sea. She thought she saw some similarities between the wall writings and the crates, however, and wished that she had some film left.

She returned to the hallway and stared in both directions. The oil lamps close to her were spaced about every twenty feet, and she counted them along the wall to her left. The hallway must be more than three hundred feet long—six hundred feet, actually, since she was standing near the center. What did that say about the size of this place?

For a moment, she was paralyzed by the reality of what had happened to her. She had no idea where she was, no idea of how large or how old this place was—and no certainty that she could leave.

Panic swept over her and she turned to go back to the black room. She froze. For one brief moment, it seemed that something had moved in the dark hallway that led back to the black room. She switched on her lantern and aimed it in that direction. Nothing. Obviously, she'd only imagined it. If anyone was there, he would surely have made himself known to her before this.

Her fear drained away and her curiosity about this place grew. She turned right and started down the lamplit hallway, telling herself that she would merely follow it to its end and then return to the black room. It didn't seem likely that she would encounter anyone. Steffen had probably just been unlucky. Despite the presence of the lamps, the area appeared to be largely unused.

She was still some distance from the end of the corridor when she heard the first, faint sounds. Somewhere in the distance there were children. There was no mistaking that joyous laughter and childish shouting. She stopped for a while and listened, then started forward again, drawn by the innocent and unexpected sounds. Despite her promise to herself, when she reached yet another lamplit hallway, she turned into it.

She could see immediately that this hallway, which was much shorter, ended at an open window, and she realized that the children must be outside. By now she could even make out individual voices, although she couldn't understand the words.

After casting a quick glance over her shoulder, she approached the window cautiously and peered out.

A large group of children, perhaps a hundred or more, were running about on a spacious playground. At first she thought that they were all boys, since they were dressed identically in loose trousers and shapeless tops. But then she realized that it was mix of boys and girls.

All the children had dark hair, though the shades varied somewhat from pure black through various shades of brown to a few with auburn hair. All wore similar haircuts: nearly shoulder length, and in a few cases, slightly longer. Only by their features could she tell boys from girls, and with the younger ones that was impossible.

She suddenly became aware of adult voices that were all but drowned out by the noise of the children: a man and a woman, speaking in a strange, guttural language she couldn't identify. She couldn't see them, however, and assumed that they must be standing directly below her, under the window.

All the while, as she'd been staring in fascination at the children, Amanda had also been aware of the rest of the scene as well. Beyond the playground was a high stone wall: black stone just like that in the room. And beyond that, reaching toward the sky, were the ragged peaks of the Dark Mountains.

She stared at them, only slowly coming to the realization that they were no longer forbiddingly high, and they were very close as well. She was in the Dark Mountains.

She drew in a sharp, quavering breath and forced her attention back to the children. At first, their dark clothing had somehow suggested poverty, but as she stared at them now, she could see that they were all clean and well fed and very healthy-looking.

And she realized something else, too. There was no sign of the usual bullies and none of the agressive behavior one invariably found in any large group of children. They played energetically, but there was a peacefulness to them that seemed strange.

She studied the playground equipment. It was all constructed of a very dark wood, rather than the plastic and metal she was accustomed to seeing, but it was otherwise familiar enough. Even the sliding boards were built completely of wood, with the slides themselves polished to a high gloss.

It felt strange, as though somehow several time periods had been compressed into one. The clothing of the children and their long hair plus the high stone wall suggested a medieval sort of atmosphere, but the playground equipment, despite being made of wood, seemed quite modern.

Thoroughly fascinated, Amanda moved closer to

the window, trying to see the dimensions of the building she was in or to see other buildings. But all she could see was a series of courtyards that were divided by lines of trees and shrubs, ending at what appeared to be a bridge. She could see only a small portion of it, but flanking it were two huge stone bowls. Bright tongues of flame rose from both bowls, and near them were huge chains. One end of the chains appeared to be attached to the far side of the bridge, which she couldn't see, while the other end angled high beyond her line of vision in the other direction.

A drawbridge, she thought. It looked like the kind of thing she'd seen in pictures of medieval castles.

Just as she was about to turn her attention back to the children, she caught a movement on the bridge. A small group of men came into view, riding shaggy but powerful-looking horses. Amanda drew in her breath audibly as she stared at the man in the lead, whose silver hair gleamed brightly in the sun.

"No," she said aloud. "It can't be!" She drew back from the window, shaking her head in denial of what her eyes had seen. Then she moved quickly to the window again—but they were gone.

She stared down at the children once more. They seemed so real—but were they? Was any of this real? Seeing him again made her doubt everything.

A loud whistle shrilled below her, making her start nervously until she realized that it was the unseen adults, summoning the children, who were reluctantly giving up their various activities. A man and a woman came briefly into view as they herded the children back into the building. He was older, with traces of gray in his dark hair, while the woman was young and attractive, with strong features and dark auburn hair that tumbled about her shoulders. They were dressed similarly to the children, in loose, dark clothing.

Within moments the courtyard was empty and the children's voices had faded away. In an adjacent courtyard, separated by trees and shrubs from the playground, two figures could be seen strolling: a man and a woman engaged in animated conversation. An older woman, leaning heavily on a cane, joined them, and the younger couple slowed their pace to accommodate her. All wore the same dark clothing, though the older woman was wearing a long skirt, rather than trousers.

Despite her fears, Amanda felt strangely reluctant to leave this place. There was a feeling of peace in these mountains, a sense of security that held at bay all the world's problems.

The thought crept up on her stealthily: Could these people be the Kassid? Was it possible that they'd lived here all these centuries, isolated and protected by their mountains? Or was she even now back in that underwater room, dreaming a vivid dream of ages past?

Remembering the room brought her abruptly out of her reverie. She checked her diving watch. She'd been gone from the group for more than half an hour. It was time to get back—or try to. She hurried along the hallways with a mounting fear that she wouldn't be able to return, even though just moments ago she'd been thinking that she wanted to stay longer.

She switched on her lantern when she reached the dark corridor that led to the room. It was empty, as before, and she ran along it, not stopping until she reached the black-and-gold room, where the door stood partly open, as she'd left it.

She didn't see them until she had stepped through the doorway. There were two men, and before she could manage more than a sound of surprise, one of them had stepped between her and the door, cutting off her escape route.

"Your camera, please," the man facing her said in a firm but not unpleasant tone. He was a black-haired giant with ice blue eyes, perhaps about her own age.

She ignored his request and simply stared at him. He wore dark, loose trousers and a fitted tunic made of a dark wool that glistened in the light of her lantern. Around his waist was a wide leather belt, and attached to it was a scabbard that held a short-bladed knife with an elaborately carved handle. His English was good, though rather heavily accented.

Then, seeing that she had no choice, she removed the camera strap from her neck and handed it to him. The other man remained somewhere behind her. He examined the camera while she stared at him.

"Who are you?" she asked, hoping she didn't sound as scared as she was.

He ignored her as he continued to examine the complex underwater camera. Then he abruptly handed it back to her.

"If you will remove the film, you may keep the camera."

Her fingers trembled as she tried to open it. Surely, then, they didn't intend to kill her. She removed the film and handed it to him. He glanced at it, then put it into his pocket and bent to pick up her air tank.

She was about to cry out in protest when she realized that he was holding it out for her to strap on. She let him help her secure the straps, then struggled to put on her flippers. He knelt to assist her once again.

"How do I get back?" she asked. "I don't even know how I got here. And where—"

"The gods will take you back when we leave," he replied, cutting off her question about where she was. But his voice remained pleasant, and she saw no aggression in the other man either, as he now moved away from the door.

Encouraged by their seeming lack of hostility, she asked again who he was.

"My name is Tarval, Amanda—and this is Jonat."

She was surprised to hear him use her name, but their willingness to talk made her want to get as much information as possible before she left this place.

"Are you Kassid?"

"Yes. Now you must go."

They both started toward the door, but stopped as she spoke again. "I saw a man outside—a man with silver hair. He was riding across a bridge. Who is he?"

"His name is Daken. He's our leader." He hesitated, then gave her a slight smile. "He has saved your life—three times now."

Then they were gone and the heavy door closed behind them. What had he meant about this Daken having saved her life three times? But Amanda had no time to think about it because in the next instant, she found herself gulping water in the room beneath the sea.

Hastily, she covered her mouth and nose with the breather, and then swam through the door—back to a world she could understand.

Chapter Three

Amanda returned to a scene much like the one she'd left, which only added to her sense of unreality. Some divers were still working to free trunks that were all but buried in the ocean bottom, while others were moving more trunks into rope slings to be hoisted to the surface. The water was nearly opaque from the disturbances they were creating, making it likely that no one had even noticed her absence. She joined two others who were attempting to maneuver a huge trunk into a sling and received only quick glances before they returned to their work.

I am not going to think about this now, she told herself firmly. *There will be time for that when I'm back on board the boat.*

But when at last she climbed onto the deck, the first thing she saw, beyond the fringe of jungle, was the Dark Mountains, distant once more, with clouds hovering about their serrated tops.

Five trunks had been hauled aboard, and two more would soon follow once they'd been freed from the sea bottom. All but three of the twelve-person expedition were back on board, and most of them were arguing with David Whitley, the expedition's leader, about opening the trunks. He was trying to contain his excitement by insisting that they wait until all trunks were brought up before opening any of them, while the others were like eager children on Christmas morning, wanting to see it all now.

Amanda did her best to summon up enthusiasm as she took shot after shot of the excited people hovering around the trunks. But even when she wasn't facing them, the Dark Mountains remained in her mind's eye, taunting her.

"This is just incredible, Amanda! The contents of those trunks could keep us all busy for years to come."

Amanda turned to Miriam Daniels, a tall, rangy woman of about forty who had the gaunt look of the long-distance runner she was. Miriam was a social anthropologist, an expert on the structure and functioning of ancient societies. She still bore a trace of her native British accent, and more than a trace of dry British humor.

"Do you think they're watertight?" Amanda asked.

"We're fairly certain that at least several of them are. They were very well constructed. Have you noticed the hinges and the locks? They're gold!"

Amanda nodded. Her diving partner had remarked on that when they discovered them. "What

71

is the wood? I can't understand how it's survived all these centuries."

"George says it isn't any wood he's ever seen, and he thinks it was treated with some type of preservative."

Amanda thought about the well-preserved wood door to the secret room and its counterpart in the other room. It was impossible to be certain, of course, but she suspected they were of the same wood.

Miriam had turned to face the mountains. "I've been fascinated with the legends of the Kassid ever since college, when I first came across a mention of them. But it seemed that the more I read, the less I knew."

"What do you mean?"

Miriam was still staring at the Dark Mountains. "I can't help thinking that someone has deliberately tried to prevent us from finding out more about them." She turned back to Amanda.

"Several of us who conducted independent research have reached that conclusion. For example, there would be references in histories from the eighteenth and even the nineteenth centuries to earlier works, but we would be told that the earlier works had disappeared.

"That wouldn't be too unusual under most circumstances, but the Menoans, in whose libraries we found the later works, have always had great reverence for their heritage, and works even earlier than the ones referenced had been preserved.

"And that's not all. The Menoan and Turvean scholars we talked to were anything but forthcoming when it came to the Kassid. In fact, they generally professed a lack of interest in them that sounded very false to us.

"And then there are the Sherbas. Most of us are convinced that they know something about the Kassid. A colleague of mine who couldn't make the trip believes that the Sherbas have a strong connection to the Kassid—or I should say, *had* a strong connection. But they won't talk—period. In fact, he believes they may have killed a private investigator he hired to find out something about them."

Amanda stared at her in shock. "What did the police think?"

Miriam shrugged. "Who knows? This was in Switzerland, where they don't have many murders to begin with and where they like to think such things don't happen. The investigator died of a massive overdose of heroin and they refused to believe he didn't inject himself."

"Miriam, if it's true that the Sherbas don't want anyone to learn about the Kassid, then we could all be in danger."

The older woman nodded solemnly. "That's why David agreed to smuggle in weapons for us. The Menoan government has very strict prohibitions against bringing in weapons, but he managed it somehow."

"But what about the guides we've hired? Can they be trusted?"

Miriam shrugged. "Who knows? Someone in the Menoan government found them for us, and our ambassador in Menoa stressed the importance to the Menoan officials of having reliable people, which in diplomatic-speak means that he said he would hold the Menoan government responsible if anything happens to us."

"You don't seem overly concerned," Amanda told her.

"Oh, I *am* concerned. We all are. But this is important work, and we've all faced dangers of one kind or another before on these expeditions. Surely David warned you of the possible dangers."

"He did," Amanda acknowledged. "But he wasn't very specific about them."

Another member of their group joined them then, staring with undisguised lust at the unopened trunks as he talked excitedly about their possible contents. Under normal circumstances, Amanda would have been just as excited as they were, but she was still caught in the grip of her solo "adventure." By now, as with the break-in at her uncle's cabin, she was beginning to doubt that it had actually happened.

Then, abruptly, she remembered the pictures she'd taken—and the film that had been confiscated by the man who'd called himself Tarval. She'd removed her underwater camera when she changed out of her wet suit, and had left it in the cabin she shared with Miriam. Excusing herself from the group, she rushed down there now. If the film was indeed missing, didn't that prove that what she'd experienced hadn't been a hallucination?

She recalled Steffen's writing about leaving his flippers behind. But losing flippers during a dive and losing film from a camera were two different matters. If she'd removed that film herself while she was in some sort of dream-trance, she would have ruined the camera by exposing it to seawater.

Her fingers were trembling as she opened the camera—and found it empty! She sank onto her bed, chilled to the bone. Maybe this wasn't completely irrefutable proof that what had happened to her was real, but it was good enough for her—especially when it was added to the growing list of strange occurrences.

Maybe it's time to go home, an inner voice suggested. *Finding out the truth isn't worth your life.*

But she shook her head, denying that warning. Miriam's revelations had only strengthened her determination to get to the bottom of this. She knew that it was quite a stretch to believe that the Kassid or the Sherbas could have been responsible for Steffen's death, but if they were, then she had to see to it that they were brought to justice.

She heard excited voices from up on deck and hurried back up there, arriving just in time to see the first of the trunks being opened. One of her other cameras was slung around her neck, and she began to snap pictures as they all crowded around the trunk. David was insisting that the items be removed one at a time for cataloging, but he was having a difficult time containing the excitement of the others.

The trunk had indeed been watertight, and was subdivided into several small compartments that held jewelry, while the remainder was filled with women's clothing—all of it apparently in excellent condition. Amanda hung back, taking pictures as the others began to examine the things item by item.

Even her untrained eye could see that the quality and lavishness of the jewelry indicated great wealth, as did the fabric and workmanship of the clothing itself. There were fine silks and woolens of beautiful design, some of them embroidered with fine gold thread. At the bottom of the trunk were several pairs of small, soft leather shoes, also stitched with gold thread.

All of the clothing was very colorful, suggesting great expertise with dyes, and Amanda thought back to the dark clothing she'd seen on both children and adults in the Dark Mountains.

Two more trunks also yielded women's clothing and jewelry of similar quality and style, and another was filled with children's clothing. There were two trunks containing bed linens of excellent quality that were somewhat yellowed, and then a final trunk filled with men's clothing.

There, too, Amanda saw bright colors and much gold embroidery, and she noted that their size indicated a man of something less than average male height of today. But when the last item was pulled from the trunk, she gasped in surprise.

Here, finally, was something familiar to her: a sweater or tunic made of that unusual black wool that glistened with silver high-lights. It was in both style and fabric exactly like the tunics she'd seen on the two men who'd accosted her—and on the silver-haired man they'd called Daken, and his companions.

It soon became obvious that the others found this item interesting as well. Someone remarked that it reminded them of alpaca, but another member of the group, who said his wife owned an alpaca sweater, told them it wasn't the same.

Amanda moved closer and touched it. She, too, owned an alpaca sweater, and she could both feel and see the difference. This was smoother, finer, almost slippery to the touch. Knitting was a sometime hobby for her, and she noticed too that the fine yarn had been twisted as it was knitted. The workmanship was the finest she'd ever seen.

She wanted to tell them that she'd seen this before, but something she couldn't explain kept her quiet. She could no longer rationalize it away by telling herself that she was protecting Steffen's reputation, because she was convinced that if any of them went into that room, they too would be transported to that strange place in the Dark Mountains.

Nevertheless, she held on to her secret—at least for now.

The group planned to depart after two nights in an old but luxurious hotel in Menoa's capital, together with their three guides, only one of whom spoke English.

In the meantime, Amanda used her time in Menoa to make contact with an elderly university scholar, Professor Purapeet, whom Steffen had met on the earlier expedition. David Whitley had contacted him, but the scholar had politely refused to see him. However, when Amanda called, his housekeeper said that he would be pleased to see her.

He was a very frail man who seemed to be clinging to life by sheer strength of will. In his softly accented English, he expressed his sorrow at Steffen's death, and then inquired about the circumstances. When Amanda told him, including the fact that the police doubted it was just another random killing, his dark eyes grew cloudy and distant.

"Did he find something?" Professor Purapeet asked, his voice barely audible.

"What do you mean?" she asked.

He explained that he knew what had been discovered beneath the sea, but was wondering if Steffen might have made additional discoveries. Uncertain just how much she could trust this man, even though Steffen had spoken highly of him, Amanda denied any further knowledge.

"I think perhaps he did find something—and he was killed for that reason," the old man said, his dark eyes now burning with great intensity.

"But what could he have found that would make someone want to kill him?" she asked.

He didn't answer her question at first, but told her that Steffen had attempted to contact him again after the group returned from their underwater explorations. Unfortunately, the professor had been too ill to receive him.

"It is possible," he went on after a coughing spasm that seemed to leave him even weaker, "that Steffen found something that would tie the Sherbas to the Kassid, though why he would have kept such a thing secret I do not know."

"Do *you* believe there's a connection?" Amanda had asked.

"Oh, yes, I'm convinced there is, although if I weren't already at death's door, I wouldn't say so. The Sherbas are very powerful here, as you may know."

"But what is the connection?" she'd persisted. "And why should they be so concerned about protecting a people who died more than six hundred years ago?"

Professor Purapeet had shrugged his thin shoulders. "Secrets can sometimes take on a life of their own, child. Have you ever seen a Sherba—or a picture of one?"

"I saw a picture," Amanda admitted, even though she was fairly certain that she'd seen one in the flesh as well: the man who'd attacked her outside her loft.

"They all wear a piece of black rock suspended on a chain. I believe that rock comes from the Dark Mountains—the home of the Kassid."

"So what you're saying is that the Sherbas worship the Kassid?"

"Exactly. And if I'm right, they would consider any intrusion into the land of the Kassid to be blasphemy. An old friend who has since died once told me that he believed the Sherbas have been behind the constant turmoil that has plagued these lands for centuries, that they stir up conflict to prevent anyone from exploring the region."

"Do you agree with him?"

He shrugged again. "I'm not in a position to know about such things. He was always more interested in politics than I was. But as I said, the Sherbas are a very quiet but very powerful force in this whole region."

He began to cough again, and this time the spasms seemed worse. His housekeeper rushed in and gave Amanda a reproving look. Amanda had started to take her leave, but found herself unable to do so without asking one final question.

"Is it possible that the Kassid could still exist, that they have lived all these centuries in the Dark Mountains?"

His coughing had once again subsided, and he stared at her with an intensity that made her catch her breath.

"There are those who believe that—but they will never admit it to an outsider."

"Where do these people live?"

"In the village of Wat Andara, in the shadow of the Dark Mountains. But do not ask, child. It could cost you your life."

As the Land Rover bumped along over deeply rutted roads, Amanda studied the map once again. The route their guides had marked out for them kept them away from the village—and from the foothills of the Dark Mountains. Instead, they claimed to be taking them to a place filled with ancient ruins that they'd seen with their own eyes.

Amanda glanced at the back of David Whitley's head. He was driving their vehicle, and Miriam was in the front seat with him, while Neville Tipton, another British member of their group, shared the backseat with her.

She'd told David about her conversation with Steffen's friend, omitting only her final question and his response. Now she regretted that, because she wanted very much to get to this village.

"David," she said, "I just remembered something else Professor Purapeet told me. He mentioned something about a village called Wat Andara. I've found it on the map, but it's not in the area where we're going.

"The professor said something about having heard that there were ruins there," she lied.

Whitely turned to her briefly. "I'll speak to our guides about it."

And they will tell you that there's nothing to be found there, Amanda thought. She understood that he had to treat the guides carefully, but she was determined to get to that village.

They drove on across flat, featureless plains toward the thick jungle forest. In the distance, the Dark Mountains were all but hidden behind a gray-white haze. The others were all eager to reach the first of the promised ruins, but Amanda didn't share their enthusiasm. Her conversation with the elderly professor had convinced her that their guides would show them nothing of real value.

Or at least nothing of real value to *her*, she amended. Her agenda was different from theirs. They could all go home happy if they found any ruins. In fact, after the discovery of the treasure-laden trunks, David Whitely was already declaring their expedition a success. But success for her meant unraveling the mystery of that room—and of the secret place in the Dark Mountains.

Her waking thoughts and her dreams were haunted by the man called Daken—the silver-haired giant. Who was he, and what role had he played in Steffen's death and in the attack on her? The man called Tarval had said that this Daken had saved her life three times, and it was those words that continued to torment her.

Assuming that was true—and she knew that was a very big assumption—what had he been referring to? One time could have been the attack outside her loft. She knew he'd been there—but had he come to her aid, or had he been in league with her attacker? Since she'd survived the attack and had somehow been carried back up to her loft, it seemed reasonable to assume that he had saved her life. But that meant he couldn't have been allied with the Sherba who'd attacked her, despite the supposition by the professor that the Sherbas acted on behalf of the Kassid.

The second time might well have been when she found herself in the Dark Mountains. But when could he have issued such an order? Very little time had elapsed between the moment when she saw him cross the bridge and her encounter with the two men in the black room. Did that mean that Daken had already known she would come there? And if so, why had he decided to spare her life, when she might well have gone back and told her companions about her discovery?

As for the third time he'd supposedly saved her life, she hadn't a clue. The only other time she'd been aware of that her life had been in danger was when the fire broke out at the cabin—and it was the wolf that had saved her then.

She thought uneasily about the connection between the Kassid and wolves. What exactly was it? Surely the man Daken couldn't be traveling around the world with a trained wolf as a companion. That pushed the unlikely all the way to the absurd. Still, she wished that she'd asked the professor about the wolves.

When they finally stopped in a small town to rest and eat, Amanda joined David Whitely as he talked to their one English-speaking guide. David already had the big map unfolded and was pointing out the village of Wat Andara.

"We understand that there are also ruins in that area," he said to the man, "and we'd like to go there as well."

"Very difficult journey," the guide said, shaking his head. "And no ruins there."

"But I was also told that there are people there who could tell us about the Kassid," Amanda put in. "And the village is very near the Shegalas," she added, using his name for the Dark Mountains.

The guide turned to her. His expression was neutral, but she saw something flicker in his dark eyes. "Who told you this?"

Amanda explained that her uncle had been on the earlier expedition and that he'd told her of a conversation with someone in Menoa. She claimed not to know the informant's name.

"Many stories—but not true."

Amanda and David exchanged glances, and his told her not to push the matter. She acceded to his silent request, understanding the tenuousness of their present situation. The guides undoubtedly had their orders from someone, and to make demands could lead to the whole expedition being canceled. Instead, she raised another matter.

"Are there wolves in the jungle?" she asked the guide.

Once again something flickered in his eyes, but he nodded. "Many wolves."

"Are any of them tame?"

He appeared not to understand the word, so she tried to explain, and finally he shook his head. "Not tame."

"How about Sherbas?" she asked. "Are there any living in this area?"

The guide shook his head, then walked away before she could ask any more questions. David Whitely stared after him.

"Now I'm really curious about that village. I'm sure he was lying about something."

Amanda nodded, pleased that her own suspicions had been confirmed. "But how can we get there, if he won't take us?"

"We can't—or at least we can't until we see what he has to show us. Then we can raise the issue again."

The days passed with agonizing and frustrating slowness for Amanda. Their caravan passed through the plains to the hills that bordered the jungle—and then they were in the jungle itself, travelling now on a dirt track just barely wide enough for the vehicles. David marked their progress on his map as best he could, telling them that he didn't trust their guides and needed to be sure that they could find their own way back if necessary.

The jungle was a strange and wondrous place. The biologists among their group were astounded at the variety of plant and animal life and had already nearly filled their crates with samples of plant species they couldn't identify, including something that looked much like Spanish moss, but which they claimed was a different species entirely.

It was on their third night in the jungle that Amanda first heard the wolves. She was sharing a small tent with Miriam, and they both awoke to unnerving howls that seemed to surround them. Miriam quickly reached for the gun David had given them, but Amanda merely sat up in her sleeping bag and listened to the rising chorus.

"I think I'd rather be hearing lions or tigers out

there," Miriam said as they sat there in the darkness. "The howls are more frightening."

"Our guide said that they won't attack a group," Amanda reminded her, thinking that her two experiences with a wolf had perhaps made her forget how frightening they could be.

"Josh says that they shouldn't be here in the first place," Miriam said. "They aren't known to inhabit any of this part of the world."

"But we know that they did live here centuries ago—in the time of the Kassid. Perhaps they sensed the coming of the earthquake and fled in time, unlike the people."

"That would make sense. I've heard animals often detect tremors before people do."

Miriam stopped abruptly and they stared at each other in the darkness, both suddenly wondering if the howls presaged an earthquake. But seconds later, after building to an unnerving crescendo, the howls abruptly ceased. Both women held their breath, then laughed uneasily when seconds passed with no more howls and no tremors.

The next morning, the talk was all about the wolf "serenade." Their English-speaking guide, however, shrugged it off and managed, after some difficulty with the language, to tell them that such things were quite common. The wolves resented their intrusion into the jungle and were trying to intimidate them. But he continued to insist that they weren't in any danger. No one believed him, and they all spent much of their time scanning the thick jungle.

Shortly after midday, they reached a small, primitive village, where they were the subject of much attention and thinly veiled hostility. The hostility didn't vanish even after David Whitley dispensed some of the Menoan currency he'd brought along among the villagers, but it did become less overt.

Following a lengthy and animated conversation between their chief guide and several of the village elders, the man told them that he had something to show them that might be of interest. But he refused to elaborate further as he led them on foot into the jungle. Amanda, who had temporarily set aside her camera to sketch some of the village children, followed rather reluctantly. She was convinced that they would find nothing of value—or at least nothing of value to her. Her sole interest was in getting to the Dark Mountains, which had been hidden from them ever since their entry into the jungle.

Amanda herself did not possess a weapon, but those who did now insisted upon carrying them. The guides, who had not known that they had weapons, were visibly upset. David explained carefully that they felt the need to provide for their own defense, rather than to rely solely upon their guides.

"No shoot wolf," the guide stated firmly.

No one had any intention of shooting anything unless it became necessary, but they were curious at this adamant warning, and Miriam was the first to inquire why they shouldn't shoot wolves, especially since they'd seen wolf skins adorning village homes.

The guide's fractured English was barely adequate to the task of explaining, but what finally emerged surprised them all. They did, in fact, kill wolves, but only certain wolves. Others were strictly off-limits, however, and the guide's fear was that they wouldn't be able to tell the difference.

"Never kill wolf with blue eyes," the man stated in the same tone.

"Blue eyes?" someone echoed incredulously. "If it's close enough for me to see the color of its eyes, I'm damned well going to shoot it."

But Amanda barely heard him because she was thinking about the wolf that had saved her life at the cabin. In the darkness, she hadn't been certain of the color of its eyes, but she'd had the impression that they were light in color, probably a pale blue.

"Death to anyone who kills wolf with blue eyes," the man stated, glaring at them as though slaughtering blue-eyed wolves was their purpose in being there.

As they made their way along a footpath into the jungle, David tried to elicit further information from their guide, but it soon became clear that the man had no intention of telling them what made the blue-eyed wolves different.

"It's probably just that," Miriam said to her. "Their blue eyes. Blue eyes must seem strange to them, since they all have dark eyes themselves."

Amanda thought that made sense, and given all that had happened to her, she was more than ever in favor of logical explanations—but she'd also become aware that there were things in this world that defied logic.

They walked on the path for what seemed a long time before Miriam remarked that they'd been going steadily uphill. The ascent was a very gradual one, and because she'd been lost in her thoughts, Amanda hadn't paid any attention.

Then the man ahead of them, a geologist, bent to take a soil sample. "This isn't volcanic," he told them.

"Apparently the lava flows never reached this area. That would explain why there are ruins in the region."

The path soon became much steeper, and at the same time widened out. The geologist stared at the hard-packed dirt and then at the surrounding trees and said that it looked as though they had come upon an ancient road. He pointed to a huge rockfall nearby.

"In that direction, it's been buried by a landslide—one that happened centuries ago, would be my guess."

"The result of an earthquake," someone else suggested, and the geologist nodded in agreement. They asked the guide about it and he confirmed that the road became visible again on the far side of the rocks. Then he managed to explain that this same road could take them to the ruins that were their destination, but it was impassable in too many places for them to get there by Land Rover.

"Too bad," he said, shaking his head. "Much faster."

A few moments later, they were all surprised when they came to the crest of a hill. One of the group, who'd been paying attention to the trees, told them that it appeared to have been cleared at one time, although that was obviously centuries ago, since even here the trees were ancient and quite tall.

At the very top of the hill was a jumble of dark wood beams, thickly covered with moss and brush and vines. The others hurried toward it eagerly, but Amanda stayed where she was, staring once more at the Dark Mountains. The day was clear and the humidity low, and they stood out in stark relief against the blue sky. The three guides had stopped as well, and when she turned to them, she saw that they too were staring at the mountains. Their expressions reminded her of the looks she'd seen on the faces of devout worshipers in church. One of them quickly lowered his hand as she turned his way, and she had the impression that he'd been making a sign of some sort.

He was a young man from the village, and through their English-speaking guide, Amanda asked what he'd been doing. The guide didn't even turn to the man in question.

"Old sign for the Kassid," he told her, then asked if she wasn't interested in the ruins that the others were now busy exploring.

"I'm more interested in the Shegalas," she told him. "Why are they associated with the Kassid, when it's clear that they lived far from there—along the coast?"

"Shegalas home to Kassid—given to them by the gods," the man told her, and then walked away. She noted that it was becoming a regular habit of his whenever she asked too many questions.

A home given to them by the gods, she thought as she turned back to the mountains. *Could it be a safe and protected place where the Kassid had survived the cataclysm and continued to live even to this day?*

She knew from her discussions with the others that nothing else provoked the level of excitement in them that the discovery of a lost and still thriving civilization could. They spoke often about other "lost tribes" that had been found earlier in the century. But they all seemed to agree that no such thing could happen now, in an era where even the most isolated parts of the world had been surveyed from the air.

And yet somewhere in those mountains was the place she'd visited by means of what had to be magic. And if magic could take her there, couldn't it also hold the world at bay?

Both excited and troubled by her thoughts, she rejoined the group to find them both baffled and excited by their discovery. And as she stared at the pile of wood beams, she understood why. Beneath the layers of brush and vines, the wood was exactly like that used for the trunks they'd hauled up from the ocean floor.

"Where does this wood come from?" David asked their guide as he held up a small piece.

The guide shrugged, but the man from the village, who apparently guessed David's question, responded promptly: "Shegalas."

"Those dark firs." The biologist nodded. "We should have guessed that before. It's amazing stuff—harder than any wood I've ever seen."

"But what is this?" Amanda asked. "It doesn't look as though it was a building."

David shook his head. "To judge from the size of the pieces, I'd say it could have been a tower of some sort."

They spent nearly an hour untangling the pieces of wood and laying them out, and in the end, everyone agreed with David. It had indeed been a tower. But what was its purpose?

"It could have been built as a lookout," someone suggested, but the others pointed out that building a tower would scarcely have enhanced the view of anyone using it. They were already on the highest ground in the area.

The man from the village was talking excitedly to the chief guide, who appeared to be trying to fend him off. David intervened, and the man took his arm, pointing some distance away along the hilltop. Amanda followed after them as the villager led the way. The villager might fear the guide, but his fear was obviously being tempered by his hope that pleasing the visitors would lead to more money.

The purpose of the tower became clear the moment they spotted what the man wanted to show them. Within seconds, all the others had joined them to stare at the huge disk.

It was shattered in many places, but there was no doubt that it had once been a very large round disk, perhaps six feet in diameter. Those in their group with knowledge of such things were astounded. They exclaimed in wonder over the quality of the glass, which was several inches thick. They found fragments of the black wood frame that had held it, and pieces of gold that had been fashioned into large rings.

As they all speculated about it, Amanda found herself wondering why the gold would still be here, since it was obvious that the villagers knew of its existence. She asked the guide that question and he waved an arm around to encompass the pieces of wood and the glass.

"Belongs to Kassid," he told her, as though that explained everything.

"They must have used it for communication," David pronounced. "Probably they had a sort of code, like Morse code. If this is as old as I think it is, that's incredible." He turned to the guide.

"Are there more of these?"

The guide said that there were two more that he knew of, both of them near the ancient road on hill-tops like this. Then David said that they wanted to take several pieces of wood and some of the glass with them for laboratory analysis. But the guide shook his head vehemently.

"Belong to Kassid. No move. Only look."

"But the Kassid are long gone—and this could help us to learn about them," someone protested.

The guide continued to shake his head. "Death to anyone who takes what belongs to Kassid."

Beside her, Miriam murmured quietly, "I wonder if he means that *he'll* kill us—or that the ghosts of the Kassid will get us."

The others gathered around the guides, arguing, while Amanda returned to the shattered lens to take some photos. The gold rings gleamed in the sunlight. David had theorized that they'd been put there to hold the ropes that turned the mirror, although the ropes themselves would have long since vanished.

She picked up a ring that was attached to a splinter of wood and studied it. Even though it had been fashioned for a purely utilitarian purpose, the workmanship was that of a jeweler. What incredible wealth the Kassid must have possessed to use gold for such mundane items!

Then suddenly, she became aware of being watched and raised her eyes to the jungle nearby. There in the shadows stood a wolf—a huge wolf with very pale eyes!

Amanda stared at it. It was nearly identical to the one she'd seen at the cabin, both larger and darker than other wolves. And like that other wolf, it simply stood there, its handsome head slightly cocked as it stared back at her.

Some fifty feet away, just beyond a fringe of trees, the others in her group continued to argue with the guide. When she turned slightly in that direction, she saw the villager behind her, on his knees. He was staring at the wolf and at the same time tracing something in the air before him with trembling fingers. She turned back again—and the wolf was gone.

She peered into the gloom of the jungle and thought she saw faint movement there, but couldn't be sure. She had no doubt, however, that the wolf had been there. The villager's behavior proved that. When she turned around again, the man had already gotten to his feet and was backing slowly away from the spot where the wolf had been. She turned her back on the spot and began to follow him, but he suddenly put out a hand to stop her, then pointed to the gold ring she still held. She nodded and then put it back where she'd found it. Nothing moved in the shadows now.

Chapter Four

His eyes were the same pale ice blue of the wolf, but there was a difference. The wolf had stared at her just as intensely, but with the dispassionate interest of an animal. The man—Daken—stared at her with eyes that glittered with a reluctant desire. Her body began to throb expectantly, wanting him to unleash that passion, no matter what the consequences.

Amanda knew somehow that this was a dream. It had to be. Behind him rose a structure that could only be fantasy: a gigantic black stone fortress seemingly carved out of the mountain itself. The setting sun reflected off thousands of windows, setting fire to them and providing a breathtaking contrast to the darkness of the stone.

He opened his wide, utterly masculine mouth and started to say something. She heard a deep but soft voice and a guttural accent before he was drowned out by a rising cacophony of excited voices.

Wanting to hear his words, Amanda fought to hold on to the dream. But it slipped away—and then she was jerked into wakefulness as Miriam opened the tent flap and let in the daylight.

"Hank is gone! No one can find him!"

Amanda focused on her tentmate, who was already dressed and carried with her the faint aroma of coffee. "What?" she asked, sitting up and trying to remember who Hank was.

Miriam came over and sat down on her own bedroll, running a hand through her hair, agitated. When she spoke again, her voice was much softer but no less excited.

"He went back up to the tower late last night to steal some fragments. He volunteered to do it because we really need something so we can date the tower. He never came back!"

Still somewhat groggy, Amanda asked if anyone had been up there this morning. They were camped at the edge of the village.

"Yes, of course. He was bunking with David, and when he didn't come back, David went after him. Hank had waited until just an hour before dawn, because he suspected that the villagers or our guides might be keeping an eye on us, and he figured that they would have given up by then."

"Didn't David find anything?" Amanda asked, fully alert now and thinking about the wolf.

Miriam drew in a shaky breath and shook her head. "It was dawn by the time David got there, but he didn't see anything. He's gone back up there now with the guides and several of the villagers."

Amanda thought about the missing man. Hank

95

was big and fit and certainly had looked as though he could take care of himself. He was also their most expert mountain climber, and they'd been counting on his expertise if they managed to get to the Dark Mountains.

"Did he have his gun?" she asked.

Miriam nodded. "If he'd fired—or if anyone else had—we would have heard the shots. Or at least David certainly would have. He says he didn't sleep at all after Hank left."

The wolf flashed through her mind again. But if the creature had attacked him, there would surely be . . . She stopped her thoughts there, not wanting to think about what the creature was capable of.

She got up and dressed hurriedly as guilt swept over her. She hadn't told the others about the wolf— and now Hank could be dead because of that.

"Do you remember what our charming guide said about what would happen if we took something?" Miriam asked, once again running her hands through her already disheveled hair.

Amanda stared at her as the guide's words came back to her. "Death!" she said in a choked voice. "I remember at the time you wondered if he meant that *he* would kill us, or that the ghosts of the Kassid would."

"Right—and I think we can eliminate the Kassid," Miriam responded bitterly as they both hurried outside to join the others—just in time to see David returning with the guides and the villagers.

David shook his head before any of them could ask the question. "Nothing—not a trace!"

"Not good to make Kassid mad," the guide stated. "Kassid magic very powerful."

David wheeled on him angrily. "I've heard enough of that, Shepta! The Kassid are long gone—and ghosts don't kill! You do as I told you and get a search party organized. He could have gotten lost in the darkness."

The guide gave him a baleful look, then left with the villagers. The other guides trailed along after him. Everyone else remained silent until finally Amanda spoke up.

"David, is it possible that a wolf could have attacked him?"

David turned to her. Amanda thought that he'd aged ten years overnight. There were deep circles under his eyes, and even his carrot-red hair looked dull in the morning sun.

"If a wolf . . . got him, we'd have found something. I even looked for wolf prints. But maybe it could have driven him off and then he got lost."

His gaze swept over the others. "From now on, no one goes anywhere alone. And make sure you have your weapons."

Someone brought him a cup of coffee, and Amanda could see his hand trembling as he raised it to his lips. "I blame myself," he said in a choked tone. "I shouldn't have let Hank go up there."

"It was his idea, David," Miriam pointed out gently. "And knowing Hank, he'd have gone even if you said no."

Amanda hovered on the edge of the group as she wrestled with her thoughts. Should she tell them about her discovery—and about everything else? And even now, would they believe her if she did? David's words to their guide indicated that he wasn't about to consider any explanation that defied logic, and she was sure the others would feel the same way. They were scientists, after all.

In the end, she decided not to tell them. It would serve no real purpose. They wouldn't believe her, and they were already on guard now.

What it came down to, she thought unhappily, was that she'd lied for too long, and now she couldn't give up her lie.

Their guides and a large group of villagers spent the day searching the jungle, but returned to report that they'd seen no sign of Hank. Then, just as they finished their report, the earth began to tremble.

It happened too quickly for anyone to react, and if they hadn't all felt it, none of them would have believed it happened. The villagers quickly made a sign in the air and murmured something in their own language.

"What are they saying?" David demanded, his voice shrill.

The guide cast a glance at the villagers. "They say that the gods are angry. But it means nothing. Happens all the time."

Amanda doubted that, given the reaction of the villagers. They seemed truly terrified. But their rapid signing reminded her of the time she'd seen the man Daken do that—just before she'd gone back to bed. If it had happened in the first place, of course. She still wasn't certain, but then, there wasn't much she *was* certain about at the moment.

They stayed at their campsite for another day, then moved on. Amanda had half expected that David would decide to end the expedition, but Miriam told her that while they all deeply regretted the apparent loss of their colleague and friend, they had work to do, and if they didn't push on now, they might never have the opportunity to explore the region again.

So they plunged ever deeper into the jungle, now on their way to what Shepta, the guide, promised were "very big ruins." There were no more earth tremors and no wolves woke them at night, but they were all watchful and edgy and their earlier enthusiasm was gone. Their guides had undergone a transformation as well. Whereas before they had often seemed surly and begrudging, they now appeared to be overly enthusiastic in their attempts to ingratiate themselves with the members of the expedition.

Amanda and the others regarded this change as further proof that the guides had had something to do with Hank's disappearance, although Amanda, at least, took advantage of Shepta's new loquaciousness to try to glean some information about the Kassid.

"Why do your people seem to worship the Kassid?" she asked him one evening.

"Kassid were favored by the gods," he responded.

"But *how* were they favored? They were still just people."

He shook his head. "More. The gods gave them gifts."

"What gifts?" Talking to him was frustrating, but she realized that was probably due to his limited facility with English.

He didn't respond for so long that she thought he must be reverting to his old silence. So she tried another question.

"Did the Kassid keep wolves as pets?"

He turned to her, his expression giving nothing

away as his dark eyes bored into her. "Not pets. Kassid and wolves are one."

Then he abruptly walked off, leaving his final words echoing in her ears. What could he mean? She found Miriam and told her what the guide had said. Miriam looked thoughtful.

"You know, Steffen believed that the Kassid and their wolves gave rise to all the stories about werewolves. It's possible that these people—and the people in the time of the Kassid—believed the Kassid could actually transform themselves into wolves. That could explain their stricture against killing the ones with blue eyes. Perhaps those are the wolves they associate with the Kassid."

She sighed heavily. "If only we could find something that would help us to understand the Kassid. Those trunks certainly contained some wonderful things, but they didn't really add much to our knowledge of the Kassid. Maybe we'll get luckier with the ruins—if they exist."

But Amanda barely heard her. She was still thinking about the werewolves that Miriam's words had conjured up. She shuddered. It was one thing to read tales or see movies of such creatures, but she wasn't at all certain that she wanted to come any closer to the source of such horror stories.

Over the next few days, she tried several times to pry more information out of their guide, but he had lapsed into his old silence once more, and gave every indication of regretting his momentary talkativeness. In fact, his attempts to avoid her became a joke among the group.

Finally, a week after they left the village, the guide

announced that they were near the ruins and would come to the ancient road again before day's end. And in fact, by midafternoon, they found themselves back on the road. It was overgrown with weeds and small trees, but clearly recognizable.

The sun was low on the horizon when they reached the ruins, and all of them stood in stunned amazement at the scene before them. Despite the guide's promise, they hadn't expected anything like this.

Rising just beyond the ruins were the Dark Mountains, now much closer than their last sight of them from the hillside near the village. They jutted up behind a series of smaller hills, dark smudges partially concealed by a veil of mist.

While the others moved excitedly toward the ruins, Amanda shot a whole roll of film, totally entranced by the scene. The mists clung thickly to the lower peaks and concealed much of the taller ones. At the very tips of the highest peaks, the dying sun touched the ever-present snow with a red-gold light.

Amanda felt as though she had stepped across some invisible boundary into another world, a world where time had either stopped or had no meaning. As her fellow expedition members began to wander among the ruins, she could almost feel this place resenting their intrusion and their attempts to unravel its secrets.

And then, as she lowered her camera, she saw the wolf again.

She couldn't be certain that it was the same wolf, but it looked much the same. And it stood just as motionless, with its handsome head cocked as it stared directly at her, ignoring the other members of the group in the distance.

Perhaps fifty feet separated them. The wolf stood on a slight rise beside the road, probably invisible to the others because of some ancient trees, but clearly visible to her—and between her and the rest of the group.

"What do you want?" she asked, standing her ground and not half as frightened as she should have been.

The animal pricked up its tufted ears at the sound of her voice, but didn't otherwise move. Its mouth was slightly open and she had the absurd sense that it was grinning at her.

Then Amanda did something she would later be unable to believe: she began to walk slowly toward the wolf, repeating her question. She carried no weapon, and subconsciously she knew that the others who had weapons were too far away to save her if the creature attacked—and yet she continued to put one foot in front of the other, coming ever closer to the motionless creature.

She was no more than fifteen feet away when she stopped beneath the small hill on which it stood. Its pale eyes had followed her progress, but not one muscle moved. Amanda stared into those eyes, and a very strange feeling came over her. Even later, in the quiet of the night in her tent, she would be stunned by the memory of that feeling that seemed to mix awe with a powerful eroticism.

Unbelievable as that feeling was, the other thought in her mind was equally impossible. What she saw in the creature's eyes was what she felt sure was the gleam of human intelligence.

And then the spell was broken as David began to call to her from beyond the fringe of trees. The wolf turned its head briefly in that direction, and for just a second she thought she saw annoyance in its eyes. Then it turned and vanished silently into the jungle.

Amanda walked among the ruins, closed off from the others by her thoughts. Around her were ancient stone walls half-buried beneath the lush vegetation. Excited voices rose and fell as new discoveries were made, the sounds sometimes echoing eerily through this long-dead place.

Had the encounter with the wolf been real? She was already beginning to doubt it, if only because she wanted desperately to deny her reaction to the creature. But if it wasn't real, if she was hallucinating in the very midst of her work—what did that say about her state of mind? Either way, she felt as though she were hovering on the very edge of sanity.

She clutched her camera with determination and began to photograph the ruins in the dying light that cast a mellow golden color over the stones, taking care now not to separate herself from the others. They represented sanity and the real world and she needed that very badly now.

She got what she was certain would be some wonderful shots. The town had sprawled across uneven ground, and as she descended into what must once have been a bustling town center, she was able to photograph ruins on the hillside against the glorious colors of the setting sun. When the light finally became too dim, she added another roll of film to her growing collection, knowing that despite everything, she might very well be doing her best work ever. And from the photos and her sketches, she might carry her painting to new heights as well.

The others were beginning to return to their vehicles to set up camp. Amanda was about to join them when Miriam appeared and suggested they climb a nearby hill for one last look at the town.

"This is wonderful, Amanda! David says it will take weeks for us to do a proper job of the place."

Amanda smiled, trying to share her friends enthusiasm. She did in fact find the ruins interesting, but her thoughts remained on the Dark Mountains. And if they were going to be here that long, they might never get to the mountains at all. She already knew that David had lost some of his enthusiasm for going there after Hank's disappearance, since Hank had been their mountain-climbing expert.

The two women climbed the hillside, wending their way through piles of stone and thick, tangled underbrush. Behind them, the sun had vanished, leaving only long fingers of pale light across the darkening sky. A tiny sliver of moon had risen above the Dark Mountains, and a few stars could be seen as well.

"Shepta says that the ancient name for this land was Balek. They were allies of the Ertrians, the people who once inhabited the plains and the coast. Some of the villagers in the region are descended from them. We really must persuade him to take us to them and interpret for us, though he says he can barely understand them himself."

"Do you think he's telling the truth?" Amanda asked. None of them trusted their guides now.

"Who knows? He did lead us here. According to him, the lands of the Balek separated Ertria from the home of the Kassid, and the Baleks lived in harmony with both."

Amanda sighed. "There's so much history here, but it seems that there's no way to tie it together and make sense of it."

"David has been pushing Shepta again to take us to the village you mentioned: Wat Andara. Shepta is saying that it's too far, and that we must return to Menoa before the monsoons. But David is convinced that there's something there he doesn't want us to find."

"This secretiveness doesn't make sense, Miriam," Amanda said disgustedly. "What could they be trying to hide?"

As she spoke, Amanda was staring at the hills beyond the town. Suddenly her gaze fixed on something and she pointed. "Miriam, look over there—on that highest hilltop. Something is there!"

Miriam followed her gaze and nodded. "You're right. It's a building of some sort. From its placement, it could be a fort. We'll have to check it out tomorrow."

As they walked back down the hillside, Amanda squinted through the gathering gloom for one final glimpse of the hilltop structure. She felt drawn to it somehow. Perhaps it was only its isolated location—a last outpost before the Dark Mountains.

She awoke in the deep of night, bathed in perspiration and certain that she'd been dreaming, although the dream itself eluded her attempts to grasp it. Was it the dream that had awakened her—or something else? A wolf, perhaps?

Miriam slept quietly only a few feet away, so she

doubted that any sound had dragged her from sleep. It must have been the dream. Still, she lay there listening and thought about the wolf. In her mind, it had become one wolf: the one that had saved her from the fire and the others she'd seen since her arrival here. That was ridiculous, of course, but somehow she'd let her mind fuse them into one.

It was a long time before she finally fell into a dreamless sleep.

"Definitely a fort—and quite a large one," David pronounced as they stood on the hilltop, staring at piles of stone and crumbling walls.

Amanda's gaze went, as always, to the Dark Mountains that now loomed closer than she'd yet seen them—save for that strange experience undersea, and that was receding more and more into the realm of dreams.

"It could only have been built here to provide protection from the Kassid," one of the others stated. "And that throws suspicion on our guide's story that the Baleks got along with their neighbors."

"So it would seem." David nodded. "Or perhaps we're just looking at an earlier time. Damn!"

The others all shared his frustration. They had found what must have been a truly remarkable civilization—and yet they'd have no chance to learn about it beyond what they could find among the ruins. The legend of the Kassid would remain just that—or nearly that. They did know, at least, that such a civilization had once existed.

Amanda was taking pictures while the others began to explore the site. There continued to be something about this place that intrigued her, though she couldn't begin to say what it was. She had taken only a few pictures when a shout from one of her colleagues brought them all together. The man held up his find triumphantly. Amanda's gasp was lost in the general excitement.

It was a knife—a knife exactly like the one she'd seen in that strange black room with the gold writings. There was no mistaking it, even though this one was still crusted with dirt. The handle was made of that same black wood and carved in an intricate fashion, just as the knives the two men had carried had been.

The man who'd discovered it made several quick thrusts in the air, then handed it over to David.

"Try it! Feel how well it's balanced, and how easily you can grip it."

David thrust and cut air with it, and then examined it. "It's the same wood as those trunks—and the tower." He hefted it, then handed it to the biggest member of their group, a man well over six feet tall.

"You try it, Mac. See how it fits your hand."

"Perfectly," Mac pronounced as he gripped it.

"The carvings aren't decorative," David told them. "The chances are that it was made to fit the grip of one individual."

"One very large individual," Miriam added. "Like the Kassid."

Amanda felt very nearly ill. She had just begun to accept the fact that she'd hallucinated that whole episode—and now here was proof that she hadn't. The others continued to examine the knife, now talking about what sort of metal the blade might have been. It was badly rusted and the tip had fallen away completely.

She averted her gaze, but it did no good. She had come here to solve a mystery—and had instead been plunged into something that defied understanding. For the remainder of the day she photographed the fortress and the ruins of the town, taking care to remain always near the others, who had split up to explore both sites.

It was time to tell David the truth. She knew that, and yet a part of her continued to resist doing so, even though she knew that her story would undoubtedly result in David's insisting that they go into the Dark Mountains in search of the Kassid.

She stared at the mountains, rising dark and brooding beyond the foothills. She *wanted* to go there, and yet . . .

Late that evening, after most of the others had gone off to their tents, Amanda told David that she needed to speak to him privately. They moved away from the tents to the vehicles, and there, in the darkness, Amanda told him the whole story.

His face was too deep in the shadows for her to read his thoughts, and even when he interrupted her with questions, she was unable to guess whether he believed any of it.

"I didn't tell you before because I know how absurd it all sounds," she finished. "But I'm telling you the truth, David. When I saw that knife, I knew that I couldn't have been hallucinating. The Kassid are real. I think our guides know that, and the villagers as well—and they're protecting them."

David leaned against the Land Rover, his arms folded across his chest. "I knew that something had happened to Steffen the last time," he said after a long silence. "And I can guess that the reason he didn't confide in me was that he thought I'd insist we go public. He didn't like what he called my 'publicity-seeking.' We argued about that a lot. He just didn't understand that unless you get the nonacademic world interested, there isn't going to be any money."

"You believe me, don't you?" she asked, more relieved than she'd expected to be.

"Yes, I believe you, even though I want to think that there's a rational explanation somewhere."

"Are we going into the Dark Mountains, then?"

"Yes," he stated firmly. "With or without our guides. But we'll have to explain the situation to the others, and let each of them decide."

"We may not be able to find the Kassid," she reminded him. "I have no idea where that place was."

"We'll start by going to Wat Andara. The guides don't want us to go there, and that tells me that our trail might begin there. If this leader of theirs—Daken—has been traveling beyond the Dark Mountains, that could be his starting point. There's probably a trail into the mountains from there."

"David, just because they let me go doesn't mean that they'll let us come there. After all, they apparently chased Steffen, and they might well have killed him. Or at least the Sherbas did, probably acting on this Daken's orders."

"But Daken has spared *you*," David mused.

"Three times, according to the Kassid I spoke to. But I can't imagine what the third time could have been."

"It would almost have to have been the fire at the cabin," David said.

"As far as I know, he wasn't anywhere around. I told you that it was the wolf who saved me."

"Maybe they're one and the same," David murmured, then made a sound of disgust. "No, of course they're not. I'm just getting carried away with this magic business."

Amanda stared at him as a chill swept through her. "Are you suggesting that the Kassid can turn themselves into wolves?"

"No, of course not," he said hastily.

Then they both jumped at a sound in the darkness behind the Land Rover. David signaled for her to stay where she was and remain quiet. He unholstered his gun and moved in that direction. Amanda held her breath, trying in vain to see into the night. A few minutes later, David was back.

"I didn't see anything. It was probably just some animal, drawn by the cooking smells."

Some animal like a wolf, she thought: *a wolf with pale blue eyes.* The one thing she hadn't told David about was her strange reaction to the wolf the last time she'd seen it. She was trying to forget that. There had to be some limits to the madness that had taken over her life.

Miriam had already fallen asleep by the time Amanda entered their tent, but sleep eluded her for a long time as she lay listening to the night sounds of the jungle, which, very fortunately, did not include the howling of wolves.

The tremors woke them both in the last hour before dawn. This time they were accompanied by what sounded almost like rapid rifle fire as the earth beneath them shook. Then the tent collapsed on top of them.

Calling out reassurances to each other, the two

women dug their way out of the bent poles and tangled heap of fabric, only to discover that all the other tents had collapsed as well and one of their Land Rovers had been toppled sideways into a ravine. In the confusion that followed, some time passed before anyone noticed that both David and his tent-mate had failed to appear from the ruins of their tent.

They were gone! When several of the men had succeeded in removing the collapsed tent, there was no sign of them. All their belongings were there—even their weapons—but the men themselves had vanished.

The confusion and fear intensified. It was Amanda who first realized that one of the Land Rovers was gone as well, and the others immediately began to theorize that the missing men had taken it. But when Amanda pointed out that their guides were gone as well, and that it was far more likely that they had taken the Land Rover, the others fell into stunned silence.

As the first pale light of dawn crept through the jungle and touched the nearby ruins with a ghostly light, they all searched for their missing comrades. Another tremor shook the area, but this time it was barely noticed as their situation began to dawn on them. Both their leader and his second-in-command were gone, as were their guides. One Land Rover had vanished as well, and another was now completely useless, lying on its top where it was wedged into a deep ravine.

Amanda had never thought of herself as being leadership material, perhaps because as an artist, she worked alone. But one look at the terrified and confused people around her propelled her into action. She persuaded Miriam and one of the men to fix breakfast, then went to search through the rubble of David's tent for his map.

The map had been given to them by the Menoan government, and they were already aware of its inaccuracies. But she knew that David had been making corrections to it as they moved into the jungle, and therefore it should lead them back out again.

When she couldn't find the map in the tent, she went to the Land Rover David had been using, but failed to find it there, either. Filled with dread, she returned to the center of their camp, where not even the smell of freshly brewed coffee could quell her pangs of fear.

This was probably the worst possible time to tell her story to the group, but she saw no other choice. If they were to survive this ordeal, they needed to know everything.

They were all silent as she told them all that she had told David the night before. And as she retold the story, she suddenly recalled the sound they'd heard that David had written off to jungle creatures. So she told them about that, too.

"It could have been one of the guides," she said, more to herself than to her audience. "Shepta had made it clear that he didn't want to take us to Wat Andara, and if he overheard David saying that he was going to insist upon going there . . ."

She let the sentence trail off as another thought struck her—one soon voiced by Miriam.

"But you knew about it—and nothing happened to you. In fact, you know more than any of us."

"But David was our leader," Amanda protested,

though somewhat weakly. "And Ted was his second in command."

In the discussion that followed, Amanda was surprised to realize that no one was questioning the story she'd told them. It was, she thought, a measure of just how traumatized they were at the moment. On the other hand, David had accepted it as well, and it wasn't as though she were a trusted colleague of long standing.

Everyone agreed that they had no choice but to retrace their path out of the jungle, hoping that even without the map they could find their way back. It would be a tight fit for all of them to pile into the three remaining Land Rovers, together with their belongings, but it could be managed.

As the two women were folding their tent, Amanda asked Miriam if they had truly accepted her story. Miriam shrugged.

"I believe you, of course—and I'm sure everyone else does as well. But we don't have all the facts yet, and when we do I'm sure it will make sense."

Amanda stared at her in silence, suspecting that Miriam did in fact speak for everyone. They didn't accept the notion of magic—or of a race called the Kassid who had somehow managed to survive unnoticed for centuries. They were in a state of shock and wanted nothing more than to return to civilization and sanity.

She couldn't blame them for that, because it was what she wanted, too. After carrying her things to the Land Rover, she paused to stare at the Dark Mountains. Whatever secrets they held, they could hold forever, as far as she was concerned.

*　　*　　*

They were deep in the jungle when they heard the thunderous explosion. The ground shook, rattling the sturdy Land Rovers—but they all knew that something was different this time. What that difference was they discovered some minutes later, when they reached the crest of a hill.

Beyond them, in the distance, was a horrific, yet eerily beautiful sight. One of the long-dormant volcanoes their guides had pointed out before had quite literally blown its top. A thick pall of smoke hung over it, and rivers of lava spilled down its steep sides, contrasting sharply with the green of the jungle. Even from this distance, they could hear the awful sounds of the lava devouring everything in its path. And as they stood there, the suddenly strong winds began to carry to them the acrid, sulfurous smoke.

They came to a halt and piled out of their vehicles, crowding together at the edge of the hill as they watched one of nature's most brilliant spectacles— too awestruck at the moment to realize what it meant for them.

But Amanda knew. Although she too was mesmerized by the sight, she knew what she had always known at some deeper level: they would not be able to leave this place behind so easily.

"We have to turn around," she said, breaking the stunned silence. "The lava flow will almost certainly reach the road."

As one, heads turned to her, her companions' childlike expressions of wonder slowly transforming into fear.

"We have no choice now," she told them. "There may be other ways out, but without a map we can't hope to find them. We'll have to go to Wat Andara and seek help there."

Their faces told her what she already feared. If the Kassid were behind the disappearances of three of their group—and they almost certainly were—then they were being forced to walk straight into the arms of the enemy.

And for Amanda, that enemy was personified by the man called Daken—never mind the fact that he had supposedly saved her life three times.

Chapter Five

The group turned back, retracing their journey to the ruins. Packed tightly into the Land Rover with four others, Amanda could feel their tension. They had now lost three colleagues, a volcano was erupting behind them, and they were about to throw themselves on the dubious mercy of the village of Wat Andara, a place where the influence of the Kassid was supposed to be very great.

She was not unaffected by this, but overriding it now was a growing anger. Given the events of the past few months, it had taken a while for her to put it all together, but now that she had—or thought she had—she was awash in righteous indignation and a determination to make the Kassid and their Sherba allies pay. Just what they had to atone for wasn't yet completely clear, but pay they certainly would.

They reached the ruins without incident, all of

them hoping that by some miracle they would find their missing colleagues awaiting them. But the ancient town was just as they'd first found it: silent, empty and clinging to its secrets.

From there on, they would be basically on their own, with only Amanda's memory of the map to guide them. She had studied the map because of her interest in Wat Andara, but that gave her only a sense of which direction to go. The others had paid no attention at all to the vanished map, and so were totally dependent on her memory to guide them.

Late in the afternoon, the caravan came to a halt at a point where a barely visible path intersected with the road they were traveling on. Amanda had become increasingly concerned, because the road they were on had taken a turn to the northeast, and she knew that the village lay northwest of the ruins.

The others waited silently for her to make the decision, with Miriam venturing the opinion that although the direction seemed right, the path itself looked barely passable and showed no signs of recent use.

They turned onto it, bumping along in deep ruts on a track that was so narrow in spots that the undergrowth on both sides brushed against the Land Rovers. As the sun slid away, the shadows in the dense jungle deepened, making them all increasingly uneasy. At one point they were forced to drive through a small but swift-running stream, pausing before they crossed it to refill their water tanks.

On the far side of the stream where there was a steep and mud-slicked bank, one of the Land Rovers got stuck, and they were forced to unload it and then push it up the hill. By the time they were ready to move on, dusk was settling over the land.

Driving along the narrow track at night was an unsettling experience. Their headlights pierced the darkness ahead of them, but on both sides the jungle had turned into an impenetrable darkness that fed everyone's worst nightmares.

Amanda was in the front passenger seat of the lead vehicle when they saw the wolf. The driver hit the brakes sharply and they all stared at the creature. It stood in the middle of the road, seemingly undaunted by the approaching vehicles. Its pale eyes eerily reflected the light, and its tufted ears were pricked in their direction.

"Incredible," breathed Miriam from the backseat. "What a beautiful animal."

"I didn't know that wolves could be that big," someone in the backseat said. "Does this look like the ones you've seen before, Amanda?"

"Yes." Not only did it look the same, but she was sure that it *was* the same.

"The headlights must be confusing it," the driver said as he began to edge slowly forward.

But the wolf didn't budge. It simply continued to stare at them. Even though Amanda knew that it couldn't possibly see her behind the bright headlights, she felt as though the creature were staring directly at her. That same strange, sensual feeling began to creep through her.

When they were within fifteen feet of the animal and it still hadn't moved, the driver reached for his gun. "Maybe if I fire the gun, it will scare it off," he suggested in an uneasy tone.

"No!" Amanda said, the single word an explosion

of sound that escaped her lips without any conscious intent on her part.

"I'm not going to shoot *at* it," the man protested. "The sound will—"

"There's something wrong up ahead," Amanda said. "It's warning us."

A stunned silence followed, and she hastily explained how a wolf had saved her from the fire at Steffen's cabin. But what she couldn't explain was her certainty that the wolf was once again warning her. The feeling was very powerful, overwhelming the other feelings that the creature had summoned forth in her.

No sooner had the words left her lips than the wolf abruptly vanished into the blackness of the jungle. Amanda picked up a flashlight and opened the door.

"Amanda, no! It could still be there."

She turned to Miriam and shook her head. "It won't attack me. I just want to see what's beyond that bend."

One of the men offered to come with her, but she refused, fearing that he might become trigger-happy. It wasn't bravery that sent her out into the jungle night, but rather an absolute certainty that no harm could come to her.

She advanced through the beams of the headlights into the darkness beyond. Behind her, the voices of the others rose as people from the other vehicles came forward to find out what had happened.

The narrow road ran along the base of a hill, curving around it just beyond the reach of the headlights. Amanda reached the curve and stopped, aiming the flashlight ahead of her.

She drew in her breath sharply. Just on the far side

of the curve, several large boulders had rolled down from the hillside and lay in the road. As she stared at them, there was no doubt in her mind that their Land Rover would have hit them before it could have stopped.

She turned around to go back to the others—then abruptly halted. The wolf was standing just off the road, staring at her. And that feeling was back—more strongly than ever.

"What are you?" she asked, her voice a mere whisper. "Why did you warn us?"

As she spoke, the animal's ears twitched and it cocked its silver-and-black head. For one irrational moment, Amanda was certain that it understood the question and found it amusing. And then it vanished into the night.

They spent the night trying to sleep in their vehicles, hoping that they would be able to clear away the boulders in the morning. It was very late by the time Amanda fell into confusing and powerfully sensual dreams of a wolf and a man with silver hair.

She was still caught in those dreams the next morning as the men attempted to move the boulders. In the more rational light of day, she saw the dream for what it was: a result of the old werewolf legend about men who could become wolves. But in all those legends, the werewolf had been still a recognizable human figure—not a true wolf.

It's not possible, she told herself. In spite of the plain evidence of magic at work that she'd already experienced, Amanda clung tightly to the belief that men could not transform themselves into wolves. That, for her, was beyond imagining.

Within an hour the men had succeeded in clearing the road, and they were once more on their way. Their compass showed that they continued to travel in a northwesterly direction. It was only guesswork on her part, but Amanda believed that they would have at least two more days' journey before they reached the village.

As dusk arrived after an uneventful day, they found a small clearing just off the road and pulled the vehicles into a circle. Everyone was complaining about the discomfort of trying to sleep in the Land Rovers, and someone suggested that instead they pitch their tents and post a guard. Two men volunteered to take shifts, and they hauled the tents out of the vehicles and set them up in a tight circle. Amanda was uneasy, but she too had suffered from trying to sleep sitting up in the Land Rover.

Once again, her sleep was filled with strange, barely remembered dreams—but this time she woke up to face a real nightmare.

It was full daylight when she awoke to find Miriam gone from their tent. She pulled herself out of the bedroll and was brushing the tangles from her hair when she belatedly realized that it was very quiet beyond the walls of the tent. The only sound she could hear was distant birdsong.

Cold terror filled her as she started toward the tent flap. And when she opened it and saw Miriam's body lying outside, she staggered backward and tripped over Miriam's bag. Then she sat there breathing deeply for a few seconds before once more getting to her feet.

Miriam's throat had been slashed, literally from ear to ear. Amanda started toward her, calling her

121

name as her brain continued to deny what she was seeing.

The next moments took on a surreal quality as she ran from tent to tent, calling out the names of her colleagues. But there was no one to hear. In each tent she found bodies, all of them like Miriam's. Most were still in their bedrolls, obviously killed before they could awaken.

Amanda staggered back to her own tent and sat there numbly. Tears stung her eyes, but would not flow. Beneath the horror, a rage was building in her. She closed her eyes, but the images of those bloody, lifeless bodies were burned into her brain. Then, after an unknown length of time, she was pulled from her near stupor by strange yipping sounds and growls.

Giving no thought at all to her own safety, she flung open the tent flap and found a pack of hyenas growling and snapping at each other as they encircled Miriam's body. They all raised their heads in her direction when she appeared, and she shrieked at them, barely recognizing her own voice. When she advanced on them, still screaming, they backed off, growling, but remained at the edge of the clearing.

Caught now in the throes of a great rage, Amanda walked over to the dead woman and picked up the gun that lay on the ground beside her. She took careful aim, then fired at the closest hyena. It dropped in its tracks, and the others scattered and ran. The sound of the gun echoed in her brain, and she let the weapon slip from her fingers, horrified at her own violence.

It was in that moment that she first realized she was now totally alone in the jungle.

"I can't leave them here," she told herself aloud. "The hyenas will come back and get them."

So she began to drag the bodies of her dead comrades into the Land Rovers, an effort that took her more than an hour and left her so tired that she barely had the strength to gather up their belongings. These she went through before stowing them in the Land Rovers as well, taking from each bag their notebooks and journals and the laptop computers several members of the group were using to store their data.

In the process, she found pictures of families and lovers, smiling faces blessedly oblivious for now to the fates of their loved ones. Except for Miriam, she hadn't gotten to know any of them well, but as she went about her gruesome task, images came back to her: the distinctive laughter of one, the habit another had of fogging his glasses with his own breath and then wiping them with a bright red handkerchief. Good people, all of them: people who didn't deserve to die in their bedrolls in a jungle.

She had nearly completed her task before it occurred to her to wonder how it was that she had been spared their fate. Had Miriam heard something and gone outside to check on it, thereby drawing attention away from Amanda as she slept, oblivious to the slaughter around her?

Finally she gathered up some food and stowed it in the remaining Land Rover, together with her own bag and cameras and the items she'd taken from the others, and she drove away.

The narrow path was deeply rutted and now began to twist and turn upon itself as she drove into the foothills of the Dark Mountains. She was grateful for the attention required to maneuver the treacherous road because it prevented her from thinking—both about what she'd left behind and about what lay ahead. Numerous times during the journey, she reached over to touch the gun that lay on the seat beside her, near an extra box of ammunition. The cool metal felt very reassuring.

She had been on the road for just over an hour when she crested a hill and saw a village below her in a deep valley. She braked sharply and stared at it, even blinking several times to be sure that she wasn't imagining it.

It had to be Wat Andara. She was sure that there had been no other village on the map. She'd obviously misjudged the distance.

The steering wheel felt hot as her hands turned to ice. The killers must have come from the village. She threw the gearshift into reverse, then stopped. She had no choice but to hope that not all the villagers were vicious murderers. There was no place else for her to go. Knowing that she could well be going to her death, she started forward, down the hill to the village.

By the time she reached the center of the small village, it seemed that every house had emptied out and a veritable parade was following her. She kept the windows closed, despite the stifling heat, and made certain that the doors were locked as well. Then she came to a stop and stared out at the faces that were peering in at her.

A tentative but welcome relief came over her as she met their stares and saw only curiosity. In the crowd that had gathered were both men and women, some carrying small babies—and a large group of other children as well.

The village appeared to be very prosperous, though quite primitive. She had already passed grazing herds of fat cows and sheep and lush fields planted in neat rows.

The people were healthy and well fed, and she immediately noticed the glitter of gold on them. Both men and women wore gold chains around their necks, and numerous rings, and all the women wore gold earrings as well.

She scanned the men carefully and saw no weapons of any kind, so she rolled a window down partway, wondering how on earth she was going to be able to communicate with them.

"Wat Andara?" she asked, waving an arm around the village.

She was immediately met by many nods and then smiles and much chatter in a language that fell pleasantly upon her ears. She could not imagine these people attacking her, but she still picked up the gun and stuffed it into her waistband before getting out of the Land Rover. Several nervous glances were cast at it, but no one ran, and no one tried to attack her.

Her head was throbbing, and when she stood up, a wave of dizziness forced her to brace herself against the door, reminding her that she hadn't eaten all day. But she had to find a way to communicate with these people, so she ignored her discomfort and began to try to make them understand her situation.

She wasn't sure whether or not she was succeeding. They continued to nod and smile and talk to each other. She tried to explain that there had been others with her, and that they'd been killed. When she drew her finger across her throat to mime the murders, she began to cry.

Her sobs were met by gasps and much excited chatter, and then two women stepped forward and touched her arm tentatively. She let them lead her to a nearby cottage, stumbling a bit as the dizziness got worse.

But even in her present condition, she wanted desperately to make them understand that the bodies of Miriam and the others must be brought out of the jungle. At the doorway of the cottage, she turned to see if anyone was going to go back for them, and breathed a sigh of relief when she saw two young men get into her Land Rover and drive off.

But her relief was short-lived, because instead of retracing her path, they drove off in the opposite direction. She ran back to the remaining group, shouting "No!" and pointing in the direction from which she'd come.

No one seemed to understand, however, so she stood there helplessly, watching the Land Rover disappear on a road that led up into the hills. Then, just as she was about to go back to the cottage, she caught a glimpse of something on the top of the hill. Fighting off yet another wave of dizziness, she squinted at it.

It was a tower of some sort, and such was her condition at the moment that it took her a few seconds to realize that it looked just like the sketch one of her dead colleagues had made to depict the fallen tower they'd found. This one, however, appeared to be in good condition.

Through the fog that was taking away her reason, Amanda tried to guess the building's purpose. The

Land Rover had disappeared from view in the thickly wooded forest, but she was sure it must be headed in the tower's direction.

One of the women took her arm and, murmuring sympathetically, led her into a neat little cottage. Amanda forgot all about the tower as she inhaled wonderful cooking aromas. She was by now so exhausted that she could barely eat the food they brought her, and tried to refuse the strange but pleasant cup of tea they pressed upon her afterward. But the women were insistent. She drank it and, within moments, slipped away into unconsciousness. A short time later, a young man came into the cottage and carried her into a tiny bedroom.

"Wake up, Amanda!"

At first the voice seemed to be that of Miriam. She'd been trying to explain to her about the strange feelings she'd had when she encountered the wolf. She ignored the summons, certain that she didn't want to wake up, but not understanding why.

Another, softer voice spoke in a language she didn't understand, and the first voice replied impatiently. It was only then that it began to get through to her that the first voice was male. She opened her eyes.

He was leaning over her, his pale, nearly colorless eyes peering at her intently. The lamp in the small room reflected off his thick silver hair. She blinked, wanting desperately to believe this was part of the dream.

"Daken!" she said in a husky voice still thick with sleep.

He merely nodded, then sat down on the edge of

the narrow bed, sending her tumbling against him as the bed sagged beneath his weight.

"I need to know what happened," he said. His tone was harsh, and seemed even more so because of his guttural accent.

She ignored the implied order as she studied what might or might not be an apparition. His words brought it all back to her in bloody detail. Tears welled up in her eyes, but she fought them back.

His was a compelling face—not really handsome, but compelling nonetheless. Even if he weren't so huge, this man would not pass unnoticed in any crowd. His face was broad and square-jawed, and he had a deep cleft in his chin beneath a wide, utterly masculine mouth. His nose was slightly crooked, as though it might have once been broken. And despite the thick silver hair, he was not that old: perhaps in his late thirties or early forties.

But for all that, it was his eyes that held her: eyes the shade of a winter sky—and at the moment, just as cold.

She was filled with a strange sense of being in the presence of something very primitive, almost feral. His speech, though harsh, had been civil enough, and yet she could not shake her unease. An aura clung to him, and it was both terrifying and powerfully sensual.

Like the wolf, she thought with horror as she moved away from him, as far as the narrow bed would permit.

For one brief moment, it seemed that something flickered in his pale eyes, but when he spoke, he merely repeated his previous words.

"They were all killed," she said. "I'm the only one

left." And to herself, she added, *But you already know that. You killed them—or had them killed.* A deep, burning rage was once more building inside her. She glanced toward the table beside the bed and saw her gun there.

His gaze followed hers and he reached over to pick the gun up. With obvious expertise, he removed the clip before replacing the weapon on the table. After pocketing the clip, he turned his attention back to her.

"Tell me what you remember."

She told him. It was easy, because there was very little for her to tell. But it wasn't easy to control her anger as she told her story. She managed it only because she knew she couldn't afford it now. She had to keep her wits about her.

"You saw no one?" he asked when she had finished.

She shook her head, afraid now to speak because the rage she felt might come pouring out. Instead, she turned her attention to more practical matters.

"I put them into two of the Land Rovers so the animals wouldn't get them, but I don't want to leave—"

"That has been taken care of," he stated, interrupting her. "They have been buried at the edge of the village."

He abruptly got up. Standing, he seemed nearly to touch the ceiling. "You will stay here tonight. Someone will come for you in the morning."

He was gone before she could reply. She heard him speak briefly to the women who'd brought her here, and then there was silence.

What had he meant when he said that someone

would come for her? Who was coming—and where would they take her?

When she awoke again, sunlight was streaming through the small window and she could hear voices both outside and inside. Delicious smells seeped around the edges of the door. Her stomach growled in anticipation, but she ignored it as she tried to sort through her confused thoughts.

Had he actually been here last night—or had it only been a part of her dream? She sat up and clenched her fists in frustration, wondering if she'd ever again be certain about what was real and what was only a hallucination. It felt as though her grip on sanity was slipping away, leaving her forever in a sort of dream-stupor.

Then her gaze fell on the gun and she recalled how he'd removed the clip. It was gone. But had he taken it, or had someone else removed it?

She got out of bed just as there was a soft knocking at the door. When she opened it, the younger of the two women from the previous night stood there smiling at her. The woman began to mime the act of eating, and Amanda returned her smile and nodded.

As Amanda ate the food that had been prepared for her, the two women hovered over her, treating her as though she were a royal visitor. Several times, others appeared at the open door and stared in at her, then vanished. She wanted desperately to know if the man Daken had actually been here last night, and finally spoke his name questioningly to the two women.

To her dismay, they both shook their heads, while at the same time making that strange gesture she'd seen the men from the other village make.

Amanda was horrified. She must have dreamed it after all, even though it had seemed so real. And that meant that no one was coming for her—and it probably also meant that no one had tended to the bodies of her colleagues.

When she had finished eating, the two women led her from the cottage and along a path. She saw a few other villagers around, but no strangers. She was wondering if anyone here might possess a radio transmitter and how she might find out, when the women beckoned her into a long, low building.

A strange but not unpleasant smell greeted her, and she stared in surprise at what must be a natural hot spring for bathing, contained inside the stone building. There were other women present, some of them with babies and young children, and everyone smiled at her. Her hostesses brought her soap and rough towels, then gestured to the bubbling mineral waters.

Amanda undressed and sank gratefully into the water, which was a perfect temperature. She lathered her body and her hair and then lay back against the curved stone sides, watching the antics of several young children and listening to the soft voices of the women.

What was she going to do? Could she persuade these people to help her get back through the jungle? She didn't know what to make of the women's reaction to her mention of Daken's name. It was clear that they recognized it, but their reaction could have been one of respect—or of fear.

Contemplation had become her enemy. She dared not think about the desperate situation she found herself in, and she dared not think any more about her dead colleagues. Most of all, she dared not think any more about the man called Daken and about the effect he had on her. To do so was to invite madness, and Amanda was convinced that she was walking a fine line as it was.

The women who'd brought her here had gone, but now they returned carrying a bundle of clothing. She belatedly realized that they had taken away her own clothing after she'd discarded it.

She climbed out of the bath and toweled herself dry, then accepted the garments they gave her: simple, loose-fitting trousers and a long, loose tunic identical to the clothing they themselves wore. Apparently these people didn't believe in undergarments, she thought with some amusement. Well, she could change into her own clothes later.

The two women led her from the bathhouse, but instead of turning back to the cottage, they continued on a path that wound around the edge of the village and up the wooded hillside. Amanda grew nervous, wondering where they could be taking her. By the time they reached the top of the hill, she understood—and she also realized that Daken's visit must have been real after all.

On the broad, flat top of the hill was the village cemetery. It was nearly covered with grave sites, each marked by simple stones engraved with indecipherable writing. In one small section, just off the path, were fresh graves, marked only by small piles of stones. She counted them and knew that her comrades had been buried here.

The women retreated some distance away to allow her privacy, and Amanda bowed her head. Her tears

132

flowed, but beneath the pain was a renewed determination to make whoever had done this pay dearly.

She lifted her head and stared at the highest peaks of the Dark Mountains, looming just beyond the foothills. The village itself lay in a deep valley from where the mountains were not visible, and she suddenly felt certain that this spot had been chosen for the cemetery because of those dark, silent sentinels.

It came to her then that if, as she believed, the Kassid and their leader, Daken, were responsible for all those deaths, the best revenge she could take would be to expose them to the world. For centuries they'd lived in their splendid isolation, and she now became determined to see that peace shattered. They couldn't possibly possess enough magic to hold off the hordes of scientists and journalists who would come running to the Dark Mountains once the word was out.

Feeling much better, she turned around—and saw that the two women had vanished. In their place stood three men—and one of them was the man called Tarval, whom she'd last encountered in the black room in the Dark Mountains.

These, then, were the "someones" that Daken had said would be coming for her.

Her first thought was to run, perhaps to find her Land Rover and take her chances in the jungle. So she sprinted down the hillside, through the forest. Behind her, she heard one of them calling her name and ordering her to stop.

She ran into the village and headed for the square, hoping that her Land Rover would be there. It was, and so were the other vehicles. She turned and saw the three Kassid bearing down on her, and so she jumped into the Land Rover and quickly locked the doors. The keys were in the ignition and the trusty vehicle started right away. Leaning on the horn to scatter the crowd that had gathered, she roared off. In the rearview mirror, she saw the three Kassid climbing into one of the other vehicles, and then they were lost to view.

She drove recklessly fast along the twisting road, reasoning that they couldn't be that skilled at driving. But she knew that somewhere ahead of her lay the obstacle that had forced the group to come this way in the first place: the volcano. She could only hope that the lava flow hadn't reached the road.

And then she realized that the volcano wasn't her only problem. The gas gauge was near empty, and she had no extra gas in the vehicle. She couldn't hope to make it out of the jungle without a refill, and the extra tanks were in one of the other vehicles.

It was then that she remembered the vehicle that had tipped over into the ravine. There was siphoning equipment in the Land Rover, but could she make it that far?

Somehow she did, even though for the last few miles, the gauge showed that the tank was empty. On the twisting road, it was impossible for her to know if the Kassid were following her, but she had no time to worry about that as she came to a halt near the ravine where the other Land Rover lay on its roof.

She grabbed a gas can and the siphon and scrambled down into the ravine. In her haste, she managed to suck some gasoline into her mouth. She turned to spit it out—and saw the wolf.

It was standing at the top of the ravine, staring

down at her with that same intent expression. She forced herself to ignore it and continued to siphon the gas from the disabled vehicle. Then, dragging the heavy can, she started back up the hillside. The wolf continued to stand there watching her. She continued to try to ignore it.

She turned her back on it and dragged the can over to her Land Rover, where she unscrewed the cap and began to lift the can to pour the contents into the tank. Just as she lifted it, the animal leaped upon her.

She rolled over, desperately trying to get away from it, shocked that it would attack her. But then she realized that *she* hadn't been the object of its attack. It stood there, between her and the gas can, which lay on its side on an incline—the precious fuel spilling down into the ravine.

She started to get to her feet, hoping to save at least some of it, but the wolf leaped at her again, then backed off. Behind it, the gas continued to spill from the can until only a trickle remained.

Amanda sat there, too stunned at the wolf's actions to fully consider the extent of her loss. Twice now, the animal had attacked her, and yet it hadn't hurt her in any way, except to knock her down. And it was plainly obvious that it had done so to prevent her from refueling her Land Rover.

"What are you?" she asked, staring at it in horror. No animal could be trained to take such an action. If it belonged to the Kassid, they could have ordered it to keep her from escaping, but how could they have taught a wolf to understand transportation and fuel?

The wolf began to advance, moving slowly with its head down. It reminded her of a dog that had just committed some unpardonable sin and was trying to get back into its master's good graces. Even its bushy tail was wagging.

Amanda was terrified, but she reminded herself that this creature had had several opportunities to kill her, but had yet to harm her. She stared into its intelligent eyes and waited to see what it would do.

It walked to her and stopped with its head scant inches away from hers—and then it began to lick her cheek! She jerked back, startled, and it moved away slightly. She put up a hand to touch the spot and came away with blood on her fingers. She must have scratched her face when the animal had knocked her to the ground.

Slowly, tentatively, she put out a hand to the wolf, and once again it lowered its head until her fingers rested on its forehead. She scratched it, and then ran her fingers through the thick ruff of fur around its neck. It made low, growling sounds that she took to be sounds of pleasure.

Suddenly it lifted its head again and its ears pricked up as though it had heard something. She listened, too, astounded that she had temporarily forgotten her predicament—and the likelihood that the men were following her. She heard nothing, but the wolf turned suddenly and loped off down the road.

She scrambled to her feet and went to check the gas can. It was empty. And now she could hear what the wolf must have heard: the unmistakable sound of an approaching vehicle.

Once more, she half ran and half slid down into the ravine. It was possible that someone had left a gun inside the other Land Rover. Several of their group had been loath to carry weapons, and often left theirs in their vehicles.

The sound of an engine grew louder and louder as she flattened herself on the ground beside the over-turned Land Rover and tried to wedge herself through the open window. Just as the sound of the engine reached a crescendo and then died, her grop-ing fingers closed around the barrel of a gun.

Above her, doors slammed, and then one of them, probably the man called Tarval, began calling to her, saying that they weren't going to hurt her.

With the gun now in her hand, she huddled beside the vehicle, knowing that they couldn't possibly see her from above. But sooner or later, they would check down here—unless they thought she'd walked off to hide among the ruins of the town. If they fol-lowed on foot, she could take their vehicle and hope it had a full tank.

She listened to their voices as they spoke in their own language. The voices seemed to be moving away. Her hopes rose, and she crawled to the rear of the vehicle and peered around. There was no sign of anyone, and they'd parked behind her, right at the top of the ravine.

She hurried up the hillside, ran to their Land Rover and pulled open the door. The keys were gone! Desperately, she thought about trying to siphon gas from it and started toward the gas can.

This time she didn't even see the wolf until it had knocked her to the ground. The gun flew from her hand. She lunged for it and found her arm caught in the powerful grip of the animal's jaws. Its teeth bruised her flesh, but she was frighteningly aware that it could do far worse.

The wolf let go of her arm and lifted its head, emitting a long, unnerving howl. Within seconds, the man called Tarval appeared, followed quickly by the others. Amanda made another attempt to reach the gun, but this time Tarval picked it up.

Then he stared at the wolf, and the creature stared at him for what seemed to her to be a very long time. She had the uncanny sense that some sort of silent communication was taking place—and then the wolf turned to her briefly before bounding off into the jungle.

"You must come with us," Tarval said, his voice surprisingly gentle. "You will not be harmed, Amanda."

She got slowly to her feet. "Where are you taking me?"

"Back to the village. We will leave in the morning."

"Leave? To go where?"

"To the Dark Mountains—to our home. You have been there before." He actually smiled at her.

"Why are you taking me there? I don't want to go there. I want to—"

"Daken has ordered us to bring you there."

"I want to speak to him. Where is he? He must be around somewhere. He came to see me last night in the village. Why has he sent you to capture me instead of coming himself?" She was so angry that her words tumbled out breathlessly.

"He is on his way home. You will see him when we get there."

Chapter Six

Amanda couldn't sleep. After a time, she gave up trying. They had brought her back to the cottage where she'd stayed the night before, where the two women had greeted her with smiles—as though she were a welcome guest instead of a prisoner.

Tarval had refused to answer any of her questions, and his companions said nothing at all. As soon as the women had gone to bed, Amanda had tried to escape again. But when she cautiously opened the door to the cottage, after listening for sounds outside, she went only two steps before coming face-to-face with one of the silent giants, who had gently but quite firmly taken her arm and ushered her back inside.

So she had waited—and then tried to escape through the window in her bedroom. But her guard was there before she'd even lowered herself to the ground. He seemed to find the whole thing rather amusing as he unceremoniously lifted her back through the window.

She lay there in the darkness, trying to think of a way out of the situation. She'd never be able to escape if they took her into the Dark Mountains. And why were they taking her there? Or more to the point, why was she still alive? She was certain that these men—or some other Kassid—had killed her colleagues, and had probably killed Steffen as well.

The answers lay with Daken, their leader. They were obviously acting on his orders. She wrapped her arms around herself, shivering as she thought about the silver-haired giant, and about her own confusing reaction to him. The man terrified her— but he fascinated her as well.

She drifted into that place somewhere between wakefulness and sleep, her mind becoming a kaleidoscope of all that had befallen her during the past few months. The images tormented her, demanding an explanation when she had none.

At some point she must have passed into sleep, because suddenly she opened her eyes and saw daylight outlining the curtains at the window. She got out of bed and peeked through them. The tentative light told her that it was just past dawn, and she began to think about another escape attempt. Perhaps her silent guard had dozed off, too.

She had her knee up on the windowsill when she heard a sharp rap at her door, followed by the now-familiar voice of Tarval.

"Amanda, it is time to leave."

She dove out through the window and raced around to the road in front of the cottage, hoping to reach one of the Land Rovers before he became impatient and entered the room. But just as she reached the road, she saw the other two Kassid, riding the ugly horses she'd seen when she'd come through the black room into their mountain home.

She turned around—and now saw that Tarval was coming toward her. He wore the amused but exasperated smile of a parent who was being forced to deal with a particularly difficult child. She wanted to lash out at him, but knowing how futile that would be, she simply walked past him, back to the cottage, where the two women were busy preparing breakfast.

Soon the women hovered about them, plying them all with more food than she could possibly eat, although her captors more than made up for her own lack of appetite. She did her best to ignore them, and they in turn ignored her, talking in their own language and then switching from time to time to the language of their hostesses.

When they led her outside, she saw that her bag had been strapped to one of the horses. "What about the rest of my things?" she demanded of Tarval, referring to her cameras and the things she'd taken from her dead comrades. "And what about the Land Rovers?"

"That will all remain here for now," he told her. "Do you know how to ride?"

"Yes, but I've never ridden horses like these," she replied scornfully as she stared at the ugly beasts.

He actually chuckled. "You will come to appreciate them as we do. They are well suited to the mountains."

In addition to being ugly, the beasts were very big,

and she grudgingly accepted his assistance to climb into the saddle. Some of the villagers were out and about by now, and Amanda scanned their faces. There was no help to be found there. It was clear that they were allied with her captors.

They rode out of the village on the same path that she'd walked the day before, when the women had taken her to the cemetery. As they passed it she turned to the fresh graves, and tears of anger welled up in her eyes.

"You killed them," she said to Tarval, who rode beside her. "And you will pay for that."

"We didn't kill them," he replied calmly, following her gaze.

"Then you had them killed!" she cried angrily. "And you won't get away with it—no matter what happens to me. People will—"

"The situation is more complicated than you can know," Tarval said, cutting her off.

But no matter how many questions she asked, he refused to explain.

They rode over the low foothills, with the Dark Mountains looming ever closer before them. The big, ungainly horse she rode proved to be very comfortable, as did the big, curved saddle. And by midday they were in the mountains, moving steadily upward on a narrow, winding trail.

The air was much cooler here, and fragrant with the aroma of the dark firs that pressed close to the trail. Amanda began to shiver from the cold air, and asked them to stop so she could put on something warmer. Tarval brought them to a halt and the men removed knitted tunics from their saddlebags, while she got out her jacket. She noticed that their tunics were identical to the ones she'd seen before: made of that strange, shimmery black-and-silver wool.

The trail wound higher and higher into the Dark Mountains, and by now Amanda could plainly see where the name had come from. Not only were the firs darker than any she'd ever seen, but in places where there was bare rock, it too was black: the same black as that chamber undersea and its counterpart in the Dark Mountains.

At first she was very nervous about riding on the narrow trail, for its edge often dropped off steeply for hundreds of feet. But before long she understood what Tarval had meant about the horses. They were remarkably surefooted and seemingly tireless. Although she had been silent for most of the journey, she felt compelled to remark upon the animals' abilities.

"You'll have reason to appreciate them even more when the trail becomes steeper," Tarval replied. "They were bred many centuries ago to live in these mountains."

Amanda tried not to let herself be affected by the haunting beauty around them, but she soon succumbed to it. Deep ravines lay in perpetual shadow beneath ancient trees, and here and there she could see traces of snow, even though it was by now midsummer. Sunlight clung to the tops of the trees like a pale, gauzy covering, and birds flitted about, filling the silence with their calls.

Then, as they rounded yet another sharp bend in the trail, she saw a wolf: obviously a mother, with two cubs. The animals were trotting along the trail, and turned to face the intruders. Knowing how ferocious mothers could be when they were defending their young, Amanda cast a nervous glance at Tarval, who still rode beside her. But he merely slowed his pace, and not even the horses seemed nervous.

The she-wolf nudged her cubs out of the way, then stood waiting for them to pass. After they did, Amanda turned in the saddle and saw it trot off down the trail, followed by the two cubs. She thought about the other wolf and reached up to touch her cheek where it had licked her. Then she realized that Tarval was watching her.

She knew he was waiting for her to ask a question about the wolf's uncharacteristically tame behavior, so, perversely, she said nothing. But that other wolf remained on her mind, thoughts of it mingling with dark tales of werewolves until she forced herself to set them aside.

Higher and higher into the mountains they rode, passing spots where swift streams tumbled over rocks in small waterfalls, and other places devoid of trees where strange flowers grew out of crevices in the black rock. Amanda began to feel as though she were traveling back in time itself. Several more times they saw wolves, sometimes standing on rocky ledges above them, and other times along the trail itself. Amanda peered at them, trying to see if any of them had pale eyes, but it was impossible to tell. The she-wolf's eyes had been dark, and it was much smaller than the wolf that had been following her. These all appeared to be smaller as well.

The shadows lengthened as the sun slipped away, and the air grew ever cooler. She was beginning to shiver inside her light jacket and wished she had a tunic like the ones the men wore.

"How much farther?" she asked Tarval, breaking a long silence.

"We will be there within the hour," he replied.

And now, for the first time, she faced the prospect of seeing Daken again. The man was a stranger to her, and yet he held the key to her future. She shuddered, thinking about the power he had over her— and she hated him for that as well.

The sky was still light, but the forest was already dark when she first saw the fires in the distance. She was about to ask Tarval what they were when she recalled the huge, flaming cauldrons she'd glimpsed that other time. And then, a few moments later, she saw the home of the Kassid.

Amanda was stunned. The scene before her was indescribable. The group had temporarily halted just after a sharp curve, and the great fortress was plainly visible in the waning light. She drew in a breath sharply, realizing in that moment that whatever she had believed about the Kassid, she had never understood them before now.

The huge fortress was literally carved into the mountain and would have been invisible now in the twilight if it weren't for the many lighted windows. Ahead of them lay a long drawbridge, flanked by burning cauldrons.

A thick, ghostly mist hung above the fortress, clinging to the upper spires and capturing the last of the day's light. Dark figures moved about in the great courtyard, where more fires burned in smaller cauldrons set amidst trees and gardens.

Staring at the fortress, Amanda understood that this place had existed unchanged for millennia—and would continue until the end of time. At a deeper level, she sensed that those who lived here were not mere mortals. The centuries revolved, the world outside changed—and the Kassid remained the same.

Tarval and the others set out again, and her own horse followed, picking up its pace now that it was near home.

They crossed the drawbridge and Amanda peered over the side into a black abyss. Just after they had passed the flaming cauldrons, they dismounted, and several young boys appeared to lead the horses away. As she was led through the courtyard gardens, people stopped to stare at her. Some smiled, while others simply stared, but she did not encounter any evident hostility. She felt like a child in the midst of adults. Even the women were taller than the average man in her own world.

My own world, she thought as they entered the fortress. Fear spread its icy fingers through her. This was *not* her world. This place belonged to Daken—and so now did she.

She was stunned by the richness of the fortress's interior. The black stone walls were hung with brilliant tapestries, and the burning wall sconces appeared to be made of gold and fine crystal. She'd expected the damp coldness she'd encountered in the cellars, but instead she found it pleasantly warm.

They walked through corridors lined with exquisitely carved doors and up a staircase with carved and polished railings. A few doors stood open, and as she passed, she could see that they were apartments, richly furnished in jewellike tones with the glitter of gold everywhere. It struck her as strange

146

that the people themselves dressed only in black, while they decorated their homes in such a rich array of colors.

They went up yet another staircase, then through a high stone archway into what was apparently a reception room. Big, comfortable-looking chairs were scattered in a semicircle around a blazing fireplace, and on the other side of the room, a huge round table was set into an alcove, surrounded by ornate but plushly upholstered chairs.

A tall, gray-haired woman appeared in an archway. She was dressed simply but elegantly in a long black wool skirt and a tunic that seemed to be a thinner version of the ones the men wore. Gold glittered at her ears and throat and on her wrists. She stared at Amanda for a long moment, then came forward and extended both of her hands.

"Welcome to our home, Amanda," she said in a low voice that was more thickly accented than the men's had been. "You must be tired and hungry after your long journey. I will show you to your rooms."

She turned back to the archway, then hesitated before turning once more to Amanda. "My name is Sheleth."

Amanda merely nodded and followed her down the hallway. She had the sudden sense that Sheleth didn't want her here, but the woman was too polite to say so.

"Where is Daken?" she asked. "I want to speak to him."

"My son will join you later," the woman said, then ushered her through another door and into a small sitting room that was just as beautifully furnished as the rooms she'd seen earlier.

"Would you like to eat now, or after you have bathed?"

Amanda replied that she would prefer to bathe first. She'd become aware of the unpleasant horse smell that clung to her, and despite the warmth surrounding her now, she was still chilled.

She stared curiously at this woman who was Daken's mother, wondering if her presence here meant that he wasn't married. On the other hand, she didn't know enough about these people to know if marriage was even part of their culture.

Sheleth showed her into a handsome bedroom with a large bed, and then led her to another door that opened into a tiny room containing a huge circular tub filled with steaming, fragrant water. The faucets, both in the tub and in the small sink, were gold, and the mirror that hung over the sink was framed in gold filigree.

Surprised to find such modern conveniences here, Amanda turned to thank her hostess, but discovered that she was alone. She was about to strip off her clothing and get into the tub when she became curious about a second door, and opened it to discover that it led into another bedroom.

The bedroom was empty, but the doors to a large cupboard stood open, and inside, Amanda saw an array of men's clothing, including several pairs of very large boots. She closed the bathroom door quickly and checked to see if it could be locked. It couldn't.

Her heart thudded rapidly in her chest as she thought about that clothing. Obviously the bedroom belonged to *someone*—and it seemed likely to her that it was Daken's.

148

It took very little time for her to guess why she had been given an adjoining bedroom, and she berated herself for not having realized before this why he had chosen to spare her life. No doubt he considered her to be an exotic prize, given how different she was in appearance from the women here.

Her anger boiled up anew. She tugged and pushed until she had moved the small but heavy towel chest in front of the door. Then she went back into her own bedroom to check for a lock there. Again there was nothing—and neither was there a lock on the outer door of the sitting room.

She dragged a chair over and wedged its top beneath the handle of the bedroom door. It certainly wouldn't keep him out for long, but at least she would be warned. She returned to the bathroom and stripped off her smelly clothing, then climbed into the tub.

She stayed in the water for a long time, thinking about him. Now that she knew why he'd spared her life, any kind thoughts she'd had toward him—and she'd hadn't had many—died. This man was her enemy. Period.

She thought about the last time she'd seen him, at the cottage, and recalled with a shudder that primitive aura she'd sensed. This man was the leader of a people who had lived unchanged for many centuries. The fact that she'd been treated gently by Tarval and the others meant nothing. They were undoubtedly under orders not to harm her—not to "damage the goods," as it were.

She climbed out of the tub, her thoughts turning to how she could defend herself against him. As she dressed in the only clean clothing she had left, she thought about his bedroom. Was it possible that she could find a weapon there—a knife perhaps? There was no way she could conceal a knife the size of the one the men all seemed to carry, but perhaps he had something smaller.

She pushed the chest out of the way and pressed her ear to the door, listening. No sound could be heard from the bedroom, so she opened the door and peered around its edge. The room was still empty. Moving quickly, she began to rummage through the drawers of a large chest that contained more clothing. Nothing. Then she went to the big cupboard.

Finding nothing there either, she was about to give up when her gaze fell on a shelf above the rack of clothing. It was too high for her to do more than touch it, so she dragged a chair over and climbed on it. It was dark up there, but her fingers quickly closed around something, and she drew it down.

A knife! Or maybe it could more appropriately be called a stiletto. The handle was sturdy, but the blade was very thin. She touched it lightly and jerked her finger back quickly. A small spot of blood appeared on her thumb. She licked it absently, wondering if she could carry the knife in her pocket without accidentally stabbing herself. Or maybe there was a sheath of some kind. She felt along the shelf again and this time came up with a slim leather sheath, fitted with a strap. Probably it was intended to be strapped to the ankle, but if she pulled away the strap, she could fit it into her pocket.

Feeling much better now, she turned to climb down from the chair and froze. Daken was leaning against the open doorway of the bedroom, his arms folded across his broad chest as he watched her with a smile. She was somehow certain that he'd been there long enough to have stopped her from getting the knife—and yet he hadn't.

He said nothing, and neither did she as she got down from the chair, clutching the knife in one hand and the leather sheath in the other.

"Your dinner is ready," he said casually, gesturing through the door that connected her rooms to his.

She just stared at him. She'd invaded his bedroom and armed herself with his knife, and all he had to say was that her dinner was ready? Was this man insane—or simply supremely self-confident? She didn't know which frightened her more.

She fitted the knife into the sheath, slipped it into the pocket of her baggy khaki trousers, and as calmly as possible walked back through the bathroom, through the bedroom and into the sitting room, expecting him to grab her at any moment and wrest the knife away.

Instead, he simply followed, then poured two glasses of wine from a beautiful crystal carafe. Gesturing to the covered tray next to it, he told her to eat, and retreated to the fireplace with his wineglass.

She picked up the wineglass and sniffed at it suspiciously. But when she saw him take a sip from his own glass, she decided it must be safe and tried it herself. The wine was wonderful, and when she lifted the cover from the tray, the delicious aromas made her almost weak-kneed with hunger.

He leaned against the black stone mantel and watched her as she tasted each item on her plate. The meat was unfamiliar, but very tender and exquisitely prepared, and the vegetables were seasoned with strange but interesting herbs. She began to eat, deciding that two could play this game of silence as well as one. She concentrated on her food and carefully avoided looking at him, although it scarcely mattered. His presence filled the room.

The silence was broken only by the sounds of the fire and the clink of silver against china as she ate. She could feel that strange aura she'd felt when he came to the cottage, although it didn't seem quite so powerful this time—perhaps because he was keeping his distance.

She ate slowly, deliberately prolonging the meal in the hope that he might leave. It had been easy enough to picture herself demanding answers from him when she wasn't in his presence, but now that her chance had come, she was increasingly fearful.

And yet, at the same time, she didn't want him to leave. This man was clearly her enemy—and a murderer to boot—and yet he intrigued her as no other man ever had and stirred within her a shameful eroticism.

She started nervously when he suddenly moved, but he had merely walked away from the fireplace to stand with his back to her at the tall, mullioned window. She noticed for the first time that despite his great size, he moved with an easy, strange sort of gracefulness, and as he stood at the window, there was an utter stillness to him that she found odd as well.

She tried to sort through her impressions of him, knowing that was important. That primitive aura definitely still clung to him, but there was something else as well, something she couldn't quite define. She thought again about his failure to take the knife from her, and found herself rather wishing that he had. At least then she would have known that he could feel fear.

She finished her meal and stood up, intending to announce that she was retiring for the night. He turned to face her, his rugged features shadowed in the dark part of the room.

"None of us here had any part in the deaths of your friends," he said in a deep but soft voice. "I don't expect you to believe that now, but perhaps you will in time."

"You're right," she replied, lifting her chin defiantly. "I don't believe it—and time will not change the truth. You killed them—or had them killed—to prevent their finding out that the Kassid still exist. But it won't work. Others will come, demanding to know what happened to our expedition."

"Wars have existed for centuries in this region. They will be told that your group was simply in the wrong place at the wrong time."

"What about the others—the three who disappeared before the . . . slaughter?"

"We had nothing to do with that, either. Their bodies will be returned to Menoa."

And what about me? she asked silently, unable to get the question out. *What do you intend to do with me?*

He stared so hard at her that she had the sense he had heard the question she couldn't ask. Then, abruptly, he broke eye contact and strode across the room to refill his wineglass. She backed up a few steps, the action wholly unconscious. He seemed not to notice.

"You have not asked about yourself," he said then,

his voice just barely audible over the crackling of the fire and the rapid beating of her heart.

"I doubt that I would get the truth about that, either," she replied defiantly, a defiance that was belied by the huskiness in her voice.

"You will remain here. I cannot allow you to carry the knowledge of our existence back to your world."

"No!" she cried. "I will *not* remain here! You can't keep me here!"

"You have seen enough of this place to know that you can't hope to escape, Amanda. You will be treated as a guest. I cannot guarantee that all of my people will be friendly toward you. Few of them have had any contact with outsiders. But none will harm you.

"You're an artist. My people have a great appreciation for such talents, and you will certainly be welcomed by the artists among them."

"I'd rather be dead than held prisoner here!"

His mouth curved briefly into a smile. "Then perhaps I was wrong to have taken that decision from you."

She brushed away her angry tears. "Why did you? Why was my life spared?"

He stared at her for a moment, then made a move as if to take her arm. She jumped back and he immediately dropped his arm. In that moment, by that small action, Amanda began to doubt her belief that he had brought her here to be his mistress. He gestured to the door.

"Come with me for a moment. I want to show you something."

She followed him out of the sitting room and down the hallway to the large reception hall she'd passed through earlier. He stopped in the middle of the room and gestured to a huge painting that hung over the fireplace. She hadn't seen it before.

"Her name was Jocelyn. She was Ertrian, a princess about to become queen at a time when war was threatening to destroy her people. She came here seeking the help of the Kassid—and drew my ancestors out of their long isolation. Together with her husband, she created an empire that lasted until the gods themselves destroyed it."

"The earthquake, you mean?" Amanda asked, staring at the portrait.

"Yes. The descendants of Jocelyn and Daken were not content to rule the empire they'd been given. They set out to conquer the world—or what they understood to be the world. Then the gods called the Kassid home. Most obeyed and came back here. Those who didn't perished, along with tens of thousands of others."

"Daken?" she asked, glancing from the man in the portrait to him.

"Yes. That was his name. We're related, of course, though I'm not a direct descendant."

Amanda turned back to the portrait. The man bore a vague resemblance to him, though it was mostly the gray hair. But the woman, Jocelyn. Her own resemblance to the portrait didn't end with shared hair color. Despite several differences, there was a strong similarity in their faces.

"She has always fascinated me," he went on in a soft, musing tone. "She was a very strong and very brave woman in a civilization that did not value such things in a woman."

She understood now—or thought she did. He had

spared her life because she reminded him of this woman, Jocelyn. She glanced at him as he continued to study the portrait, thinking that she had just learned something important—something that made him seem more human.

He turned to her. "As you have probably guessed, you were spared because of your resemblance to her."

"You have just admitted that you lied, Daken. If you spared me, then you obviously *did* have something to do with the deaths of the others."

He shook his head. "You're wrong, but the explanation is very complicated. I did not order their deaths, but I did have something to do with your being spared."

His final words echoed in the charged silence, a silence filled with other words that went unspoken. She saw nothing in his pale eyes, but she felt something throb between them, as though with a life of its own. She turned quickly and started back to her quarters, but his voice stopped her.

"You are free to come and go as you please, but do not go to the *azherwa*—the black room. You cannot escape that way. If you try, you will drown."

"I'm aware of that," she replied coldly. She had in fact thought about it.

Daken watched her walk stiffly from the room, then turned once again to the portrait. Had he told her the truth? He wasn't sure, but he knew he'd given her the answer he'd given himself.

For the first time in a life of total self-confidence, Daken was uneasy. He'd become the leader of his people nearly five years ago, at the age of thirty-five.

Ten years before that, he'd been chosen by his predecessor, and when Torven had retired, his selection had been confirmed by a unanimous vote of the people.

The position of leader was no popularity contest. If it were, neither Daken nor many of his predecessors would have been elected. Instead, the choice was made on the basis of certain qualities of leadership that had served their people well over the centuries.

The leader's power was absolute, although it was expected that he would heed the advice of his council of advisers, of which some were appointed by him and others elected by the people. The leader himself was elected for his lifetime—or until he chose to retire.

It was also customary for the resigning leader to be quite frank about the shortcomings he saw in his chosen successor, and Torven had been. He'd warned Daken that the youth had a tendency to "let his mind trample his heart," when both were necessary for a great leader. Daken had taken this to be a subtle disapproval of his failure to take a mate.

The truth was that although women were invariably attracted to him, they ended up marrying someone else because, as one outspoken former lover had put it, "I want a man who's there, Daken—and you're not always there for me."

So at forty, he remained alone. Not always alone, of course. There were always women who were more than willing to share his bed. But none of them shared his heart. He wasn't generally troubled by the situation, however. The desire to produce an heir was not strong among his people, since each of them individually owned no property, save for personal items. And, of course, the position of leader wasn't hereditary.

The other flaw that had troubled Torven was Daken's restless nature. Daken was the first leader of his people who had actually ventured out into the world beyond the Dark Mountains, and Torven had voiced the fear that this could loosen his ties to the gods.

Daken had been forced to admit that there was some truth in this. He was fascinated by that other world, though he was also repelled by it. And until recently, he'd given precious little thought to the workings of the gods, believing them to have lost interest in his people after the great destruction centuries ago.

Now, however, he began to sense that the gods were once more taking notice of the Kassid. They hadn't spoken to him directly, as they had previous leaders, but still, he sensed something.

All around him, Daken felt the gathering of great forces—and his uneasiness was shared by others as well. It had all begun with Steffen Lescoulans. The gods had permitted him to discover the existence of the Kassid, thereby setting in motion a chain of events that had led to Lescoulans's death—and now to the presence of Amanda. Another flame-haired woman from the world beyond the mountains, and one just as determined as Jocelyn had been, though one whose only goal at the moment was to escape, and to tell the world about the Kassid.

He turned away from the portrait and went instead to the window. The cool night air brought to him the songs of the wolves that echoed through the

Dark Mountains. He longed to be out there now, to be free for a time from the feelings that were bedeviling him. But he didn't dare go now. She could already sense that other part of him, that one secret of the Kassid he didn't intend to reveal.

Amanda decided to take her jailer at his word. He'd said that she was free to come and go as she pleased, and she intended to do just that.

Sheleth had brought her breakfast and informed her that some clothing would be ready for her by the next day. The woman had been polite but formal, and Amanda wasn't certain whether it was just her nature or a sign of disapproval. At any rate, Amanda's attempts at conversation had gotten her nowhere.

She was relieved and disappointed in about equal measure that there was no sign of Daken's presence in the large apartment. Her continued ambivalence about him annoyed her. What was she to make of what he'd said—and what he hadn't said? He claimed not to be responsible for the others' deaths, and at the same time admitted that he *was* responsible for her life having been spared. Furthermore, he struck her as being far too intelligent not to realize the conflict there.

She stood in the large reception room, staring at the portrait and hearing his words: the only time she'd felt a genuine warmth in him. Well, she supposed it was inevitable that a people locked up in these mountains would live in the distant past. She, on the other hand, had the present and the future to consider.

She left the apartment and began her first exploration of the huge fortress. The place was an incredible maze of corridors and staircases and numerous doors that led out into the courtyard. Within a few minutes, she'd made so many turns that she knew she'd never find her way back again. But that didn't trouble her. Surely she could find someone who could guide her.

She encountered people everywhere, although they were scattered throughout the fortress. A few startled her by greeting her in English and using her name, but most either smiled or nodded and went on their way. Daken had said that not everyone was happy about her being here, but she saw no overt hostility as she continued her aimless wandering.

At one point, drawn by children's voices, she went up a short staircase and found herself in the wide corridors of what was clearly a school. The classroom doors were open, and as she passed, voices ceased and both students and teachers turned to stare at her. When she heard English words floating out from one classroom, she paused short of the open door to listen. The children sounded young, but their fluency was impressive.

Still, she wondered why a people determined to live in isolation would bother to learn English.

She reached the end of the corridor and found herself at the edge of a wide-open space with tall windows. A small group of teenage children were scattered about the room, working intently at large canvases set on easels. A tall woman of about her own age moved among them, talking to each student. The canvases she could see from where she stood were impressionistic, and one or two showed some real talent.

Suddenly the woman turned in her direction, perhaps alerted to her presence by one of the students. She spoke a few more words to a young girl, then made her way across the room to Amanda.

"Hello, Amanda. I'm Jessa. I've been eager to meet you."

Amanda returned her smile, recalling what Daken had said about the Kassid artists' interest in her. Jessa's English was excellent, almost without accent.

"Come over here and let me get us some tea. The students don't need my attention for a time."

She led Amanda over to a wide window seat and poured two cups of tea from a pot that stood on a nearby table. After handing one cup to Amanda, she took a seat beside her.

"I thought that perhaps Daken would bring you here, but it seems that you found your own way."

Amanda acknowledged that she'd been exploring the place and said that she hadn't seen Daken this morning.

"He's probably at arms practice." Jessa nodded. "It's that time of the month."

"Arms practice?" Amanda echoed in confusion.

Jessa shrugged. "It's a tradition, that's all. All of the Bet Dawars practice with their knives each month at this time."

"I don't understand. Who are the Bet Dawars?"

For one brief moment, Jessa gave her a startled look. Then she covered it with a smile. "I'm sorry. You don't know our language, of course. It simply means the men who've chosen to join the defense force—not that it's needed. As I said, it's only a tradition."

She hurried on to talk about her students and to

ply Amanda with questions about her own work, but Amanda thought she seemed in too much of a hurry to change the subject, and filed away that thought for further consideration.

At one point, Jessa laid a hand on Amanda's arm. "I know this must be difficult for you, but I think you could be happy here. My people have great reverence for the arts, and everyone will be happy for the contributions you can make."

"Then you know that I'm here as a prisoner?"

Jessa nodded sympathetically. "Of course. We all know that—and we know about your friends' deaths. But Daken says that there is no other way—that we cannot let you go back to your world and tell them about us."

"The world will find out anyway," Amanda protested, knowing it would be pointless to make any promises. "Surely you don't believe that you can live here without discovery forever."

"We can if the gods so will it," Jessa stated calmly. "And so far, at least, they have."

Unable to counter that, Amanda asked if she'd ever been out there, beyond the Dark Mountains.

"Yes. Twice. I visited the great museums in America and in Asia and Europe. Like most of us who have gone out, I found it exciting. But then the need to be back here came over me, as it does with us all."

"I don't understand what you mean by 'need.' Are you speaking of a feeling that comes over you?"

Jessa nodded. "The Dark Mountains are more than just our home. We draw our very life's breath from this place, which was given to us by the gods when they left this world."

"Are you saying that the gods actually *built* this

place?" Amanda asked, thinking of her first glimpse of the great fortress and how it seemed literally to have been carved out of the mountain by a giant sculptor.

"Yes. We could never have created it ourselves. I think even your science would have difficulty doing that."

Amanda nodded her agreement, even though she couldn't bring herself to believe that it was created by supernatural beings, either.

"Has anyone ever tried to stay away from here?" she asked curiously.

"No, although Daken has been away for rather long periods of time—or at least he had before he became leader. That troubled my grandfather, who was the leader before him."

"How did he become leader?"

Jessa explained their system. "Grandfather believes that Daken has many of the same qualities as the other Daken, our great leader, and that, like him, he may be ruling in a very difficult time for us."

"What do *you* think of him?" Amanda asked.

Jessa smiled. "Daken is not an easy man to like. I respect him, of course, but he is often distant and seems to live too much in his mind, rather than in his heart."

"Is he married—or do you have such a thing here?"

"No, he isn't married, and yes, we do have marriage. Marriage is for life among us, so we are very careful about whom we choose as mate. Daken is not married because he guards his heart too closely."

Amanda had many other questions for this willing source of information, but Jessa forestalled her by rising from her seat.

"The class is nearly over and I should check their work. Will you join me? They all speak English, and I'm sure they would welcome your criticism."

So she spent the next quarter-hour examining the students' work and offering suggestions. Most had only minimal talent, but a few showed some promise—and one young man exhibited true greatness. She enjoyed the session, having always thought that she would like to teach at some point.

The students left and a group of young children bounded into the studio. Jessa looked at them with exasperated amusement. "This is really just playtime for them—and a lot of work for me. You may stay if you like."

Amanda thanked her but said that she thought she'd continue her exploration. She also said that she wanted to see Jessa and the other artists soon, and Jessa promised that she would.

As she left the classroom area, weaving her way through children who were already as tall as she was, Amanda's thoughts turned back to the beginning of their conversation. She felt certain that Jessa hadn't intended to tell her of the Bet Dawars, the "defense force," and wondered what she could have been hiding.

It seemed likely to her that arms practice would be outside in the courtyard, so she began to search for an exit. She wondered if Daken's statement that she could go anywhere had included spying on their defense force.

Chapter Seven

Amanda found her way out into the courtyard, a huge area divided into sections by rows of trees and shrubs, beneath which were neat flower beds. Just to her right as she walked out into the bright sunshine was the playground area she'd seen on her first visit here. A group of young children were playing under the watchful eyes of an older couple. They smiled and greeted her. She returned the greeting, but did not linger. She was determined to find the Kassid defense force.

Jessa had said that it was nothing more than tradition, but Amanda suspected there was something she wasn't saying, though she couldn't begin to guess what that might be. There was something faintly amusing about the notion of the Kassid defending themselves against modern weaponry—unless, of course, they possessed weaponry of their own that she had yet to see. She wondered if Daken's self-confidence could be mere self-delusion. Still, Jessa had said that he'd spent considerable time in her world. He must know how pitiful their defenses here were.

As she reached the outer wall of the courtyard and turned to look back at the fortress, she was as awed as she had been the first time she'd seen it. This was indeed a place for all time, and she came very close to believing that it had indeed been created by gods.

By the time she'd walked through the entire courtyard, she was inclined to think that Jessa must have been mistaken. She'd seen no men-at-arms anywhere. Standing now at the wall once again, she studied the fortress. It was so vast that it was difficult for her to absorb all the details, but now she saw that near the far end there appeared to be another courtyard, surrounded by a high wall. It was several levels above where she stood, and that, plus the stone wall that curved around it, made it impossible for her to see into it—or even to judge its size accurately.

She began to follow the wall of the courtyard in that direction. It curved sharply at one point, and then straightened out again, and now she saw that there was yet another section of the fortress beyond that upper courtyard. It climbed high into the mountain, and at its end was a stone turret, surrounded by yet another wall. In that courtyard was a tower—a wooden tower like the one on the hilltop near the village.

Now she understood the purpose of that other tower. The mirrors were turned in the other direction, but she had no doubt that the people of Wat

Andara used this means to alert the Kassid to any intruders.

Between the turret and the walled courtyard some distance below there was a broad expanse of glass that jutted out from the mountain. It looked to her very much like a greenhouse.

She turned her attention back to the wooden tower, wondering if it represented the end point of a system that had once spanned the entire region, before the great earthquake and the volcanic eruptions. The wrecked tower in the jungle suggested that was indeed the case. Hank had lost his life trying to steal a piece of that ruined tower in order to determine its age, while she could probably find out merely by asking.

Amanda was suddenly overcome with a cold fear that made her knees tremble and forced her to sit down quickly on one of the stone benches nearby. For a time, thanks to Jessa and her own fascination with this place, she'd been able to forget her situation, and that made it all the more painful to remember it now.

Don't think about it, she told herself. *You're alive and you're safe and you* will *find a way out of this.* Then, before she could start to think about Steffen and her murdered colleagues and her life back home, she got up and started toward a door below the upper courtyard that led into the fortress.

Inside, she climbed stairs whenever she found them, unable to guess just how high up the courtyard was. She wondered how even the Kassid could find their way around in this place, where hallways curved and sometimes angled sharply or ended abruptly.

After she had walked for what seemed miles, the sounds of voices began to fade, and she guessed that she was now in an unoccupied portion of the fortress. Before, she'd passed what were clearly living quarters, as well as the wide entrance to an enormous library that she intended to explore later. But she was determined at this point to find that upper courtyard and see if that was the site of the arms practice.

Then, after listening to nothing more than the sounds of her own boots striking the stone floor, she began to hear voices again in the distance. Men's voices. She followed the sounds up yet another staircase.

At the top of the staircase was an enormous empty room. Inside opposite where she stood uncertainly, were three sets of double doors that lay open to a courtyard filled with men in black.

She stepped into the room, but angled away from the doors into a far corner, hoping she wouldn't be spotted. Then she peered out the long, narrow windows.

There were easily several hundred men out there, engaged in hand-to-hand combat. She gasped as a man near her lunged at his opponent, whose defense was just a second too late. Then she realized that the knives, while similar in appearance to the ones they usually carried, were in fact blunt.

She watched them secretly for some time and realized that every man there possessed that same easy, athletic grace she'd seen in Daken. Moving still closer to the window, she scanned the courtyard, but didn't spot him. From this vantage point she couldn't see everything, however, and so assumed that he must be at the far end somewhere. She did, however, see both Tarval and the other man who'd been with him that time when she'd encountered him in the black room.

Many of the men were facing in her direction, but the sun was striking the window and she felt confident that they couldn't see her. So she moved from that window to the next one, which was closer to the first set of doors, hoping she could spot Daken.

She still couldn't see him, but suddenly something struck her as she scanned the group. Every man she could see clearly enough to ascertain the color of his eyes had the same pale eyes as Daken.

She frowned. Surely it was just a coincidence. But now that she thought about it, she couldn't recall having seen any of the Kassid women with eyes like that—and very few men. The Kassid all had dark hair and bronzed skin, which made light eyes even more noticeable.

Very curious now, she began to watch individual men, waiting for them to turn in her direction. And every one of them had the same nearly colorless eyes.

This discovery made her very uneasy, although she wasn't sure why. Perhaps it was only that their eyes reminded her of the wolf. Then she frowned again. Speaking of wolves . . .

The art they'd found in the underwater ruins had shown wolves and people together, and yet she hadn't seen a single wolf in all her wanderings in the fortress. In fact, she'd seen no animals of any kind.

She was still mulling that over when Daken came into view at last. Like the other men, he was wearing a light, sleeveless tunic and loose black trousers. In the midst of this group, he didn't stand out quite so much, which made her realize that the men here were among the largest of the Kassid.

He had his back to her as he stood perhaps fifty feet from a large target that had been painted in bright colors on a large, well-stuffed sack of some type. He turned to the man next to him and said something, and the other man promptly reached down into his boot and pulled out a stiletto like the one she'd taken from his cupboard: the one she in fact had in her pocket at this very moment.

The man handed it to Daken, and with one quick and fluid movement he threw it at the target. Amanda's eyes widened as the stiletto struck the small red circle in the center of the target. He hadn't even taken time to aim!

After retrieving the knife, he repeated the throw several more times with the same result, then handed the stiletto back to its owner, who then proceeded to do likewise. Daken watched him for a moment, then turned away, moving in her direction as he talked to some of the men. She moved back a bit from the window, even though she was still certain that he couldn't see her.

As her eyes remained glued to him, Amanda saw that no one seemed to be showing him any deference. If this was a defense force, he must surely be its commander, and yet she saw no indication of that. She was wondering if there might be a different commander for the military, when suddenly he turned to stare straight at her.

Amanda took a few quick steps backward, poised to flee—then stopped. She wasn't going to run away from him. She refused to give him the pleasure of knowing that she feared him. A moment later he appeared in the open doorway, silhouetted against the bright light. Behind him the men continued their training with their antiquated weapons, and she felt more strongly than ever that she had fallen through a hole in time. Struggling against that disorientation, she lifted her chin defiantly and spoke in a contemptuous tone.

"Surely you don't believe you can defeat a modern army with your knives."

He took a few steps toward her, and once again she had to fight against the urge to flee from this man.

"No," he said, shaking his head as his pale eyes bored into her. "We leave our protection to the gods."

For just a moment, his calm, certain tone kept her silent. Then she gestured angrily to the scene behind him. "Was it some of them who murdered my friends?"

"I've already told you that no one here had anything to do with their deaths."

"Forgive me if I don't believe you, Daken—any more than you would believe me if I promised not to tell the world about you."

"Then we seem to have reached a stalemate, Amanda. Neither of us is able to believe the other."

"I want to leave here, Daken!"

"That's not possible."

Suddenly her anger boiled over and she forgot about everything but her need to vent her rage on him.

"You're living in the past. You're a fool, Daken, if you think that you can re-create that time by finding yourself a woman who reminds you of her!"

Before the words had left her lips, she knew her

mistake. But it was too late. Her accusation hung there between them, filling the silence. Fearing that her words might drive him to violence, she slid her hand into her pocket and closed her fingers around the stiletto.

"Perhaps you too are living in the past—but a different past. Out there, men seize women they want. That does not happen here."

His words, dripping with contempt, shocked her. She didn't know what to say to him, though it seemed clear that he was awaiting some sort of response. Then, finally, he spoke, this time in a far less harsh tone.

"When you come to know our history, you will see that it is very different from your own. If you have stepped back in time, it is not to your history—but ours." He gestured to the men in the courtyard.

"This is part of our history, too—a tradition we follow, even though the need no longer exists."

She felt herself relax—as much as she could in his presence. The confrontation was over—for now, at least. And a part of her she despised listened to an echo of his words. He hadn't said that he didn't want her, only that he wouldn't take her by force. She turned to the courtyard.

"All the men out there have blue eyes, like yours."

As she turned back to him, she knew that for one brief moment, she'd caught him off guard. It was an observation he hadn't anticipated. Finally he merely nodded, offering no explanation.

"Why is that?" she demanded.

"More tradition. Blue eyes are supposed to be given to those most favored by the gods because that is the color they chose for the heavens."

"I haven't seen any women with blue eyes," she said in a challenging tone.

"No, there are none."

"So women aren't favored by the gods?"

To her surprise, he laughed. "*All* Kassid regard themselves as being favored by the gods—both men and women. You cannot bring your own beliefs here, Amanda, based as they are in a long history of the mistreatment of women. Men with blue eyes are simply endowed with special qualities that are needed for fighting. It is no more than that."

Yes, it is, she thought, but didn't say. *You're a very clever man, Daken, trying to use history to deny the truth.*

"Is the leader always chosen from among the men with blue eyes?" she asked curiously.

"Yes, because part of that leadership involves leading our forces into battle."

"You're not telling me all of the truth, Daken. What about the wolves?"

She saw him stiffen briefly, and a bone-deep chill ran through her. She wished that she could take back the words, though she wasn't sure why. But it was too late, so she pressed on.

"We found artifacts beneath the sea, and they showed wolves living with people. You must have kept wolves as pets at one time."

"No. We do not keep pets of any kind."

"But you must have trained wolves," she persisted, fighting that coldness inside her. "A wolf prevented me from escaping when Tarval and the others were after me. It couldn't have—"

"Wolves are sacred to us," he replied in a clipped

173

tone made harsh by his accent. "We have a . . . special relationship with them."

"Especially the blue-eyed ones?"

"With all wolves—but especially the blue-eyed ones." Then he turned abruptly toward the door. "I must return to the men."

It can't be true, she thought desperately. *They can't turn themselves into wolves! It just isn't possible!*

And yet, deep down inside, she knew that it might be true. This man—and probably the others out there as well—were not human.

Amanda stood quietly as the two Kassid women took her measurements. Another woman entered the room carrying a large selection of fabrics. She was surprised and delighted to see bright, shimmering colors. Sheleth had provided her with a small supply of the loose, dark clothing they all wore, but it seemed that the drab moths became colorful butterflies at festival time.

Jessa had explained to her that next week they would be celebrating midsummer, one of their two big festivals of the year. There would be games and art exhibitions and craft sales and dancing. The festival lasted for three days and climaxed with numerous wedding ceremonies. June, it seemed, was wedding time even here in the Dark Mountains.

When the seamstresses had finished taking their measurements, Amanda examined the fabrics. They were all beautiful, soft and lightweight and as luxurious as anything she'd ever seen. She was wondering where they got such fabric when Jessa came in.

"Choose the green," Jessa suggested, picking up a

bolt of pale green fabric. "It will bring out the green in your eyes."

Amanda agreed with her. The shade was so delicate, like the tentative green of early spring. "Where does this fabric come from?" she asked. "I haven't seen any animals or anyone weaving." Of course, there were still parts of the fortress she hadn't yet explored.

"It's done at one of the other homes, and that is where the animals are raised as well."

"You mean there are other fortresses?" Amanda asked in astonishment.

"Two more," Jessa confirmed as they left the busy quarters of the seamstresses. "Both are much smaller, of course. And everyone will be coming here for the festival."

They walked out into the sunlit courtyard just as a group of men rode across the drawbridge. Amanda shaded her eyes with her hand and peered at them.

"Who are those men?" She could tell, even at this distance, that they weren't Kassid because of their size.

Jessa glanced at them and grimaced. "Sherbas—come to see Daken. I hope they don't stay for the festival."

"Why not?" Amanda asked, thinking about the man who'd attacked her outside her apartment. She'd nearly forgotten about the mysterious sect.

"The festival is supposed to be fun—and I'm afraid that the Sherbas don't understand that."

"I've heard of them, but what is their connection to the Kassid?"

"Oh, it goes back more than a thousand years. They were a small tribe that was defeated in a war, and then sought refuge in the Dark Mountains. Our people helped them—and now it seems that we can't rid ourselves of them. I don't envy Daken, but at least he'll be able to get away from them quickly."

"What do you mean?"

Jessa seemed momentarily surprised. "Hasn't he told you? The men—the defense force, that is—will be leaving the fortress for the next week. They'll return just in time for the festival."

"I haven't seen much of Daken," Amanda admitted. That was actually an understatement. The man had been avoiding her quite successfully.

"Tell me more about the Sherbas," she asked, not wanting to discuss Daken. Jessa had already shown great interest in her relationship with him.

"There really isn't much to tell." Jessa shrugged—unconvincingly, Amanda thought. "They live all over the world. When we leave here, we stay in their homes. They worship us, and most of us find it unpleasant." Jessa sank down onto a bench.

"There was a time many centuries ago when they were our eyes and ears to the outside world. In a way, they still are. But we needed them then to ensure our safety. Now . . ." She sighed heavily.

"Let's talk about something more pleasant. Everyone is pleased that you will be doing sketches of the children at the festival. You're much better at it than any of us are."

Amanda smiled. She'd already sketched some of the Kassid children. They were delightful. "I think it's because I see what you don't see," she told Jessa. "At home, I see so many children who've been forced to grow up before their time. But here I see the innocence that all children should have. Perhaps that's what I capture."

And it's what I truly love about this place, she thought as they watched some children playing hide-and-seek. There was such gentleness and goodness here. There was no crime, and no television to bring violence and horrors into this place.

By now she'd learned that Daken was right: she could not see this place through the filters of her own history. The Kassid were different, and had always been different. In fact, they were now as they had always been: an egalitarian society that took it as a given that the weaker among them should be cared for.

She'd also learned through her discussions with Jessa that women had never been oppressed in Kassid history. Men and women were truly equals here, and always had been, and whatever else they might do with their lives, the raising of children was viewed by all as being the most important task for men and women alike.

Only when Amanda had questioned the tradition of always electing a male leader, since only males had the requisite blue eyes and the special blessing of the gods, had Jessa's words rung false. She'd given Amanda the same explanation that Daken had, but hearing it again did not satisfy Amanda that it was the truth. She knew that the Kassid were still guarding their secrets—no doubt on the orders of Daken.

Amanda reminded Jessa that she'd promised to take her up to the greenhouse. She'd tried to find it herself, but hadn't yet succeeded. That particular part of the fortress was largely unoccupied, and even more of a maze than the rest of the huge structure.

As they got up from the bench, Amanda shaded her eyes and stared up at the tall, crenellated tower several levels above the greenhouse.

"Could we go up to the tower as well? It doesn't appear to be too far from the greenhouse." She wanted to see the signal tower and wanted also to see what must be the most spectacular view in a fortress that offered many.

To her surprise, Jessa shook her head. "We'll have to ask Daken before we can go up there. The tower belongs to him. No one goes up there without his permission, except for the *bozhrans*—the ones who signal—and they go at set times."

"I don't understand." Amanda frowned. "Do you mean he has rooms up there?"

Jessa nodded. "The leader has always used the tower as a place to be alone. The tradition supposedly started with the other Daken, our Great Leader. But I'm sure he'll give permission, and we can go up there while he's gone."

"Where are they going?" Amanda asked curiously. Jessa had said that the defense force—the Blue-Eyes, as she had begun to call them to herself—would be away from the fortress for some time.

"Just out into the mountains. They go always at this time of year."

Amanda stared up at the tower, wondering if that was where Daken had been hiding himself for the past few nights. He certainly hadn't been in the apartment, unless he'd come in quite late. She wondered if he took women up there. She'd become quite curious about that situation, though she hadn't asked Jessa any questions.

The Kassid, she'd discovered, had a rather unusual

code of ethics where sexual matters were concerned. It appeared that everyone had affairs, beginning somewhere in their teens. But when they married— generally sometime in their late twenties or early thirties, they were invariably faithful to their spouses, and divorce was unheard of among them. Illegitimacy also did not exist among them, since they had discovered herbal potions that provided foolproof birth control many centuries ago.

Amanda and Jessa made their way around one of the areas of greenery that separated the various portions of the courtyard—and came face-to-face with the visiting Sherbas. Amanda stopped in her tracks as the memory of the attack outside her apartment came back to her again.

She saw quickly that none of these men could possibly have been the attacker, however, since they were all much older. But they were dressed the same, right down to the gold chains with the piece of black rock that she now recognized as being nothing more than the stone that was all around her here.

The Sherbas stared at her as well, and their expressions indicated the first true hostility she'd seen since her arrival in this place. She lifted her chin and stared right back at them as Jessa tugged at her arm and reminded her that they had a long walk up to the greenhouse.

Then Daken appeared in the open doorway that led into the central portion of the fortress. Amanda's gaze shifted to him in time to see him look from her to the visiting Sherbas again with a very grim expression. The Sherbas immediately turned away from her and bowed to him, making signs in the air as they did so. Daken favored them only with a brief nod before turning to go back inside, followed now by the Sherbas, who had to scurry to keep up with his long strides.

"He doesn't seem very happy to see them either," Amanda remarked as they walked on.

"He isn't, but they're here at his order. They wouldn't come otherwise. Daken is far less tolerant of them than my grandfather was when he was leader."

"Then why did he summon them?"

Jessa affected a shrug. "I don't know. No doubt he has some business with them."

Amanda cast a sidelong glance at her new friend, thinking that she did indeed know. As the two became closer, Jessa's ability to lie to her effectively diminished. Much as she wanted to press the matter, Amanda let it go. She valued Jessa's friendship and genuinely liked her, and therefore didn't want to force her to lie.

She thought about the Sherbas as they began the long climb up to the greenhouse, and she belatedly realized that while they certainly weren't pleased to see her there, neither did they seem at all surprised. Obviously they must have known of her presence somehow.

Within moments, Amanda was totally lost in the maze of corridors, and she asked Jessa how often children got lost in the fortress.

"Not often. They learn to read the numbers almost as soon as they learn to walk. Besides, very young children would never be in a deserted area anyway."

"What numbers?" Amanda asked, but saw the answer just as she got the question out. About two feet up the wall at the intersection of two hallways, something was carved into the stone. She hadn't noticed it before because it was below eye-level, but she realized that it would be at just the right height for a child.

Jessa pointed to it and explained that children had only to follow the numbers backward to reach the nearest exit or one of the wide corridors of the main floor.

"I'll write them down for you, if you like," Jessa offered. "I should have thought of that before."

During the first part of their long climb, they had passed through a deserted area Amanda had already seen on her way up to the courtyard where the Blue-Eyes held their war games. But now she and Jessa had gone off in another direction, and as they passed various open doorways, she saw men and women at work inside, cleaning.

"This section is used for the people from the other homes who will be coming for the festival," Jessa explained. "Usually the adults stay in here and the children sleep in tents in the courtyards. It's great fun for them. And of course, many of them stay in the homes of friends or relatives here."

A short time later, Jessa pushed open the big doors into the greenhouse, and warm, humid air filled with a tantalizing mixture of aromas and rich, damp earth rushed out at them.

"We grow some things in here yearround," Jessa explained. "But most vegetables are grown outside in the summer months."

"Where?" Amanda asked. She hadn't seen any vegetable gardens.

Jessa laughed. "So you haven't found everything yet, despite all your explorations? On the rooftops.

Just about every rooftop has a garden. Most of them are reached through the apartments of those who tend them, which is why you haven't seen them."

They strolled along the neat rows of raised beds, with Jessa pointing out the various herbs and explaining their purposes.

"Centuries ago, the Sherbas made their living by trading the herbs we gave them for the other things they needed. They wandered all over Ertria and Balek and even into Menoa and Turvea, selling their herbs and picking up information for us."

"How did they escape the earthquake?" Amanda asked.

"Not all of them did. A few Kassid died as well, because they didn't heed the call to come home. But it happened in the early spring, at a time when most of the Sherbas were here. They came here several times a year to refill their wagons with herbs."

"I'm told they live very well. How do they get their money?"

"Oh, we gave them gold. We have plenty to spare."

"Where is the gold mined?"

"Deep in the mountain under one of the other homes. But no one mines it anymore. The Sherbas have more than they need, and we certainly don't need it."

Amanda walked over to the wall of glass and rubbed away some of the moisture, then drew in a sharp breath at the sight. The Dark Mountains marched off forever, it seemed, their snow-covered peaks lost in mist.

What a magical place this is, she thought. Day by day, it seemed that the beauty and peacefulness settled more deeply into her. But it frightened her to think that such a thing could happen, because it suggested that she had resigned herself to being a prisoner here forever.

I must not let that happen, she told herself. I cannot let myself forget that despite what he says, Daken is surely responsible for many deaths—including Steffen's.

But she couldn't help wondering uneasily if the forces that Jessa claimed always drew the Kassid back to their home could be working on her as well.

After Jessa had snipped some herbs for herself and some for Amanda to take back to Sheleth, the two women made their way back down to the courtyard and went their separate ways. Jessa lived in a distant part of the fortress that contained small apartments set aside for single people and older couples who no longer needed or wanted much space.

The scent from the herbs she carried in a damp burlap sack tickled her nose pleasantly. She'd already forgotten what they were called, but Jessa had said that Sheleth would be pleased to have them.

Daken's mother continued to be polite but distant, and Amanda still didn't know if that was simply her nature or whether she was displeased at having an outsider thrust upon her. It was even possible that her behavior was the result of her lack of facility with English.

Jessa had told her that Daken's sister and her family would be coming from one of the other fortresses, or "homes," as Jessa called them, and now Amanda wondered if she should volunteer to stay with Jessa to allow the family some privacy.

On the other hand, she found herself rather curious about Daken's sister, whose existence had remained unknown until Jessa mentioned her.

She crossed the courtyard to the covered walkway that ran along the exterior of the fortress in this section, and was about to turn the corner to go inside when she suddenly heard Daken's voice. Startled at his harsh tone, she stopped, realizing that he must be in one of the rooms just inside. Peeking around the corner, she could see that both the big double windows were open.

He was speaking in his own language, so she couldn't understand any of what he was saying, but it was clear that he was angry, and she assumed that the objects of his anger must be the Sherbas she'd seen earlier. That was confirmed a few moments later when she heard another male voice, speaking in a placating tone.

She stood there unseen in the shadows, wondering just what they'd done to incur his wrath. Their attempts to soothe Daken certainly weren't working. His tirade continued and sounded all the harsher in the somewhat guttural Kassid tongue. Amanda smiled a bit, rather enjoying the thought that the arrogant Sherbas were the recipients of his wrath.

Thinking about them brought back to her again the attack by one of them. She frowned. Was it possible that the Sherbas were also behind the deaths of her colleagues—and of Steffen?

No, she thought, that couldn't be the case. If it were, they surely would have killed her as well. The look they'd given her made that plain enough. Besides, Jessa had said that the Sherbas worshiped the Kassid, and if that was true, it didn't seem likely that they'd do such a thing unless they'd received orders—orders from Daken. The conversation she was listening to only reinforced her certainty. They were clearly terrified of him.

A bell rang inside, startling her. The conversation had ended rather abruptly, but now she heard Daken speak briefly to someone: a different male voice this time. Perhaps he'd summoned someone. She crossed to the other walkway to avoid being seen and went into the fortress. But no sooner had she entered the building than she very nearly collided with Daken.

"Sorry," he murmured, picking up the sack of herbs that she'd dropped.

"They're for your mother," Amanda told him, fighting the conflicting emotions that always accompanied a confrontation with him. "Jessa took me up to the greenhouse."

At that moment the group of Sherbas passed them, accompanied by a young man she'd seen with Daken before. This time they didn't even glance at her. Daken's gaze followed them until they disappeared, and Amanda couldn't quite suppress a shudder at his barely leashed anger. She started toward the stairs, then stopped, remembering that Jessa had said she would need his permission to go up to the tower and he would be leaving tomorrow. It probably wasn't the best time to be asking, but given his rare appearances in the apartment, it might be the only opportunity she'd have.

She turned on the stairway and found him staring at her. Her mouth opened and then closed when she saw the anger still in his eyes and his big fists clenched at his sides. Then, just as she was about to turn away again, his expression softened.

"I'm not angry with you, Amanda," he said in a

gentler tone than she'd yet heard from him. "Is there something you want?"

"Yes," she replied, now staring at him from eye-level as she stood on the stair. "I'd like to go up to the tower, but Jessa said that we'd need your permission. I thought perhaps we could go up there while you're gone. She said you'd be away for a while."

"Of course. You may go there anytime you want." He paused for a moment. "In fact, I'll take you up there now if you like."

There was something in his tone that made the simple offer sound far more complex. Amanda hesitated, thinking of the isolated tower.

"Thank you, but I should get these herbs to your mother."

Two teenage girls appeared in the doorway and Daken turned to them and said something. One of the girls immediately smiled and nodded, then extended her hand to take the sack of herbs.

"She'll take them up to Mother," Daken told her.

They walked back outside together. Still reluctant to go up there with him, Amanda protested that he must have many other things to do.

"Nothing of importance. The walk will do me good."

Chapter Eight

The people who had been cleaning the empty apartments had gone, and they were now completely alone. Amanda slanted a glance at her silent companion, wondering why he'd offered to bring her up here when he seemed not to want her company. Before she'd learned about the ways of the Kassid, she would have feared there could be another reason, but she no longer worried about that.

Perversely, as soon as she'd stopped fearing that he might rape her, she had begun to wonder if he was at all attracted to her. But she didn't like to think much about that, because to do so meant that she also had to examine her feelings toward *him*. And those feelings remained mired in confusion.

She cast about for a safe topic of conversation. She wanted to ask him about the Sherbas, but given the argument she'd overheard and his anger, that didn't seem wise. So she asked instead about his sister, telling him that Jessa had mentioned she would be coming for the festival.

"Nenna is five years younger than me," he said. "She's a weaver, and so is her husband. That's why they live at Donelvy. They have a four-year-old daughter, Janissa."

"Do you see them often?"

"I visit the other homes every month or so, but they come here only twice a year for the festivals."

He lapsed into silence again and she made no further attempts at conversation. It was difficult enough for her to keep up with him, let alone talk at the same time. The numerous staircases made it even worse, because the steps were too widely spaced for her. Still, she did her best, and was therefore surprised when he noticed her difficulty and slowed his pace.

Then, just when she was certain that she couldn't climb another step, they reached the end of a winding corridor and he pushed open a heavy door to reveal a narrow set of steps that disappeared in a tight curve.

"Is this the last set of stairs?" she asked, gasping.

He nodded with a smile. "Now you don't need to worry about gaining weight during the festival."

She laughed, surprised to hear him make a joke. "I think I've already gained weight, thanks to your mother's wonderful cooking."

"It's been my good fortune to have the best cook of all for a mother. And she will outdo herself during this festival."

"I was wondering if I should perhaps ask to stay with Jessa when your family is here," she said as she started up the narrow staircase behind him.

"That isn't necessary. The apartment is large, and I'm sure my sister will be eager to meet you."

What a charming conversation we're having, she thought with a shake of her head. *One would almost think that I'm an honored guest, instead of a prisoner.*

When she reached the top of the staircase, Amanda stopped to catch her breath and to stare in astonishment at her surroundings. They were in a large, circular room that was richly furnished with dark-paneled walls and the ever-present crystal-and-gold wall sconces. A thick, multicolored rug covered the floor, and big matching pillows were piled in front of the stone fireplace. Light poured in through narrow stained-glass windows, and a door opened out to a stone courtyard.

"This space was created by the first Daken, and has been used by our leaders ever since." He paused and then his voice changed slightly. "There are many demands upon me, and sometimes I come here to get away from them, just as my predecessors did.

"I am sorry that I have spent so little time with you, Amanda—to help you learn about us and be comfortable here. But I knew that Jessa had become your friend."

He was avoiding her eyes, and Amanda thought about Jessa's description of him. She was touched by his attempt to apologize, but in the next instant she reminded herself—and then him—that she was still a prisoner here, no matter how kind her jailer.

"Are you spying on me even here?" she asked.

He gave her another of those brief smiles that lingered in her mind. "No, I'm not spying on you. There's no need for that. You're the subject of much discussion."

Then he gestured to the door. "Come outside to see the view. I assume that's why you wanted to come up here."

She stepped through the doorway into a cool wind—and beheld a panorama that literally took her breath away. Only a few snowcapped peaks seemed higher than the spot where she now stood, and from here, she could see where the Dark Mountains ended and the lower foothills began. She could also see the volcano that had cut off their escape from the jungle. Smoke still hovered above the crater, and below it, the green of the jungle was gone, replaced by blackened sticks that had once been mighty trees.

"Have there ever been earthquakes or eruptions up here?" she asked.

"No. We've felt the earthquakes from time to time, but only as slight tremors that did no damage. The gods have always protected the Dark Mountains."

She walked over to the low stone wall that bordered the small space and leaned over to peer down into an impossibly deep abyss.

"Be careful," he warned. "Some people become dizzy staring down there."

She drew back as a falling sensation came over her, catching her by surprise. She'd never suffered from vertigo before—but then she'd never seen a sheer drop of thousands of feet before, either. Instead, she turned around to stare at the wooden tower with its many mirrors.

"We found one of these in the jungle," she told him. "One of the men tried to take pieces of it so that we could determine its age and study the quality of the glass. He disappeared."

"Those towers are sacred to many people—though not to us."

"Do you know what happened to him—and to the other two who disappeared before . . . before everyone was killed?"

"Yes. They are dead as well, and their bodies will be taken to Menoa to be returned to their families."

"Who killed them?" she demanded.

"The man who attempted to steal from the ruins was killed by the villagers. I'm told that you were all warned not to touch the tower. The other two and the rest of the group were all killed by your guides."

"Acting on whose orders?"

"The Sherbas," he said after a long pause.

"And they were acting on *your* orders," she stated.

He looked distinctly uncomfortable, and for a time she thought he wouldn't respond. By the time he did, he'd turned away from her to stare out at the mountains.

"It's a complicated situation, as I told you before. Centuries ago, the Kassid protected the Sherbas. Now they protect us—or believe that they do.

"The guides were under orders from the Sherbas to keep you away from the Dark Mountains by showing you various ruins. But one of them overheard you talking to someone in the group about Wat Andara and how you should go there.

"According to the Sherbas, the guides then acted on their own to prevent that—by killing everyone."

"Except for me," she reminded him.

"Except for you," he admitted. "That's why I don't believe the Sherbas."

"What do you mean?"

"The guides had obviously been told to spare your

191

life—which means that the Sherbas must have ordered them to kill everyone else if it became necessary."

"But why not me? They hate me. I could see it in their eyes when they came here."

"They knew of my, uh, interest in you because I stopped one of them from killing you outside your home."

"So you *were* there. I wasn't sure."

He merely nodded, then began to talk about the signal tower and how they had once provided communications for the entire empire. Amanda had many more questions, but she sensed that she would get no more answers now. Eliciting information out of Daken was a delicate matter.

"The remaining towers are used for communications between the homes and with Wat Andara," he finished.

"Why don't you just get radios?" she asked. During her travels through the fortress, she'd been searching for one, hoping that she could use it to get help.

"Because radio signals would alert the outside world to our presence. Besides, a decision was made long ago not to bring the outside world here in any form. We are isolated.

"We know that the Dark Mountains have been photographed from the air. I've seen copies of the photos myself. But the mist protects us."

She lifted her head. It was true. Even when the sky was clear, that portion over the fortress was always enshrouded in mists. She was sure that there must be a scientific reason for it, because she still found it difficult—despite his claims—that his gods actually existed.

She walked around the signal tower and stared down into the big courtyard, then let her gaze travel along the sinuous curves of the fortress itself, as it hugged the mountain. It was all too easy to believe in his gods when she saw it like this. She wrapped her arms around herself and shuddered, wanting to cling to a world she could understand.

"Come back inside," he suggested. "You aren't dressed for this wind."

She followed him through the door, assuming they would leave the tower. But he lit the logs in the fireplace, then poured some wine. Amanda felt the first faint stirrings of uneasiness—an uneasiness vying with excitement, though she tried to deny it. The small, circular room had a rich, voluptuous feel to it that was heightened by the setting sun, which struck the stained-glass windows and filled the space with a warm, rosy light.

Instead of handing her one of the gold winecups, he set them both on the hearth. "The wine will be better if it warms first."

And I will be better if I get out of here right now, she thought as she became unbearably aware of his presence and of their isolation. But she made no move to leave.

He sank down against the cushions, and after a moment's pause she did likewise, taking care to keep as much distance between them as possible. It scarcely seemed to matter, though. Delicate, powerful threads of desire connected them. Or did they? Was the attraction all one-sided? She very much wanted an answer to that question, but feared knowing it. Instead, to break the heavy silence, she told him about being fitted for a gown for the festival.

193

"The fabric is beautiful. I've never seen anything finer."

He nodded as he reached for the winecups. "The fabric you chose was created by my sister."

"How do you know that?" she asked in astonishment, having a sudden vision of him hiding behind the draperies in the seamstress's quarters.

"As I told you, you are the subject of much discussion."

"I chose it only a few hours ago, Daken."

He laughed, a rich, deep sound that filled the room. "You chose a pale green—almost exactly the color of your eyes."

"That's right. Are you saying that someone rushed down to tell you that? I thought you were busy with the Sherbas." A wild thought came into her mind that he could see through walls—or read her mind. She was badly shaken to realize that she could even think such a thing.

"I was merely guessing. Mother showed me the fabrics that Nenna had created, and I thought that one suited you well."

"I see." And she was shamelessly flattered. He'd been avoiding her, but obviously she'd been on his mind.

"I am curious about something," he said, balancing the winecup on his knee as he sprawled comfortably in front of the fire. "What is the origin of the name Lescoulans—your mother's family?"

She was surprised by the question, but explained that no one knew. "My uncle tried to trace its origins, but he never wholly succeeded. He always thought that perhaps the family might have originally come from this region, and that the name underwent a transformation over the centuries. But that seems rather unlikely, because none of us looks at all like the people here."

"That's true," he replied thoughtfully. "But the Ertrians were a fair-skinned people who looked very different from other tribes in the region."

She hadn't thought about that. Now, remembering Jocelyn, the woman in the painting, she realized he was right.

"Do you think it could be an Ertrian name? But I thought they were all killed in the earthquake."

"Most were, but even then the Ertrians were a sea-faring people, and it seems reasonable that some of them could have been out to sea.

"I'm no student of Ertrian history, but there are some here who are, and in the library vaults are some ancient Ertrian books that go back to the time of Daken and Jocelyn. I will ask our Ertrian scholars to search them for any name that sounds similar to Lescoulans. It seems somehow familiar to me."

"That would be incredible," she said softly, thinking about that underwater city. "Steffen would have—"

She stopped abruptly as tears stung her eyes. Even after all this time and all that had happened, she still had difficulty accepting his death.

"Were you very close to your uncle?" he asked.

She nodded, swallowing the painful lump in her throat. "My father died when I was very young, and Steffen became both my father and my best friend."

He was silent, and when she had regained control of herself, she glanced over at him. He had turned away from her to stare into the fire.

"Did the Sherbas kill him, too?" she asked in a choked voice.

"Yes," he replied, but didn't turn back to her. "He had found the *azherwa*—the sacred room—in the old Ertrian palace, and for reasons known only to the gods, he was transported here—as you were later. We had thought that the room was destroyed in the earthquake."

"But he told no one!" she cried angrily.

"He must have told you."

She shook her head. "He didn't tell me. I found a journal, just a few pages that he'd written about it. And a map he'd drawn."

"They were at the cabin?"

"Yes." Amanda knew that her question was inevitable, but knew also that she didn't want to ask it. "You were there, weren't you?"

He searched her face carefully as he nodded. "Yes. I followed you there, thinking that I might find it."

"I don't understand what happened that night, Daken."

Her words hung in the air between them and echoed loudly in her own brain. She could feel the tension in him even as she felt it in herself.

"The gods have granted us certain powers when we leave the mountains," he said, slowly and with obvious reluctance. "It is their way of protecting us in the world outside."

She waited for him to say more as her very bones turned to ice. Then, when it seemed he intended to say nothing more, she asked, in a voice barely above a whisper, "What powers?"

"I sent you back to bed," he replied.

She stared at him in horror until he averted his

eyes. For a moment she thought he would say more, but he remained silent.

She set down the half-drained winecup and got clumsily to her feet. "I would like to leave now."

He, too, got up. "I don't have those powers here, Amanda."

"Is that supposed to reassure me?" she asked angrily. "Because it doesn't."

They stood there, separated by perhaps four feet, staring into each other's eyes—and trying to see more. Her horror and anger were mixing explosively with an emotion of a very different sort. Then she flinched as he raised his hand, curving his fingers and grazing her cheek lightly.

"Don't hate me, Amanda. I am only a man."

He dropped his hand quickly, but she continued to feel its caress. And in the lengthy silence as they descended from the tower, she heard his words over and over. But she didn't believe them. And later, when she was away from him, she wondered why he had asked her not to *hate* him, rather than not to *fear* him. The difference seemed important, but she didn't know why.

Daken stood on the rocky ledge, his head raised to the nearly full moon. He couldn't see the others, but he could feel their presence nearby in the midnight darkness of the forest. His thoughts were muted, sluggish, as they always were when the Other took over. It was not an unpleasant sensation, however; in fact, it was one he welcomed. Or usually welcomed. This time was different, and he knew, even though the thought formed slowly, what the difference was.

He lowered his head and stared off to the left. There was nothing to be seen except the faint outlines of the peaks against the star-studded heavens. He knew she was there, miles away in his home. His sense of direction was infallible.

The others were restless, wanting to move on, to climb the highest peaks and scale the treacherous rocks near the waterfalls. He could feel their tense energy and their impatience with him. They wouldn't move on without him because he was their leader, but part of leadership was knowing when and how to exercise it.

Even though his thoughts were sluggish, his images of her were startlingly clear: that defiant tilt of her chin, the way the light through stained glass set fire to her hair, the awareness of her body beneath the shapeless clothes. And most of all, the horror in her eyes when he admitted to having used his powers on her.

A mistake, he thought, though the brain of the Other lessened his regret now. Two mistakes, really. He should have taken away her memory of his visit to the cabin that night. But he'd been foolish. He'd thought he would never see her again, and he'd wanted her to remember him. A very human foolishness, from a man she no longer considered to be human.

And if she knew the whole truth? He shuddered slightly, and not from the cold wind that buffeted him. She might already have guessed, but was refusing to accept that knowledge.

The silent voices of the others broke through his pained musings, and he climbed down from the ledge to join them in their mindless freedom.

*　　*　　*

"They are staying for the festival," Jessa said, pulling a face as they both looked out the window to the courtyard, where the black-robed men walked among the flower beds. Behind them, the children in Jessa's art class worked diligently at their easels, their thoughts no doubt on the freedom to come.

"Daken told me that they were the ones who killed my friends," Amanda said. "The Sherbas, I mean. I don't know if these particular men were responsible."

"He told you?" Jessa turned to her in surprise, then resumed watching the Sherbas. "I didn't think he would tell you that. It is a shame we all feel—especially Daken, I think."

"And they had my uncle killed as well," Amanda went on, her voice taut with anger.

Jessa glanced at her, but said nothing.

"If what Daken said is true, I don't understand why he couldn't have prevented it—why he can't control them."

Jessa sighed. "There was a time when we could control them—but that was long ago. When they spread themselves throughout the world, they said it was because they needed to be our eyes and ears out there, as they had once been here. But then they became . . . corrupt. Protecting us has been their mission, you see, and they will stop at nothing. It is not Daken's fault. We all know that, although some would have him move against them."

"How could he do that?" Amanda asked curiously.

"By himself, he couldn't. But with the Bet Dawars and the help of the gods, he could. Still, there is great risk in that, and Daken is a cautious man, as befits a leader. Grandfather says that it is often the work of the leader to tame the anger of his followers."

Jessa got up from the window seat, and Amanda followed her as they began to examine the work of the class. She was especially eager to see the work of one student: the only child in the class with blue eyes. She'd been watching his work and believed he had greatness within him. But when they came to him, she saw that he'd done very little, and what he had done, while still competent, was lacking in the skill and beauty she'd seen in some of his previous work.

"Myen's mind seems to be elsewhere today," she commented after the children had left the studio.

"It is," Jessa confirmed. "He is but one year away from being able to join the Bet Dawars in the mountains. Still, if I am right, art will never be his life's work."

"What do you mean?" Amanda was surprised. Jessa agreed that the boy had talent, and she knew enough about the Kassid by now to know that they always encouraged talent of any kind.

"I think he will one day be leader. Daken has already taken notice of him."

Amanda thought about the boy, Myen. She, too, had sensed something in him beyond his talent. Perhaps it was the way the other children deferred to him, or perhaps it was something more. She couldn't say, but it surprised her that she, too, had felt what Jessa obviously felt. The difference was that she hadn't considered that possibility.

"Still, that doesn't mean that his art shouldn't be encouraged," Jessa went on. "It's very important for a leader to have something that gives him pleasure—

and a chance to escape his burdens for a time. My grandfather had his woodcarving—and, of course, his children. And Daken has the *leithra*."

"What is that?"

"A musical instrument. It's similar to a . . ." She frowned. "I cannot remember the name." She drew an outline in the air. "An instrument with strings."

"A guitar?" Amanda prompted in surprise.

"Yes. That is it, except that a *leithra* has more strings. It's very difficult to play. He sings, too, though not often. His voice is quite good."

"Daken?" she asked in astonishment, unable to imagine such a thing.

Jessa laughed. "He even composes music. Grandfather says that as a boy, Daken was always torn between his love of mountain-climbing and his music."

She grinned at Amanda. "Perhaps you can persuade him to play and sing at the festival. From what I've heard, he is quite taken with you, though of course that makes it very difficult for him."

Amanda didn't have to ask what her friend meant, because she knew. For all that she was being kindly treated, she was still a prisoner here—and one still liable to escape. In fact, she'd been wondering if the opportunity might present itself during the festival.

Later, as she walked back to Daken's quarters, she thought more about the possibility of escape. The festival would begin in three days' time. The fortress would be crowded and everyone would be busy. She'd already noticed that there didn't appear to be any guards posted at the great drawbridge, an omission that seemed rather strange to her.

She'd finally found the stables, and she thought that it shouldn't be difficult to find her way back to

Wat Andara. It was a treacherous trail, but easy enough to follow.

But that, she thought, would be the easy part. Even if the Land Rovers were still there, could she find them and take one without being captured by the villagers? As soon as her absence was discovered, a message would be sent to the village via the tower.

A part of her wanted to ignore this opportunity, to stay here. And now that she understood the situation with the Sherbas, she no longer blamed Daken for the murders. But in a sense, that only gave her added impetus to escape.

Jessa had said that Daken was "quite taken" with her, and she knew that was true. She had seen the desire in his eyes in the tower, had felt her own response, even through her horror at learning that he possessed supernatural powers.

Amanda shuddered. If he were only an ordinary man . . . But then, she'd known from the first time she'd spotted him that he wasn't.

As she walked through the courtyard, she stared off at the Dark Mountains, but thought instead about the concrete-and-steel towers of her home, the city, and held fast to that image, because it represented a world that, however imperfect, was understandable.

Then, as she turned toward the entrance to the fortress, the Sherbas came out. She glared at them. Whether or not these particular ones were responsible for Steffen's death and the deaths of her colleagues didn't matter. And as an outsider here herself, she felt no need to treat them kindly.

They walked toward her, their eyes on her. The one in front, a tall, ascetic man with a long nose, stopped, and the others stopped as well. Amanda felt no fear.

No one else was around at the moment, but she knew others were nearby. Still, her hand slid into her pocket and closed around the hilt of Daken's stiletto.

"You do not belong in this place," the man said in flat, unaccented English. "This place is sacred to the Kassid—and to us, their servants."

Amanda stared at him defiantly. "I am not here of my own free will—as you surely know. And if you are indeed servants of the Kassid, you're very bad ones."

"You should have died," he said in a hiss. "And if you leave this place, you will. There is nowhere you can go that we will not find you and stop you from revealing our masters."

Ice pierced her spine as she wondered if they had somehow tuned into her thoughts. Daken hadn't said that they possessed any powers, but she couldn't be sure.

"Daken will not allow any harm to come to me," she replied coldly, even though she suddenly wondered if that were true. If she did escape, he might well set them on her.

"Do not be so certain," the man said with a sneer. "He will do what he must to protect his people—as he has already done."

They all swept past her in a rustle of black robes, leaving her to stand there staring after them. What had they meant? Daken hadn't ordered any deaths. He'd told her and Jessa had confirmed it.

But they could both be lying, a dark voice whispered inside her head. If Daken told Jessa to keep the truth from her, she would. He was her leader.

Amanda hurried up the steps and into Daken's quarters, wondering if he might have returned in her

203

absence. She knew he was due back sometime today.

But when she entered the apartment, it wasn't Daken that she found there. Instead, his sister and her family had arrived. Nenna and her daughter were seated on the floor in the reception room, playing a game with brightly colored blocks. Amanda would have recognized Daken's sister even if she'd encountered her elsewhere. The resemblance to her mother was very strong.

"Amanda!" she cried, getting gracefully to her feet. "How nice to meet you at last." She reached out to take both of Amanda's hands and hold them briefly to her heart in what Amanda knew by now was the Kassid way of greeting.

Amanda let go of her suspicions as Nenna began to talk about the festival and about how pleased she was that Amanda had chosen one of her fabrics for her gown. They both joined the child, Janissa—a beautiful, dark-haired girl with huge, heavily fringed black eyes. Nenna explained the game they'd been playing, which was designed to improve coordination skills for the four-year-old. Then, when Janissa began to yawn, Nenna picked her up.

"Come with me. I have something to show you as soon as I put her to bed."

The child protested sleepily in the Kassid tongue, and Amanda heard Daken's name in there. Nenna kissed her and responded, then translated for Amanda.

"She wants to see Daken and she was disappointed that he wasn't here when we arrived."

Amanda followed her back through the hallway to a small room, where Nenna laid Janissa down in a child-size bed with a bright coverlet. After a few more protests, the little girl closed her eyes and they left the room. Nenna went to a larger bedroom across the hallway and opened a large, soft leather bag.

"This is for you," she said, handing Amanda a folded piece of fabric.

"It's beautiful!" Amanda exclaimed, running her hand over the soft, luxurious material. In fact, she'd never seen anything so glorious in her life. The background color was the same muted green as her gown, but woven into the fabric were thin threads of gold that formed an intricate design. She peered at the designs, frowning. They seemed familiar. She asked Nenna about them.

"You've seen them before," Nenna confirmed. "They are in the old language of the Kassid—before we simplified it."

"The black room," Amanda said, now recalling where she'd seen them.

"Yes. The *azherwa*. How terrifying that must have been for you."

Amanda merely nodded. That time seemed long ago. She studied the designs and saw, finally, that it was only one design, repeated over and over again. And as she unfolded the fabric, she saw that it was a large triangle, fringed on all sides with the fine gold thread.

"The design is our word for peace, except that it doesn't really translate very well. It means more than peace." She shrugged. "I do not have the words in your language for it. Perhaps Daken will be able to explain. It was his suggestion that I use that word."

Daken, she thought as she thanked Nenna profusely and sincerely and Nenna said she could use the garment for the cool evenings.

"What is your name for it?" Nenna frowned.

"Shawl," Amanda told her, still fingering the fine fabric and thinking about Daken. Had he lied to her—or did the Sherbas merely want her to believe that?

Daken did not return that evening. Amanda learned that Nenna's husband, Varlan, was with him in the mountains, which she assumed must mean that he too was a Blue-Eye. No one seemed unduly concerned by their failure to return, however.

She left them rather early in the evening, to give Nenna some time alone with her mother. She was tired, but decided to go for a walk in the courtyard before retiring. Perhaps the fresh air and exercise would stave off the dreams she'd been having.

The dreams were strange. She would awaken in the middle of the night, her body slick with the sweat of fear. But she could never remember what it was that had frightened her. And each time she awoke, she would hear the distant howls of the wolves echoing through the mountains.

She heard them often at night, but when she awoke after one of the dreams, she would feel a strange sort of yearning to be out there, running free through the forest. The feeling was amazingly strong and powerfully erotic, throbbing within her and reminding her of those encounters with the wolf before she came here.

She left the fortress and strolled through the gardens in the cool night air. The courtyard was lit at night by smaller versions of the huge cauldrons at the drawbridge. She'd learned by now that this light—and all the light and heat within the fortress as well—was provided by oil that was pumped in from wells directly beneath the fortress.

On this night, though, the lights were unnecessary. Overhead, the moon was huge and full, bathing the courtyard in its harsh illumination. Many people were out enjoying the pleasant coolness of the evening: both young and old moving about from shadows to light, totally without fear. According to Jessa, there was no crime here at all, and if Amanda hadn't already decided that the Kassid were utterly without pretensions of any kind, she would have doubted that statement.

What would happen to these people if the world encroached upon them? she wondered. How long would it be before the quiet night would be filled with the discordant sounds of boom-boxes blaring forth rock music? How long before television would find its way into the Dark Mountains? How quickly would rebellious teens form gangs to prey on the weak?

She would keep their secrets, even though the temptation to tell the world about these remarkable people would be very great.

Her thoughts turned to Daken. She would miss him, even though she hardly knew him. The silver-haired giant would never leave her mind, always there to remind her of what might have been.

She shook her head to dislodge those thoughts. Daken was beyond her understanding, a man and yet more than a man—a being who walked along the very edges of reality.

The wolves had been quiet, but suddenly they filled

the night with their voices once again. She stopped, startled at how close they seemed—as though they were just beyond the walls of the fortress. Of course, sound could be deceptive up here in the mountains, but still . . .

She noticed that others had stopped and were listening as well. The strange sounds rose and fell, almost as though they were singing. She couldn't begin to guess how many of them were out there, but it sounded like dozens, perhaps hundreds.

The utterly alien music seemed to glide over her and settle deep inside her, summoning that aching, yearning feeling again.

I must get out of here, she told herself, *before I lose all sense of reality. I must find a way to escape.*

But those thoughts brought back the memory of the Sherbas' threat. And thoughts of them in turn produced a reprise of the one man's statement that Daken would do what he must do to protect his people—what he had "already done." She didn't want to believe that—and yet she had just admitted to herself that Daken was unknowable.

The wolf serenade continued beyond the wall, rising and falling in a rhythm that seemed to match the beating of her heart. She turned and hurried back inside.

Amanda awoke slowly in the depths of the night, drifting between sleep and wakefulness, between dreams and reality, sensing that she was being summoned even though she heard no voice.

In the dream part, her naked skin was caressed by soft, thick fur, and then, as she edged closer to wakefulness, she would be repelled by the dream. In her dream, the pale eyes that bored into her were those of the wolf. But then they became Daken's eyes, filled with that raw desire she'd glimpsed so briefly. Daken and the wolf, over and over again.

Finally she opened her eyes, certain that she'd heard a sound. She sat up in bed, her head turning toward the open window, expecting to hear the haunting songs of the wolves. But the night was silent.

Water, she thought groggily. *It was a splash that woke me.* She was suddenly sure of it, and turned slowly toward the door that led into the bath. She'd stopped barricading both doors some time ago.

Daken! He'd come back. Fear and excitement vied for control of her thoughts—and of her body as well. She was still straining to hear any sounds in there, any indication that he had returned and was bathing—when the door began to open slowly.

The room was dark, but not so dark that she couldn't see his huge, dark silhouette as the door opened wider. A hot, damp scent of herbal soap tickled her nose as she sat there in bed, paralyzed, not really certain that she hadn't once again retreated into her dreams.

There was light in the bathroom, and it leaked briefly into her bedroom before he closed the door silently behind him. He was naked except for a towel draped around his waist. His silver hair looked dark, plastered against his head.

He moved soundlessly across the thick rug, then stopped abruptly. Her heart thudded noisily in the interval before he spoke.

"I'm sorry. I thought you were asleep."

She drew the covers up around her neck, shivering. "Why . . . ?"

The question died away into meaninglessness. She understood why he'd come—understood it deep inside herself, in the throbbing core of her womanhood.

"I—just wanted to see you. I didn't intend to wake you." His voice was low and husky and she could actually feel his discomfort.

But now she could feel something else as well: that same alien, primitive feeling she'd had when he'd come to the cottage in Wat Andara. It washed over her in waves, inundating her. She shuddered.

"I didn't mean to frighten you," he said, still apologizing—but not leaving.

The charged silence that followed was broken by the cries of the wolves. But they were distant this time, far off in the mountains. She turned toward the window. Daken and the wolf. She shuddered again.

"They were very close earlier," she said without turning back to him. "It sounded as though they were singing."

He said nothing. She felt him waiting and felt his hunger reach out to touch her, envelop her, push her back to the dream. In a slow motion that seemed to take forever, she turned back to him. He hadn't moved, and yet she felt that he had.

"Yes," she said, then "yes" again, the words running together in the electric silence. She felt the power of that single word—and its irrevocability.

He stood totally still for one long second, then fumbled with the towel—and finally flung it away.

Her fingers trembled as she continued to cling to the covers, and then she let them go.

She expected him to leap at her as the image of the wolf slid through her mind again. But he moved slowly across the room, stepping through a band of silvered moonlight that painted his big, hard body.

He stopped at the side of the bed—not uncertainly, but rather as though he wanted to savor the moment. That strange aura was overpowering now—far stronger than it had been before. Fear mingled explosively with desire as their eyes locked for a moment, and then his gaze slid down to caress her naked throat, shoulders, and her breasts, and she felt her nipples grow taut beneath his gaze.

He drew back the covers slowly, exposing the rest of her, then eased himself into the bed, stretching his long, hard, hair-roughened body over hers—reminding her again of the wolf-dream.

She could feel the war within him: raw, primitive hunger battling an innate gentleness. His lips sought hers greedily, bruising them, even as his hands moved gently over her. The contrast was incredibly erotic. She melted and flowed against him, arching beneath his touch as strange cries came from her and were quickly swallowed by his hard, demanding mouth and tongue.

Arms and legs tangled, they rolled on the bed until her weight was resting on him and his lips sought and found her achingly sensitive dark nipples, then teased them. His soft tongue alternated with sharp teeth, the sensation stopping just short of pain, and spreading fire within her.

Amanda soared into a realm of pure sensation, giving up the last shreds of control over her body, exchanging that control for the power she had over him. He trembled at her slightest touch, offering himself to her as she gave over herself to him.

She seemed to become him, to be reduced to his hard, throbbing shaft, while at the same time never losing her awareness of her own femaleness and its power to satisfy his hunger. And all of it was surrounded by that powerful sensation of something preternatural, something as timeless as the Dark Mountains themselves.

Then the two halves merged as he thrust into her, choosing the exact moment when her own need exploded and carried her over the edge into oblivion. With each powerful thrust, he seemed to surge closer and closer to her very soul, then merge with her completely.

"*Kazhena,*" he murmured, the sound soft and thick as he held her to him.

She didn't ask what it meant. Instead, surrounded by his warmth, she slept, drifting off to the renewed wolf songs in the mountains. But this time, there was no yearning to join them, no aching for that freedom.

Chapter Nine

When Daken entered the apartment with his giggling niece perched on his shoulders, Amanda immediately knew two things—two very important things: last night had not been a dream, and Daken regretted it.

She had awakened alone in her bed—alone and confused. Her body told her that the memory wasn't a dream, but even now, Daken often seemed not quite real to her.

Added to that uncertainty was the fact that what she remembered seemed too wonderful to have been real. Amanda had known other lovers, but what her memories and her body told her about last night's lovemaking banished forever thoughts of those men.

So she'd waited, hoping that he might return, and had gotten out of bed only when she heard the others, including the child, Janissa, now protesting as Daken deposited her gently on her feet.

The regret was in his eyes, though she saw it only briefly because his gaze slid quickly away from hers. At first she was angry. How dare he come to her bed, and then behave this way? If it hadn't been for the presence of the others, she would have confronted him then and there.

But her anger gave way quickly to a sense of shame. She had invited him—not into her room, but certainly into her bed. A burst of indignation and self-righteousness would have been very satisfactory right now, but she was too honest to delude herself.

So she took the only course of action open to her at the moment. She left the apartment and the happy family scene and wandered alone through the courtyard, which was filled with people coming in from the other fortresses to be greeted by their friends and families. Many of them stared at her unabashedly, making her feel even more alone. She was now dressed in the dark clothing of the Kassid, but her red hair and her pale skin gave her away—not to mention her diminutive size. Weaving her way through the groups of tall Kassid, she felt like a lost and abandoned child.

But she was also more determined than ever to take advantage of the chaos of the festival to escape. All that remained was for her to choose the time, and it seemed to her that the first night of the festival might be best. People would be in high spirits, and everyone would be busy renewing old friendships and family ties. She was certain she could slip away unnoticed.

Feeling somewhat better, she found her way to

Jessa's apartment, then joined her and several other artists who were deciding which of the children's work should be displayed in the studio. There were dozens of paintings to choose from, some of which had only just arrived with families from the other fortresses.

Amanda threw herself into this task enthusiastically. She truly liked Jessa and her friends, and knew she would miss all of them. That made this time all the more precious to her, and their warm, easy acceptance of her chased away any feelings of isolation.

She spent the entire day with the group, even staying to join them for a communal dinner in the studio. Although she stayed because she enjoyed their company, she also realized that she needed to establish a pattern of being away from Daken's quarters, so that her final absence would be less likely to be noticed.

After dinner, one of the musicians who had joined them brought out his instrument, and Amanda saw a *leithra* for the first time. It was a wonderfully ornate instrument and obviously quite difficult to master. But the sound was beautiful, deep and rich, and she complimented the musician warmly after he'd played a particularly haunting melody.

"It was written by Daken," he told her. "I do not sing as he does, but still the melody is beautiful."

The name went through her like a shard of ice. Jessa had told her that he not only played the *leithra* but had also written compositions, but she would never have believed that such music could be produced by him. And yet, as she thought about their lovemaking last night, she knew that he was indeed capable of great depths of feeling.

But she reminded herself that he remained her enemy. No matter what he felt for her, he would do whatever was necessary to prevent her escape—perhaps even to the extent of siccing the Sherbas on her. And they'd made it quite clear that they would show her no mercy.

It was very late by the time she finally left the studio and said her good-nights to the others as they made their way back to their apartments. She hoped that by now Daken would have gone to bed, and although she intended to barricade her door, she doubted very much that he would come to her again.

As she walked across the now-deserted courtyard, passing by the section where the children slept in tents, she wondered *why* he regretted what had happened. Did he believe that he had forced himself on her—or was he regretting a momentary weakness that had driven him into the arms of a very willing woman?

It was a question that would not be answered, however, because she had no intention of asking. Her earlier urge to confront him had vanished completely. She wanted only to stay away from him until she could escape.

She climbed the stairs and started down the hallway to his quarters. Ahead of her she could see that a light was still on in the reception room. The door hadn't been closed in all the time she was here, and a soft light spilled out into the hallway. Hoping that it had been left on for her, she approached the doorway cautiously.

He was there, stretched out in a big, comfortable

chair that he'd pulled over to the fireplace, his feet propped on a low footstool. She stopped and held her breath. His face was hidden from her by the curved back of the chair, but something in his posture suggested that he might have fallen asleep. His hand dangled over the arm of the chair, his fingertips just above a half-full wineglass.

She hesitated, calculating her chances of getting past him to the hallway that led to her bedroom. The floor was thickly carpeted, so she might be able to make it. But if he was waiting for her, he would probably awaken at some point and come looking for her. The chair barricade would warn her that he was coming, but it certainly wouldn't prevent him from getting into her room.

She didn't want to talk to him about it—not now and not ever. She didn't want to hear him say he regretted what had happened, no matter what the cause for his regret. She wanted only to leave the Dark Mountains and carry with her the memory of one glorious night in his arms.

So she turned around and walked quickly down the quiet hallway, down the stairs, across the courtyard—back to Jessa's apartment, where her friend opened the door immediately.

"Could I stay here tonight?" Amanda asked the moment Jessa ushered her in.

"Of course—but why?"

"It's . . . complicated," Amanda said. "But I just don't want to go back to . . . back there."

"Back to Daken, you mean?" Jessa asked in confusion.

Amanda nodded, wishing that her friend wouldn't push her for more information, yet knowing that she would. Jessa obviously found it strange that Amanda would be on her doorstep at this hour.

"I just don't want to see him, and he was there—waiting for me, I think."

"I don't understand."

No, you don't, Amanda thought. In a similar situation in her own world, a woman would have quickly assumed that Daken had tried to force himself on her. But that couldn't happen here, so it was understandable that Jessa would be confused.

"We . . . made a mistake last night, and I just don't want to talk to him."

"Last night?" Jessa echoed, a strange look coming over her face. "You mean that the two of you made love when he came back?"

"Yes. It shouldn't have happened. He didn't force himself on me, of course, but . . ." She trailed off as she belatedly became aware of Jessa's expression.

"What's wrong?" she asked.

"Nothing," Jessa said quickly—too quickly, Amanda thought. Then she started toward her bedroom. "Let me get you a blanket and pillow. You'll be comfortable on the . . ." She stopped and gestured to the sofa, her command of English temporarily deserting her.

"Sofa," Amanda said. "And I'll be fine. Thank you."

But after Jessa had gone to bed, Amanda lay on the sofa and pondered her friend's strange behavior for a long time. Why had she seemed so surprised that they'd made love? She'd already said that Daken was interested in her, and had tried several times to find out how Amanda felt about him.

* * *

Daken woke up when a log fell in the fireplace. The ornate gold clock on the mantel showed the time to be just past three A.M. He stretched, then stood up, momentarily uncomfortable in his body. She must have come back and gotten past him, which he found rather surprising.

He went down the hallway and paused outside her door, then opened it carefully, not wanting to awaken her. But she wasn't there. He frowned. He knew that she'd spent the day and evening with Jessa and her friends, so she must have decided to spend the night in Jessa's apartment.

He closed the door again and stood there uncertainly. She couldn't have left the fortress, and wherever she was, she was in no danger. Still, he was tempted to go over there.

Finally he went on to his own room, wondering what she'd told Jessa—and more important, what Jessa had told her. Jessa knew his orders regarding Amanda, but it was conceivable that she would disobey them—and if she did, he had only himself to blame.

He stood at his window, listening to the distant sounds of the wolves, part of him longing to be back out there, while the other part wanted something very different: to be next door in Amanda's bed. Instead, he stripped off his clothes and got into his own bed, cursing himself for the weakness that had led him to such a mistake.

Amanda waited the next morning until she could be reasonably certain that Daken would be gone, then left Jessa's, promising to return soon to help with the art displays. As she left Jessa's apartment, she thought that she really understood for the first time that old adage about going from the frying pan to the fire. Jessa had asked nothing more about her reason for staying over, but she'd questioned several times whether Amanda was all right, and she continued to seem confused about something.

And now, if Daken was home, Amanda would undoubtedly be forced to endure more questions she didn't want to answer.

She hurried through the bustling courtyard and in through the entrance that led to Daken's quarters—only to find him coming down the stairs.

He paused momentarily when he saw her, then continued toward her. She managed to fix a smile to her face, even though her heart was racing and her treacherous body was already threatening to melt at the mere sight of him.

"I stayed at Jessa's last night," she said brightly, forestalling—or so she hoped—any questions from him. "We were up late and I didn't want to disturb anyone."

He said nothing as he stopped at the bottom of the staircase, but his pale eyes were busy searching her face—warily, she thought.

"I promised to help with the art displays as soon as I bathe and change," she told him, at the same time moving past him to start up the stairs.

"Amanda," he said in a low voice that would have stopped her even if he hadn't put out his hand to lightly grasp her arm.

The heat of his body flowed through her, leaving her with the insane wish that he would pick her up and carry her back to bed right now. Standing on the stairs, she was at eye-level with him, and when she met his gaze, the world blurred into the magic of that night.

"I intended to tell you that I'm sorry about what happened," he said in a low, intimate voice that sent tiny curls of heat through her. "But I'm not sorry. I wanted it to happen, but I should have waited."

"Why?" she asked, not understanding.

He hesitated, once again searching her face. "Did I frighten you?"

"No," she replied, shaking her head for added emphasis. "You didn't force yourself on me, Daken. I invited you into my bed."

He continued to stare at her, started to say something, then stopped. The uncertainty in his eyes troubled her—and reminded her of Jessa's confusion. What was going on here? What didn't she understand?

Several people hurried past them, and then a group of children came running down the stairs. Amanda had been about to demand that he explain, but suddenly she was afraid, without understanding why. She repeated that she had to hurry back to the studio and fled up the stairs. When she turned around at the top, he was still standing there, staring up at her.

The question she hadn't asked continued to hammer at her as she soaked in a warm bath. She was certain that both Jessa and Daken had been troubled by the same thing—but what was it?

By the time she had dressed and was on her way back to Jessa's, Amanda had decided that she was more likely to get the truth from Jessa. And perhaps it would be easier to hear from Jessa's lips as well.

Two young girls were just leaving the studio when

Amanda arrived. More paintings had been added to the collection, and Jessa was walking among them, studying them carefully. No one else was there at the moment. They were probably busy setting up their own displays in the great hall downstairs.

She went over to the table near the windows where Jessa always had a pot of tea, and poured some for herself, then glanced out the window just in time to see Daken emerge from the fortress below her. She wondered if he could have been up here to see Jessa. She herself had come through the building to the studio after stopping first at Jessa's apartment.

"Was Daken here?" she asked as Jessa joined her for some tea.

"No, I haven't seen him," Jessa replied. But she avoided Amanda's eyes as she spoke and her response seemed too quick.

"Jessa?" Amanda put out a hand to touch her friend's arm. "I need to know why you seemed so shocked when I told you about Daken and me. Surely it couldn't have surprised you."

Jessa continued to avoid looking at her. "It didn't," she said quickly.

"But something bothered you about it—and something's bothering Daken as well. I saw him earlier."

"You must talk to him about it, Amanda."

"I'd rather talk to you. In spite of what happened, Daken still frightens me."

Now Jessa did look at her, and her expression was one of surprise. "He'd never harm you, Amanda."

"He admitted to me that he has . . . magical powers. He said that he doesn't have them here, but . . ."

"That's true. I didn't realize he'd told you about that. But the gods only grant those powers to defend himself when he's away from the Dark Mountains."

"You've been away from here, too," Amanda said. "Do *you* have such powers?"

Jessa hesitated, then shook her head, looking very uncomfortable. Amanda felt guilty about putting her friend on the spot, but she was determined to get to the bottom of this. "Do you mean that only Daken has them?" Amanda asked, finally.

"No. All the Bet Dawars are granted such powers."

The Blue-Eyes, Amanda thought, and once again felt the fear that was warning her to end this questioning. But this time she ignored it.

"What are you hiding?" she demanded. "And why does it matter now if I know your secrets? Who could I tell?"

"It isn't that," Jessa said softly. "But you must go to Daken for your answers."

"He was here, wasn't he? And he ordered you not to talk to me about this."

"Yes, he was here," Jessa admitted.

"I'm sorry, Jessa. I don't want to get you into trouble, and you're right. I will talk to Daken."

Amanda was happy to see her friend relax, but now she herself had lied. She wasn't going to speak to Daken about it. Instead, she was going to leave this place and its secrets. And she wasn't going to wait any longer. The festival didn't really begin until tomorrow, but it seemed to her that everyone had already arrived, and tonight would do just as well.

She spent most of the day helping Jessa and the others, all the while making her plans. It would be best, she thought, to wait until very late. The stables were in an isolated portion of the fortress, so she didn't anticipate any problem getting a horse.

Food for the journey was another matter, but she knew that Sheleth and Nenna were preparing huge quantities of food for the festival. Surely she could sneak into the kitchen tonight and take a few things.

She was still somewhat concerned that there might be guards posted somewhere that she hadn't seen, but she decided that was a chance she would just have to take. She'd studied the fortress carefully, and couldn't imagine where they'd be. As nearly as she could tell, all the windows that faced the drawbridge were living quarters, and there was no sentry box of any kind.

Once again she joined Jessa and the others for dinner. They all spoke English in her presence, and she appreciated their kindness in this and many things. Everyone was in a festive mood and Amanda did her best to imitate their gaiety, but she alone knew that this was the last time she would see them.

Finally, though, she could keep up the act no longer and, pleading tiredness, she said her goodnights, which were really good-byes, and left them in the studio, with the haunting music of the *leithra* following her.

Reluctant to return to Daken's quarters and risk another confrontation with him, she began to roam the courtyard. Many others were out enjoying the pleasant night, and everywhere she went she heard laughter and saw people enjoying themselves beneath a bright, full moon. Her own mood was badly split between nervous eagerness to put her plan into action and sadness over leaving this enchanted place.

She walked deeper into the courtyard, close to the

wall, and turned to stare back at the great fortress with its many lighted windows. Would the time come when all this would no longer seem real to her? She supposed that could happen, because at the moment, her home, with its noise and dirt and crime, didn't seem real either.

The contrast was too sharp, she thought—too boldly drawn for her mind to grasp. How tempting it would be to tell others of this place—and yet she knew that she'd never do that. The one gift she could give to the Kassid was the gift of her silence. And no matter what Daken's role might have been in the deaths, she would keep their secret.

Daken. She wrapped her arms around herself as memories slipped through her with a soft heat. She wondered if she might be in love with him. She hadn't allowed herself to consider that before, but now that she would soon be gone . . .

No, she told herself, *you can't be in love with him. He has already admitted to having powers that no man should possess, and who knows what other secrets he still holds? Love is built on trust, and you don't trust him. Furthermore, he obviously doesn't trust you, either.*

A single wolf howled in the distance, and she wrapped her arms even more tightly around herself, shuddering, allowing herself only a brief glimpse into the darkness of her own mind before she thrust her thoughts back into the abyss. It simply could not be.

Suddenly she had the sensation that she was being watched: the same feeling that had come over her those times at Steffen's cabin. The wolf. Could it be here? She whirled around, her eyes searching the darkness where the wall and the tall evergreens cast deep shadows.

She saw movement there, where the wall curved close to a clump of dark firs, and she braced herself, expecting the wolf. But the figure that emerged was much larger.

Her heart thudded noisily in her chest and her mouth went dry. She had stayed out here to avoid him, but he had found her. And as he walked toward her, becoming more visible now in the moonlight, she stared into his pale eyes and felt herself staring once again into an abyss of horrors.

"Have you been spying on me?" she demanded angrily, the accusation out of her mouth before she could stop herself.

"I've been watching you," he replied as he stopped before her. "There's a difference."

"A very small difference," she said, the anger now gone from her voice as his nearness smothered it with other feelings.

"Surely you should be spending your time with your family," she countered, somehow having gotten herself into a confrontation she'd wanted to avoid.

"I've been with them most of the day and evening," he said mildly. "They would have welcomed you as well."

"I was busy with Jessa and her friends."

"And busy avoiding me as well," he said with a smile.

"Yes."

"Do you regret what happened night before last, Amanda?"

"Yes . . . no. I don't regret it, but it shouldn't have happened."

To her surprise he chuckled, a deep sound that seemed to vibrate through her. "Perhaps my English isn't good enough to understand the difference."

"Why did it happen, Daken?" she asked, knowing that she should have ended this conversation before it reached this point, but now realizing that she both wanted and needed to know how he felt about her.

"It happened for the only reason such things should ever happen. We wanted each other."

"Then why did you say that you should have waited?"

"I was wrong about that," he replied, but now his gaze slid away from hers.

Several wolves howled, their voices rising and falling in an eerie chorus. He turned to stare in that direction, and she shivered, recalling how she'd heard them the night he returned. It was the only time she'd heard them so close to the fortress.

He turned back to her and she saw the hunger in his eyes. Her legs trembled and her pulse raced wildly. Every fiber of her being cried out for his touch. The very air between them seemed to throb with electric energy.

She stepped toward him, only just barely aware of the movement. For one heartbeat he seemed to hesitate—and then she was in his arms, surrounded by him, engulfed in the strength and heat of his body.

"Amanda," he muttered roughly, his accent more noticeable now. "By the gods, I cannot stop wanting you."

His hand trembled as he threaded his fingers through her hair and drew her face up to meet his lips. His kiss was hard, driving, demanding—but his body trembled against hers.

"Come with me now—back to my bed," he murmured against her ear.

She nodded, not trusting herself to speak, and he released her, then seized her hand and started back to the fortress, nearly dragging her along behind him until he finally slowed his steps to accommodate his longer stride to hers.

As they turned a corner, they very nearly collided with the group of Sherbas, who quickly stepped aside, inclining their heads and making a sign. Daken said nothing to them, but his grip on her hand tightened almost painfully.

The sudden appearance of the Sherbas reminded Amanda of her plan to escape tonight, but the memory was short-lived. One look into Daken's eyes and she forgot everything but her hunger for him, a hunger that fed on his desire.

The reception room was empty and the apartment quiet as they hurried through to his room, driven by their need. In a small, rational part of her brain, Amanda feared the firestorm that seemed to surround them, but the rest of her longed to be consumed by that fire.

It was a wild coming-together. They shed only the necessary items of clothing before falling together onto the big bed in a tangle of fabric, arms and legs. She arched toward him and he drove into her, pushing them both over the edge into a shuddering, welcome oblivion.

"*Kazhena*," he murmured, still trembling as he held her close.

"What does that mean?" she asked in a husky voice.

His mouth curved in a smile and his fingers caressed her cheek. "It is a term of endearment. It means 'gift of the gods.' "

He began to remove the rest of her clothing, his fingers gently grazing her heated flesh, his lips following. Their passion was not yet spent, but had instead been curbed to a glowing warmth that made room for tenderness.

Naked now, they played at lovemaking, teasing, taunting, enjoying each other. Amanda knew somehow that she was seeing a side of this man that no other had ever seen: the part of him that wrote beautiful music.

She spotted the *leithra* standing in a corner and wished aloud that he could play for her. Still naked, he climbed out of bed and returned with the instrument.

"Won't you disturb the others?" she asked.

He shook his head as he adjusted the strings. "The walls are very thick, and I will play softly."

She lay naked in the tangled heap of bedcovers and clothes, both of them bathed in the silvery moonlight as he played, his silver hair glowing as he bent to the instrument. Even played softly, the *leithra* had a wonderfully rich sound that caressed her ears.

"Did you write that?" she asked when he stopped.

"Just now." He smiled.

She sat up, astonished. "Just now? You mean you were composing it as you played?" She was sure that he must be teasing her, taking advantage of her lack of familiarity with Kassid music. There'd been no hesitancy, no stumbling.

"Yes. It seems I was . . ." He paused, obviously searching for the English word. "Inspired," he finished with a smile.

"Play it again," she ordered, still not quite believing him.

He did, then set the instrument aside.

"Will there be words?" she asked.

He shook his head. "Sometimes words are inadequate. Music is the way we speak when there are no words."

"But it must have a name," she protested, the artist in her overwhelmed by the ease with which he could create such beauty.

"It has a name: 'Amanda.' It is meant to be you—all the things for which I have no words in your language—or in mine."

Chapter Ten

The great hall was filled to overflowing. The huge carved doors had been opened to the courtyard, and the musicians in the balcony above filled the evening with glorious sound. A flowing river of color filled the space as the Kassid cast aside their customary dark clothing for all the colors of the rainbow and the glitter of gold.

Amanda touched the fine gold chains that encircled her throat as her eyes sought him out in the shifting sea of people. Daken had given her the delicate necklace only hours ago, before he left to see to the final preparations for the evening's festivities.

Then she saw him, making his way slowly through the crowd, his eyes already on her. She smiled, thinking of his sister's comment about his attire. Nenna had said that left to his own devices, her brother would have simply exchanged one dark tunic for another. But she'd made him a new tunic in a pale, shimmering silver wool that was a perfect match for his hair, then edged it in an intricate gold design.

He stopped before her, his gaze dropping to the rounded swell of her breasts above the low neckline of the gown. She'd been surprised to see the normally modest Kassid women wear such décolletage, though their gowns were certainly no more daring than the current high fashion in her own world.

"You are beautiful," he said simply.

"Thank you," she replied huskily. Then she swept an arm around the great hall, where huge urns of flowers filled the air with their fragrance and garlands of shiny dark leaves with tiny white blossoms were strung everywhere. She hadn't yet found out what they were.

"Everything is beautiful," she told him. "This hall seemed so grim before."

"This festival is about beauty." He smiled. "About beauty and . . ." He frowned, searching for the word. "It is a celebration of life and love. Ah, *sensuality*. That is the word I sought. A feast for all the senses."

Amanda thought that he'd found the perfect word for it. The music that drifted down from the balcony was uniquely sensual: high, light notes over a deeper, darker beat. The mingled fragrances of the flowers added their own voluptuous note. Even the golden wine that flowed in great abundance had a silken feel and an intoxicating aroma.

The Kassid themselves seemed different somehow. Despite their usual dress, they were not a somber people, but on this night they seemed carefree, and at the same time seductive. For both men and women, loose, nearly shapeless clothing had been exchanged for formfitting pants and tunics and gowns with plunging necklines.

The music came to a halt, and suddenly people were moving around more purposefully. Daken took her arm. "It is time for dancing."

"But I don't know your dances," she protested as he led her toward the center of the great room, where other couples were gathering.

"Just let your body move with the music," he advised her, drawing her into his arms.

The music began again as the lights dimmed in the hall. Later, when she thought about this night, Amanda would be certain that Kassid magic had been at work. The music changed tempos dizzyingly, moving from a slow, sensual beat to soaring, hauntingly beautiful melodies. She was unaware of any conscious effort to move in a given pattern, but she moved nonetheless, her body fitted against his and then turning, whirling, their only contact through clasped hands.

His mouth sought and found hers and she arched against him, teasing him with her closeness before moving away again, caught up in the music. Then, with clasped hands raised high, they swayed, bodies brushing lightly, his hard angles fitted to her soft curves.

Amanda was scarcely aware of her movements as the music seemed to enter her and join them together with its powerful sensuality. And she was completely unaware of the other couples in the great hall and out in the courtyard beyond. They too were lost to everything but the music and the celebration of their bodies.

It seemed that it would go on forever, but then the

music slowly drifted away, until the dancers were hearing it only in their minds. Daken drew her to him one more time and kissed her softly, and as the lights in the hall grew brighter, she once more became aware of those around her, who also seemed to be struggling out of a trance.

The hum of conversation began, and laughter once more filled the great hall. Daken held on to her hand as he led her toward the corner, where huge casks of wine were set up. Then he left her there, at the edge of the crowd that was gathering, and she backed away into an alcove, still caught between the dream-dancing and reality.

What had happened? Was it magic? All around her people were just as they had been before. It was as though the aura of sensuality that had hovered over the celebration had suddenly been thrown into sharp relief during the dance, only to retreat now to its former subtlety. Had they all felt what she'd felt, but being Kassid, simply accepted it?

Despite sharing the experience with the celebrants, Amanda now felt more than ever alienated from them—and from Daken, even though her body continued to call out for his. And it was in that moment, as she was trying to sort out her feelings, that she heard the low voice behind her.

"What kind of woman would share the bed of a man who ordered her uncle's death?"

Paralyzed by the voice and by the words, Amanda was slow to turn, and when she did she saw only a dark shadow moving off into deeper shadows. But she recognized that voice: it was the Sherba who'd spoken to her before.

She looked around wildly for Daken and saw his

silver head in the midst of the crowd gathered at the center of the room. Then she turned again and ran after the Sherba. But she was soon lost in the maze of hallways in this part of the fortress, and the sounds from the great hall had faded away, contained within the thick stone walls.

Finally she found her way outside and saw that she was not far from the entrance she used to reach Daken's quarters. The magic of the music was gone, leaving her with only the cold certainty that it *had* been an enchantment, and reminding her once again of the Kassid's secrets.

I must leave, she told herself. *If I stay, he will only use his powers again to keep me here.* It scarcely mattered whether it was the power of his desire for her or magic; to her, it had suddenly become all the same. She couldn't trust him.

And a voice that she'd ignored all this time was telling her that the Sherba was right: Daken *had* ordered Steffen's death. She'd always known that, but she'd tried desperately to ignore it. Steffen had threatened the security of his people, and Daken had had him killed. She, too, threatened that security, but he'd chosen to bring her here, instead of having her killed. But it amounted to the same thing: he would do what must be done to protect his people.

She ran back inside and up the stairs, then down the empty hallway to his apartment. She knew it would be empty. Everyone was at the festival, and little Janissa was with an older cousin at the children's party.

She stripped off her gown and dug through the cupboard for the clothes she'd worn here. After dressing hastily, she went to the kitchen and gathered up some food: bread, cheese and fruit, putting it all into a sack. She didn't bother with water, since she knew there was a faucet at the stable as well as oiled leather canteens that could be attached to the saddles.

When she reached the top of the stairs, she paused. Daken might well be out in the courtyard by now, looking for her. In order to reach the stables she would have to pass through the courtyard just outside the great hall. So instead she began to make her way through the fortress toward the stables.

By now, thanks to the time she'd spent exploring the fortress, Amanda had developed a certain degree of familiarity with the immense place. After only a few false starts, she found herself on the downward-sloping hallway that she was sure would lead to the stables. She saw no one anywhere along her route.

No one was in the stables either when she pushed open the heavy door and walked into the dimly lit interior that was filled with the sweet smell of hay and the distinctive odor of the animals. Like everything else here, the stables were large, but she'd already found the horse she'd ridden here, distinctive because of an unusually shaped star on his forehead.

She set down the sack of food and dragged the heavy saddle from its place in the nearby tack room. After giving the animal one of the apples she'd brought along, she threw the saddle on him and tightened the girth, then filled a canteen and tied it to the leather thong on the saddle alongside her sack of food. Then she led him outside, pausing in the open doorway to peer around.

There was no sign of anyone, and she had only to cross a hundred feet of open space before she would be on the bridge. She climbed into the saddle, literally hauling herself up onto the horse's back because it was so much taller than any animal she'd ridden before.

The sound of its hooves striking the wooden planks of the drawbridge seemed very loud to her, and she kept turning in the saddle, expecting to see someone pursuing her. But no one came, and in a few minutes she was across the bridge and onto the trail.

When she reached the spot where she'd first seen the fortress, Amanda brought the animal to a halt without consciously intending to do so. Very faintly, across the space that now separated her from it, she could hear the music and the laughter. The fortress was mostly dark tonight, except for the bright lights around and in the great hall and the burning cauldrons in the courtyard and at the entrance to the bridge.

Amanda felt tears stinging her eyes, blurring her final view of this magical place. For one brief moment, all that she loved about the Kassid very nearly made her turn back, and when Daken's image filled her mind, she actually began to turn the horse's head.

"No!" she said aloud, loosening the reins again. "I do not belong there—and he does."

She kicked the animal lightly and it obediently set off down the trail under the bright moon. She resisted the temptation to turn for one last glimpse of the home of the Kassid.

"She is gone and he is searching for her."
"Then it worked—as I thought it would."

"But why did she believe you?"

"Because she already knew the truth. She needed only to hear it."

"If he finds out that you told her . . ."

"He will not find out. Only she could tell him—and she will soon be dead."

"Still, he might guess."

"But he will have no proof, and Daken does not act without proof. He has spent too much time among them to be able to think clearly. His choice was a mistake. And her presence here proved that. Leaders before him would have had her killed, too. We must help the gods protect the Kassid."

Daken felt the emptiness in the apartment the moment he walked in. He'd expected to find her here, and was still carrying the two glasses of wine, not really displeased that she'd come back here.

Except that she wasn't here. He walked down the hallway and stopped in the doorway to her room. Her gown lay in a heap on the bed, and the soft dancing shoes that seemed child-size to him were on the floor.

He stood there, thinking. Was it possible that she'd left the fortress? But why? He'd stopped worrying about that after the first night they'd spent together, certain that she was bound to him as he was to her.

He shouldn't have left her alone after the dance. She'd probably been frightened about the effects of the music, and he should have realized that. His mistake was in believing that she'd become so much a part of him that she understood everything—and might even be willing to accept the secrets he still kept from her. But there was one he never intended to reveal to her.

He went back to the great hall to seek out Jessa, hoping that she might know something. But when he found her she said she hadn't seen Amanda since much earlier in the evening.

"Has she gone—run away, I mean?" Jessa asked in alarm.

"I think she may have," he admitted reluctantly.

"Daken," Jessa said, laying a hand on his arm. "I think you do not understand what goes on in her mind—or in her heart. She has been confused by what she's seen and felt here. And she is confused as well by her feelings for you. When you find her, you must be honest with her—about everything. If she loves you, she will accept the truth in time."

Daken nodded uncomfortably, already too much aware of his mistakes. He thought that Jessa was probably right. Amanda *could* learn to accept what he was in time. But he feared that she'd never accept the role he'd played in her uncle's death.

"We must go after her," he told Jessa, then went to seek out some of the Bet Dawars and give them their orders. Because it was festival, he kept the number small, not wanting to deprive all of them of the celebration.

They stepped out into the courtyard and heard the first warnings from the wolves.

When she first heard the wolves, Amanda brought the horse to a halt. A chill slithered through her as their cries rose and fell, seemingly on all sides. She thought about the wolf that had prevented her from escaping before. Could it be out there now?

She urged the horse forward, eager to put some distance between her and the wolves. Thanks to the brilliant moonlight, she'd made good time thus far, but now the trail was in deep shadow as she descended into a ravine. She let the animal find its way and thought about what lay ahead. It occurred to her that there must be vehicles of some kind in the village of Wat Andara. How else could Daken and other Kassid reach the outside world? And if there were vehicles, then there must also be a gasoline supply.

She knew it would take her the night and at least part of the next day to reach the village. When she did, she would find a safe place to hide and perhaps get some sleep, and then she would sneak into the village after dark.

It was going to be tricky. In all likelihood, Daken would send a signal in the morning to the village to be on the lookout for her, and she had no doubt at all that the villagers would hold her captive if he ordered it. Furthermore, he might already have guessed that she'd escaped and could be coming after her.

Perhaps she'd made a mistake by leaving tonight. Tomorrow night would have been better because she could have stayed away from him more easily, and then have gotten an earlier start. But if she'd stayed, she would have spent another night in his bed. . . .

Her breath escaped in a sob. She'd been gone for only a few hours, and yet she already missed him and ached for his touch. Had he cast a spell on her? She shivered and kicked the horse to speed it up, knowing it would do no good. The animal moved at its own speed as it sought sure footing on the treacherous trail.

She was just thinking that at least she'd left the wolves behind when the chorus started up again. They must be following her! The howls were still coming from everywhere, and they were just as close as before.

She frowned. They sounded different this time—more excited. Her horse pricked up its ears, though it had ignored them the last time. She reached into her pocket and grasped the hilt of the stiletto, knowing it didn't really offer her any protection, but still reassured that it was there.

Abruptly the cries of the wolves ceased, and then, in the ensuing silence, she heard something else. It sounded like a horse's hoof striking a stone somewhere above her on the trail. She was deep in a ravine, having just come down a particularly steep portion of the trail that had several switchbacks.

She brought the horse to a stop and stared up through the trees at the trail behind her. It was dark down here, but up there the moonlight bathed the forest in silver light. And she thought she saw something move.

A few heartbeats later, she was certain of it. Someone was coming down the trail. She could see the horse and the rider, but only fleetingly as they moved in and out of shadow.

Amanda thought quickly. Should she try to outrun whoever it was, or get off the trail and hope she wouldn't be seen? The latter course seemed best. So she leaped from the saddle and led the horse off into the thick woods, stumbling over the uneven ground in the darkness. After leading the horse deep into the woods, she tethered it loosely to a tree and moved away from it, back toward the trail. She knew that

241

the animal might well whicker when it heard one of its brethren, and she wanted to make sure that it wouldn't lead whoever was following directly to her.

But who was it? She was nearly certain that it wasn't Daken, because his hair would have been a dead giveaway in the moonlight. Besides, though she'd seen the figure only briefly and at a considerable distance, the impression she had was of someone much smaller.

A Sherba. The thought struck her with a chill. Would they dare come after her here in the Dark Mountains? She had thought she wouldn't have to worry about them until after she'd left the Kassid lands—but maybe she was wrong.

If it is a Sherba, she thought, he has come after you for one reason: to kill you! Daken or any of the Kassid would merely take her back to the fortress, but she wouldn't get any leniency from the Sherbas.

Concealed behind some thick shrubs, she watched and waited. The wolves began to howl again, their voices seemingly frantic. She couldn't begin to guess how close they were, because the sounds echoed weirdly in the ravine, but they seemed closer than before.

It was almost as though they were issuing a warning—but to whom? Were they telling her of danger—or guiding the man who was following her? Or were they simply protesting the human presence in their woods?

Unfortunately, their unearthly howls prevented her from hearing the approaching rider until he was just opposite her hiding place. The night was too dark for her to see more than shadows amid shadows. And then, from somewhere behind her, came the sound she dreaded most: the whicker of her horse.

For a moment she held her breath, hoping that the rider hadn't been able to pick out that one sound from among the cries of the wolves. But the rustling in the darkness stopped—and she suddenly knew that he had.

Long minutes went by as she strained to see into the darkness. She drew the stiletto from her pocket and wondered if she could use it. If her pursuer was a Sherba, he would almost certainly also have a weapon of some sort, and probably one far more deadly. That meant that her only hope lay in surprising him.

Besides, she had to be certain that it was indeed a Sherba and not a Kassid. It seemed unlikely that Daken would send someone else, rather than coming after her himself—but she couldn't be sure.

The howls reached a crescendo—and abruptly fell silent, leaving her to listen to the rapid thudding of her own heart as she stared into the darkness. And then she saw him—not more than thirty feet away and moving in her direction.

A Sherba, she thought. He was far too small to be Kassid, and even though he was dressed entirely in black, his clothing looked different, too.

He passed by her hiding place and moved deeper into the forest, but not before she glimpsed something in his hand that looked very much like the deadly knives the Kassid carried. Out on the trail, his horse whinnied—and her horse answered. The Sherba turned quickly in that direction.

She knew that she might be able to hide from him in the darkness, but if he took her horse she would be left with no transport and no food. She clutched the stiletto tightly and began to creep through the woods, stepping carefully to avoid signaling her approach.

Never in her life had she expected to be in the position she was in now: forced to kill to save her own life. Rationally, she could justify it as self-defense, but could she actually plunge the stiletto into him?

He was just ahead of her now, moving toward a patch of moonlight that had managed to penetrate the depths of the ravine as the moon sailed higher in the heavens. Her horse was only a short distance away.

Amanda didn't allow herself to think. When he reached the small clearing and was sharply outlined by the moonlight, she ran toward him, the stiletto raised. She very nearly made it—but at the last moment a twig snapped beneath her foot, and the Sherba whirled around sharply just as she struck.

The thin blade caught him on the tip of his shoulder and he screamed in pain—but he also raised his own knife. Amanda sidestepped just in time, and his knife slashed through air. Then he struck again, and this time the blade came closer as she once more flung herself out of its path. But she'd moved too quickly and she lost her balance, and suddenly he was there, looming above her in the moonlight.

She could feel the force of his hatred as he raised his arm again. But at the same time she saw something move behind and above him, on the steep slope. Daken! She saw the silver hair, and then he was lost in the shadows again as he scrambled down the bank.

Once again her assailant brought the knife down,

and once again Amanda managed to move out of its path and scramble to her feet. But she was standing on the edge of a steep slope that fell away to a stream, and the Sherba was coming at her again. Daken was too far away to save her. She could see him again as he continued his descent from the trail.

She turned her attention back to the Sherba as he forced her ever closer to the edge of the slope. She let herself fall backward partway down the slope, then grabbed an exposed tree root. The Sherba hesitated only briefly and then started down the slope toward her. Above him, she suddenly saw Daken again, but he was still too far away.

The Sherba lunged forward, his knife raised—and suddenly a huge gray wolf was on him, snarling as it leaped upon him and buried its gleaming fangs into his throat.

Amanda stared in disbelief as the wolf and the Sherba rolled down the rest of the slope, the Sherba's screams echoing upward. She was so stunned by the wolf's sudden appearance that it took a few seconds before she realized that she was safe. Then she turned, expecting to see Daken above her.

No one was there. She called his name again and again, but there was no response. Below her in the darkness, the shrieks of the Sherba had ceased. And then she saw the wolf again, the silver tips of its fur gleaming in the moonlight as it started back up toward her.

"Daken!" she said, her voice a mere whisper as the horror took hold of her. In a shaft of moonlight, she saw the wolf's pale eyes as it stopped. That dark part of her mind that she'd tried to ignore opened wide— and she knew what she'd known for a long time now.

The wolf remained motionless on the steep slope. She stared at it through a haze of tears as she tried to accept the truth. Then she turned and fled up the bank, hoping against hope that she would find Daken up there. But when she reached the top no one was there, and her last, faint hope vanished.

She ran through the woods until she reached the trail—and the horse left there by the Sherba. Only when she had climbed on its back did she turn to stare back into the woods, but the wolf hadn't followed her.

She fled down the trail, followed by the memory of the pleading look in the wolf's pale blue eyes.

The others found Daken sitting at the top of the slope. The body of the Sherba lay below him.

"She is gone," he told them. "Let her go. Tell the villagers that she is to be allowed to leave."

One went to do his bidding, and the others returned to the fortress, understanding that he needed to be alone.

Daken sat there until the moon had set and the first tentative light of a new day crept through the forest. His foolishness weighed heavily upon him. He had believed she could accept what he was, as Jocelyn had come to accept her Daken so many years before.

But it was wishful thinking: the thoughts of a man who'd been foolish enough to listen to his heart. Jocelyn had lived in a different time, a time when the magic of the gods was closer, more understandable.

He'd saved her life, but he had lost her. He got slowly to his feet as a man, but it was a large gray wolf that padded noiselessly through the forest.

* * *

Amanda rode through the night and into the dawn, down out of the Dark Mountains. To keep her mind from returning to that scene in the forest, she fixed it on her home and her work and her mother, who must surely believe her to be dead.

By midday she had reached the hillside overlooking the village of Wat Andara. There she turned once more, but this time the Dark Mountains were enshrouded in mist, barely visible.

Keep to your plan, she told herself. *Find a place to rest and then go into the village after dark.*

She skirted the village on the hilltop and then a small adjacent valley, and came upon a narrow, swift-running stream shaded by ancient trees. She let the horse drink and then tethered it to a tree and sank to the mossy bank, tired and numb. Within moments, sleep carried her away.

When she awoke, it was to darkness—an impenetrable darkness, cold and dank. Instead of the soft, mossy bed, she lay on a hard stone floor. She began to push to her feet, confusion and fear swarming over her. Where was she? Obviously she'd been captured, but what was this place? And then she gasped as she saw the glitter of gold in the darkness.

The walls and ceiling seemed alive as her eyes traveled over the ancient writings—and the drawings of wolves. She was in the room the Kassid called the *azherwa*. Daken had found her—but why had he brought her here?

The thought of the man resolved into the image of the wolf, and she drew in her breath on a ragged sob. *He isn't a man*, she told herself. *He's a creature from*

247

a nightmare—and now he's brought you back here.

Suddenly the golden writings and drawings began to glow even brighter, until she was forced to shade her eyes from the glare. At the same time she felt something: a deep sort of humming that seemed to be just at the limits of her hearing, but could be felt in her body. A moment later the air in the room began to stir, whipping against her. And then she felt a presence.

She backed into a corner, trying desperately to see in the darkness and the glare of the gold writings. And then her eyes picked out a familiar gray head.

He didn't appear to have seen her yet as he picked himself slowly up from the floor. The wind had ceased as abruptly as it had arisen, and the walls now cast only a soft glow. Daken had his back to her as he stood—and now she saw something different— something wrong.

His hair was longer and it didn't curl at the ends, and that led her to notice other differences as well. He wasn't quite so tall and he seemed to be thicker through the middle as well. Confused still more, she stood silently in the corner and watched as he remained motionless in the center of the room for a few seconds, then started toward one wall.

It took her a few seconds to realize that he had opened a door, because it was as dark beyond as it was in the room. The door closed behind him with a barely audible click. Suddenly fearing that she would be trapped in here forever, she rushed to the spot where the door was now invisible and felt along the wall until her fingers closed over a latch.

When she pulled it open, the space beyond was lit by a flickering light, which she quickly saw was a torch being carried up the stairs by Daken.

"Daken!" she cried, unable to believe that he would simply walk away from her.

He stopped just as he reached the curve in the staircase, then turned around slowly. Amanda clutched the door frame as shock made her legs tremble. It wasn't Daken! Or rather, it *was* Daken, but the Daken of the ancient portrait. He stared at her with a frown, then turned and resumed his climb up the stairs.

Amanda understood—and didn't understand. She knew now that she wasn't in the sacred room at the fortress, but the other room at the bottom of the sea. Except that there was no water. And the other Daken had seemed for a moment to see her, but had turned away.

This was a dream. She was still sleeping on the bank of the stream, awaiting her chance to escape. She began to move toward the stairs even before she'd made a conscious decision to follow this man who was and wasn't Daken.

The torchlight had vanished and she stumbled up the stairs, then saw a pale flicker in the hallway at the top. When she reached it, she saw him turning into another hallway and she hurried after him. Several sets of stairs and many hallways later, he pushed open a door and she could see light beyond it. The door closed behind him and she followed, opening it to see that she was now at the intersection of two hallways—wide hallways with floors covered by richly colored rugs and walls hung with tapestries and lit by flickering sconces that smelled of kerosene.

He was striding down one hallway toward an open archway at its end. A young woman appeared, scarcely more than a girl, her pale hair drawn back into a white cap. Amanda saw him nod to her, and the girl curtsied and continued to walk toward Amanda. A moment later she passed by without a glance and vanished down the other hallway.

Amanda walked down the hall toward the archway, and as she approached it she could see the splendidly furnished room beyond. It was empty, but she could hear voices coming from another room: a man and a woman's, speaking a language she didn't understand but was certain couldn't be Kassid.

The door to the room stood partly ajar, and Amanda went to it, but stopped when she saw the two figures locked in an embrace. She started to turn away, then stopped. This was a dream, after all—and *her* dream at that.

After a moment the woman broke away and began to speak again. It was Jocelyn—though an older Jocelyn than she'd seen in the portrait. Her red-gold hair, in the portrait a shade or two lighter than Amanda's, was now threaded with gray, and laugh lines were etched into her fair skin.

Daken—the other Daken—went over to sit down on the edge of the big bed, and Amanda saw his face clearly for the first time. It was a harsh face, and lines were carved deeply into it, but he was still compelling. And the harshness was softened by the light of love in his eyes as he watched Jocelyn move about the room, talking animatedly in her indecipherable language.

It was Jessa who had explained to her that these two people had once used the sacred rooms to travel back and forth from the Dark Mountains to Ertria. As leader of his people, Daken had to remain at the fortress. Jocelyn, on the other hand, was the ruler of the Ertrians, and a woman with many plans.

Probably she was talking about some of those plans now. Amanda actually smiled as she saw the look of long-suffering patience on this other Daken's face, before he finally reached out and caught her around the waist as she paused in her pacing.

She stopped speaking and smiled at him, then knelt before him to help remove his boots. When she had finished, he leaned forward and kissed her tenderly.

Amanda backed out of the room, feeling like a voyeur even if it *was* her dream. A wave of envy washed over her. Jocelyn had known what he was—and yet she hadn't run away. But they were from a different time.

She walked through the palace, passing servants who didn't see her, and guards who didn't stir at the sight of a strange woman dressed in khaki trousers and a bright, jungle-printed T-shirt. She was invisible—a time traveler.

The palace was grand, though she felt it lacked the enduring majesty of the fortress in the Dark Mountains. Or perhaps it was only that she knew it had not endured, and now lay at the bottom of the sea in a jumble of silt-covered stones.

She came to a set of stairs leading upward and wondered if they might take her to the roof. A warm breeze swept down the staircase, suggesting an opening above. She climbed the stairs and found herself standing beneath a brilliant sky, with the last of the day's sunlight throwing streaks of crimson and purple across the heavens.

The palace was on a slight rise, standing above a

broad plain. Cultivated fields swept nearly to the horizon in three directions, with the sea bordering the sprawling town on the other. She turned in a slow circle, frowning as she realized that she'd hoped to see the Dark Mountains from here. But the land had changed. The spot where she stood was now far out to sea, and the Dark Mountains were lost beyond the horizon, where low hills rose.

As she stood there, studying the town and its busy harbor, an uneasiness stole over her. She'd expected to see the Dark Mountains and had forgotten about the havoc that would be wreaked upon this land centuries from now. Wasn't that strange for a dream? If she'd forgotten about it, why was it this way?

Have I really gone back in time? she asked herself as the uneasiness edged closer to real fear. She didn't want to think about that and the capriciousness of the Kassid gods, but she could not deny their powers.

She began to walk along the outer wall of the palace on a narrow walkway, her gaze drawn more and more to the harbor, where many tall-masted ships rode at anchor. The urge to visit the harbor became irresistible and she left the walkway, taking a set of stairs that ended in the big courtyard.

A few moments later she passed unnoticed by more guards and was in the large park that surrounded the palace, walking down the hill to the town. The streets were mostly empty, although here and there were taverns where crowds were gathered. Closer to the palace, the houses she passed were large and surrounded by stone walls, but as she made her way toward the harbor they became smaller, often mingling with closed shops. No one she passed gave any indication that they'd seen her.

She stopped at a corner as she saw a large black wagon being pulled by two handsome black horses. In the driver's seat sat a man wearing a long black hooded robe—and a gold chain from which was suspended a black rock. A young boy, also dressed in black, rode next to him. Sherbas.

She felt a sudden jolt of fear, even though she reminded herself that she was invisible. The wagon moved toward her, and she saw that it contained boxes of greenery. Herbs, she remembered. The Sherbas had traded herbs given to them by the Kassid as they traveled around gathering information.

Suddenly, when the wagon was nearly abreast of her, the man turned in her direction and reached up to touch the stone. Amanda's heart began to pound noisily in her ears, and a chill swept through her. The wagon continued on its way, but the driver turned in the seat, staring at her. Finally, he turned away and the wagon disappeared around a corner.

Strange, she thought. First Daken had seemed for a moment to hear her, and now the Sherba sensed something. Had she felt like a ghost to them?

She continued down the street, which ended at the harbor. There were perhaps a dozen ships at anchor, several of which were being loaded. She stopped to watch one of them, her attention snagged by the bright red hair of a man who stood on the deck, apparently supervising the loading. Then, as she stood there wondering why this particular ship, no different from its neighbors, should hold such interest for her, the last of the crates were loaded and the man with red hair walked down the gangway, taking out a small bag from which he dispensed coins to the workers.

She had stopped in the shadows of a closed shop that appeared to sell rope and stared at him as he began to walk in her direction. What was it about him that had drawn her attention, apart from that fiery red hair?

He passed quite close to her, but did not turn in her direction, so she began to follow him. He moved through the town with a purposeful stride, greeting and being greeted by others. After a time, she realized that they were back on the fairly wide street that led up to the palace. And a moment later the man stopped at the locked gate to one of the large houses that were surrounded by stone walls.

He drew out a key, fitted it to the lock and opened the gate. He paused as a man in uniform and on horseback hailed him. While the two men talked, Amanda slipped through the open gate. A moment later, she heard it clang shut and saw the man coming toward her.

She was directly in front of him now, less than ten feet away, and she drew in a sharp breath as she saw what it was that had drawn her to him. Except for the bright red hair, he strongly resembled her uncle.

His steps slowed as he stared directly at her, his brows knitting together in an expression that reminded her even more of Steffen and brought a painful lump to her throat. After a moment, he shrugged his shoulders and started toward her again. She stepped quickly from his path.

The front door was opened by an older woman who appeared to be a servant. The red-haired man stepped through, saying something that made the woman laugh, and Amanda once more slipped past during the diversion. Inside, she looked around with interest.

The house was an incredible mishmash of different styles. Furniture with clean, amazingly modern lines sat side by side with the heavy, ornate furniture she'd seen in the palace. Amanda supposed that in the hands of a skilled decorator, it might have worked, but here the effect was jarring.

A slender, brown-haired woman appeared, and Amanda immediately recognized the soft, shimmering wool in her simple gown. It was clearly Kassid in origin.

The couple went up the stairs and Amanda remained behind, reluctant to become an unwitting observer of more intimacy. Instead she wandered about the downstairs rooms, examining the furnishings with mounting curiosity.

She was recalling what Daken had said about the likelihood that some Ertrians had managed to escape the devastation that would later befall the area. They were a seafaring people, and it seemed likely that some of them had been safely at sea when the cataclysm had struck.

Here, then, in all likelihood, was the answer to her family's origins that Steffen had sought in vain all of his life. The red-haired man was obviously a successful shipowner, and that would save the family— or at least some of them.

Amanda paused before a display of tiny animals that she realized were carved from bone: scrimshaw. She'd seen displays of this art form a few times. She picked up a whale, its body curved so that it rested on its belly. Her throat tightened as she stared at it and thought about her discovery.

Once again the thought came to her that this was not a dream, that she was being shown all of this for a purpose. Tears welled up in her eyes. Were the gods tormenting her because she'd run away from their servants, the Kassid—and from the man they'd chosen as leader? Or was this only a dream after all, born out of her own doubts and confusion?

She fled from the house, out into the warm night. But once she had reached the street again, she stopped, not knowing where to go or what to do. Maybe the gods were being more cruel than she'd thought. Maybe they had condemned her to spend eternity wandering through the ancient past.

Finally she started up the broad thoroughfare that led to the palace on the hill. This dream—or whatever it was—had begun in the sacred room, so she would go back there.

That, however, proved to be much easier said than done. When she climbed up from the cellars of the palace before, she'd merely followed Daken—the other Daken. Now she was on her own. After wandering about for what seemed like hours, she finally found her way to the place where Jocelyn had met him. The door to the bedchamber was now closed, and Amanda stood there in the outer room for a long time, imagining the two of them making love, and reliving her own time with her own Daken.

But then it wasn't Daken she saw in her mind's eye, but the wolf, its pale, intelligent eyes pleading for understanding.

She ran from the room and fled down the hall to the doorway that led to the stairs. After several frustrating wrong turns, she was in the palace cellars. At first it was very dark, and she couldn't find any torches, but her eyes gradually became adjusted to the darkness. Or did they? It seemed to her that there was some light down here, even though she couldn't find its source.

After a time, she realized that the light was leading her. Each time she came to an intersection in the maze of corridors and stairwells, one way seemed brighter than the others. At last, she was running down the narrow, winding staircase to the heavy, carved door.

She opened the door and stepped into utter blackness. The door swung shut behind her. The deep vibrations began and a cold wind tore at her clothing. On the walls and ceiling, the gold writings began to move.

Chapter Eleven

Amanda awoke to damp, earthy aromas and the musical babbling of the small stream. She heard her horse whickering impatiently. The moon was bright overhead, though when she squinted up at it, she could see that it was on the wane.

She raised her hands to brush her hair from her eyes and realized that she was clutching something in one of them. Even before she opened it, she knew what she would find, but still she stared at the tiny whale, unable to believe it was there.

She cupped it in the palm of her hand and stared at it as the moonlight gave it a pale, ghostly color. The dream was real. She had actually traveled back to the time of Daken and Jocelyn—and she'd unlocked the secret of her own origins.

She understood that she'd been given an opportunity no one else might ever have had. Steffen and her dead colleagues would have been ecstatic. But she was frightened and shaken to her very core—not only by the dream-that-wasn't-a-dream, but by all of it: the mighty fortress that could not have been created by the hands of man, the music that wove erotic, magical spells, and by a man who wasn't a man.

"I want to go home," she said aloud, then added, in a softer voice, "please!"

She got to her feet and a wave of dizziness washed over her. Food. She had to eat. And the increasingly impatient noises from her horse reminded her that it, too, required food. She untied the animal and let it drink from the stream, then took a drink herself. Remembering that there was an open field some distance back, she retraced her steps and set the animal free, knowing it wasn't likely to run off when it was hungry and there was grass in abundance. Then she sank down in the meadow and ate as well.

The moon was already high in the sky, so it must be late. That meant it was time for her to make her foray into the village, to see if she could find a vehicle and some gas. Even if she did, she would still have several days' travel through the jungle before she would reach the town in Menoa and roads that would take her to the city and the airport.

It seemed a very long way, but perhaps no longer than the journey her mind must make to carry her from the Dark Mountains. It was far shorter than the journey her heart would have to make to forget Daken.

The village was dark and quiet when she entered it an hour later, leading her horse and moving stealthily along its edges. She was seeking a large building at one corner of the village that she had assumed was a stable, but which might also have housed some vehicles.

When she finally found it, the first thing she saw was an old gas pump standing near the doors. Parked beside the pump were three Land Rovers, none of which had belonged to her expedition. After watching from the shadows for some time to be certain no one was around, she once more tethered the horse and went over to them. Inside were long, dark, zippered bags—and on those bags was the imprint of the U.S. Army.

Tears sprang to her eyes as she tried to count them. Instead, she looked at the names written on the canvas. All those who had died in the massacre were there. Their bodies must have been returned to the American embassy. And then she saw another bag, folded and unused, and she choked back a sob, knowing that it had been intended for her.

On the front seat of one of the vehicles, she found a slim leather attaché case, and when she opened it, she saw that there were photos of all of them: their passport photos, greatly enlarged. Along with them were some papers, all of them bearing the seal of the U.S. Department of State.

She pushed the attaché case aside and crawled into the seat, crying. She was safe. She was going home. The long nightmare was over.

But after a while she began to think again. She had to have a story. It emerged slowly, woven from a tapestry of truths, half truths and lies. She had survived the massacre because Miriam had gone outside their tent and drawn away the attention of the killers. She'd driven the Land Rover until it ran out of gas, and had then wandered through the jungle to this place that she remembered from a map.

Having created her tale, she went over it and over it until it took on a certain degree of truth because she *wanted* it to be the truth. Then she got out of the vehicle and took the horse into the stable, finding an empty stall in the rear of the long building. The horse was the only problem with her story, but she knew she could trust the villagers not to reveal its presence. They too were protectors of the Kassid.

Then, since she had no idea where the Americans might be, she returned to the Land Rover to wait with her dead colleagues.

Daken watched helplessly from the deep woods as the vehicles drove away from the village. He'd gotten only a quick glimpse of her as she walked in the company of four Americans. If only he'd come sooner . . .

No, he thought, danger or not, she would still have chosen to go with them. And he would not have forced her to come back to the safety of the Dark Mountains—a safety that was suspect in her eyes, after that attack by the Sherba.

The primitive brain of the Other urged him to take her, reminded him that she belonged to him. But its power was waning by the second because he'd become a man again after the swift run down from the mountains.

Which was worse, he wondered: to fear for her life out there, where he couldn't protect her, or to have brought her back, to see the horror in her eyes each time she looked at him?

He thought that she'd be careful. She was smart, and she would guess that the Sherbas would still be trying to kill her. But she didn't know how skillful they were—and how desperate.

Daken clenched his fists helplessly as the caravan passed out of view. His advisers were counseling patience, saying that he must not allow his personal feelings to lead him astray. But he knew in his gut that they were wrong. The Sherbas were out of control. The others didn't understand because they hadn't traveled beyond the Dark Mountains. They didn't know the power the Sherbas had gained for themselves with Kassid gold. And they couldn't be expected to understand how that power had become their reason for existence, not the protection of the Kassid.

Their leader had claimed that the attack on Amanda was a terrible mistake, the tragic result of too much wine-drinking by a young novice whose stability was already under question. The man had groveled and begged forgiveness, and all but Daken had believed him.

He clenched his fists again, then drew in a deep breath and summoned the Other. A moment later, a large gray wolf was streaking through the forest toward the Dark Mountains. The pain of losing her became, for the moment, bearable.

Amanda sat on the floor of her loft back in the city, surrounded by newspapers and magazines. The few friends she'd seen since her return ten days ago had teased her about what they viewed as an uncharacteristic burst of egotism. Her mother had merely raised an eyebrow.

She had endured all this without comment, because she could not explain to any of them why she was obsessed with what was being written about her. But the truth was that she needed to know whether or not her story was being accepted, and she needed to know as well if any pressure might be exerted on the government to seek revenge for her colleagues' deaths.

If it was true, as a fellow artist had once remarked, that everyone gets his or her fifteen minutes of fame, Amanda had gotten more than her share. Her phone hadn't stopped ringing since her return. She had, from the first, used the machine to screen her calls, and each time she ventured out she was accosted by photographers and reporters. Everyone, it seemed, was fascinated by the diminutive redheaded artist who was the sole survivor of an ill-fated expedition to the Land of the Kassid.

The Kassid themselves came in for a great deal of coverage as well—and that troubled her most of all because it could easily translate into more expeditions to the Dark Mountains. She could only hope that the fate of her own expedition would prevent that. And her hopes were furthered by reports of renewed and ferocious fighting along the borders, near the area they'd explored.

Those reports lent credibility to her story of silent killers in the night, and although she regretted the loss of life from the outbreak of fighting, she knew it had come at a most convenient time—perhaps too convenient, since she herself had seen no evidence of such fighting. She suspected the Sherbas were behind it—with or without Daken's blessing.

Daken. The mere thought of him was still too painful to be borne. But back here, in the real world that she understood, he was slowly beginning to seem unreal again, together with the great fortress in the mountains.

But Daken still owned her dreams. Each night he came to her, his pale eyes shining with desire, his big hands so gentle on her body. But the wolf came, too—and when that happened, she would awaken with a cry of horror and sit trembling in her bed until the image faded.

She finished reading the articles one last time, then gathered up all the newspapers and magazines and tossed them into the trash. It seemed to be over. There were no new stories, and this morning there'd been only two phone calls and no one lurking outside her loft. She was glad for the fickleness of the public's interest.

But *was* it over? There was still the matter of the Sherbas, and the possibility that they might try again to kill her. Surely, though, they must realize by now that she had no intention of telling the world about the Kassid.

If Daken and the wolf came to her in her dreams, the Sherbas filled her waking thoughts. She never went out at night, and even during the day, she was always looking over her shoulder. She'd even upgraded her home security system.

Still, she tried to return to her normal life and to her work. But her muse seemed to have deserted her. She painted every day, but she knew the work wasn't good. She told herself that she needed time, but she fretted that she'd never again feel that surge of adrenaline that told her she was creating something good.

* * *

It began two weeks after her return. The first incident left her shaken, but after the second episode she became truly frightened. She'd made a lunch date with a poet friend who supported herself by writing advertising copy for a major firm. As she waited in her friend's office, she went over to the window and stared down at the street, some forty stories below.

And suddenly she was on the small balcony outside the tower at the fortress, looking down at the deep, dark abyss beyond the stone wall. The vision was scary enough, but what accompanied it was even worse. Every fiber of her being ached to be there. The power of that feeling was beyond anything she'd ever felt. It vanished instantly when her friend entered the room and spoke to her, but she was badly shaken.

Then, a few days later, she was walking through midtown in the shadow of giant skyscrapers—and suddenly she was no longer on a paved sidewalk, but on a narrow, winding path, with the Dark Mountains looming over her. And once again she felt that incredible yearning. This time the spell was broken as someone brushed against her on the sidewalk, where she had apparently stopped in confusion.

For a time, she tried to convince herself that what had happened could be explained away as mere memory: the natural longing for a place she had truly loved in many ways. But when a similar incident happened a few days later, she began to fear that supernatural forces were at work.

She remembered what Jessa had said about how the Kassid were "called" home if they'd been out in the world beyond the Dark Mountains. But she wasn't Kassid, and the Dark Mountains were not her home.

Amanda wanted it to be over. She wanted to resume her life here—a life she had loved. She wanted to enjoy her friends, instead of finding them lacking by comparison with the friends she'd made among the Kassid. And she wanted Daken to become no more than a distant memory, instead of a large, dark shadow that refused to go away and a dream-lover who came to her every night.

But the incidents continued. One evening she forced herself to attend a friend's party. The large, airy loft space was filled with people. Jazz played in the background, weaving through the buzz of conversation and bursts of laughter. And suddenly she was back in the great hall, and the music she heard was the sensual melodies of her last night in the fortress. She ached to be back there, and yearned for Daken.

There was no one to whom she could go for help, not even her mother, who could be counted on to keep the secret, but whose practical nature would prevent her from believing her daughter's story. Instead she would worry that the episode had unhinged Amanda's mind.

So she began to think of escaping from the city for a while—going out to her beach house, which she hadn't visited since Steffen's death had set all the madness into motion. It was the place she had always gone to seek peace when the city began to overwhelm her.

Still, she knew that the idea posed some danger. There were other cottages nearby, but she couldn't be certain they would be occupied, and the place was not as secure as her loft.

In the end, she decided to go, reasoning that if the Sherbas still wanted to kill her, they would surely have made some attempt by now. She'd been back for over three weeks.

In a concession to her continued uneasiness about the mysterious sect, she borrowed a gun from a friend. He didn't question her request, apparently assuming that she was still suffering from the trauma of the expedition.

When she returned to the loft after picking up the gun and some art supplies, she stopped just inside the door, her eyes frantically searching the big, open space. Daken! She had the uncanny sense that he was here.

She searched the place, even looking behind the shower curtain and peering under the bed. He wasn't there, and nothing had been disturbed. Or so she thought until her gaze fell on the tiny whale, which sat amidst her books on the apartment's built-in cherry shelves.

A thrill that was part fear and part joy swept through her as she saw the small clean spot in the light film of dust on the shelves. Normally a meticulous housekeeper, she'd dusted that spot only once since her return—just before she'd placed the whale there. And she hadn't touched it since, though she'd looked at it many times. There was no doubt that the whale had been moved.

She tried desperately to think whether it could have been moved by anyone else. She'd had few visitors since her return, and none of them had commented on the whale. Furthermore, the bookshelf was built into a corner of the loft where she kept her antique cherry desk, rather than in the space she used for entertaining.

She picked up the whale, and for a moment his presence became palpable in the loft—so real that she once again searched for him, her heart racing.

"Daken," she said aloud. "Are you here?"

Then she sank onto a sofa, embarrassed at her outburst, but still frightened. Was it so unreasonable to believe that a man who had controlled her mind and sent her off to bed that night at Steffen's cabin could make himself invisible? Or that a man who could turn himself into a wolf could suddenly materialize here?

Her very bones felt cold. How could she have let herself believe that she might be falling in love with such a . . . creature?

She replaced the whale on the shelf, then quickly packed her things. She hadn't intended to leave until the next morning, but if she left now, she could be at the beach house before dark.

The drive took more than two hours. For most of the journey she was constantly scanning the cars behind her, although she knew she couldn't hope to spot anyone following her in the heavy traffic. But when she left the expressway, she paid close attention to the vehicles that exited after her.

Instead of taking the most direct route to the beach, she chose a circuitous route that would make it easier to spot anyone following her. Finally, when she was sure that no one was, she drove to the cottage.

She felt even safer when she saw a car in her neighbors' driveway. The cottage was owned by two gay men, Peter and Greg, who had a computer consulting business, and they were rarely out here during the week. As she was unloading her car, they both came walking up from the beach and invited her over for a drink, obviously eager to hear about her adventure.

Amanda wasn't exactly eager to tell her tale again, but since she liked them both and was grateful for their presence, she accepted. As it turned out, they'd read the newspaper reports and had seen the one TV interview she'd granted, so they didn't really press her for too many details. As they all sat on the deck overlooking the beach, she asked casually if there'd been any strangers around. Unlike many beach enclaves out here, none of the cottages were rentals, and consequently everyone knew everyone else by sight.

It turned out that they'd arrived only a few hours ago and hadn't seen anyone. They even nodded their understanding when she laughed off her concern, saying she was still feeling a bit paranoid.

"There was a report on the news a couple of hours ago about the fighting over there," Peter told her. "It sounds like you got out just in time. They said it was the same area where your expedition had been. Apparently an entire village was wiped out."

"It wasn't Wat Andara, was it?" Amanda asked in alarm. Surely Daken would never permit that.

"No. It was another village, but I don't recall its name."

She didn't know its name, either, but she suspected it was the one near the ruined tower, where they'd lost the first of their group. She wondered if

269

it was retribution or merely the random destruction of war.

Who was behind this latest outbreak of fighting? Was it the Sherbas acting on their own—or Daken giving orders? He'd never admitted to stirring up trouble in the region, but it was certainly convenient for such a thing to be happening now. Any attempts by the Menoan government to find the murderers would be impossible, no matter how much the State Department protested—and she knew they had.

She accepted their invitation to stay for dinner, then joined them for a stroll along the beach. From what she could see, only one of the other cottages was occupied at the moment, and the private beach they shared was completely empty.

"Do you think you'll ever go back there?" Greg asked as they walked on the hard-packed sand just above the high-tide line.

"No," she replied firmly.

"Well, I can't blame you, considering what happened. But surely someone will go there again, after the fighting has ended. We have a friend who's an anthropologist, and he said that your group's discoveries have stirred up a lot of interest in the wolf-people. What are they called?"

"Kassid," Amanda told him, struggling to avoid a shudder at his reference to "wolf-people."

They paused at the fence that marked the boundary of their beach. Peter shook his head. "It's hard to imagine that the Dark Mountains will remain unexplored much longer. If it weren't for the fighting, there'd already be climbers all over them."

Yes, Amanda thought—and that is undoubtedly why the fighting goes on. How could Daken and the

Sherbas justify letting so many people die, just to protect themselves?

After two days Amanda began to relax. By the time the weekend came all the cottages were occupied. She went into town to buy some groceries and saw no sign of the Sherbas—or of Daken. Of course, she couldn't be certain that the Sherbas would be dressed in black as she'd seen them before, but she doubted they would cast off their gold chains with the chunk of black rock from the Dark Mountains, and given the casual summer attire everyone wore, it would be difficult to hide them.

She even began to paint again, and for the first time since coming home felt the tentative return of her muse. But the painting that began to emerge was disturbing. Even Peter and Greg commented on its dark, foreboding character as she was working out on the deck. Nevertheless, she continued to paint, hoping that by transferring her dark memories to canvas, she could rid herself of them.

After spending most of the morning painting, she went down to the beach with a sketchpad. Her other neighbors had a bright, pretty six-year-old whom she'd promised to sketch. As she worked on the drawing and chatted with the little girl, Amanda found herself thinking about the Kassid children.

How very different they were. At six, her neighbors' child seemed already to have lost much of her innocence, even though she was the daughter of affluent parents and was hardly a product of the inner city and all its pain.

She finished the sketch and the little girl thanked her and ran off with it to show her parents. Amanda watched her, feeling a surprising jolt of sadness. Was it sadness that this child couldn't have more of a childhood—or was it something more? Although she was at an age where most women began to hear the ticking of their biological clock, she'd never really given much thought to having children, even though she enjoyed sketching them. Now, thinking about the contrast between children here and Kassid children, she knew that she didn't want to have children in this world where they were robbed of innocence and forced to face at an early age a hostile adult environment.

These thoughts led her quickly to other thoughts that were never far from her mind: her dreams of Daken. She'd gone to a party the night before and had met a man—a weekend guest of one of her neighbors. She'd liked him right away, but she'd felt none of the things she should have felt.

There will never be anyone else for me, she thought through a haze of pain. And she wondered what it said about her that she could love such a creature.

She began another sketch in an attempt to bury her pain. But the pencil seemed to have acquired a life of its own as it moved rapidly over the paper. She knew almost immediately what she was doing, yet seemed powerless to stop herself as Daken's strong features began to take shape. And by the time she was finally finished, her tears had already smudged the drawing. Angry with herself, she flung the sketchpad down and sat there staring at the gray-green ocean while the breeze dried her tears.

* * *

Daken moved soundlessly in the shadows, avoiding the open expanse of beach. Twice, dogs began to bark excitedly inside houses, their frightened tones telling him that they knew of his presence even if their masters didn't. Finally he reached the cottage next to hers, which was dark and thankfully free of dogs. He settled down beneath the deck to wait: a perfect spot, since it had a clear view of most of her cottage.

Lights were on inside, though he saw no sign of her. He'd passed by a cottage where a party was in progress and wondered if she could be there. But the instincts he trusted implicitly were telling him that she was in her beach house, even if he couldn't see her.

And then, suddenly, he did see her. She'd apparently been out walking on the beach, because she was now climbing up the slight rise to her deck. He retreated further into the shadows under the neighboring deck, his eyes never leaving her. His longing for her was dulled by the brain of the Other—but it was still there, mixing dangerously with a primitive possessiveness.

He didn't like it that she'd been out walking alone. That seemed to suggest that she no longer worried about the Sherbas. He understood, though. She undoubtedly wanted to forget, and the fact that nothing had happened thus far would have given impetus to that urge.

But Daken had known from the beginning that they wouldn't come after her right away. They would guess that she was being careful then, and they would also be reluctant to go after her when her name was so much in the news.

She had now reached the stairs that led up to the deck, no more than a hundred feet from his hiding place. He let his eyes feast on her slim legs and trim bottom as she started up the steps—and then suddenly stopped. He was thinking about those legs wrapped around him, about her soft, female body arching to him, and he was slow to question why she had suddenly stopped.

Then she turned and stared in his direction. He didn't move, certain that he was well concealed. She had only human night vision, while his was greatly augmented. But she had sensed him, just as she had at the cabin. He should have expected that.

She stood there for what seemed an eternity, then abruptly turned again and ran up the remaining stairs to the deck, disappearing from his view. A cry of disappointment welled up in his throat, but he caught it before it could escape.

Amanda stood in the middle of her small living room, her arms wrapped tightly around herself. She felt it again: that same feeling she'd had at Steffen's cottage those times when she'd seen the wolf. She knew now that it hadn't really been simply a wolf, but it was easier to think of it as such.

He couldn't be here! How could he have found her? She was overreacting. There was no reason for him to be here. If he'd wanted to stop her, he could have done so long before she left the Dark Mountains. She'd taken some solace from the fact that he'd let her go, reasoning that it must mean that he trusted her—and he must know by now that she hadn't betrayed that trust.

She wondered if she should go to the party after

all. She hadn't gone because she didn't want to see the man she'd met last night, and be forced to face once more her fear that she would spend the rest of her life alone, even though that possibility had never troubled her in the past.

It's not that I'm afraid I'll be alone, she thought. *It's that I'm afraid I'll never be able to get him out of my mind.*

She decided to stay home and read one of the books she'd brought along, but before she settled down, she went back out onto the deck. This time she felt nothing—no sense at all that she was being watched.

Barely an hour later, she was dozing off despite the author's best efforts to hold her interest. She stretched and yawned. The sea air seemed to have this effect on her every time she came out here—a sort of natural tranquilizer.

The cottage was still warm from the day, and she was reluctant to close all the windows. So she compromised and closed all but the two bedroom windows. Because the cottage was built on a slope, both were nearly a story above ground level, which made her feel safer.

Unfortunately, now that she'd given in to her sleepiness, she found herself wide-awake. After tossing and turning for a time, she flung back the covers and padded on bare feet through the darkened living room to the deck. Wearing only a silk shift, she stepped out into the pleasant night. In the distance she could hear the sounds of the party she'd passed up: conversation and laughter that made her feel alone and isolated from the world she'd so desperately wanted to come back to.

Then suddenly she heard something. The sound was too quick, ending too abruptly for her to know what it was. She whirled around, seeking the source. It had sounded close—between the cottages, she thought.

She froze in indecision, then bolted for the living room and locked the glass door. In that instant she'd felt something: not the same sensation as before, although that might have been a part of it, but something else.

Danger, she thought as she waited for her pulse to slow. What had stirred her into action was a sudden certainty that she was in danger.

She went to the one side window in the living room and peered out. But the slope beside the cottage was too dark for her to see anything. Still, she stood there watching, searching the darkness for shadows, for movement.

Paranoia, she told herself. If there was anything out there, it was probably one of the neighbors' dogs. There were several people who regularly brought their pets with them and allowed them to run free. If she'd stayed on the deck, she would probably have been greeted by the party-givers' golden retriever and his buddy, a Dalmation. She'd seen them both earlier on the beach.

She went back to bed, and this time must have fallen asleep quickly. She knew that only because she was awakened less than an hour later by a pounding at her door, and her Peter's voice shouting her name.

When she opened the door, she found Peter and Greg standing there, and Peter had a gun in his hand. She was shocked to see him with a weapon, but probably no more shocked than he would be if he knew she also had a gun with her. They all pretended to be safe out here, but pretense was all it was.

"What's wrong?" she asked, opening the door to let them in.

"I . . . we were worried about you." Peter looked at his partner, as though for support.

"Why?"

"It was a *dog*, Peter. You woke her up for nothing."

"You didn't see it as well as I did. Dammit, it was a wolf!"

Amanda felt herself grow cold inside long before her neighbor said that word. But she strove for calm and asked where they'd seen the animal.

"It came up from the side of your house—the other side, not the side that faces us. We were walking home from the party when we saw it."

He meant the side of her house where her bedroom was—where the windows were open. Once again she struggled for calm and asked where it had gone.

Peter gestured toward the dead end of the road. "That way. There aren't any lights down there, so I couldn't see it for long. I ran into the house and got the gun."

"Then we came back out and heard the wolf drive away," Greg stated dryly.

"What do you mean?"

"We heard a car door slam and then an engine start up. Greg's trying to be funny."

"But if you heard a car, you must have seen it. It would have gone right past you."

Peter shook his head. "It must have been parked at the dead end of Sandpiper."

"Oh." She remembered now that the enclave next

to theirs had a street that dead-ended only a couple of hundred yards from their street. In between was a sandy strip with some rare beach grass, which was why the two streets had never been joined even though they all shared the same beach.

"It was a wolf," Peter repeated. "I saw one once, out in Idaho. They move differently from dogs. And it was a big one—much bigger than the one I saw. I think I should call the police."

"Right," Greg said. "You'll make their day—or night. You saw where it went. It was a dog and it belongs to someone on Sandpiper."

"Peter, you must have been mistaken. There couldn't be any wolves out here." But she knew there had been—and now knew as well that it hadn't been paranoia. But why was he here, outside her bedroom window?

"Do you have a flashlight?" Peter asked.

She nodded. He asked her to get it. She did and they went outside, around the corner of the house and down the slope. Greg complained that it was pointless. So what if they found tracks? They knew there'd been a dog out there.

They found the tracks quickly—just below one of the bedroom windows. Amanda stared at the indentations in the sandy soil, fighting tears. Why was he here? She couldn't believe he'd come to harm her— but if he hadn't, then why had she felt that urgent sense of danger out on the deck?

Daken drove slowly along dark, deserted side streets, searching for a place to leave the body in the trunk. He was already far enough from Amanda's cottage that she wouldn't be drawn into any police investigation. The man had carried no identification of any kind, except for his *meera,* and Daken had already removed that. He knew that the police had many other ways of identifying a body, but he was certain that the Sherba assassins left no trail.

He felt no remorse for having killed the man who'd been sent to kill Amanda. What he did feel was a growing anger at those who'd sent him—and he knew that he needed to control that anger. The Sherbas had to be destroyed, but he needed a clear head to make his plans.

Off to his left he spotted a grimy industrial area, lit only by a few weak lights and obviously deserted at this hour. He turned into it, then quickly extinguished the headlights so he wouldn't be seen by any passing traffic. Then he got out to scout the area, and discovered that the ocean was just beyond it, lapping at a seawall. Better still. It would probably be a few days before the body was discovered.

He returned to the car and opened the trunk, then lifted the man's lifeless body easily, carried it to the seawall, and dropped it into the ocean unceremoniously. It wasn't exactly the sort of funeral the arrogant Sherba would have hoped for, but Daken had no intention of commending the man to the gods. They'd deal with him in their own fashion.

That unpleasant task taken care of, he got back into the car and turned around, heading back to the seedy little motel where he'd taken a room earlier. He was tired and still somewhat disoriented, the result of having made the transformation too many times.

He'd been careless, and that troubled him. The two men who'd seen him when he'd foolishly returned to her cottage would almost certainly tell her they'd seen a wolf—unless they'd thought he was only a large dog.

He'd gone back there because he'd wanted to be near her for a little while, to sit outside her bedroom window and imagine that she was dreaming about him, as he dreamed about her. He'd been so lost in his murky thoughts that he hadn't even heard the men, as he easily should have with his heightened senses.

He pulled into the motel and went up to his small, shabby room. Finding any room at all out here at this time of year had been a problem he hadn't anticipated. Most of the times he'd ventured out into the world, the Sherbas had taken care of everything, getting him the powerful sports cars that were his secret passion, reserving elegant suites in the best hotels, or putting him up in their own lavish homes.

Fortunately he'd established a sizable bank account for himself, and had even obtained the little plastic cards that passed for money so much of the time in this world. Long ago he'd decided that he should prepare for such emergencies, since he'd always harbored suspicions about the Sherbas. He'd even managed on his own to obtain an American passport. He'd been fascinated with the United States ever since his first visit here years ago. It was a strange and jarring place, capable of a greatness he thought it had yet to achieve.

He stripped off his clothes and showered. He was tired, but he knew he wouldn't be able to sleep yet. He wasn't wholly settled into his own body again. So he put on fresh clothes and left the motel, walking through quiet neighborhoods until he reached the public beach.

Off to the east, the sky was beginning to lighten as he walked along the deserted beach. It didn't occur to him to worry about being out here alone. His size alone was probably enough to deter any attackers, but if that didn't work, he had other ways of dealing with them.

The first rosy rays shot into the eastern sky and he sat down on the beach to watch the spectacle. The color made him think of her—and thoughts of her led inevitably to pain. How could he make her understand that he was what he was—and that, for all his differences, he was still a man?

The horror on her face when she'd discovered his secret was a raw wound inside him. And if she ever learned the role he'd played in her uncle's death . . .

As the sun rose slowly at the edge of the sea, Daken began to feel the first, faint stirring of a desire to return to the mountains. It would get much worse, and probably very soon. And yet he couldn't leave her here, at the mercy of the Sherbas, who would certainly send another assassin.

Chapter Twelve

It was there again! Amanda dreaded coming home, because nearly every time she did she was certain that Daken had been there in her absence. It had been this way for the past three days—ever since she had returned from the beach house. Nothing was moved. Nothing was missing. But she knew he'd been there. She could feel his presence lingering in the loft like a silent threat.

And she could think of it no other way. Her heart wanted to believe that he couldn't harm her, but her mind told her that she was being foolish. If he believed her to be a threat to his people, he would do what he had to do.

Each time she went out she searched the crowds for him, not certain what she would do if she spotted him. But it was a decision she had yet to be forced to make.

She tried not to think about how he'd gotten in. Her security system was state-of-the-art, and yet it hadn't deterred him. At times like this, when she sensed his presence, she wondered if he could make himself invisible—and whether he might be here even now.

She accepted the fact that she could not hide from him. If he'd found her at the cottage, it would do no good to flee again, though she was greatly tempted to do so.

The morning after her neighbors had seen him at the cottage, she had actually hoped that the body of a Sherba would be discovered somewhere in the vicinity. Then she would have known that he was merely there to protect her, as he'd been before.

But it was a foolish hope. There had been no human footprints where they'd found the prints of the wolf, and she'd found nothing anywhere else around the cottage either, though the front yard and the other side would not have shown them as well. The previous owner had brought in topsoil and planted grass there. In any event, no bodies were found.

She even thought about hiring a bodyguard. Thanks to Steffen's money she could easily afford to do so. But how could she expect a mere man to defend her against the likes of Daken? It wouldn't be fair to put an unsuspecting bodyguard into such a position, and she certainly couldn't tell him the truth.

At least, she thought grimly, the hallucinations had stopped. She was no longer being visited by visions of the Dark Mountains, though she still had moments when she returned to the loft and felt Daken's presence.

But if the hallucinations had ended, her dreams had not. He was always there, waiting for her, his pale eyes lit with passion, his big hands rough yet gentle on her body. Each morning she would awaken to a warm, voluptuous feeling, only to have it shatter as she faced another uncertain day.

The man she'd met at the party had called her and informed her that he'd managed to get some highly prized tickets to an Off-Broadway show they'd discussed. She'd agreed, albeit reluctantly, to a theater-and-dinner date, hoping that for this one evening at least, she could pretend to again be the person she'd once been.

The show proved to be as good as its reviews, and over a late dinner afterward, her companion was as likable as she'd found him to be the first time. It was the kind of date every single woman hopes for—and rarely finds. They discovered shared interests and the conversation flowed easily. But Amanda knew it ended there. He was obviously attracted to her, but she could not summon a spark of interest in return. It was as though something in her had died—or had been stolen away by a man who wasn't a man.

She invited him up to her loft, certain that she would feel Daken's presence there once again and hoping that her companion's presence would drive it away. She knew she was using him shamelessly and that the invitation could be construed as an invitation to spend the night. But she had already sensed his basic decency and was certain that he would accept the invitation for what it had been: a chance to continue their conversation over espresso.

As they got off the elevator and she unlocked the door to the loft, they were both laughing over the recent public response by an artist acquaintance of hers to a conservative senator who had condemned her work on the floor of the Senate. But the laughter was cut off abruptly as a figure rose from her sofa to face them.

He was dressed casually in a pale gray silk jacket that was nearly a perfect match for his hair, which gleamed beneath the track lighting. He simply stood there staring at them, his face expressionless but his stance suggesting a coiled snake, ready to strike.

Her companion put a protective arm around her waist and started to say something.

"Leave," Daken ordered, his voice low but threatening.

"Amanda?" the man asked, staring from Daken to her. "What's—"

"Do as he says, Rick. I'll be fine."

He dropped his arm from her waist, but didn't move otherwise. She started to tell him again to leave, fearing what Daken might do. But her words came out as a strangled cry when she saw Daken raise his hand and trace something rapidly in the air. Rick seemed to stiffen, and then he turned and walked out. Amanda started for the door.

"Wait!" Daken ordered.

She pushed the door shut, then turned to face him. "I wasn't leaving. What will happen to him?" She'd seen the dazed look on his face and was worried that he might roam around like that, an easy target for attack.

"He will be himself in a few minutes."

She leaned against the door to fight the fear that was making her legs tremble. "Are you here to kill me, Daken?" Her tone was that of one who had nothing left to lose. And then she did see something in his face: shock—and perhaps pain as well.

"No. How could you think that?"

His accent seemed stronger, making his words sound rough. But she was sure now that she both saw and heard his pain, and she let go of her fear. But that only made space for other feelings that were just as dangerous—or perhaps even more so.

"Then why are you here—and why have you been sneaking into my apartment when I'm not home?"

What she now saw was something she'd never expected to see in this supremely self-confident, even arrogant man: embarrassment.

"I—just wanted to be here," he said in a voice that was barely above a whisper. "I didn't think you'd know."

"I knew. Just as I knew when you were outside at my beach house cabin."

"I don't understand that."

"Neither do I." She had moved away from the door and walked over to the corner where her desk stood. In the desk was the gun she had yet to return. She believed him when he said he wasn't here to kill her, but she still didn't know why he was here, and enough uneasiness remained for her to want some protection. Her gaze fell on the tiny whale on the bookshelf: the first indication she'd had of his presence here. Without consciously intending to do so, she picked it up, and when she turned back to him, she saw him staring at it.

"Where did you get that?" he asked.

"From an ancestor, I think. I can't be sure."

He frowned, and she told him about her "journey" back through time. "I thought it was just a dream, but then I discovered that I had this. I hadn't intended to take it. I'd just picked it up, and then forgot to replace it.

"So I'm probably Ertrian, or part Ertrian. You said once that some of them might have escaped because they were at sea."

He merely nodded, so she went on, knowing that none of this was really important now, but not wanting to hear his reason for being here. "Steffen spent most of his life trying to discover the family's origins, but he never found anything very conclusive. He'd begun to suspect that we might have come from that part of the world." She paused, taking a deep breath.

"Did you have Steffen killed, Daken?"

She saw him tense and felt the very air between them become brittle. And she knew. The knowledge fell into her like a cold, hard lump of ice.

"It was a mistake, Amanda."

"A *mistake?*" she repeated, her voice rising. "Whose mistake, Daken—yours or the Sherbas'?"

"Mine," he replied softly, his eyes still on her.

"Are you saying that *you* killed him—or that you ordered him to be killed?" she asked, though it made no difference.

"I ordered it."

Amanda felt both cold and hot with rage at the same time. She moved behind the desk, then reached into the drawer and took out the gun, aiming it at him with a shaking hand. His eyes shifted briefly to it, then back to her face again. If the gun frightened him, he didn't show it.

"Tell me why," she ordered. "He hadn't told anyone about his discovery. You knew that. You even attended his lecture."

"But he was coming back—and we knew that he intended to try to come to the mountains. He would have told the others sooner or later."

Hot tears were stinging her eyes, making him a blur. She wiped them away with her free hand. "Why didn't you just *talk* to him, Daken? He would have kept your secret."

"The Sherbas convinced me that he wouldn't. They were certain that he intended to show the others his discovery, and then come to the mountains."

It could have happened that way, she thought through a haze of pain and anger. She knew that Steffen must have been greatly troubled by his failure to tell them about the room. If he'd lived, he might well have led them to it to see if they, too, experienced what he had.

"Our leaders have always done things they were not proud of, simply to prevent outsiders from coming into the Dark Mountains. We are sworn to protect our people, so we allow the Sherbas to keep the wars going, century after century. Steffen is not the only one who died for that cause."

"It's wrong, Daken! You cannot buy your people's safety with the blood of others!"

To her considerable surprise, he nodded. "I know that now, but I did not know it in time to save Steffen's life. It was difficult enough to allow such things when those who would die were faceless and nameless—but now I know that it must stop."

"What will you do?" she asked, her anger lessening somewhat as she began to grasp the enormity of the problem that faced him. She could never forgive him for having Steffen killed, but if it had taken that to make him understand, then some good had come from her uncle's death.

"I don't know yet. I must go home and speak to the gods." His mouth curved briefly into a fleeting smile.

"Unlike past leaders, I have never consulted the gods about anything. It always seemed to me that they had deserted us long ago, left us to make our own decisions.

"Most of our people haven't traveled to the outer world as much as I have. They haven't seen all that I've seen. They don't know the wonders brought about by science. But I think the price for having them ourselves may be too great."

She nodded, thinking of the children. "So you will let your gods decide."

"Yes."

She put down the gun, surprised to see that she still had it in her hand.

"Could you have fired it at me?" he asked.

"I . . . don't know." She couldn't have, but she didn't want to admit it.

"You couldn't have, Amanda—even now that you know the truth about your uncle."

But I can't love you, either, she said silently. "Are you going home now?"

He nodded. "And you are coming with me."

"No!"

"You must come back to the Dark Mountains until I find a way to deal with the Sherbas. By now they will be sending another assassin."

"*Another* assassin? What are you talking about?"

"I killed the first one they sent, and by now they will know that. I caught him at your beach house."

"My neighbors saw you—but they didn't see anyone else." She avoided looking at him now as the image of the wolf filled her mind. "And I didn't find any . . . any human footprints," she continued hesitantly.

"By the time they saw me, I had already killed him and carried his body away. I scattered the footprints. Then I came back."

She thought about the sound she'd heard on the other side of the house—and that sudden sense of danger. "I won't go with you, Daken. I'll take my chances here."

"No. You will come with me. I promise that I won't . . . touch you again, and I promise to let you go as soon as I have dealt with the Sherbas. But I cannot stay here to protect you any longer. I must go home."

"No." She stared at him and saw regret in his eyes—and then saw him raise his hand. Her own hand shot out toward the gun, but he knocked it away from her, so that it sailed across the room to land noisily in a corner.

She stared at it in horror as it flew through the air, and then she turned back to him. A numbness was spreading through her. She cried out in protest and the sound died away, echoing in her ears.

"I'm sorry," he said, and his voice seemed to be coming from a very great distance. She was still on her feet, still able to see and hear him, but something had gone from her. She couldn't seem to move. Her mind and her body had somehow become disconnected.

"Don't be frightened. It's only temporary. I would put you to sleep, but I don't want any problems at the airport."

His soothing tone filled her brain, but she ignored

it, trying desperately to get her body to respond to her orders. He reached out to take her arm, then paused for a moment as he stared at the bookshelf behind her. A moment later he placed the tiny whale in her hand.

Amanda drifted in and out of a semistupor for the next hour. She was aware of being led from her apartment to a waiting limousine. Then she knew nothing until the long car reached the airport, where it rolled to a stop next to a small, sleek jet. When they got out of the car, a man in a customs agent's uniform was waiting for them. Daken drew out a passport, and told her to get out hers.

"It's in your purse," he instructed, then turned to the customs agent. "She's just had a terrible shock and the doctor gave her a tranquilizer."

Liar! her brain screamed, but her mouth refused the word. She fumbled through her bag, certain that her passport wasn't in there and hoping that would mean they'd be detained. But it was there. Just as her fingers touched it, Daken took the bag from her, removed the passport and handed it to the agent, who merely glanced at it before handing it back.

She willed her legs to run, but they wouldn't. She tried to form words, but her lips did not move. Tears of frustration rolled down her cheeks, but that only brought her a look of sympathy from the customs agent as he bid them a safe journey.

Daken took her arm again and told her to get onto the plane. Her feet obeyed him, even though her mind tried to stop them. The interior of the plane was small, but luxurious. Daken had to bend over as he guided her into a seat because of the low ceiling; then he fastened the belt securely around her. When that was accomplished, he touched her cheek, brushing away the curls the breeze had blown there. That simple gesture, which in another situation would have been a treasured sign of affection, in this case became yet another reminder of her utter helplessness.

"Sleep now," he said gently. She looked up to see him make another gesture—and then the world slid away into darkness.

Amanda struggled up out of sleep, only to fall back again, repeating the process several times. But each time her consciousness stirred, she felt her mind trying to warn her. But about what? It seemed so much easier to sink back down into blissful oblivion.

It was the sound, finally, that drew her back. Jet engines. She was on a plane. By the time she opened her eyes, her mind had retrieved it all, and she recoiled in horror at what he'd done to her.

The only illumination in the small passenger cabin came from low lights along the edges of the seats facing the aisle. Daken sat across from her, his own seat fully reclined. She watched him for a few seconds, trying to hate him and coming very close, despite the familiar stirrings. His face was turned away from her, and he appeared to be asleep.

She willed her hand to unbuckle the seat belt, and to her surprise it obeyed. It felt like a small miracle. Then she told it to find her hairbrush, and that worked, too. Another miracle. That strange lassitude was gone. He'd given her back to herself. Tears of joy sprang to her eyes and she brushed them away, embarrassed and angry. But she knew that she would never again take for granted the millions of cells in her brain and the nerve pathways that connected it to her body.

She looked out the window and saw that they were flying into the dawn—a spectacular sight she'd always loved on overnight flights to Europe. They weren't going to Europe though; they were going back to the Dark Mountains. But even in the depths of her anger, she felt a tiny thrill of anticipation.

She turned from the window and looked at Daken again. He hadn't moved. Then she thought about their conversation—about his admission that he'd ordered Steffen's death. But her earlier anger had vanished. In its place was a bottomless pain. How cruel could life be that it had conspired to give her this: a man she loved who wasn't a man, and who had killed the only other man she'd truly cared about? She could not forgive him, and could not forget what he was, yet she couldn't stop wanting him.

She got out of her seat to seek the bathroom she assumed the plane must have, moving quietly because she didn't want to disturb Daken. She wasn't ready for another confrontation, or another display of his inhuman powers. And because her eyes were on Daken, she was slow to realize that they were not alone in the small cabin.

Two seats behind her was another man, also asleep. He was of average height and slim, clad in a dark suit and shirt. Suspended from his neck was a gold chain with a black rock.

Amanda was at first frightened, and then confused. Her gaze flitted several times between the two men as she stood in the aisle uncertainly. Why would a Sherba be aboard this flight?

Seeing a door that must be a bathroom, she made

her way carefully back along the aisle, past the sleeping Sherba. Then, after using the toilet, she stared at herself in the small mirror, wondering how the familiar person who stared back at her had gotten into such an incredible mess. How could a life change so dramatically—and so irrevocably—in such a short time?

Since she hadn't brought her purse to the bathroom, she brushed her tangled hair as best she could with her fingers and thought again about the Sherba. He didn't look old enough to have attained a high position in the order, but then she didn't know how they chose their leaders. Maybe he was just an emissary, or maybe he was a renegade whom Daken had enlisted to help him wage war against the leadership.

She returned to her seat and stared out the window again. It was daylight now, and through wispy clouds she could see the gray-green ocean. Her stomach growled, reminding her as she sat there staring down at the water that she hadn't eaten for some time. She wondered if there might be any food aboard.

Something was nagging at her, preventing her from trying to find a galley. What was it? A sense of wrongness. Then suddenly she realized what it was. The two great oceans were different. The Pacific was blue, and the Atlantic was the dull gray-green she saw below her now. But when she'd traveled before to the Dark Mountains, they'd flown over the Pacific.

She frowned. Perhaps they were taking a different route because the plane was smaller and required more stops to refuel. But still, the different route, combined with the unexpected presence of a Sherba, made her uneasy.

She looked over at Daken again, wishing that he would wake up. But he slept on, his big chest rising and falling slowly beneath his well-tailored suit. She actually smiled when she saw the expensive gold watch on his wrist. For a man of the mountains, he certainly traveled the world in style.

Except that he isn't a man, she reminded herself. *How must he feel as he walks among ordinary mortals who would run away from him in horror if they knew the truth? As I do myself,* she thought with the familiar combination of repulsion and attraction.

Having spotted an alcove just behind the door that led to the cockpit, she got up again to see if she could find something to eat. The Sherba was still asleep behind her.

She discovered a coffeemaker and a small refrigerator that contained thick, plastic-covered sandwiches, together with a pitcher of iced tea and an assortment of fruit and cheeses. In a small overhead cupboard were some Styrofoam plates and a small supply of liquor, as well as containers of soup that could be heated in the tiny microwave.

She selected some soup and switched on the microwave, her mind going back again to the strange route that they were taking. She stared at the cockpit door. The microwave beeped, but she ignored it and instead tapped on the door. There was a muffled response from beyond, so she opened it.

Both the pilot and copilot turned toward her. She hadn't seen the pilot before, but she vaguely recalled that the copilot had been out on the tarmac when they arrived.

"I was wondering where we are," she asked.

The copilot glanced toward the array of instruments. "We'll be landing in Dublin to refuel in about a half hour. Then it'll be about four hours to Geneva."

Amanda waited for him to say how long it would be after that until they reached Menoa, but he said nothing. She started to ask him, but a sudden caution kept her silent. Instead, she thanked him and closed the door again.

She carried her meal back to her seat. Both men were still sleeping peacefully. She ate and tried to ignore her growing uneasiness. Why hadn't Daken said anything to her about the Sherba? She was sure that no one else had been aboard when they got on the plane. It was too small for her not to have noticed him, unless he was up in the cockpit, which seemed unlikely.

She tried to reconstruct the conversation at her loft. Daken had said he must get back to the Dark Mountains, and he'd said that he was going to consult with the gods before deciding what to do about the Sherbas. So why were they going to Geneva? She seemed to recall having been told that the Sherbas had their headquarters there, or perhaps it was something she'd read about them.

She finished her meal and carried the remnants back to the galley.

Then she paused beside Daken. With her eyes still on the sleeping Sherba, she touched Daken's shoulder lightly. No response. Clamping a hand around his shoulder, she shook him, then shook him harder still. He didn't move. She lifted his hand and dug her fingernails into his palm—and still there was no response.

Suddenly the drone of the engines changed to a whine, and a few seconds later a bell dinged, followed by the copilot's voice stating that they would be landing in Dublin in a few minutes and reminding them to fasten their seat belts.

Amanda glanced back at the Sherba and saw him begin to stir. She dropped Daken's lifeless hand and hurried to her own seat. Behind her, she heard the whir of the Sherba's seat being brought up, and then the click of the seat belt. She reached for her own belt, then stopped. If she fastened it, he would hear, and then he'd know she was awake.

Her heart thudded noisily as she sat there, staring at Daken. Could he be sleeping—or was he unconscious? She couldn't believe that anyone could have harmed him. It was nearly impossible to think of Daken as being anything other than invulnerable. But all her instincts were telling her that something was wrong.

Down they went through a fine mist, and then the fabled green of the Emerald Isle was beneath them. The plane landed smoothly and began to taxi toward the terminal. Amanda used the noise of landing to cover—or so she hoped—the sound of her seat moving as she brought it back to the reclining position it had been in when she woke up. Then she turned her head toward the window and feigned sleep, all the while listening for sounds behind her.

She heard nothing as they moved toward the terminal, but suddenly she felt a presence and knew the Sherba must be in the aisle between her and Daken. She struggled to remain still as she thought about

Daken's helplessness. The Sherba wouldn't kill him. However much the order might dislike him, he was still a Kassid. But if she was right and they'd been kidnapped, then what was their purpose?

The plane came to a stop and now she heard the Sherba move on, toward the cockpit. She risked turning her head and then opening her eyes. Daken was still there, and still not moving. For a moment, she stared at his chest, relieved to see its slow rise and fall.

The cockpit door opened and she heard low voices, but could not make out the words. Her thoughts turned to escape—but only briefly. She couldn't leave Daken, and besides, it wasn't likely that she could get away herself in any event. Furthermore, if she tried, the Sherba was quite likely to give her whatever drug he'd given to Daken.

Her only hope, she thought, lay in feigning sleep for as long as she could, and then pretending to be frightened and compliant. She couldn't begin to formulate any plans until she knew the situation.

The Sherba passed by again and once again, and she pretended to be asleep until she heard him fastening his seat belt. The plane refueled and taxied back to the runway. Moments later they were airborne once more.

Amanda watched Daken, hoping that whatever drug they'd given him would begin to wear off. And then a chilling thought occurred to her. When Daken did awaken, he would certainly be able to escape, thanks to his supernatural powers. But the Sherbas would know about that. They surely realized that the only way they could keep him in captivity was to keep him drugged—and that meant that she was completely on her own.

She decided to see if she could find out anything from the Sherba. But what tack should she take? Should she pretend to believe that she was still Daken's captive, being carried against her will back to the Dark Mountains?

That, she decided, might gain her some sympathy from the Sherba. Or at least it could make it seem that she was naive, which fit with the persona she wanted to project now: naive, frightened, compliant. The classic victim.

She moved her seat into the upright position, then got up. The moment she stepped into the aisle, she pretended to be shocked to see the Sherba sitting there, staring at her. She glanced from him to the unconscious Daken, her expression one of confusion.

"There has been a change of plans," the Sherba told her, his English slightly accented.

"What . . . what do you mean?" she asked, wide-eyed, turning again to Daken.

"We are going to Geneva."

"But . . . but I don't understand. He told me he was taking me back to the Dark Mountains." She hoped she wasn't overplaying her role.

The Sherba regarded her silently for a moment, and she feared that he had seen through her charade. "Why was he taking you back to the Dark Mountains?"

"He told me that my life was in danger—that you were going to . . . to kill me." Since it was true, she had no problem acting frightened.

The Sherba made a dismissive sound. "We have no

interest in you, Amanda. It is true that we feared the worst when you escaped. That's why one of our members, acting on his own, tried to kill you. But you have had many opportunities to reveal the secret of the Kassid, and you haven't done so. He lied to you. He was taking you back for his own reasons."

Amanda thought fast. A small voice inside told her that the man just might be speaking the truth. After all, she had only Daken's word that they were still after her. Finally she nodded.

"Yes. I told him that, but he insisted that he was only trying to protect me."

"He ordered the death of your uncle."

She nodded again. "He admitted that, before he . . . put a spell on me and took me to the airport."

"Daken is a very clever man—far more worldly than his predecessors. And for that reason he cannot serve his people well."

"I don't understand," she said sincerely, taking a seat across from the Sherba.

"He has allowed himself to become involved in the outside world, even to the extent of taking you as a lover. The leaders before him were content to rule in the Dark Mountains and leave everything else to us. Perhaps you know something of our history?"

"A bit. I know that the Kassid helped you many centuries ago, and then you became their eyes and ears to the world."

"Exactly. And as the world became ever more complex, we established ourselves throughout it. We exist to protect the Kassid from incursions by the outside world—and we've been very successful. Or we were, until your uncle's expedition arrived on the scene."

He paused, frowning at her. "We still do not understand how your uncle gained the permission of the gods to travel from the *azherwa* in the old palace to the Dark Mountains."

"I don't understand either—and neither did he. But I traveled that same way." She could see that he hadn't known about that, because his frown deepened.

"Could it be because of our Ertrian heritage?" she asked.

His dark eyes widened. "Your family is Ertrian? How could you know that?"

She told him about her dream that wasn't a dream, then went back to her seat and got the little whale from her bag. "I know it wasn't just a dream because when I woke up, I still had this. I picked it up in the home of a man I believe was our ancestor."

The Sherba took the whale and examined it closely, then nodded. "Yes, I have seen these before. The whale was a favorite subject for Ertrian seamen. This particular species of whale has been extinct for many centuries, but once flourished in the waters off that country. We have a small collection of such carvings ourselves."

"I know that it seems incredible, but if my ancestors were seafarers, then it's certainly possible that they escaped the earthquake."

"Indeed. We've always believed that some must have escaped. For many years we tried to track them down, but then we turned our attention to other matters." He paused, staring at her with an intensity that was very disquieting.

"The gods must favor you, Amanda—perhaps because of that Ertrian heritage. If we had known that your uncle was Ertrian . . ." He left off with a dismissive gesture.

"That is the past, and it cannot be changed."

Amanda was thinking that the gods' "favor" was definitely a benefit at the moment. "Why are you taking us to Geneva?"

"We intend to persuade the Kassid to elect a new leader—one who will lead as those before Daken did."

Meaning that you want someone who won't interfere with your war-making, Amanda thought. Aloud, she asked why she, too, was being taken there.

"There was no help for it," he said, a bit too smoothly. "Daken had cast a spell on you. When this is all settled, you will be permitted to go home, if that is your wish."

"Of course it's my wish," she said with false indignity. "I told you that he kidnapped me."

"Then you have no feelings for him?" the Sherba asked.

Amanda thought about lying, but decided that to the extent possible, she should be truthful. "Yes, I have feelings for him—but I cannot forgive him for ordering my uncle's death—and I cannot accept . . . what he is."

"Ahh," said the Sherba, nodding. "So then he has told you about the Bet Dawarzha: the transformation."

"He didn't have to tell me. I found out when he rescued me."

"Yes, it is difficult for anyone in the modern world to accept such a thing—and that is all the more reason why the Kassid must be protected from that world."

Amanda nodded. "That's why I would never reveal their existence. I was taken there against my will, but I came to love the Kassid—to admire them, really. But I don't belong in such a world."

"I think you may have some difficulty persuading Daken of that."

She saw the opportunity and seized it. "Then you aren't going to . . . to kill him?"

The Sherba looked horrified, which confirmed her earlier belief that however devious they might be, they would never kill a Kassid.

"No, of course not. The Kassid are the servants of the gods. We only want the chance to persuade them to elect a new leader, and we can only do that if Daken isn't there."

"Will they do that, do you think?" she asked curiously.

"It is possible—even probable," he said, then lapsed into a silence that suggested he wasn't about to reveal to her any more of their plans.

"And then Daken will be allowed to return to the Dark Mountains?"

"Of course—if he chooses to do so. He may decide to remain in the outer world. If he does, we will, of course, assist him in any way."

"But he couldn't do that. He told me himself that he can't stay away from the Dark Mountains for long."

"That is for the gods to decide. If they choose to do so, they could take away his need for the Dark Mountains—and his other powers as well."

The Sherba got up to get some coffee and offered to get her some as well. Amanda thanked him, then sat there thinking about what he'd said. Why did the thought of Daken stripped of his powers and remaining in her world disturb her so? Wasn't that what she wanted? Hadn't she secretly wished that Daken could be an ordinary man?

In the time she'd had to think about it, she'd come to understand that while she could never truly forget his role in Steffen's death, she had come to accept it. But what she still couldn't accept was that the man she loved wasn't a man at all.

The Sherba brought her coffee and she sipped it, listening to the low rumble of the jet's engines. It shocked her to realize that her life had undergone such a serious change that she no longer found it to be surreal. And yet here she was, on a luxurious private jet in the late twentieth century, thinking about ancient gods and a man who had supernatural powers.

Chapter Thirteen

It took four strong men to carry Daken from the plane to the waiting ambulance. The Swiss authorities were shown his passport and told that he was under heavy sedation because of pain and was being taken to the private clinic whose name appeared on the side of the ambulance. As desperate as their situation was, Amanda could not help appreciating the irony: Daken was now on the receiving end of the treatment he'd accorded her earlier.

The Sherba from the plane, whose name she had yet to learn, had said he was a doctor, and he'd given Daken another injection several hours ago.

She wanted desperately to accompany Daken because she didn't want to be separated from him. But she knew that she had to continue with the role she'd been playing if she had any hopes at all of winning the Sherbas' trust. It had probably been a mistake to have admitted that she had any feelings for him at all, but she'd feared that the Sherbas who'd seen them together at the fortress would contradict that.

So she went willingly with the man from the plane into a waiting limousine, and made no inquiries at all about Daken.

"We will try to make your stay with us as pleasant as possible," the Sherba told her.

"Thank you. I appreciate that. But I'm sure you will understand that I'm eager to return to my own life as soon as possible."

"Of course." He nodded. "It will not be long, I think."

He chattered on, pointing out various sights in this city that Amanda had never visited and had no interest in now. It did occur to her, however, that Geneva was largely French-speaking, and that could be important if she were able to escape—or perhaps even to communicate with servants if there were any. She was fluent in French, having spent a year studying at the Sorbonne.

She nodded politely and ventured several compliments. Geneva was quite lovely, situated as it was on such a beautiful lake. But she would gladly have traded all this perfection for Manhattan anytime. And all the while, she tried surreptitiously to see if the ambulance remained behind them.

Or at least she thought she was being surreptitious. Apparently she had underestimated the Sherba.

"You are worried about him," he said.

"Yes, of course I am. I've already told you that I have some feelings for him. Besides, if anything happens to him, the Kassid might well blame *me*."

306

"Nothing will happen to him."

"But you can't keep him sedated forever. Surely that's dangerous."

"We are being careful. I assure you, Amanda, that we would consider his death at our hands to be a grievous sin—one that would destroy everything we stand for."

Once again Amanda found herself believing him. The Sherbas were clearly zealots; of that she had no doubt. But like other religious fanatics, they were true to their beliefs. It was only the actions that flowed from those beliefs that were reprehensible.

Furthermore, she now doubted that she herself was in any danger. She considered it entirely possible that Daken had lied to her about a Sherba assassin being at her beach house. Such a story served his purpose too well. He wanted her to stay with him in the Dark Mountains and used the excuse of protecting her to persuade her to return there.

And as for the attempt on her life when she'd escaped from the fortress, well, Daken himself had told her the same story this Sherba had given her: that it was the act of a single, overly zealous young man. Of course, Daken hadn't believed it.

They left the city behind and drove through lush, rolling countryside. The ambulance was still behind them, so it appeared that she would not be separated from him.

What should she do? Might it not be best simply to wait them out, to see if they were successful in persuading the Kassid to replace Daken?

She was just beginning to think about that when they turned suddenly. The limousine halted briefly before an elegant wrought-iron gate; then the gate swung open and they drove through. The ambulance followed. She hadn't seen any sign on the stone pillars.

"Is this your home—or whatever you call it?" she asked.

"We call them communities—and yes, this is our world headquarters."

"I don't understand why you would have your world headquarters here, instead of closer to the Dark Mountains—in Menoa, perhaps?"

"A decision was made many years ago that it would be wisest to avoid being linked with the Dark Mountains. From time to time the order has drawn the attention of various journalists and others, and we wished to make certain that we did not unwittingly draw that attention to the Dark Mountains as well."

"But surely you can't believe that the world will stay away from them forever?"

Rather to her surprise, he heaved a deep sigh. "No, we don't believe that. Or rather, we don't believe that *we* can hold back the world forever. But we will do so as long as possible, and then trust that the gods will help their servants as they have done in the past."

"Daken seems to believe that the gods have lost interest in the Kassid," she said, recalling their conversation on the subject.

The Sherba nodded. "That is another reason that Daken is unsuited to being leader of his people. His travels in the outer world have made him less devout."

She decided not to point out that he and the rest of his order lived in the "outer world" and had certainly not suffered any diminution of their devotion. It was generally not wise to point out such discrepancies to fanatics, and however pleasant this man was, he was definitely a fanatic.

After a long drive through a forest and then formal gardens, they came to a stop before a very imposing stone house that was surrounded by smaller buildings. The ambulance drew to a halt behind them.

"We have prepared an apartment for you. I think you will find it comfortable," the Sherba said as he assisted her from the car.

She nodded, wondering if his "you" was singular or plural. But she didn't dare ask for fear of appearing overly concerned about Daken. He was carried from the ambulance and into the house. The Sherba led the way.

Amanda was astounded by the luxury around her. This was more like a palace than a house: marble floors and richly carved wainscoting, beautiful Oriental rugs, magnificent tapestries—and an art collection that could rival that of any museum.

"You are impressed?" The Sherba smiled as they waited for the elevator.

"Of course. I'd very much like to see the rest of your art collection."

"You are free to come and go as you please, Amanda—provided, of course, that you don't try to leave the grounds. Our security is quite good, by the way. But I think you would not try to escape as long as he is here."

She said nothing, but she wondered again if her efforts to conceal her true feelings about Daken had been in vain.

The Sherba stared down at the unconscious Daken

as they all got onto the elevator. "I also think that he will never willingly let you go."

"Why do you think that?" she asked, avoiding looking at the subject of their discussion.

"I personally do not know him well, but those who do say that he is deeply in love with you, and that that has never happened to him before.

"You must understand that although the Kassid are a kind and gentle people, they are descended from a race of warriors. The Bet Dawars, like Daken, were the mightiest warriors of all. The gods created them for that purpose, and it was under the first Daken that the great Kassid-Ertrian empire was created. Warriors are by nature very possessive. Daken believes that you belong with him, and he will fight to keep you."

The Sherba's words were still echoing in her mind later, as she stared at the unconscious Daken. It was strange, but she'd never thought of him as being a warrior. It was an archaic term that conjured up all sorts of bloody images, and yet she recalled the eerie feeling she'd had the day she watched the Bet Dawars at arms practice: a feeling that she was seeing the past come to life.

Now she couldn't get that image out of her mind, where it joined all the other images she had of him: the great gentleness, the arrogance she'd seen, the supernatural powers—and the wolf. How could such a being exist?

The Sherba's statement that Daken was in love with her didn't surprise her, however, even though he'd never spoken those words. She knew he loved her. And if the Sherba was right when he said that Daken would fight to keep her . . .

She knew he would never take her by force, though the Sherba had seemed to be suggesting that he might. But it wasn't that simple. He surely knew how she felt about him. In fact, he might understand it better than she herself did.

She continued to stare at him, but as before, she saw both the man and the wolf: the gentle, wonderful lover and the wild, vicious creature. Once again, she asked herself the unanswerable question: how could she have fallen in love with him?

She left his bedside and began to roam around the spacious apartment. It was impossible to imagine such an elegant prison—but a prison it was. The Sherba was right. She could not escape and leave him behind.

She turned her attention back to the thoughts that had been interrupted earlier. What was the likelihood that the Kassid would be willing to select another leader? She wished that she knew more about their politics. Was it possible that they would agree with the Sherbas that Daken had become too "worldly" and was therefore willing to put their safety at risk?

She thought they just might do that—and the fact that he had brought her to the Dark Mountains could be held against him as well. Still, Daken had traveled in the outside world before his election.

It also seemed to her that the Sherbas might be misjudging the influence they could bring to bear. Like most fanatics, they undoubtedly gave little thought to the feelings of others. And she knew that the Kassid regarded them as somewhat of a nuisance, though perhaps a very necessary nuisance.

The truth was that she couldn't begin to guess what would happen, and the only person who could was unconscious.

She was deeply worried about that, too, despite the Sherba's assurance that the drugs would do no permanent damage to Daken. Already they'd hooked up an IV to feed him and supply the necessary fluids, and various monitors as well, but that did little to reassure her.

Where, she thought angrily, were the gods of the Kassid now, when their presence was so very much needed? They had transported her from the underwater chamber to the Dark Mountains and then had sent her on a time-journey, but now it appeared that they'd lost interest. It rather reminded her of the notoriously fickle gods of ancient Greek and Roman mythology. On the other hand, she didn't much like the notion that there were beings out there somewhere who could control her destiny.

After looking in on Daken once again, she left the apartment just as two maids were coming in, carrying armloads of clothing. They told her in French that all of this was for her, and she almost responded in French before she caught herself and feigned ignorance, then hurried away.

She spent the next hour touring the main building, or at least the rooms that seemed to be public. Dark-clad male and female Sherbas passed her, all of them pausing to greet her by name pleasantly with offers of assistance.

She was enthralled by their art collection, which included several masterpieces that she knew had been auctioned for millions of dollars in recent years. The collection was a strange mixture of periods and styles: everything from the great masters to the Impressionists and even a few contemporary giants like Rauschenberg and Rothko. If it was true that money was power, then the Sherbas' power was far greater than she'd previously supposed.

Furthermore, their collecting didn't end with paintings. There was everything from ancient Greek and Chinese vases to Fabergé. A friend had once remarked after visiting the British Museum that it appeared that the British simply carried the world home with them, and after touring the Sherbas' home, Amanda decided that the British had been amateurs at raiding the world's treasures.

In the library she discovered the treasures of Ertrian civilization that had been the object of their ill-fated expedition. The room was vast, and nearly half of it was given over to the Ertrian collection, including ancient volumes kept in temperature-and humidity-controlled cases. There was more Kassid and Ertrian history here than there was in the Dark Mountains.

Amanda became angry as she moved through the displays. People had died because of this treasure— including Steffen. And all the while the Sherbas had been in possession of this secret collection. She was staring at a beautiful gold vase embossed with a design that featured both wolves and the Kassid when she became aware of a presence behind her. She turned to find the Sherba who'd brought her here.

"This is wrong!" she blurted out before she could stop herself. "This belongs to the world—not locked up here in secret."

"If the world were to see it, the Kassid would be in grave danger," he replied mildly.

Knowing that he was right, Amanda said nothing more about it. Instead she asked his name.

"Forgive me. I didn't realize that I'd forgotten to introduce myself. My name is Tranar."

Amanda frowned. "What sort of name is that?"

"It is a Kassid name. We all take Kassid names when we enter the order."

"But where do you all come from? How does the order find you?"

"Many of us are original members of the tribe, but they augment the order with some outsiders. Their selection methods are unknown to me, but I believe that they try to recruit from all the world's races or nations. At least it seems that way to me."

"Then what were you before you joined the order?" she asked.

"I am Dutch by birth, and I was a practicing physician whose hobby was archaeology. I met a member of the order on a dig. We finance many such undertakings, you see.

"I was told that the Sherbas' archives contained information about the Kassid, and I'd always been fascinated by the legend. But it wasn't until after I joined the order that I learned they are more than legend. The journey into the Dark Mountains is a sort of pilgrimage for us, and it changed my life."

"We certainly have that in common, then," Amanda commented wryly.

Tranar smiled. "Exactly. And you feel as we do: that the Kassid must be protected."

Amanda found herself unable to respond. He was right—except that she was unable to go to the lengths to which they had gone and would go to protect the secret existence of the Kassid.

Nevertheless, after Tranar had excused himself and she continued her perusal of the huge library, Amanda found herself thinking uneasily about his comment. She was beginning to understand the Sherbas better—at least those like Tranar, whose interest in ancient civilizations had undoubtedly led him to accept actions he might otherwise have found reprehensible. She had been called upon to do no more than lie to protect the Kassid, but knowing the devastation that would be wreaked upon them if their existence became known, would she do more?

Did the end justify the means? It was an old question, and one that mankind had never truly answered.

"Have you received an answer from the Kassid yet?" Amanda asked Tranar two days later as he made one of his regular visits to check his unconscious patient.

His worried expression gave her the answer before his words did. "They have told our leaders that they will choose no new leader as long as Daken is alive and chooses to remain leader. Some of us had feared this would happen, because the Kassid believe that their choice is dictated by the gods."

As long as Daken is alive, she thought with a chill after Tranar had departed rather hastily, saying that they still hoped to persuade the Kassid to change their minds. He had said it would be a grievous sin to kill Daken—but might they not consider committing that sin in their zeal to protect the Kassid? Might they not be able to justify the death of one Kassid to benefit the entire race?

Amanda knew that she had to do something—and quickly. Tranar's worried expression and his reluctance to talk about it told her that time was running out. But what could she do?

She went into Daken's room and stared at him, shuddering as always at the tubes and wires and machines that never failed to remind her of her father's protracted death. As she sat on the edge of the bed, holding Daken's limp hand, she realized that he was the only one who could do anything to save himself—and quite possibly her as well. But how could he do anything?

Her gaze fell on the wastebasket beside the bed, which was half-filled with the debris left by the nurse who tended to him. In it lay the discarded syringe from the injection Tranar had just given to Daken.

Could she do it? Did she dare try? Her mind whirled with the possibility. She knew the routine by now. Tranar came in twice a day to give Daken his injection—but the injection itself was prepared by a nurse, who always came in just before he did.

She had to try. The risk was great, but the risk of inaction was even greater, unless the Kassid gave in to the Sherbas' demands. But how long would it take for him to regain his senses, and what kind of shape would he be in when he did? Of course he would have her to help him, but their escape from this place depended on his powers. She knew by now that escape in the ordinary sense was impossible.

Nighttime would be best, she decided. The nurse and then Tranar came in at 10:00, and then did not return until the same time the next morning. The machinery that monitored his condition had alarms, and she had been instructed to call Tranar immediately if any of them went off.

She studied the monitors, wondering if the alarms would go off to signal *any* change, or only a deterioration. It seemed likely that it was the latter, but she decided that she'd have to disconnect them just to be on the safe side. She had no idea how loud they were, and she knew that the apartment next to this one was occupied.

She must do it tonight. It was dangerous to wait any longer. At any time the Sherbas could decide to kill him. She was certain that had been the meaning of Tranar's worried expression. Either that, or he feared that prolonged use of the drugs could harm Daken.

During the day the nurses were in and out fairly frequently, but at night there was only one visit. Most of the time the nurse had come and gone by the time Tranar arrived, but one time they had been there together. She could only hope that wouldn't happen tonight, because if it did, her plan wouldn't work.

The day passed for Amanda with agonizing slowness. Anxious to keep up the appearance of what had become her normal routine, she visited the school for the Sherba children, sketching them as she had been doing for the past few days, and then giving the sketches to the delighted youths. Then she went for her afternoon run on the property, taking the path that wound around the borders near the high fence. This was how she knew that escape on her own was impossible. She was no security expert, but the fence was at least ten feet high, with only one gate, and she could see devices that had to be motion detectors mounted at regular intervals on the concrete pillars.

Following her evening jog, she showered and went to her room. She knew that she would get no sleep this night, and it was essential that she keep her wits about her. Still, she was certain that she wouldn't be able to sleep now—and was therefore greatly surprised when she awoke to darkness as someone tapped lightly on her door.

She had been dreaming—the first time since she came here. And the dream continued to haunt her as she opened the door to find a maid who held a dinner tray toward her. Amanda thanked her and gestured for her to leave the tray in the dining room, then closed the door again and began to dress as she thought about the dream. Following the dream that hadn't been a dream when she'd returned to ancient Ertria, she'd begun to place far more importance on such things.

She could remember only fragments, but she knew that she'd been back in the Dark Mountains. Daken was there as well, standing at the bridge, near one of the flaming cauldrons. She was on horseback, preparing to leave.

What came through from the dream into reality was her pain, her agonizing uncertainty. And then one last glimpse of Daken, still standing near the fiery cauldron, but he was now nothing more than a receding shadow.

Amanda shivered as she felt a chill settle deep into her soul. She knew what the dream had been telling her. She would lose Daken.

Until she had been kidnapped and brought here, Amanda had accepted that loss. She had made her choice and she would have lived with the pain of his loss and gotten on with her life. But something had changed. As she'd sat for hours at his bedside, she'd begun to believe there might be another way—some way that would allow her to live in both worlds. After all, Daken himself did that.

It wasn't until she was forcing herself to eat her dinner that she realized she'd come upon the same solution that Jocelyn had found with *her* Daken. She'd been unwilling to give up her home in Ertria and her position as ruler of her people, but thanks to the *azherwas*, the sacred rooms that linked the Ertrian palace to the Kassid fortress, she'd been able to lead a double life.

In the modern world, jet planes had replaced the *azherwas*, though ironically with considerably less efficiency.

As to her feelings about Daken's supernatural powers, well, perhaps seeing him as he was now had changed her opinion of that. Or so she hoped. There would be time later to deal with that—after they got themselves back to the Kassid fortress.

She didn't realize how long she'd lingered over her dinner until she heard the outer door open and realized that it must be the nurse. Her heart began to thud rapidly as she waited for sounds of the woman's departure and prayed that Tranar wouldn't come early.

The moment the outer door opened and then closed again, Amanda dashed for her room, where she took from her night table drawer the syringe she'd stolen from the wastebasket earlier and cleaned and filled with water. She hurried to Daken's room.

A new syringe filled with the drug lay in a tray. She

held it up with shaking hands and saw that it contained less fluid than the one she had prepared, so she went into the adjoining bathroom and squirted out enough water to bring it to the same level. Then she ran back to Daken's bedside and snatched up the drug-filled syringe, replacing it with the one she'd prepared. The outer door opened again just as she was hurrying down the hallway to her own room to hide the syringe.

When she returned to Daken's room, Tranar had just picked up the water-filled syringe. Holding it up, he turned to greet her. Her whole body was trembling, but to her amazement her voice sounded perfectly calm as she greeted him.

Then he turned back to Daken, and she held her breath as he slid the needle into his arm. Her plan had worked. She turned and left Daken's room, and a few seconds later Tranar followed her. He often stayed for a few moments to talk to her, but he didn't this time. She saw the tension in him and was certain that she'd put her plan into operation at the last possible moment.

As soon as he'd gone, Amanda returned to Daken's room, her eyes going immediately to the monitors. How soon would it be before anything registered? She guessed that Tranar was probably using the minimal possible dosage to keep him unconscious, so it probably wouldn't be long. She pulled the plugs on the monitors.

Then her anxiety began to take over. What if her actions had killed him? What if he had to be weaned gradually from the drug? Or what if he came to, so confused that he couldn't help them to escape?

The next few hours were the longest of Amanda's

life. She sat on the edge of the bed, studying his face and holding his hand, her fingers pressed firmly against the pulse point in his wrist. But her own blood was pounding through her so loudly that she couldn't be sure whose pulse she was feeling.

It was just past midnight when she thought she saw his eyelashes flutter slightly. But when the movement wasn't repeated, she decided that she'd imagined it. But twenty minutes later, his hand that she still held twitched slightly, and the other hand that lay on the bedcovers moved restlessly.

Her fear escalated. What if he had a seizure? She very nearly picked up the phone to call Tranar and confess her trick. But she stopped herself by reminding herself that his life was already in jeopardy.

After those brief movements he was quiet again, but she thought that his pulse rate was rising. Unable to sit there any longer, she got up and began to pace around the room, pausing at the windows that faced the gardens. The moon had risen: a bright, nearly full moon.

Then suddenly she wasn't staring at the gardens here. Instead she was staring down from her room in the fortress into the gardens there, where the small cauldrons of flaming oil twisted in the night breeze and distant snowcapped peaks gleamed beyond the high wall.

She blinked—and the image was gone. Suddenly she heard a sound behind her—and whirled around to face a nightmare.

In the dim light of the room, she could just barely make out Daken's form on the bed. But superimposed over it was the wolf! And as she stared in paralyzed terror, the forms shifted. The wolf became clearer and Daken faded, until she could just barely make out the outline of his body. Then the scene was reversed, and it was the wolf that became a mere shadow.

This shifting back and forth went on for many minutes that were punctuated only by her pounding heart. Amanda was both fascinated and horrified as she stood there, scarcely breathing lest she draw attention to herself. Neither Daken nor the wolf had looked in her direction. It almost appeared that they were wrestling with each other.

And then, as her brain began to function again, she realized that that was probably the case. Daken was coming out of his long sleep—and so, too, was the part of him that was a wolf. She knew she should be pleased, but what she felt instead was a renewed recognition of what he was.

Now both man and wolf were thrashing about, and the stand that held the IV bag she'd forgotten to disconnect was about to crash into the nightstand. With a cry she ran toward them and grabbed it. The wolf turned suddenly toward her, baring its teeth. Fangs gleamed in the low light.

"Daken!" she cried, her voice urgent but low. "Daken, it's Amanda!"

The pale eyes of the wolf studied her for what seemed like hours, but could only have been seconds. And then, gradually, the animal faded and she could see only Daken, staring at her through those same pale eyes.

Her hands shook as she struggled to disconnect the IV. But she babbled on, telling him what had happened and what she'd done. He remained so still that she feared he'd lost consciousness with his eyes open. But when she grasped his wrist, she could now feel a strong, steady pulse—or thought she did, anyway. Her own blood was roaring in her ears, nearly blotting out her chatter.

She stopped abruptly when he suddenly grasped her hand in a powerful grip that was nearly bone-crushing. She cried out in pain, and he immediately loosened his grip. A frown creased his brow. He tried to say something, but all that came out was a croak. She tried to extricate her hand from his, so that she could get him a glass of water, but he merely tightened his grip again.

"I want to get you a glass of water," she said slowly. "I won't leave."

Relief flooded through her as she had her first indication that he understood. He nodded and released her hand. She ran into the bathroom and filled a glass. When she came back he was struggling to sit up in the bed. And now, after her brief absence, she became aware of the aura she'd sensed several times before.

The wolf, she thought, wondering why she hadn't realized it before. Even though the wolf was gone, its presence lingered—as it had on those other occasions.

She started to hold the glass to his lips, but he took it from her and held it in both hands as he drank greedily. She noted that his hands were shaking slightly, but not even as much as hers had been—and still were.

As he drank, his gaze roamed around the room. Then he handed the glass to her and fell back against the pillows. "Tell me again what has happened," he ordered in a hoarse voice. "Speak slowly, so I can understand."

Then he abruptly raised himself up again, the movement so fast that she unconsciously took a few steps away. "Are you all right?"

She nodded, ashamed of her reaction, and came back to sit on the edge of the bed. When she wouldn't meet his eyes because she didn't want him to see her fear, he cupped a hand beneath her chin and forced her to look at him. She thought she saw both pain and confusion in his eyes before he released her and asked again that she tell him what happened.

So she did, slowly and carefully. He asked no questions, but each time their eyes met, she felt certain that he was absorbing it all.

"I was afraid that they would kill you. Tranar said they wouldn't because that would be a grievous sin, but I was afraid they would find a way to justify it."

Daken nodded, but said nothing.

"I knew that the only hope we had of escaping was if I could bring you back so you could . . . use your powers." She averted her eyes. He reached for her hand, but still said nothing.

"We have some time," she told him. "No one will come until morning."

He had lain back against the pillows, but now he roused himself again. "Help me to the bathroom, and then leave me for a few minutes," he said as he swung his legs slowly over the edge of the bed.

"Are you sick?" she asked with alarm, even though he looked surprisingly healthy.

"No. But my mind is not working as well as it should. I want to take a shower. That may help to clear my head."

He stood up and took a few careful, hesitant steps. She wrapped her arm around his waist and walked with him. That aura still clung to him, and she felt the same powerful reaction she'd felt before: fear mixed with desire. He wrapped an arm around her shoulders as they made their way across the big bedroom.

Then he dropped his arm as they reached the open doorway to the bathroom. "Leave me now," he said.

She thought he seemed too weak to be on his own and hesitated. He gave her the merest ghost of a smile. "I must think."

She nodded, knowing that he was actually saying that he couldn't think with her there. Still, she was reluctant to leave him, and after he had closed the door she remained outside, fearing that at any moment she would hear a crash.

She heard the shower and retreated to the bed, sinking down and breathing in the scent of him that lingered there: the man-wolf scent that both attracted and repelled her.

The image of that struggle between the two parts of him flooded back. How could she ever keep them separate again—and what would happen if she couldn't? She wondered if he were aware of what she'd seen.

Daken stood beneath the hot spray, trying to clear the cobwebs from his brain. But instead of considering what to do, he found himself lingering on his thoughts of her. He'd seen the fear in her eyes that he was certain wasn't a result of their situation. That must concern her, surely—but what he'd sensed went beyond that.

He cast his mind back, trying to recall the first moments of consciousness. It seemed to him that the other had awakened first. Yes, he thought, that was what had happened. The gods only knew what she'd seen as he struggled between his two selves. No wonder she was terrified.

But then he smiled, his mind turning to her clever trick with the needle. Yes, he had not been wrong about her. She was every bit as resourceful and strong-willed as Jocelyn had been.

Still, he was angry with himself for his failure to protect her. His memory was hazy, but he could now vaguely recall that just after they'd taken off, a Sherba had come out of the cockpit, aiming some sort of weapon at him. He'd been watching her, lost in his thoughts, and so was slow to react. There'd been a blinding pain—and then nothing. What were those weapons called? He'd heard of them. The Sherba had reached him and pushed it against him. The weapon discharged a powerful electrical current. Stun gun. Yes, that was it. And then the drugs.

He stepped out of the shower and began to towel himself dry, forcing his thoughts to the matter of their escape. Already he felt better, clearer in his mind, even though every muscle in his body ached from disuse.

He wrapped the towel around his waist and went to find his clothes.

Amanda turned from the window when the door opened. She'd been about to go in and check on him when the shower had stopped. He stood there, naked except for a towel around his waist, and she felt her bones begin to melt. They stared at each other across the room—and then she was suddenly in his arms, her body thrust against his, his mouth bruising hers. The towel slipped away and she felt him grow hard against her.

"There's no time now." She gasped, tearing her mouth from his.

"We have a few moments. It isn't enough, but it will do. I need you." His already hoarse voice was made even more so by his urgency.

"But you're not well," she protested as he began to lead her to the bed.

He smiled at her. "Then give me your strength."

They struggled with her clothing, both of them clumsy in their eagerness as the flames of passion licked at both of them. He drove into her and she welcomed him and he covered her mouth and swallowed her gasps of pleasure as she arched her body, sending him deeper and driving them both over the edge all too quickly.

Amanda was still struggling to find words when he kissed her tenderly. "I do not want it to be this way with us, *kazhena*, but sometimes the need becomes too great and I cannot be gentle."

She stared into his pale eyes and in her mind she saw instead the eyes of the wolf staring back at her. She didn't know if he saw her fear, but with another quick kiss, he left her and went to the closet, making a sound of satisfaction when he saw his clothes there.

This will not work, she thought, denying the pleasure he'd given her body. *I cannot forget what he is.*

"What are you going to do?" she asked, her thoughts of what he was leading her back to their situation.

"We are leaving. Get dressed, *kazhena*."

"But how? I told you about their security. What will you do?" She had no doubt at all that he could get them out of there, but she wanted to prepare herself to see him in action.

"I will do whatever is necessary—and no more. Since it is nighttime, that might not be much."

She stared at him, recalling how he'd said she could give him her strength. Perhaps somehow she had, because he seemed very much himself again. Even his movements were no longer stiff and awkward.

"I can't believe you have recovered so quickly," she remarked as she got out of bed and began to dress. "Anyone else would surely have needed a day or two to recover, after being drugged for so long."

"I am not anyone else," he replied simply, now dressed and watching her closely.

"No, you aren't." She glanced at him, then averted her gaze quickly.

A silence fell between them as she finished dressing. Then he asked if she knew where the garage was. He said that he'd been to the Sherbas' headquarters before, but it was long ago, and his memory of the place wasn't clear.

"Yes. It's not far—on that side of the house." She gestured. "But it's not attached. We'll have to go outside."

They left the apartment and started down the hallway. Amanda didn't know what she feared more: the sudden appearance of a Sherba, or what Daken would do if that happened. She slanted a glance at him. He walked confidently down the hall, giving no indication whatsoever that he feared anything.

He *doesn't* fear anything or anyone, she thought. But instead of making her feel secure, that certainty only frightened her still more.

They reached the main floor without incident, and Amanda had just begun to think they could at least get to the gate without being confronted, when suddenly a tall Sherba appeared.

The man stared at Daken as though he were seeing a ghost. Out of the corner of her eye, she saw Daken raise his hand—and the man fell heavily to the floor. She stopped, staring at him, but Daken took her arm.

"He isn't dead. Come."

They stepped out into the night. Amanda felt terribly vulnerable. The house had been dimly lit, but the exterior had bright floodlights that created an artificial daylight. Daken started toward the garage, then stopped abruptly. She scanned the area, trying to see what had brought him to a halt.

"Wh—?" She got no farther before he placed a hand over her mouth. Then he began to turn his head slowly. She still heard nothing and saw nothing.

And then, looking in the direction he was facing, she did see something: dark shapes moving in the shadows of the woods beyond the garden.

"Dogs!" she whispered. She hadn't seen any, but they must be used to patrol the grounds at night. She squinted, trying to see them better. There were a lot of them, far more than she would have thought necessary. How could he deal with so many of them?

"Not dogs," he replied in a normal voice that held a note of quiet satisfaction.

And then she knew. The wolves moved out of the shadows and loped toward them in that loose, easy gait that could make them seem much slower than they actually were. Within a few moments they were surrounded by more than a dozen of them—and every pair of pale eyes were turned to Daken.

He said nothing, but she knew that he was communicating with them. Then, abruptly, they turned as a group and vanished into the night again. Daken took her arm once more and began to stride quickly toward the garage.

"If it weren't for me, you would join them, wouldn't you?" she asked in a strangled voice.

"Yes. But we will both join them soon."

They entered the garage through a side door, and Daken then opened the door to a dark Mercedes. She got in, and as she waited for him to get in on the driver's side, she saw that there were no keys in the ignition. She told him that as he settled himself into the seat.

"They're probably in the house, but I don't know where. Maybe—"

Her words were cut off abruptly as the car started. This time he hadn't even made a gesture. She swallowed hard and then felt an irrational sense of relief when he used the opener to raise the garage door.

He backed out, turned and sped down the long driveway. She told him that although there was a sentry box at the gate, she'd never seen a guard there. But she hadn't been down there at night.

The driveway made a long curve through the woods, and then the gate loomed ahead of them, lit by large globes on stone pillars. The sentry box was lit as well, and she could see a figure in there.

Daken was traveling fast, and he didn't slow at all as the gate came ever closer. Amanda unconsciously pressed her foot to a nonexistent brake as she saw the guard opening the door.

When they were less than fifty feet from the imposing gate, it suddenly opened—not in the slow motion she'd seen before, but in an explosion that ripped it from the stone pillars with a shrieking sound. The shocked expression on the guard's face mirrored her own as Daken drove through, then turned left in a squeal of tires.

"Where are we going?" she asked when she could find her voice. Things were moving too quickly. She hadn't planned anything beyond their escape from the compound, though she'd hoped she could somehow guide them to the airport.

"To the airport," he confirmed.

"Do you know the way?" she asked, gripping the door as he took a curve at an alarming speed. How much driving experience could he have? She feared that he would kill them both as she thought about the many curves ahead.

"Yes. They gave me directions. A plane is waiting."

She didn't ask who "they" were. Of course he meant the Bet Dawars. She realized that she was dangerously close to hysterics when she had to fake a cough to conceal a giggle. She was thinking about a planeload of wolves waiting for them.

Daken suddenly reached out to take her hand briefly. "I am sorry if I'm frightening you."

"What's frightening me right now is your speed," she replied. "You can't have driven enough to—"

She stopped abruptly as he slid through a sharp curve, not even bothering to release her hand. Then he laughed—a sound so improbable that she was certain the drugs must have done something to his mind after all.

"You are now witness to my secret . . . what is the word? A bad habit?"

"Vice," she said, staring at yet another curve coming up.

"Yes, that is the word. I like to drive good cars." And even as he spoke, he expertly maneuvered the curve.

"No wonder the Sherbas say that you are too worldly," she muttered, then turned to look out the rear window. "Will they come after us, do you think?"

"Yes, but they will not follow us into the airport. They would not want to cause trouble there."

They came up behind another car and Daken slowed impatiently, getting far too close to it. But a moment later the other car signaled and then pulled over. He sped up again.

"Did you do that?" she asked suspiciously.

"No. It wasn't necessary."

A few moments later, she saw him looking in the rearview mirror and she turned to see headlights approaching. They were on a straight stretch at the moment, and she could tell that the car was gaining on them, even though Daken was traveling very fast.

"Is it them?"

"I think so," he said grimly.

Amanda turned again. She couldn't believe that the other car could possibly be catching up to them, but the gap between them was narrowing by the second. Then they entered a wooded area and the road once again became winding. The other car was closer still, only a few car lengths behind them now.

Suddenly the rear window shattered and something struck the headrest above her seat. She cried out in surprise. Daken said something in his own language, then told her to get down.

"Now they have gone too far!" he said, his voice colder than she'd ever heard.

A moment later she heard a strange sort of *whump!* and peeked around the edge of the seat. The shattered rear window was lit with orange flames. At first, she thought their own car was on fire, but then she saw what appeared to be a fiery pinwheel leave the road and careen off into the woods.

She climbed shakily back into the seat, the vision of the flaming car still spinning in her brain and his cold anger echoing in her ears.

Neither of them spoke as Daken drove on through the outskirts of the city, past the dark, shining waters of the lake, and on to the airport. Amanda closed her eyes, willing herself to calm down, trying to forget exploding gates and cars that turned into fireballs. The whole scene was replaying in her head like a bad movie—except that in the movies, there was at least a pretense of a scientific explanation.

She opened her eyes as Daken slowed at the entrance to the airport. A few minutes later he came to a stop near a plane much like the one that had carried them here. Beside it stood a group of suit-clad men with blue eyes—men who had been wolves the last time she'd seen them.

Chapter Fourteen

Amanda pressed the button to lower her seat into a reclining position and closed her eyes, hoping against hope that she could sleep. Beyond the windows of the plane, the first tentative light of a new day could be seen.

It was an effort doomed to failure. Instead of a dreamless sleep, her brain reproduced the images of the past few hours: the Sherba dropping in his tracks in the marble foyer, the iron gate ripping from its post, the exploding car. All of it caused by the man who sat across the aisle from her, watching her. Even though her eyes were closed and her face was turned away, she could feel his gaze.

Most of all, though, what she saw was the struggle between man and wolf when he'd awakened: the graphic, horrifying proof of what he was.

All around her was more proof of that. She was

overwhelmed by the auras of the Bet Dawars, confined as they all were in such a small space. The sensation rubbed her nerves raw, but it had a very powerful sensuality as well.

Suddenly she recalled Jessa's shock that Daken had made love to her the night he'd returned from his trip into the mountains. Now, finally, she thought she understood why her friend had been surprised. They had, of course, gone into the mountains as wolves. No doubt it was them she'd heard that evening, so close to the fortress.

Jessa was surprised because she knew that Daken wanted to keep his secret from her, and she'd obviously known as well that Amanda would sense the difference in him—and might guess its cause.

Her mind drifted, filling up with images of that night—of his fierce, passionate lovemaking. Both the man and the wolf had been present that night. She shuddered, and yet could not deny the magic—a dark magic that had drawn her irrevocably into his world.

Without consciously intending to do so, she turned her face toward him, and opened her eyes to find him staring at her. Not a single word had passed between them since the incident with the car. Tarval, the Bet Dawar she'd first met in the *azherwa*, was among the group, and he had inquired whether she was all right, but other than that, she'd been ignored by all of them as they conversed urgently in their own language.

Now her eyes met Daken's and unspoken words hung in the charged air between them, an atmosphere already made nearly unbearable by the presence of the Bet Dawars. She could think of nothing to say, and perhaps neither could he. She turned away again.

What would happen now? Would there be all-out war between the Kassid and their erstwhile protectors? The significance of those shots fired at them was slow to dawn on her. Tranar had said that to kill a Kassid would be a grievous sin—and yet the Sherbas had shot at them.

She listened for a time to the low, urgent conversations around her, wondering if that was what they were discussing. Daken's voice mingled with the others', and she thought that he sounded sad. Or perhaps he was merely tired. There must be some lingering effect from the drugs. Still, as she listened to the unfamiliar words and the strange cadences, she thought the others sounded angrier than he did. At least she heard no more of that cold anger she'd heard before he had set the Sherbas' car on fire. She hoped that she would never hear that again. It had carried a total absence of human feeling.

At some point she fell into a blessedly dreamless sleep, waking only when the whine of the jet engines told her they were about to land. She brought her seat up and looked out the window. They were descending over a broad, sun-drenched plain, and up ahead she could see a landing strip flanked by several ramshackle buildings. She had no idea where they were.

Something had changed in the atmosphere of the cabin. The man-wolf aura was still there, but there was a palpable excitement, a ferocious eagerness. She turned from the window and looked over at Daken, but he was turned away from her, looking out his window. She would have asked where they were, but as the jet descended, the noise level made conversation impossible.

They landed, then taxied toward the buildings— and now she saw a cluster of planes, all of them small, sleek jets similar to the one on which they were traveling. And then she saw the dark-clad figures: big, powerful men in dark suits. When the plane rolled to a stop, they all turned toward it and she saw several hundred pairs of pale eyes watching them.

Suddenly she saw a familiar figure move through the crowd toward the plane: Jessa! What was going on here? She barely recognized her friend, clad as she was in a fashionable pale suit with a skirt that stopped at midthigh. And she was carrying a large leather travel bag.

Amanda turned to question Daken, but the Bet Dawars were crowding the aisle between them as they hurried off the plane to join their comrades. Daken, however, remained seated until all of them had gone.

"Jessa will accompany you back to the Dark Mountains," he said before she could open her mouth.

"Where are you going? Why are they all here?"

Daken unfolded his long frame from the seat, then stood hunched over, his shoulders nearly touching the low ceiling. "We are going to destroy the Sherbas," he said in a voice devoid of emotion.

Amanda stared into those cold blue eyes and felt her blood turn to ice. "Daken, you can't! Not all of them are responsible for—"

"The children will be spared. We can take away their memories of us and place them with foster families in Menoa. I have no time to debate this with you now, Amanda. We must move quickly."

And before she could say anything more, he was gone and Jessa appeared in the open doorway. A moment later the pilot pulled up the stairs and the door was closed. Jessa smiled at her uncertainly as she took the seat Daken had vacated.

"They can't do this!" Amanda said, her voice shrill. "Stop them, Jessa! The Sherbas aren't all bad."

"I couldn't stop them even if I wanted to, Amanda," Jessa said sadly. "The gods—and Daken—have decreed it."

Then conversation became impossible as the engines revved up and they began to lumber back to the runway. Within a few minutes they were airborne. The plane banked sharply and turned in a wide arc, and Amanda had one last glimpse of the Kassid fighting force, gathered in a circle around their leader, Daken.

When the engine noise had died down to a low drone, Jessa reached across the aisle and laid her hand on Amanda's arm. "Are you all right?" she asked with obvious concern.

"I wasn't harmed," Amanda replied, which wasn't the same as saying she was "all right." "Why are they doing this? Not all the Sherbas can be guilty."

Jessa sighed heavily. "This day has been coming for a very long time, according to my grandfather. The Sherbas have become evil. They proved that when they captured Daken and then tried to demand that we choose a new leader."

"But that's not a good enough reason to kill them all, surely!"

"As far as my grandfather and Daken's advisers are concerned, it is. We elect our leaders, but we believe that our choice is dictated by the gods, working through us. So not only did the Sherbas go against *our* wishes, but they also went against the gods themselves."

"One of them told me they did it because they believed Daken had become too 'worldly,' and that made him unfit to rule."

"Yes, they told us that as well. But what they really meant is that Daken won't tolerate their methods of protecting us any longer. And we knew they would try to kill him if we refused."

"They tried to do that," Amanda admitted, then told her the story of their escape.

"Oh!" said Jessa, clearly surprised. "I thought that the Bet Dawars rescued you both."

Amanda shook her head, then slowly and haltingly told her friend what had happened when Daken started to awaken from his drug-induced sleep. Jessa stared at her, obviously fascinated.

"You have seen what no one has ever seen, so far as I know. And how terrible it must have been for you—or had you already guessed?"

"I knew—but I didn't want to know," Amanda admitted.

"I don't understand," Jessa said, frowning.

No, you wouldn't understand, Amanda thought. Self-deception was not part of the Kassid way, and because they lived easily with their magic, neither could Jessa truly understand why it had been necessary for Amanda to deceive herself.

"Do the Bet Dawars rarely . . . change in front of others?" she asked.

Jessa shook her head. "No. It does not happen often, you see. When they are young, when they first become able to make the transformation, they are like children with a new toy, and go as often as possible into the mountains. That was the problem with Myen, the young artist whose work you admired.

"But then, as they grow older, the need comes upon them far less often."

"But why does it happen in the first place?" Amanda asked, even as she wondered how they could be sitting here discussing such a thing so calmly.

"Wolves were the favored animals of the gods when they lived among us. They loved them for their speed and ferociousness and their many other good qualities. So when the gods left this world, they decreed that there should always be among us some who felt a special kinship with the wolves, and who could also defend us against any enemies.

"No one knows why some children are born with the talent, and a father who is a Bet Dawar does not necessarily produce a son who is one. It just happens to about the same number in each generation, and our leaders are always chosen from among them."

"And they're never female," Amanda pointed out, thinking that seemed unfair—especially among a people who otherwise seemed to be remarkably free of sexism.

Jessa smiled. "No, and that has caused a few arguments, believe me. The gods are both male and female. Some think they are both at the same time. I suppose it happened that way because it is always the men who must fight."

"It's always the men who *start* the fights as well," Amanda reminded her.

"That is true, but that's their nature. And even in ancient times, Kassid men fought only when it became absolutely necessary to defend our home."

"Which is what they believe they're doing now," Amanda said grimly. "You said earlier that both Daken and the gods agreed that the Sherbas must die. How do you know that?"

"The Bet Dawars told me that he agreed. They can communicate with each other through their minds. Unfortunately, that didn't help them find him, because of the drugs. They simply guessed that he would have been taken to Geneva. When they couldn't reach him with their minds, there was great fear that he might be dead, even though the Sherba leaders who came to the Dark Mountains said that he'd merely been drugged."

"Would Daken disobey the gods?" Amanda asked her friend. "I'm not sure. He has never been very devout. Most of us aren't, actually. We pay little attention to the gods, because like Daken, we believe that they have lost interest in us. But the message they sent that the Sherbas must die was felt by every one of us. The Sherbas will expect retribution."

"It's wrong, Jessa! I don't care what your gods told you. And besides, in the long run it won't work. Sooner or later there will be other expeditions into the Dark Mountains."

Jessa nodded sadly. "I think we all know that. We may even be hastening that day by killing the Sherbas. But now that the gods have spoken to us again, we know that they will protect us."

Amanda said nothing to that simple but heartfelt declaration of faith. What could she say?

After a short silence, Jessa spoke again. "What will you do?"

"I thought we were going back to the Dark Mountains?" Amanda asked in surprise.

"We are. Daken wanted to be certain you were safe until the Sherbas are gone. He feared that if you returned to your own home, they would capture you to prevent any action he might take against them. But he will not hold you captive, Amanda."

"When the Sherbas are gone, I will be the only one left who knows about you."

"Yes, that was discussed. There are some who think that you should be forced to stay with us, but we know Daken will never agree to that. He let you go before and he will do it again, no matter how much he loves you.

"I know you would never betray us—and Daken knows that as well. But I hope you will stay."

Amanda said nothing. Once again she saw that struggle between the man and the wolf. And now Daken was about to spill innocent blood.

Several days later, the news was filled with accounts of mass murders—or perhaps mass suicides—at the lavish compounds of the ancient order of Sherbas. The police were at a loss to explain the cause of death, and autopsies carried out all over the world yielded no information. What struck almost everyone as being singularly odd was that no children were found, although it was known that many children had lived within the compounds.

The media was filled with information and speculation about the Sherbas. In the U.S., several enterprising journalists dug up some scholarly articles that suggested a connection between the Sherbas and the Kassid—and then it was discovered that

Amanda was missing, as reporters tried to contact her because of her ill-fated expedition.

Swiss authorities discovered that the Sherbas had amassed a fortune far greater than anyone had previously imagined. Billions of dollars were either secreted away in bank vaults or invested in various enterprises around the world. According to the investigators, it would take months to determine the exact extent of their holdings.

Pictures of their lavish compounds were published, showing to the world their vast art collections. But it was said that nothing had been found that could explain their beliefs. Perhaps there might be something in the ancient volumes found at their Swiss headquarters, but it appeared that at least part of this collection was missing, and it seemed likely that the Sherbas had carried their secrets to their graves.

Then another piece of information surfaced. Papers were discovered in the vaults of the Swiss bank where they maintained their chief account. It was deemed to be authentic since it bore the seal of the order as well as the signature of the current leader.

The papers stated that, in the event that the order was disbanded, their assets were to be liquidated and the entire fortune was to be distributed to charities worldwide. The Swiss banker assigned to their accounts was named to head this undertaking, though he claimed to have known nothing about it. However, he stated that he would, of course, do as he was told.

The signature was real. The leader of the Sherbas had signed it just prior to his death, and the papers had then been placed in the bank vault by a Bet Dawar who had no trouble at all in bypassing the bank's elaborate security systems.

None of the charities who would receive this largesse had any idea that it actually came from vast quantities of gold mined centuries ago in the Dark Mountains by a people believed to be long gone. Nor did they know that the idea to distribute the Sherbas' wealth had come from a man with supernatural powers who had walked often among them.

Her arms braced on the waist-high stone wall, Amanda stared down into the abyss. The sheer drop was thousands of feet to the bottom of a ravine filled with the dark firs that were unique to this region. She ignored her slight vertigo, drawn to this highest point in the great fortress.

She'd been back in the Dark Mountains for three days, and during that time had scarcely spoken to anyone other than Jessa. She had requested that she be given another place to stay so that she wouldn't have to return to Daken's quarters, and an apartment near Jessa's had been made available to her. She even avoided Jessa as much as possible, and her friend seemed to understand and did not force herself upon Amanda.

Instead Amanda spent most of her time up here in the tower, alone except for the regular intervals when someone came to exchange messages with the other fortresses.

The Kassid went about their normal business, but even in her own unhappy state, Amanda thought that she detected a difference in them. She'd asked Jessa about it, and Jessa said that they were all mourning the deaths of the Sherbas. She had said it quite sincerely, which left Amanda wondering how one could mourn the deaths of people whom one had destroyed.

Perhaps guessing Amanda's thoughts, Jessa had said that everyone understood why the Sherbas had to die, but it was still painful because her people were not murderers.

"Long ago we mourned the deaths of those we killed in battle," Jessa told her. "Not the leaders, of course, because they were guilty of aggression, but those who followed them. It is the same with the Sherbas."

Jessa also told her that there was an uneasiness among the Kassid now, since most of them had long since stopped considering themselves to be servants of the gods, who had for centuries now required nothing of them. But the gods had spoken again—and everyone worried that still more might be required.

Amanda herself caught some of this uneasiness, quite apart from her own concerns. She had the strange sense that things were somehow coming to an end for the Kassid, though she couldn't define it any more clearly than that.

But mostly she thought about herself—and about Daken. She felt keenly the burden of being the only one left beyond the Dark Mountains who knew about the Kassid's existence, save for the handful of villagers and Menoans who had quietly revered the Kassid for many centuries.

She longed to return to her home and try to pick up the shattered pieces of her life—and yet she knew just how difficult that would be. In fact, it seemed utterly impossible.

As for her thoughts of Daken, she was, as always, confused. She loved him, and yet she could not forget that he had blood on his hands: the blood of her beloved uncle, and now the blood of the Sherbas as well. And, of course, she could never forget that the man she loved wasn't really a man—or was not entirely a man.

She moved away from the abyss, knowing that she was drawn to it by the parallels it held to her own life. She walked over to the other side of the tower balcony and stared down at the courtyard. It was late afternoon, and a market day. Dark-clad figures moved among the many stalls or stopped to chat with friends. Children, just released from school, scampered about or played in the playground area. Flowers bloomed in the gardens, and she could see a group of musicians, though she couldn't hear them. It reminded her of Daken and how he'd played the *leithra* for her once after they'd made love.

She turned away, intending to go down to the market herself to find something for her evening meal. There would be freshly caught fish and wonderful vegetables from the rooftop gardens. Then she saw the tiny figures below her begin to stir, gathering in groups and then moving toward the drawbridge. She shifted her gaze to the bridge.

The Bet Dawars were returning: dark-suited men on foot crossing the bridge in loose groups. Even at this great distance, she thought she caught a glimpse of silver hair in their midst.

Daken felt her gaze touch him and began to scan the courtyard. But crowds were gathering and she was so small that he wouldn't be able to spot her even if she was there. He didn't know what caused him to look up at the tower. Perhaps it was only that he thought of it as being his refuge, and one he needed badly at the moment. Or perhaps he sensed her presence up there even before he caught a glimpse of red hair reflecting the sunlight.

At first he felt anger that she should be up there, even though he'd invited her to go there whenever she wished. He knew that he would lose her soon and he didn't want her memory to linger there.

Then he let go of that anger, knowing that her memory would be everywhere because his heart would not let it go. As a Kassid, Daken was uniquely vulnerable in this situation. His was a race for whom permanence had been a given for centuries, and so he was less prepared than ordinary men to accept that change and letting go were a normal part of life.

He would insist that she stay here for a few weeks, pointing out that if she were to return to her own world now, she would once again be besieged by journalists seeking information about the Kassid.

They had remained in the outer world long enough to watch and read the reactions to the Sherbas' deaths and to gauge the level of danger the massacre posed to them. It appeared that the story was already dying down, relegated to the back pages of newspapers and to no more than brief mentions at the end of newscasts. Any connection between the Sherbas and the Kassid had vanished completely.

Nothing would be found among the collections of the order to renew that interest. They had taken all books that dealt with Ertrian and Kassid history. Those volumes were now in crates left in the temporary care of the villagers of Wat Andara until men and horses could be sent after them. The Sherbas' children, fortunately few in number, since most Sherbas had dedicated themselves to lives of celibacy, had been given over to the care of Menoan families with ancient ties to the Ertrians and the Kassid. Kassid gold would provide for their futures.

The Bet Dawars had first returned to the Dark Mountains as wolves, eager to climb the rocky ledges, run through the ancient forests and drink from the sparkling pools at the base of waterfalls. It was a welcome release after the bloodletting, and a ritual the Bet Dawars had always followed.

Unlike the others, Daken would have preferred to remain out there. More than any of them, he sought the release from pain that the Other offered. The Other could remember her, of course, but it was incapable of the complex emotions that troubled the man.

When they had transformed themselves before returning to the fortress, the talk had been uneasy: a strong sense that more was to come, though no one knew exactly what that was. Daken didn't feel it himself, though he knew that could be because his thoughts had turned immediately to Amanda.

He needed her. He wanted her. He loved her. And yet he would lose her.

Amanda spent a largely sleepless night in her small apartment, expecting his knock on her door at any moment. Once, she thought she could actually feel his presence there, just outside her door. She got out of bed and started through to the small living room, then stopped, unwilling to take the final few steps and open the door. But memories of his lovemaking became so powerful that for a time it seemed that he *was* there in her bed, his long arms around her and his mouth covering hers.

When morning came she dragged herself reluctantly from the bed she'd shared with his ghost and decided that she should not wait for him to approach her. So she bathed and dressed and then went to his quarters. But Sheleth, as inscrutable as ever, told her that Daken had gone to his *abarda*. Amanda was unfamiliar with the word, and Sheleth's English was inadequate to the task of explaining, but she finally decided that it must be a sort of office—perhaps the room where she'd once listened outside while he berated the Sherbas.

So she went down there, grateful to be able to confront him in a more formal setting. The door was open, so she walked in, then stopped when she saw that he was not alone. The small group of men and women gathered there she knew to be his advisers. All of them turned to her, and Amanda saw pale flames leap into his eyes in the seconds before he controlled them and rose to greet her.

"I will come back later," she murmured, taking a step backward as though to escape the searing heat of desire that had flashed so briefly.

"No. This can wait."

She tried to protest, but the advisers had already started to rise from their seats and file out. Several avoided looking at her. One or two gave her tentative smiles, and one woman touched her arm briefly in a friendly gesture. And then the door closed behind them and she was alone with Daken.

In flat, unemotional tones, he told her what had happened and also told her about the media's reaction. She listened, thinking that he might have been a general, reporting to his superiors. By the time he had finished, she had chosen to fix her mind on the children as a way of avoiding the rest of it.

"They won't remember their parents—or their earlier lives?"

He shook his head. "No. It is better for them that way."

In spite of everything she'd seen, Amanda discovered that she could still be shocked and appalled by the extent of his powers.

"But Daken, they will know at some point that their memories have been stolen from them. That could cause them all sorts of trauma."

"What would you have us do, Amanda?" he asked coldly. "Should we have killed innocent children?"

Perhaps she took a step back, or perhaps she merely mentally shrank from him—but whichever it was, he saw it and his tone softened.

"I did the best I could do for them. They will have loving families and will lack for nothing."

"I wish to leave, Daken—as soon as possible." There. She'd spoken the words, words that conveyed far more than their actual meaning.

He merely nodded, averting his gaze. "I ask only that you wait a week or two. If you leave now, your reappearance will bring on questions about us."

She nodded reluctantly, seeing the wisdom of that. "One week, then. You said that the media is already losing interest, and I can avoid them by staying with my mother or at my beach house for a time."

He nodded again, still not looking at her. Unspoken words began to fill up the space between them. She turned quickly and walked to the door, pausing only for a heartbeat before opening it and hurrying away.

It amazed her how easily she was able to avoid him for the next week. Daken and the fortress were so inextricably linked in her mind that she'd forgotten just how vast the place was. Once, when she was in the greenhouse with Jessa, gathering some herbs, she saw him with a small group of men, riding across the drawbridge into the mountains. And another time she looked out the window of her tiny apartment and caught a brief glimpse of him as he crossed the courtyard.

But at night he was always there in her dreams, so that each morning she would awaken, less certain about her decision to leave. She didn't take his avoidance of her as a sign that he wanted her to leave; rather, she knew that he had placed the decision squarely on her shoulders. That was his way, though there were many times when she wished otherwise.

The week that she had thought would be the longest of her life had in fact passed swiftly. She had avoided going back to the tower since his return, but on what would be her last afternoon in the Dark Mountains, she made the long climb one last time. It wasn't likely that he would be there during the day. In fact, she doubted that he was in the fortress at all, since she'd seen him riding out again early in the morning.

She entered the circular tower room and breathed a sigh of relief to find herself alone, ignoring the small disappointment born of a wistful, romantic notion of a final meeting here. A few moments later she heard footsteps climbing the stairs, and her heart began to thud noisily in her suddenly constricted throat. Had he seen her and followed her up here? Would he beg her to stay? What would she say?

But it was only the young men who operated the signal mirrors. She followed them out to the balcony and watched as they hauled on the ropes that adjusted the mirrors. Shading her eyes against the bright sunlight, she saw the series of flashes from the nearest of the other fortresses. The young men ignored her, talking among themselves as one of them wrote on a tablet and the other began to send a return message. Finally, their work complete, they bade her farewell and left her alone.

On this, her last day here, Amanda avoided the abyss and instead stood for a long time at the other side of the balcony, where she could see nearly all of the fortress and the series of courtyards far below.

I will paint this place, she thought, wishing that she'd brought along her sketchpad. But it wasn't really necessary. The great mountain fortress was etched indelibly on her mind, down to the smallest of details: the rooftop gardens, the myriad tiny turrets, the twinkling panes of the huge greenhouse, the way the structure hugged the Dark Mountains, becoming nearly invisible in places where the shadows of late afternoon had lengthened.

And beyond it, the other peaks of the Dark Mountains, now in late summer finally losing most of their snowy caps, standing out starkly against a sky that was losing its blue as the sun slipped away.

Then, too, there was what could never be captured in a painting: the cool, fresh air that seemed always to carry with it a hint of deep, dark glades, and an indescribable sense of timelessness and peace.

And she thought as well about winter here, when the snow would lie many feet deep on everything, bringing the dark firs into stark relief and piling up on the many walls and lintels. She would never see it, but she imagined it now. Jessa had told her of their other great holiday, in midwinter, when everyone dedicated themselves to self-improvement, and the ancestors played their pipes out beyond the walls.

Tears leaked from her eyes and slid down her cheeks, to be dried by the freshening breeze that was growing cooler now that the sun was gone. She shivered and turned away, going back into the tower room. The bottle of wine Daken had poured from that one time they'd been up here together was still there, and she now poured herself a goblet, then sat down on the pillows before the cold hearth.

Amanda awoke to a terrifying vision. Flames were leaping in the darkness, and a shadowy figure crouched between her and the fiery tongues. Paralyzed by her fear, she could do no more than cry out.

Her voice seemed barely audible over the crackle and hiss of the flames and some other sound she hadn't yet identified, but it was enough to draw the attention of the hunched figure. He turned toward her, and now she saw the gleam of silver hair beneath a dark hood. Then the tower was briefly and brilliantly lit, and thunder reverberated off the stone walls. The other sound, she realized now, was rain pelting the glass doors that led to the balcony.

In those first few seconds after she realized it was Daken, he seemed to be part of a dream, sent to taunt her in her last hours in this enchanted place. But when the last traces of her unplanned nap slipped away, he remained very much there.

"Jessa was worried. She said that she hadn't seen you since this morning. Then Tesca told me that you were up here when they came up to signal."

She nodded. Lightning flashed again, throwing his rugged face into brightness for one brief second before leaving it in shadow again. He picked up the empty wineglass beside her and got up to refill it and fill one for himself.

"Everything has been arranged for your departure tomorrow morning," he said, handing her the glass.

She tried to hear regret in his voice, but it wasn't there. Had she been wrong all this time about his feelings for her? She accepted the wine and murmured her thanks. He sank down beside her, maintaining the careful distance of an acquaintance or even a stranger.

The tower was lit even more brilliantly than before, and this time the crash of thunder was so loud that she started involuntarily. He smiled at her.

"This is no place for someone who fears storms. Would you like to leave?"

She shook her head quickly. The storm didn't really frighten her, and somehow it seemed appropriate that her last memory of him should be in this tower, with his gods hurling thunder and lightning at them.

He sipped his wine, seemingly content to let the sounds of the storm fill up the silence between them. When he moved suddenly, she jumped, but he didn't notice because he was busy removing the oiled cape.

"I'm sorry, Daken." The words just popped out before she could stop them.

He turned to her and his wide mouth curved into a sad smile. "It is best. You belong to the world out there, Amanda."

"But you hate that world," she protested. She'd listened to him talk about the injustice and the poverty and the destruction of the environment.

"No, I don't hate it—or at least I don't hate all of it. There is much I dislike—as I've told you. But there is much that is good, too.

"Living here requires the mind of a Kassid. Because of you, I can understand that now. People in the world outside—especially Americans like you—are always striving, always wanting change. Here we strive as well, but only to perfect ourselves in a world that remains the same. I think there is a very big difference.

"And we have had many centuries—since the beginning of time—to accept who and what we are. We do not think of ourselves as being different because we have always been this way. Our magic is a part of us—and it could never be that way for you. I don't know what happened when I was awakening from the drug, but I think you must have seen both parts of me, and of course that scared you. How could it be otherwise for you?"

"I saw . . . both," she said, trying unsuccessfully to supress a shudder at the terrible memory. "It seemed that you were fighting—or wrestling."

"In a sense I was. My mind had been clouded by the drugs, but I think they affected the two parts of me differently. Such a thing would never happen under normal circumstances. The Other does not surface unless I wish it to, and it leaves when I choose to send it away."

Outside the storm continued to rage. Wind rattled the glass doors. Suddenly it seemed to her that all that needed to be said *had* been said. He understood, and in the way of his people, he had made his peace with it. She envied him that.

"I would like to make love to you one last time," he said in a low voice that barely carried above the sounds of the storm and the crackling of the fire. "It seems to me that we have had too little time for tenderness because the need has been too great."

She was nodding even before he had finished. It was what she wanted, too. And now they could come together in total honesty, knowing that there would not be another time for them.

They undressed slowly, hands and lips caressing bare flesh, taking time because time was the gift they could give each other now. And even when they were naked, with the firelight flickering over them and warming them, they moved slowly.

But Amanda could feel the fierceness of the wolf in him, the primitive hunger to possess completely, even though he seemed to control it effortlessly, as he had said he could do.

A long moment could pass in merely tracing a finger along soft curves or hard angles, and gentle kisses took forever to deepen into fierce possession. Amanda had never felt so cherished—and knew that she would never feel this again. Tears welled up in her eyes and spilled onto her cheeks, and he kissed them away with silent understanding.

And when finally he entered her, they moved to another plane of slow, gradually escalating passion, wrapped in each other's arms, their bodies melting together. She expected a sudden explosion of passion, a hot, fierce climax—but it didn't happen that way. Instead they slid together off the edge of the world and then stayed there for what seemed an eternity.

In the aftermath, they held each other in silence because words would have been an unwelcome—and unnecessary—intrusion.

Chapter Fifteen

Amanda saw the newscast only because she was at her mother's, waiting for the arrival of the new love in her mother's life, who was taking them both to dinner. The TV was on in the kitchen as her mother prepared a cheese tray to accompany their cocktails. In fact, if her mother hadn't suddenly stopped talking to stare at the small screen, Amanda might never have known. She hadn't paid much attention to the news since her return nearly a month ago.

"Experts say that the eruptions could presage much greater explosions from the chain of volcanoes that surround the Dark Mountains. There have been minor eruptions in the region from time to time, but this latest outbreak is far more violent and destructive. Fortunately that area is almost completely unpopulated.

"This is the same region that was recently in the

news when an expedition seeking traces of the lost civilization of the Kassid was attacked by guerrilla fighters, and all were killed except for an American artist."

The words of the news anchor slid through her brain, but Amanda's attention was focused on the photographs. They were aerial shots, and even a satellite photo. She hadn't realized until now that the volcanoes actually encircled the Dark Mountains, which were barely visible through the thick smoke.

"Amanda?"

Her mother's voice drew her attention only when the scene on the screen shifted to an economic report. Her mother hugged her tightly.

"How glad I am that you're safe here."

But was *he* safe? Amanda didn't have the faith in the gods that the Kassid had, and what she saw terrified her.

Her mother's new love arrived, and Amanda did her best to be pleasant to him. He was in fact a very nice man, and it pleased her that after all these years her mother had finally found someone. But the evening was a nightmare for her as images of the great fortress crumbling to dust or swallowed by lava flows tortured her mind.

After dinner they returned to her mother's apartment, and her fiancé left shortly thereafter. Amanda got up to leave as well, wanting only to be alone with her terrified thoughts. But her mother's words stopped her.

"You don't like him, do you? I was so sure that you would."

Amanda stared at her mother's tears—and began to cry herself. It took several minutes for her to convince her mother that she *did* like her stepfather-to-be, and then her mother wanted to know what had caused her to cry.

It all came out over the next hour, in fits and starts and much retracing of incomplete information. She didn't feel that she was betraying the Kassid; this was her mother, after all. And in any event, she was now convinced that the days of the Kassid were numbered, that the strange solace she had found in thinking of Daken in his mountain home would be gone.

Her mother sat quietly through it all, asking only a few questions. And when Amanda finally finished, Amanda asked her mother if she believed her.

"Of course." her mother said simply. "It makes no sense, but I do."

"Perhaps the reason you can believe me is that we're Ertrian," Amanda said through her tears. "Maybe there's some sort of genetic memory at work. I think that had something to do with Steffen's and my being able to travel through the *azherwas*—the sacred rooms."

Her mother nodded. "I was always fascinated by Steffen's stories about the Kassid and about Ertria. At the time I thought it was only his own enthusiasm rubbing off on me—but it could have been more."

They talked some more and her mother asked her to stay the night, but Amanda went home, feeling relieved of her burden, but still frightened for Daken.

News of the volcanic eruptions dwindled away over the next few days as nothing more seemed to happen. Amanda now became fixated on the news and was rarely far from a radio or TV. Finally, four days after the first report, there were new eruptions—

and this time, earthquakes as well. One powerful tremor occurred just off the coast, and from the map she saw on CNN, Amanda guessed that it was quite close to the lost city. A later newscast confirmed this, mentioning Steffen's expedition.

Unable to cope with her fear and with the coldness that was spreading inside her like a living thing, Amanda withdrew into herself. She tried to paint, but found herself standing for hours before the easel with the brush drying in her hand. She ignored the calls from her mother and from her friends. She thought about going to her beach house, but the summer season would be in full swing. Occasionally she wandered the city streets, scarcely noticing the heat and humidity that drove sensible people out of the city in August. Several times she found herself miles from her loft, with no knowledge of how she'd gotten there.

The news reports continued. Some experts suggested that what was happening now mirrored the great cataclysm that had destroyed the Ertrian and Kassid civilizations centuries ago.

Her mother appeared late one afternoon, as Amanda sat watching yet another satellite photograph. Amanda had forgotten to return her call. After one look at her daughter, she packed a bag and insisted that she come home. Amanda consented, if only because she knew that she wouldn't have to keep up any pretense with her mother.

After forcing herself to eat at least part of the dinner her mother had prepared, Amanda went to her old room in the spacious apartment and stood looking down at the view she'd always loved. Their co-op was in an elegant old building that overlooked a park, but as she stared out at the greenery, she saw instead an endless stretch of mountains: the view from the tower, as she'd seen it the morning she left.

They had not made love that morning, as though they both feared that they could not equal the perfection of the night before. And Daken had not been the one to take her down out of the mountains. Instead they said their good-byes at the bridge, and when she had turned one last time, what she saw was the dream she'd had: Daken, standing beside the flaming cauldron, with the great fortress behind him.

The vision faded and she turned away from the window, praying that it meant he was still safe, that his gods were continuing to protect him. Without bothering to undress, she stretched out on the bed, hoping that here, amidst the pleasant memories of a much happier time, she could get some sleep. The muted chime of the doorbell reached her ears. Her mother hadn't mentioned that she was expecting Thomas, her fiancé, but it was probably him.

She drifted toward an uneasy sleep, then bolted awake as her mother tapped at her door and then opened it. Amanda sat up and switched on the bedside lamp. Her mother wore a very strange expression that Amanda couldn't decipher, but in her present frame of mind immediately decided must presage disastrous news.

"He's here, Amanda."

Amanda frowned uncomprehendingly, assuming she meant Thomas, but wondering why she'd come in to announce that.

"It's Daken. He wants to see you."

"No!" she cried. It couldn't be. Her mother

wouldn't play such a cruel trick. It must be some Sherba who'd managed to escape the Kassid's wrath and who'd come to exact revenge upon her.

"It can't be Daken, Mother," she whispered, reaching for the phone to call 911.

"But it *is* him, dear. You described him very well."

Amanda's hand hesitated, poised over the phone. And then he was in the doorway, with the light from the hall making a silver halo around his head.

It's a dream, she thought. *I'm asleep. There will never be an end to this torment.*

"I can't stay long," the dream that was Daken said, still not moving from the doorway. "But I had to come, to see you one last time."

Her mother moved quietly past him, and then he advanced slowly into the room.

"One last time?" she echoed, still afraid to let herself believe that he was actually here.

He nodded, his pale eyes never leaving her face. "I have come to say what I should have said before you left. But I believed that it was the will of the gods that you should leave—and that it was best for you as well.

"I love you, Amanda. My heart has not belonged to me since you came into my life. I can never be merely a man, as you would like me to be—but I love you and cherish you."

She said nothing. Was he real?

He stared at her, and then a slight frown creased his brow, followed by a tender smile. "I am real. This is no trick. The gods have granted me this little time to come to you."

She remembered that he'd said he couldn't stay. "What little time?" she asked, her joy that he was really here now tempered by the certainty that he was going home to his death.

"You have heard about the earthquakes and eruptions?"

She nodded, unable to speak.

"The gods are even now casting their greatest spell—to protect us forever. No one will ever find us, because we will not be there."

She leaped from the bed. "No, Daken, you can't go back there to die! Stay here with me! We can—"

"*Kazhena*, I did not mean that we would die. The gods are casting a great spell over the Dark Mountains. Perhaps I lack the words in your language to explain it. For us, everything will be the same as it has ever been. And if, when the earthquakes and the eruptions cease, people come into the Dark Mountains, they will see them as they have ever been. Except that we will not be there. Or we will be there, but not there. Do you understand?

"That is why I have come now, and why I must return quickly. Once the spell has been cast, it will no longer be possible to travel between the worlds."

She nodded her understanding—such as it was. "And the gods told you to come and tell me this?"

"No. I asked them to give me this time, and they granted my request, perhaps because they understand that I left words unspoken between us."

Amanda took a deep, quavering breath and shook her head. "I don't think that's why they let you come, Daken. I think they let you come so that I could return with you."

She saw the hope leap into his eyes and knew that it had been buried there all along.

"I cannot ask that of you, *kazhena*. You would be

trapped there as I will be. Your mother—"

"My mother will understand. I broke my word to you and told her everything. She has had me until now, and she will know that I am happy."

"Are you sure?" he asked, his eyes searching her face intently.

"I'm very sure. I love you, Daken—*all* of you—and I will go with you, even beyond this world."

Futuristic Romance

Star-Crossed

Saranne Dawson

Bestselling Author Of *Crystal Enchantment*

Rowena is a master artisan, a weaver of enchanted tapestries that whisper of past glories. Yet not even magic can help her foresee that she will be sent to assassinate an enemy leader. Her duty is clear—until the seductive beauty falls under the spell of the man she must kill.

His reputation says that he is a warmongering barbarian. But Zachary MacTavesh prefers conquering damsels' hearts over pillaging fallen cities. One look at Rowena tells him to gird his loins and prepare for the battle of his life. And if he has his way, his stunningly passionate rival will reign victorious as the mistress of his heart.

_51982-8 $4.99 US/$5.99 CAN